Praise for Cretaceous Clay!

"a science fiction-fantasy thriller with an added dose of murder, mystery and mayhem ..." – Wendy, Goodreads

"funny, witty dialogues were enough comic relief in all the strange and sometimes scary crime scenes ... if the saying of starting with a blast is true, then this series is bound to become a hit!" – Lydia P., Goodreads Top Reviewer

"a very vivid imagination and I would definitely read another one of his books ..." – Angel S., Goodreads Best Reviewer

"the Black Dwarf takes what we expect from the fantasy genre and reforms it into something new and exciting. ..." – C. P. Bialois, Author of *The Sword and the Flame, Call of Poseidon, and Skeleton Key*

"a wonderful imagination in the life-and-death situations ..." – Erlinda C. N.

"a nonstop read. It took me three hours without putting it down to read from front to back! This book kept me flipping the pages wanting to know more!" – Misty A., Goodreads

~~~~~

~~~~~

Also by D. A. Knight

Cretaceous Clay & the Ninth Ring

Available from Amazon.com, CreateSpace.com, and other great retail outlets!

~~~~~

Coming Soon!

Cretaceous Clay & the Yellow Stone

~~~~~

Cretaceous Clay

& the

Black Dwarf

~~~~~~

D. A. Knight

~~~~~~

Stonewald, LLC

Greenville, Texas

CRETACEOUS CLAY AND THE BLACK DWARF

Published by Stonewald, LLC

Copyright © 2013 ALAN BROOKS.

Publisher's Acknowledgements

Cover Designed by Stonewald, LLC

Cover Art: Copyright 02-28-13 © Yevgen Timashov / Vetta Collection / iStockphoto.com / Standard License

Editor: Tina Musial

Map of Nodlon: Copyright © 2013 ALAN BROOKS.

Softcover Printed by CreateSpace, Charleston SC, an Amazon.com Company

Author's Website: **BlackDwarves.com**

ISBN-10: 0-9893861-2-0 (Paperback)
ISBN-13: 978-0-9893861-2-8 (Paperback)
ISBN-10: 0-9893861-0-4 (eBook)
ISBN-13: 978-0-9893861-0-4 (eBook)

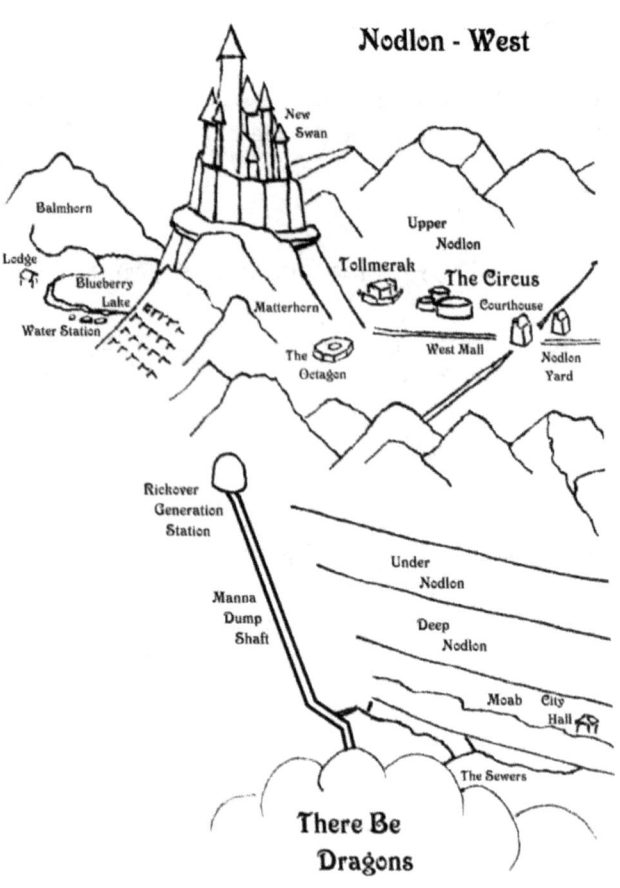

Nodlon - West

New Swan

Balmhorn

Lodge

Blueberry Lake

Water Station

Matterhorn

Upper Nodlon

Tollmerak

The Circus

Courthouse

The Octagon

West Mall

Nodlon Yard

Rickover Generation Station

Manna Dump Shaft

Under Nodlon

Deep Nodlon

Moab City Hall

The Sewers

There Be Dragons

Nodlon - East

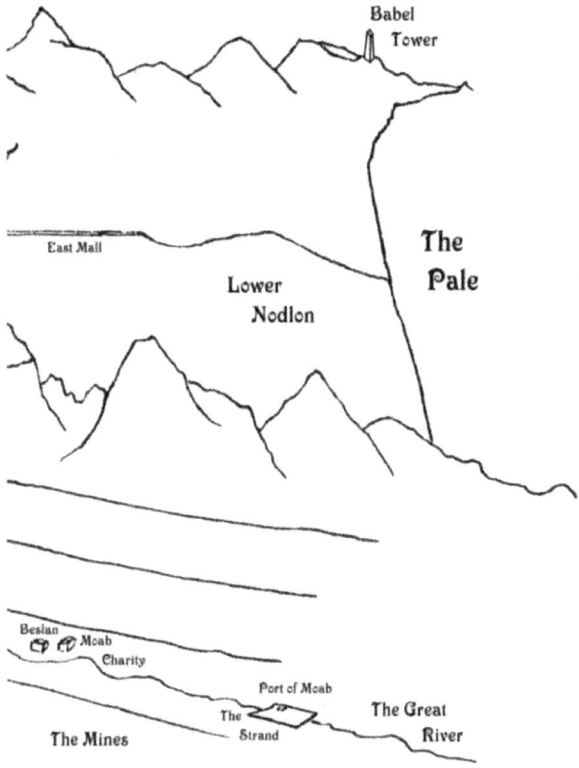

Babel Tower

The Pale

East Mall

Lower Nodlon

Beslan

Moab

Charity

Port of Moab

The Strand

The Great River

The Mines

Contents

Cretaceous Clay

& the

Black Dwarf

Call Me

"Call Me!" laughed the nymph.

Evan sank onto his couch and watched her on his vid screen. She danced across the screen and bounded over puff balls and spinning flowers. "All your hopes can come true!" Was she real, or was she just a sprite created out of the mind of a graphic artist? "Don't be blue, dreams can too!" He turned off his vid, but he still saw the nymph and heard the jingle.

"Call me," she called.

For forty nights, he watched. For forty nights, she repeated her rhymes. "Call me! call now! Call me if you want to be alive!"

The jingle rang in his head. At work and at his apartment, the tune repeated over and over. It would not let go. He stuck his fingers in his ears, and it played. He tried to drown the tune with music, and it played.

Insomnia plagued him, and the little tune rang when he tried to sleep. The rhyme was magical in its power. It repeated endlessly. It would not stop. He needed help to sleep with the tune playing all the time. He was struggling to stay awake at work, and he needed rest.

Throwing aside his pillow, he rubbed his face, and sat up. Awake in the dark, the jingle left him alone for a minute. He sighed with relief, and sat in the dark. An electronic glow lit the apartment. He had a computer, a vid, a theatre system, and a clock. His furniture was sparse, but tasteful.

Curling his toes, he went to the bathroom without turning on the lights. He opened his medicine cabinet and searched for something to help him sleep. He needed to take the edge off. Taking each bottle out of the cabinet one at a time, he read the labels by the tiny power light on his toothbrush. After stacking a small pharmacy on the edge of his lavatory, he found the right bottle. Carefully, he took one pill, sipped some water from the faucet, and swallowed it. Placing all of the bottles back in the cabinet, he relaxed hoping the drug would reward him with sleep.

He closed the cabinet, and saw his clock reflected in the mirror. Opening the bathroom door wider, he peeked out and looked for his clock. It sat on his nightstand at his bedside facing the bathroom. *The cord must have caught in my sheets. I must have pulled the clock away from the bed when I sat up.*

Taking small steps, he walked to his refrigerator, and opened it. Inside was very little, but he was a bachelor, so what would anyone expect. He had the essentials: Pizza and sparkling water. He took a bottle of water and drank a slug. Screwing the cap on tight, he put the bottle back, and closed the fridge. Patiently, he stood in his little kitchen waiting for his eyes to adjust.

He had just moved in. It was expensive, but he wanted to be noticed. He wanted to show off. He had a good job, and he wanted every dwarf girl in Nodlon to know it. That's why he moved. He just wanted someone to love him, but he knew it was hopeless, and he wondered why he cared.

And then he heard it. Something heavy bumped a wall. But he dismissed it. It was just the neighbors next door. Perhaps they were getting up and starting their day early.

Slowly, with his toes curled, he walked across the apartment to his bed. At the foot of the bed, he climbed in and crawled over the covers. Lying down, he curled up with his pillow. He shut his eyes, and tried to clear his mind.

The floor thumped below him. He sat up bolt straight, clutching his pillow.

Nerves! He breathed slowly, calming himself, and he suppressed the feeling. He lived in an apartment building now. He had left the dorms. Dorms were just a place to warehouse biots. But the dorms were quiet. Dorms were just quarters for others dwarves like him. He was not used to the noise. It was just the neighbors.

The apartments on the Bio-Soft campus were pre-war.

The walls were thin he told himself. The apartment must be over a century old, or maybe two. The dorms were new. But his apartment was expensive and well built. *Yes, but the dorms were insulated better*. But, then, he had never heard his neighbors in the dorm.

He pulled up his blanket and curled up again with his pillow. Rolling over, he looked directly at the time. He had not moved the clock. Or had he? Maybe he had moved it when he was startled by the thump on the floor. Or could he? How would he have moved the clock?

Slowly and gently, he reached across his bed. He felt for the switch on his lamp, and switched on the light. The shadow was on the wall. It was as tall as a goblin, and it was on the wall next to his closet door. He blinked, trying to think. Nothing stood between the light and the shadow. He tried to yell for help, but his mouth would not move. He tried to turn his head, but he was paralyzed.

He closed his eyes. He wished it to go away. He opened his eyes, and the shadow was gone.

Composing himself, he tried to make sense of it. He was just tired, he told himself. Sleeplessness was affecting his senses. Slowly, the fear faded, and he could turn his head. He peeked out from his blanket and looked around. His saloon doors were open. He could see most of his studio from his bed. There was nothing there.

He climbed out of bed. He checked his front door and found it locked. A peek in the bathroom confirmed it too was empty. The closet door was closed. Cautiously, he opened it, and found only his clothes and his bathrobe. He knelt to see if the intruder was hiding behind his clothes. Nothing there except his sneakers, shoes, and his boots. No one was in the apartment.

He felt tingles run up and down his back, and he closed the door. Looking around again, his clock was just as he had left it. Nothing was amiss.

"Nightmare," he muttered, "I was just having a

nightmare." Shaking, he went back to bed, curled up with his pillow, and left his light on.

Perchance to Dream

Constellations twirled around Clay. He soared through the stars and he searched for his mother. He called her name. Stars passed him by, and the starry night passed overhead. He could not find her and he fell to Earth. Dwarves surrounded him, and he struck at them with lightning. They fell back until a dwarf warlock appeared. He attacked the foul lord with flames and ice. The dwarf fired a tornado at him. He ducked, and the whirlwind hit a mountain. The mountain erupted, and lava flowed. The dwarves ran, and the warlock escaped. A volcano was beyond his powers. He wanted to fly, but the volcano exploded and sent mountains into the sky.

"Jack," called his mother.

I'm here. The volcano disappeared, and the dream faded. He opened his eyes. Moonlight flooded his bedroom with a pale light. The smoke alarm blinked in the hall. He twisted his head. Struggling to move, he turned just far enough to see his bedroom door.

"Jack," she said, "be calm Pumpkin, it's only me."

"Mum," he mumbled. He tried to call her. A bead of sweat rolled down his brow. Supine, he tried to rise. Cold air settled over his bed, and he saw a shadow in the hall. The shadow moved quietly into his room, and stepped into the moonbeam revealing a woman in a white gown. She was an elf, fair and lovely, and familiar just as he remembered her. In the cool moonlight, she shined snow white.

"Mum!" his shout gurgled on his lips.

"Pumpkin," her blue eyes twinkled, "childhood ends. For a time, you will battle a dwarf, and then you will face the dragon. Many will be lost, but Nodlon will be saved. Afterwards, you will go into the starry night for three days." Stars and constellations swirled across his ceiling. The Milky Way rolled until it crowned her. "None know with whom you contend. Enmity lies between us and the dragon's servants."

Still frozen, he tried to cry out.

"None of your questions can I answer now," she shook her head, and smiled.

"Be true and brave and you will not fail me. Whatever may come; we shall meet again on a sunny day." Giving him a simple wave, she left.

"Mum!" he cried.

He forced his muscles to move, and gradually he sat up. He searched his condominium, but she was not in the apartment. She was gone. What did he expect? Three years had come and gone since she had passed.

His patio door was open. He stepped into the cool, morning air. The stars blazed in the clear mountain air. Orion was high and the moon waxed in the east. A low earth orbiter on a red-eye flight to Elysium split the sky with a contrail reflecting the distant sun.

He tried to clear his head standing in the cold air. He had no idea. He could not be sure.

Was his interest in the supernatural any more than a morbid obsession with a dark chapter in human history? No, he had to find out why. In all the solar system, he alone was blessed with magic. Blessing or curse, magic was his life. He had studied history, science, and nature. When those offered no explanation to his magic he had investigated the supernatural, the paranormal, witchcraft, alchemy, and the occult. He had learned nothing about himself.

His mother's appearance to him was just another strange event in his strange life. He was a magician. Thinking of the supernatural, he wondered, *was she a dream, or did I see a ghost?* Again a cold tingle ran up and down his spine, and he recalled her words. Then, he remembered his mother. *She was so real! Did I really see my mother?*

Willing himself to be calm, he looked down on the twinkling lights of Nodlon. It would be a long day.

The Apple

Evan Labe stood in front of his door and looked up and down the hall. Deep in the night, his neighbors slept and, he felt an insubstantial bond with those who watched the late-night vid while others slept. Sucking in a deep breath, he opened his front door. He checked behind the door, in the bathroom, and in the closet. Nothing unusual was in the apartment.

Night after night, Evan returned to his studio apartment, turned on his vid and watched the nymph sing her rhymes. Nothing had happened since he had seen the shadow, but he was still worried.

He flopped in his lounge chair, gazed around his quarters, and he pondered his fate. He had had enough. He picked up his remote, and said, "Vid on."

"Call me!" Her refrain echoed. She smiled sweetly, and batted her eyes, "Hungry? Angry? Lonely? Tired? Call me! Call now!" she teased. How could she be lying? Smiling from the glowing screen, the nymph swayed from side to side and her skirt shook as she danced. "One can be two, when genes are new!"

New Gem's numbers floated across the screen. The nymph dared him to pick up the caster and call her.

"New Gem will make a new you. New genes! New Gem!" He snatched his remote, and yelled, "Stop!"

Obediently, the vid screen froze. He picked up his caster, *I have nothing to lose*. Frozen on his vid screen, the New Gem numbers taunted him. Pressing a key on his caster, he stored the number on the screen.

"Oh, vixen, you are pneumatic."

He dialed the number, and a soft beep warned him the connection was made. A chamber ensemble began playing from his caster, and he waited, helpless to do anything else. How could he pay for gene therapy? Seconds passed, and they seemed an eternity. Thinking he had lost his mind, he almost hung up.

"A biot you are, and a biot you'll be. There's no escaping who you are," he argued.

"New genes, New Gem," a young goblin interrupted a cello, "How may I help you?"

"Hi, I'm Evan Labe and I saw your number on an infomercial."

"Oh, good, my name is Sally, and I just need some information." Quickly he gave her far more personal data than he wished.

"Can you come in for an appointment tomorrow morning? I have a nine-thirty or an eleven. Would any of those do?" He agreed to an early appointment, and silently hoped he could get a pass.

Princess of Nodlon

Nodlon lay at Virginia's feet, and its blue lights flickered in the gathering twilight. Her home was a castle built on the artificial mountain at the west end of the city. At the valley's other end on the northern spur stood Babel Tower. The tower rose above the mountains and marked the city's modern edge. Beyond it was the Pale, the abandoned suburbs of a more exuberant, more confident age. The tower was home to Nodlon's nouveau riche, and to its most enigmatic resident, Cretaceous Clay.

Soon, she would be off to see Clay perform. He was a sensation. She had seen his show many times, but tonight was different. Tonight, she hoped to enlist him in her scheme to win popular support for the emancipation of the biots. If her father knew what she was doing, he would ground her until she graduated from college.

She sighed. The city had begun with a dream. She knew the story by heart.

Thornmocker was a mining mogul whose family had made their fortune carving coal out the roots of the Rocky Mountains of Wyoming. He wanted to create a perfect resort for the planet's most perfect people. The city's infrastructure for the staff and industry was built into the mines. The valley became a playground for the elite.

At the head of a valley carved out of the mountains by an ancient glacier, he built a manna generator into the mines. To hide the cooling towers, he built an artificial mountain, and atop the mountain, he constructed a fairy castle. The frothy mix of architecture was once a hotel for the Solar System's elite. Now it was home to the King and his family, and since she was the King's daughter, it was her home.

The castle was much too big to live in alone. They shared it with Nodlon's nobility, her father's bureaucrats, and all of their servants. Among the hundreds of luxurious suites, the King's family occupied the highest one in the tallest tower.

No utopia of men is without a price. Someone had to build and maintain Nodlon. Who better to build Nodlon than biots?

Biots were superior to humans in every imaginable way, and many feared they were the logical successors to humans on the ladder of evolution. Such fears drove humans to demand limitations. Synthetic biological androids were the perfect cogs in Thornmocker's machine. Human-like creatures with no family and no home besides what the company provided. Less than animal in status, and more than human in capacity, no one dared to defend them.

Still, they were supposed to be soulless creatures with no complaints. But the pressure of lives spoiled by hopeless loneliness could not be contained. Nodlon groaned with the suffering of biots, and the heart and soul of the city festered.

To contain the threat, Thornmocker constructed Tollmerak. Tollmerak was a school for biots at the center of the nurseries. There he hoped to chain the hearts of the biot children and harness the only true resource: their mind and spirit. But even his cunning mind had no antidote for the ghosts in the machine.

Rebellion exploded, and the world burned. The Regressive Wars nearly wiped out the solar system, but Nodlon survived. The city owed its survival to its two chief assets: Its vast underground industrial base and to Tollmerak, the school, which tempered Nodlon's culture and warded off a rebellion.

~~~~~~

"Princess, your guests are here."

"Great, Anna, let's go." Anna handed her a shawl, and she slipped it on.

"Tonight, we're having a good time. Call me Virginia, please."

"Yes, ma'am."

Virginia peeked out of her door and saw no one in the hall. The two girls left her suite, and tip toed towards the exit. Anna hobbled in her tight gown, her heels clicked and clacked across the marble floor.

"Never wore any high heels before?" Virginia stopped her.

"No, ma'am, it's my first time."

"Follow me, and do as I do. If you keep making that racket, we'll never get out of here without getting caught."

"Virginia!" said her father in that tone, which told her he had overheard.

"Yes, daddy?" she turned around and sighed.

Her father was King of Nodlon, and he was used to command, but she never felt like one of his subjects. Once in a while he barked, but they both knew she was the apple of his eye. After her mother passed away, he had doted on her. Still, he tried.

"Where are you going, young lady?"

"To see Cretaceous Clay, it's the last Winter Show for this year."

"Yes, I saw the bill on your expense report. Maybe my tax collectors should audit Jack Jack and his Clay-players." Her father looked chagrined.

"Oh no, I bought the entire upper balcony and gave away the tickets to the biot students at Tollmerak. As a princess, I need to invest in popularity."

The old man's eyebrow lifted, and he nodded. "Likely as not that may be true, certainly cannot hurt your reputation. All right, I'll approve the expenditure, but ask first next time."

"Okay, great," she made to leave, but he put out his hand to stop her.

"Stop evading the issue, my future politician. Virginia, I've told you to take protection when you go out."

"Oh, dad, how can we relax with those stiffs hanging around?"

"Virginia, how can I relax worrying about my baby coming home as a stiff?" Two goblins with shoulders as wide as a door appeared from an inconspicuous nook dressed in evening attire.

"Dad," she whined. If she wanted to go out tonight, she had to stop him before he began lecturing her on politics and decorum, poker and diplomacy, and war versus the economy. Someday, she might be Queen of Nodlon, he would say, and she had to be ready. True, but tonight, she was still a teenager, and she had a date with a dreamy officer candidate studying at the Naval Academy.

"We think Martian agents are operating in Nodlon. With Nogora threatening to blockade Saturn, I cannot let you wander the city without security."

"Dad, I'm packing a mini-blaster right here," she patted her purse; "I could take out Genghis Khan and have juice to spare."

Her father crossed his arms, and she knew she had lost. She had no idea why he was more worried now, but then again she was not privy to his security briefings.

She sighed and rolled her eyes, "Daddy, I'll take big and thick, but I think you're overreacting." The goblins immediately put on their sunglasses.

Her friends waited in the lobby. Millie and Burt made a matched set, and Zachary was stunning in his uniform. And with them was a black dwarf who looked terribly uncomfortable in his tuxedo.

"Hi, Millie," she hugged her friend. "You must be Burt."

"Yes, princess," Burt bowed and kissed her hand.

She giggled, and looked the dwarf in the eye. "And who might you be?"

He looked down at his shoes, and bowed low. "Nicholas, ma'am," said the dwarf, "I'm Master Decatur's yeoman." He scratched the black microchip in his forehead nervously, and then put his hands behind him.

"Well, Nicholas, this is Anna. She's filling in for Nadia my handmaiden who is out sick. Would you mind escorting her?"

"No, ma'am, if it's all right with her." Nicholas spoke softly and never looked up.

"Anna, will accompany Nicholas?" The maid nodded and mumbled something inaudible. Virginia took her hand and squeezed it. "We're having fun tonight. Let's all be friends."

"Now that we all have a date, let me introduce our chaperones. Sorry, about that, but daddy seems to think we need an escort. Sylvester, Karl, say hello."

"Hello," they said in unison.

She started to say something and thought better of it. "Sylvester and Karl may look tough, but in reality, they are. I don't think we'd be any safer if we had a pair of Mark Five's." Millie giggled, and the boys squirmed under the glare of the sunglasses. They took the King's private elevator to the garage, and piled into one of the black airships from her father's fleet. A stylish flyer would be cool, but she knew her security detail would never fit in her sporty, little Andromeda even if she could get Sylvester to agree.

Bread and Circuses

Fans jammed the Circus chanting, "Jack! Jack! Jack!" Electric riffs tore the air, and bass drums drowned out the fans with heart-pounding balls of sound. The Rockhounds levitated over the auditorium, and the crowd leapt to its feet screaming. Many fans wore costumes based on the characters Cretaceous Jack had created.

Virginia pushed the dwarves to the front of the royal box. *The dwarves would have stared at the back of the elves' heads all evening.* Sylvester and Arnold took their places, and the rest of her guests settled in for the evening.

Zachary slapped Burt on the shoulder. "There's no sign of a waiter. Let's get the drinks," said Zachary. Everyone called out a favorite, and the young men departed in search of refreshments.

The curtain shield dissolved to reveal a mock castle. Goblins, elves, and dwarves in a myriad of costumes waved from the parapets. The drawbridge dropped and the crowd thundered as Clay dashed from the castle, and waved to the fans. The Rockhounds lowered the beat, waiting for the magician to hit his mark on a round stage in the center of the auditorium.

Teenage girls screamed and cheered. An elf reached over the barrier to touch the drawbridge and pitched over the barrier. Jack jumped between the stage and the rail and the yelling subsided.

Kneeling over the prostrate girl, he assisted her, "Are you all right?" The question blared over the public address system. Assured she was fit, he helped her up. The crowd cheered.

He levitated back to the stage. More girls swooned and rather than risk a stampede of frisky teenage girls, he retreated.

"Welcome everybody! Let's just have a good time, and we don't want any accidents tonight."

Zachary and Burt returned with drinks and snacks. "Did we miss anything?" asked Burt.

"No, they're just getting started," said Virginia.

Millie giggled. "Some kid tried to brain herself to touch Jack's breeches."

With a flick of his wrist, the magician began the show. Leprechauns and trolls, nymphs and dragons came alive. Illusions and dancers cavorted together across the stage and around the auditorium.

He created an ice board, and surfed around the Circus. Jack's board left an icy path. As he flew, seven flaming rings formed over the audience. Jack jumped through the rings. Her stomach jumped as the magician zipped through the flames.

Dwarf ballerinas danced along the path with nyads, dryads, and fauns. Snowflakes fell from the roof and an elf maiden dropped from the ceiling.

Zooming across the Circus on his ice board the magician caught the falling elf. He set her on the icy path, and she joined the ballerinas. She pirouetted around the path, bounding over the animals, and dancing with the dwarves.

Goblins in black leapt from behind curtains onto the stage and cracked blazing fire whips. Balls of fire burst over the stage. Trolls and malevolent elves joined goblin sorcerers and imperiled the mage and his dancers. Fire and ice in operatic proportions filled the evening as the magician fought and vanquished each of his imaginary foes.

All too soon, the show wound up to the climax. "Dragon!" chanted the crowd.

The Rockhounds broke into a new beat, and the crowd screamed.

High above the Circus, a tornado dropped through the halo of stage lights hanging over the Circus. Lightning flashed. The tornado dipped to the stage. Out of the tornado a red dragon attacked the mage. Clay battled the dragon. He pitted his magic against the dragon's nuclear breath. After several gags, he summoned a sword, and vanquished the dragon by piercing the soft spot over its heart.

The magician levitated over the dragon's ruin, and pushed his ice board through a victory lap. Thinning to translucence, the illusions dissolved into a mist, and the mage closed the show with an astronomical display. The Milky Way swirled over the fans, and they sped through the stars in the outer spiral arm. The stars zoomed into the solar system, onto the Earth, and dissolved into a mist.

Clay landed on the end of the drawbridge. Bowing deeply to each section of the stadium, he thanked the fans. "Next week we begin our spring show. Come and see Celia, Easy Cooper, and all the way from the Moon, our special guest the Minotaur! Also, in honor of May Day, I will be appearing on the mall at the Renaissance Faire to autograph your vids, tee-shirts, and anything else your mother will let me sign." Hooting and hollering joined the chorus of cries and thunderous applause.

Clay waved at the royal box, and a spotlight fell on the princess and her entourage. Embarrassed, Virginia stood up and waved. "Everyone stand up," she muttered. "That means you Nicholas, go ahead, wave back at everybody." Enthused by her appearance, the crowd screamed and applauded.

"Put your hands together," shouted Clay. "Welcome your favorite and ours, Princess Virginia!" In the balcony, the girls screamed.

"Princess Virginia generously supported our show tonight. On behalf of all of you, and especially from my heart, I want to say thank you." Clay bowed and then rejoined the cast.

Biots

A faded bronze star graced Jack's dressing room door. The rest of the cast shared two large locker rooms, divided between the men and the women. Given the division of labor, his dancers had plenty of space, while the men waited for the showers. He did not think of himself as a prima donna, but he had taken the star's room for the privacy. A locker room was hardly the place for a shy, introverted elf.

Two burly goblins guarded his door in black tuxedos and sunglasses. He thought of the Crown's legendary men in black, and wondered if his taxes were paid. Jack briefly suppressed an urge to flee.

"Evening, Mr. Clay," said one with a spray of gray on his temples, "Please go in." The other goblin tapped the door box. The door slid aside. "Princess Virginia hopes you will join her. She looks forward to seeing you."

From the goblin's tone, Jack had the feeling that refusing the invitation was not an option.

Inside, Jasmine leaned back in one of the makeup chairs, and the Princess occupied the other. They were discussing the advantages of whale bone corsets over plastic ones.

For a princess, Virginia looked more like a child than an heir-apparent to the throne. She cut a petite figure in a pink gown with a matching tiara, which clung desperately to a pony tail that fell to her waist.

"Princess Virginia," he said, placing his hand over his heart, "I am honored." Bending a knee, he knelt and said, "How may we help you?"

"Recover, Master Clay," said the Princess. "Please, call me Virginia."

"Why of course, Virginia," said Jack. "My friends call me Jack. It's easier to pronounce than Cretaceous and much easier to spell."

"Master Jack it is, sir," she placed her hands in lap, and

introduced her friends. The shy, young man in the naval uniform tugged at his collar. The others teenagers mumbled as the magician greeted them, and stumbled into an awkward silence. The two dwarves hugged the wallpaper.

"Virginia, thank you for coming," said Jack trying to break the ice. You enjoyed the show, I hope?"

"Yes," she spoke so softly he could barely hear. "And I saw my coat of arms flying from the castle. Was I the damsel in distress?"

"Thank you, Princess," he smiled. "Please don't mistake my show for a political statement. We flew your banner for your kindness in supporting the show."

"Oh," she said with a hint of disappointment, "father asked what I wanted for my birthday, and I told him I wanted to go to your show with friends."

"King Justin must have been surprised. Not even I can afford to buy the upper balcony."

"Daddy was surprised, but he can't say no to me. I pretty much blew my expense account, but I told daddy I was buying popularity. From his expression, I know he was impressed with my political calculations."

"It's very generous of you. Tollmerak called my publicist to find out what was going on. Not to be ungrateful, but wasn't there anything you wanted for yourself?"

"Master Jack, what can a princess want? I'm hardly deprived," she giggled. "I have my own Andromeda flyer and the best view of the city from the tallest tower."

"My lady, I'm sure the King is proud of you," he said, impressed. "Such maturity is rare for one of such tender years." Nodlon's aristocracy rarely showed any such humility in public, much less their offspring.

"Flattery will get you almost everywhere, Master Jack."

"If you're not here for autographs, how can I help?"

"Daddy said I'd make a great politician."

"My lady, I agree with your father, but aren't you a bit

young to be canvassing for support? The King is forty-seven years young and fit as a fiddle."

"Master Jack, I am not here to gain the support of the biots. I need support for the biots. May I ask a service of you off the record?"

"Off the record, Virginia?"

"Daddy doesn't know I'm here to ask for your help. This is very sensitive, and no one must know I came to you. I'm sure you can appreciate the delicacy of these matters."

"I promise no word of what you share tonight shall pass my lips."

"The council postponed consideration of daddy's manumission plan. The Council thinks there's no time for discussing the plight of biots."

"What of Mars?" he asked. "War is in the air."

"Master Jack, it has nothing to do with the war. Baron Voltaire and his accomplices in Parliament simply want to delay a vote."

"Perhaps they're right? Mars is hell-bent to start a war. The colony was a poverty-stricken dictatorship when I was born. Now it's a threat. Their ambassador warned the Middle Kingdom and the Empire of the Sun to mind their own business. Elysium declared neutrality. Now Nodlon stands alone. None of us can enjoy the gift of freedom, if we haven't got the gift of life."

"We will win," she asserted. "Though my heart fears the cost may be high in blood and lives. But we will win. Will we then rebuild Nodlon with free labor or indentured biots?"

"Princess Virginia, surely we must defend Nodlon. If your father must defend Nodlon, all of us must support him regardless of personal political differences."

"We have a majority in the Parliament. He knows the council wants to manumit the biots and extend citizenship to them. The war is an excuse to stall manumission. They hope the war will end the movement, and they won't be held accountable."

"The Baron won't give up easily. I've met him. He's been a guest here at the Circus. He's a cunning genius. He has fingers in every vice in Nodlon. If we expose his abuse of biots, his immoral enterprises will crater, and his revenues will fall. And he has many followers who enjoy the services his businesses provide. He will fight, and he will lie. If his followers don't act, he has goons and thugs who will."

"Heady stuff," Jack said. "Who's filling your head with subversive thoughts?"

"No stain can be washed away without effort. Master Cato says the Baron will blame us for his crimes, and future history will tell the story of how little my father did for the synthetic people. Likely as not, he's right. It's happened before."

"Virginia, what made you think of me, I'm not a politician?" Clay waved his hands in futility. "Many Nodlon's think there's nothing special about being human. They think humans are just animals who pollute the planet."

"A well-known entertainer posted his opinions under a thinly disguised pseudonym on a subversive website. Biots laugh, cry, bleed, and they dream. Biots are people, too, Master Jack."

"Princess, you've caught me," Clay expressed mock surprise. "Guess my opinions are hardly confidential when I post them on Clay-net."

"Yes, Master Jack," said the little princess. "If you lead, the people will follow. You will be their champion. Use Clay-net to support manumission. Help the biots! And the Crown will support the people's champion, too. I promise you that." She pulled ring from a pocket in her sash, and held it out to Jack. "Take this," she said, offering him the ring. "My signet ring bears the seal of the House of Justin. The ruby represents the heart of a virgin. Take the ring as a sign of my favor. All who love me will honor the sign."

"My lady," Clay gulped, wondering if a teenager had the

power to give away the ring. "What makes you think I am the people's champion?"

"Because you care, and you can help," she coughed, and her cheeks flushed. "My father cares, but he prepares for war. I care, but no one must know I am the source of this information."

"Princess Virginia," said Jack, "I love your spunk, and I'm grateful for friendship, but what has any of this to do with a magician? I do illusions, fireworks, and special effects." Clay waved his hands. "Look ma, no technology." He cocked a wry smile and mocked himself, "Hey, mage, shut up and pull a rabbit out of a hat. And I can't even do that by the way without an old vaudevillian sleight of hand trick." To illustrate, he picked up his hat and feigned pulling a rabbit out of it.

"We need to oppose the Baron openly. If Nodlon's human citizens can criticize him, and speak against him, openly and without fear of personal destruction, the biots may have a chance. Create that pressure, Master Jack. Mock him, humiliate him, scorn him, and make Nodlon laugh at him, and he'll melt like a wicked witch. We won't have to rely on me pretending to get an autograph from Jack Clay to leak the Council's business and betrayals."

"To push the Baron, we need pressure, lots of pressure. More than a few laughs can drum up. The Baron is no tin-pot dictator like Nogora who will implode if a jester mocks him."

"Master Jack, change is in the air. Everywhere you go, it's at the malls, in the stalls, and on the walls, and it's on the Net," she said. "We can shut down speech anytime. We can harass anyone or intimidate them into submission, but we cannot mend broken hearts. Nodlon's heart is broken. Her children cry in the night. I can hear them." A tear ran down her cheek.

Clay quickly handed her a handkerchief and she daubed her eyes.

"Thank you. I can see the children in my dreams. I know what goes on in Deep Nodlon, and it's got to stop." Her face flushed, and she tried to control her emotions. "The Crown wants what's best for Nodlon. My father wants what's best for Nodlon. And I want what's best for Nodlon. We have a majority in Parliament and almost a majority on the Council. Will you help us?"

"As you command," Clay knelt, and accepted her ring. "I want what's best for Nodlon too, though I'm not sure what I can do." He put the ring on, and bent to kiss her hand. "I will do what I can, Princess."

"Master Jack, please," she smiled. "Would you mind autographing our tee-shirts?"

"Oh, not at all, Princess," he autographed shirts, posters, and vids for all of the Princess' friends. Even Sylvester and Karl stepped forward.

Sylvester held out a shirt with Jasmine imperiled by his blue dragon. "Would you sign this for 'Julie' Mr. Clay?"

"Sure Sylvester. Is she your daughter?"

"My wife, Mr. Clay. She's a big fan."

"Anything else?" Clay held out his hands, "I'll sign anything your mother will let me sign." A chorus of 'thank you' greeted him and no one stepped forward. Mentally checking, he was one person short. The Princess Virginia held back nervously.

"Nothing for the Princess? Don't you want something signed too?"

"Well," she reached into her bag, and pulled out a tee-shirt. On the front, he and Jasmine burst from a circle of fire. He autographed her shirt.

The Princess held out her hand, and Clay gently kissed her. "Shake silly," she giggled, "Protocol is for occasions of state."

He bid her and her friends farewell four or five times and ushered them out of his door.

Jack and Jazz

Closing the dressing room door, he spun on his heel, flopped against the door, held out his arms and looked up to heaven. "Good grief, now she wants me to free the biots."

"No need for histrionics boyfriend," Jasmine mocked him. "She's right you know."

Jack slipped behind a Shoji screen to change. Stretching himself to his full height, he looked over the screen at his fiancée. "I may be Personality Web's Biot of the Year, but if I cross the Baron, I'll be swimming with the cave crabs at the bottom of the Ninth Ring of Nodlon." He emerged in a working elf's coveralls.

"You're the people's champion, Jack." She took his hand. "See she even gave you a ring to prove it. I haven't even given you my ring yet, and you're taking friendship rings from strange teenager girls."

"She's not just a teenage girl. She's the heir to the throne of Nodlon. It wouldn't do for the court jester to cross her." He hugged Jasmine, and she pushed him away.

"Boys are so black and white," she grinned to reassure him. "Let's go," she said, and threw her things in her bag.

"I'm right behind you."

They walked empty halls and stairs to the lift lobby and down to the parking garages far below.

His flyer sat in a reserved spot. White with golden pin stripes, and a smooth wedge for a nose, her sporty curves broke the sound barrier even while parked. Clay allowed himself the conceit of a little pride. For seventeen years, he worked to get where he was. He had started doing special effects at the Circus, and performed on the sidewalks on Nodlon's great mall. He moved on to pubs, private gigs, and the annual faire. Now he had a star's parking space in the Circus garage. He entertained thousands, and kept hundreds employed.

He thumbed the remote and the little flyer unlocked itself.

Her generator purred. Clay circled the flyer, and stood next to Jasmine's door. It was an unnecessary show of gallantry. The machine sensed her presence and opened her door.

"Ever the gentle ham," Jasmine laughed. She gave him a peck and climbed in.

He climbed into the driver's seat and disengaged the autopilot. He put the flyer into ground effect mode, and the levitators lifted her off the pavement.

Guiding the flyer onto the eastbound level-way, he merged with the traffic and slid into the fast lane. In the morning's wee hours, only a few vehicles shared the road. Unimpeded, he pushed his speed to the limit and let the flyer cruise on ground effect. Overhead, the blue lights of Nodlon illuminated the level-way.

~~~~~~

"Another dwarf is missing. I heard it on the news." Lights flashed across Jasmine's face.

"How many does that make?"

"Mercury News said more than forty dwarves have disappeared since the year began. Now they're saying the rash of runaways began earlier, but only a few ran last year. They think they're running away, because no one can find them. If they were in the city, their chips would have set off a sensor somewhere. No one has any idea where they could go."

"I hope they're safe too. Unscrupulous traffickers abuse runaways." Clay tapped his forehead. "They reprogram the chips, and the hapless biot cannot disobey them."

"Mercury News says the new case is different. They're calling it the Zodiac case because of a sign left at the scene. A psychologist claimed the missing dwarf was psychotic."

"Nonsense, I refuse to believe a voodoo doctor. The guy probably has never lived with a biot. Dwarves are extremely stable. Have you ever known a crazy dwarf?"

Jasmine watched the level-way's signs pass by. The lights twinkled on the sparkles in her hair. "Nope."

They were not going far. He followed the eastbound level-way through Under Nodlon, and turned north onto California Parkway following a ground car. Shifting to fly, the engine purred. He juiced the flyer, and they rose into the low flight lane. After a few blocks Babel Tower was in sight. Within minutes, they were home.

~~~~~~

Jasmine's apartment was a few floors below his, but as their wedding approached, her stuff collected in his penthouse. She dumped her load unceremoniously on his dining table.

He poured himself a root beer and stepped out onto his patio. Nodlon glowed blue under a dome of bright stars. His root beer was imported from the no man's land beyond the Pale. Aromatic and frothy, it made a good substitute for an adult beverage. Jazz hated drinking. He watched himself around her. She thought beer was fattening and might lead to heart disease. He smiled. Beer was one thing he would miss after their wedding.

"What happened to your hand?" Jasmine asked. She pushed him into a dining chair.

Blisters bloomed where a fire whip had marked him.

"I tried to catch a fire whip. It's my own fault. I was having fun and missed my mark. My mistake shouldn't ruin everyone's evening."

"You've got to be more careful. Let me take a look at that."

"Yes, doctor."

"I'm a nurse, not a doctor," she corrected him. "If I were your doctor, I'd report you to the authorities for stupidity. Magician practices magic without a brain."

"Thanks for not telling anyone."

"No problem," she quipped. "It's a minor burn. I'll get my first aid kit." She disappeared down the hall, and returned with her bag and the tools of her profession. She applied a salve, and bandaged his wound. The pain stopped so fast it made him wonder how he managed.

"Dibs on the shower." Snatching up her case and satchel, she took off towards his bathroom. "And no peeking Romeo," echoed down the hallway. Faintly, he heard the shower running.

He admired the view. Babel Tower was the not the tallest skyscraper in Nodlon. That honor went to the New Swan. The castle glittered in the moonlight. Nodlon was a fantasy built over the greatest coal mine on earth. Thornmocker's creation was fantastic for those enjoying the fruit of the apple. For those who toiled below to make everything function, the benefits were few and far between. Not that Under Nodlon, Deep Nodlon, or Moab lacked charm. Many of the finest shops were underground, and the Port of Moab drew tourists from as far away as the Space Station of Ur.

Deciding it was better to feed his girl than lose her, he left the patio. Shotgun's instructions were under a magnet on his fridge. His butler had prepared home-made spaghetti sauce, garlic bread, and a Caesar salad. For desert, he had bought a flan from Snuffie's.

Shotgun probably thinks I'll burn the custard. He boiled water for the pasta, zapped the sauce, and placed the garlic bread in the oven. He tossed everything on the dining table onto the couch, and set the table for two. He lit a candle, and put out water goblets with a lemon slice just in time.

Jasmine wandered back with her hair in a towel, struggling with her locks. "How's dinner coming?" Standing in the middle of the room, she bent over sideways and squeezed her silky hair with the towel one last time, and hung the towel over a dining chair. "I'm starving."

"Shotgun's got us all fixed up. He's prepared a spaghetti dinner."

Opening his refrigerator, Jack found a salad, and set it on the counter. Then he selected a couple of bowls, forks, and knives. "Pick a seat." He brought out the salad, and quickly divided it between them.

"Looks great, and smells better." She breathed deep enjoying the pleasant aromas. "Is any of this your doing or is it all Shotgun's?"

"All of this is Shotgun's work, except the flan. The flan's from Snuffie's."

"What did I tell 'ya? Aren't you glad I hired him?"

"Hey, I'm the one paying him." He smiled, "He's great. Cooks, cleans, keeps me in threads; and he keeps my computer updated too. He said he spent some time working for the university as a technician." He leered mischievously. "My only complaint is he's not a girl."

"Too bad for you, you've got enough girl trouble with me around. Where is he anyway, did you give him the night off?"

"Goldie has plans for him. I told him not to show up again until she was done with him. He hardly takes any time off even when I give it to him."

"Good. I'm glad I hired you a butler, but it's a bit creepy when I want you all to myself."

"I pay him well," said Jack. "No that quip's not fair, I'm glad you hired him too. He's an excellent cook, and a brilliant technician" Wandering back into the kitchen, he picked up the spaghetti, and the flan, and returned to the dining room. "He's better than an employee. He's a friend.

"Has he told you about what happened at the university yet?"

"No, not exactly, as I understand it, they think he hacked some files."

"Personnel files are what he hacked. The agency told me he was searching for genetic codes."

"Makes sense, if you can prove someone is not fully human I suppose that could be valuable."

"Blackmail?" Jasmine put her fork down. "Black dwarves are notoriously reliable and honest. Shotgun is not the type, Jack. He was after something or someone. Anyway, I knew he'd make a perfect addition. One girlfriend, one butler, and one sporty flyer parked at the best address in Nodlon this side of the Matterhorn. All you need now is a cat."

"Keep the cat. What made you think I needed Shotgun? I mean why him?"

"He's not just a typical geeky, black dwarf, he's a real nerd. Clay-net recommended him. And he's a big fan and a believer in the movement. Shotgun's one of our first Clay-net subscribers, and he's posted subversive material on Clay-net since we launched."

"Biots are people, too." He said it. It was the defacto motto of Clay-net. The phrase was not original with him, but Clay-net had put it on everyone's lips.

"Yeah, that's right. And, Shotgun is a special guy. He needed a break, and you needed someone to keep you from overloading."

Eating their early morning dinner, they talked of plans. Plans for the week, plans for the summer, and plans for life floated back and forth across the table.

"What will you do when I get pregnant?"

He put down his fork and grinned. "Promote Goldie. She's not as good as you are, but she's mastered a triple pirouette. Keep it all in the family I say."

"No, silly," Jasmine's eyes twinkled. "If Shotgun keeps feeding us like this, we'll have to go on a diet." She looked at him. "You know what I mean. I'm not talking about who will replace me in the show."

Clay closed his service, and began clearing the table. "Did you enjoy that?"

She handed her plate to Jack. "Yes, but I can't stay. I've got to be at the hospital by two, and I'm not going to make it if I don't leave now."

Taking her in his arms, he hugged her. "Why work there?"

"Because, Jack Clay. I have to do more than just dance." She squeezed him.

"You're not just a dancer. You're my partner. I pay you a fortune, and I rely on you to help me write the gags and skits."

"There's more to life than money, Jack." She gazed out at the blue lights of Nodlon and her green eyes sparkled. "At the Circus, I'm just a dancer in sexy tights. At the hospital, I'm helping people. I'm an Assistant Director of Nursing and I'm contributing to something important."

"Making people laugh is important." Irritated, he looked away. A sense of shame dropped over him. "People need to laugh. It brightens their day, and adds color to their lives. For some, it's all they have."

"I'm sorry. I didn't mean it that way." She squeezed his hand.

"Yes you did, and you're right. Nursing is more important than magic shows. I know that. My talent is magic though and it's the only talent I have. You're a one woman band of talents; dancing, singing, piano, nursing, and you speak three languages. And you can stop an asteroid in free fall! What can I do?" Was his love true or mere vanity? "Sorry," he said. "Maybe I'm just selfish and jealous. I'm going to marry you and I don't want to share you with your patients."

"You're honest, too, and that's worth something. Not many boys have any humility these days." She reassured him with a hug.

He blushed. "Summer seems so long from now. I can't wait," he complained.

"You're just going to have to," she grinned. "If it helps, I can't wait either." She stood on her toes, and gave him a quick kiss. "After we're married, you can have me."

"So, does that mean you'll quit working at the hospital, or I can see you there during visiting hours?"

"Come on, walk me to my car." She squeezed him again.

Cutting the embrace short, she pushed him away. She collected her satchel, grabbed her keys, and headed out the door. Together, they rode down the lift to the garage.

"Speaking of visiting hours, I want you to come by. There's a girl I want you to meet."

"Anything to help the sick, I'll be there."

"Make sure you are. She's a suicide."

"A suicide? If she's a suicide, how can I visit her? Wouldn't that be encouraging bad behavior?"

"She's a red dwarf named Melissa. She swallowed a bottle of pills and died last Friday. Fortunately, her agency had her chip feed tied to a manned emergency board. When she stopped breathing, they couldn't believe it but they called emergency anyway. She'd been dead about a quarter of an hour when the medics found her. They shot her up with Afterlife and she's making an excellent recovery. Never thought I'd say chipping was a good idea, but at least in this case it saved one person's life."

"Why would she hurt herself? That's got nothing to do with a chip. Should I be chipping you?" He smiled lamely, not sure where this was going. He felt uncomfortable. He hated chipping, and he railed against the practice on Clay-net. Usually, agencies only chipped their biots to track their whereabouts. But humans never had to accept a chip for a job. Biots were not so lucky.

"Just be there. Be your happy, plucky self, and leave the brilliant, depressed introvert at home. You don't want to know why a kid tries killing herself. Besides, it's confidential."

They reached Jasmine's roadster, a fully loaded Europa III in electric pink with a brown convertible top. "You didn't answer my question, Jack Clay."

"I love children. That's why I love my job. I love making kids laugh, and offering a nice clean show. You know, I'm not faking that. And I laugh at my own jokes, and I cry at the sad parts. But being a father? Being a dad? I'm not sure. I never knew mine."

He broke off. The pressure was terrible. He felt the tears in his eyes, and he bit his lip. Phaedra had taught him not to yell or curse in the company of women and children.

"You're a good elf, Jack Clay, and you'll make a good dad." She puckered up. "Kiss." She tossed her satchel into the back seat, and climbed in.

Leaning on her roadster, he kissed her and stepped back. "Love, you too."

Blowing him another kiss, she waved, guided the roadster out of the garage, and she was gone.

Nimrod

Nimrod soared over the mountains of Zagros. Sherry, his roc, beat the air with her wings rising over the ridges of the eastern face of the mountain of Nisir. Flocks of sheep and goats bolted as he and Sherry glided overhead. Spying a ram with horns as long as a man's arm, his fingers twitched.

"Soon, my pet, you will feast on fresh meat."

Stowing his riding crop, he circled the roc above the herd, and clinched his saddle between his knees. Unslinging his war bow, and drawing a bolt from his quiver, he armed himself. His bow was strung with dragon's hair. Brass cowls protected the bow's tips from this toughest of threads. He set the bolt's notch in the nock and clasped the grip. Thus armed, he took Sherry's reins in his free hand and flicked.

Knowing his intention from long training and many lashes, she dove. The herd scattered. With his free hand, he refined her dive. Gently he guided her towards the herd's proud patriarch. A magnificent ram sprang upon the ridge of Nisir and bolted down the cliff. He imagined his trophy hanging in his suite above the fire.

He kicked Sherry into a dive, and matched the ram's descent. As fast as the ram ran, the roc dropped from the sky. The ram scrambled for shelter under a ledge hoping to escape the roc's reach. Sherry's shadow crossed the ram's path, and its horns dipped. The ram knew it was too late.

Nimrod drew the dragon's hair taught. The ram dodged, evading the imminent attack. He waited for the shot. He led the ram, and for a second he held his breath. He released the bolt. The bow string sang.

The bolt cut the air and struck home. It drilled through the ram's heart. Stricken, the ram toppled down the cliff. He somersaulted over a ridge towards the floor of the Dead Sea, and Nimrod cursed. Then the ram slammed into a small outcrop. Its broken body bounced once and stopped. He slung his war bow and whooped with joy. He little wanted to descend to the floor of the Dead Sea of Umber to recover his prize.

He squeezed Sherry with his knees. The roc needed no encouragement. She enjoyed this part of the hunt.

The roc landed and Nimrod leapt from her back. Stones dislodged by his sandals rained off the rocky ledge. Shards of shale, feldspar and dolomite slid off and cascaded down the mountain. Sherry waited as he unsheathed his hunting blade. In short work, he field dressed the ram and lashed his bloody trophy to Sherry's side. Rolling up the hide, he stuffed it into a sack cloth brought for the occasion, and lashed it beside his trophy.

Mounting his steed, he jiggled her reins, and cooed, "Dinner my sweet, enjoy your reward." Released from his restraint, the roc tore the carcass to bits and swallowed the pieces whole. Carefully, she pecked at the outcrop rescuing every morsel. Finished, she purred and cocked her head to see him.

"Yes sweetie, you've done well." He scratched Sherry behind her ears, and tugged on her reins.

With a leap, Sherry launched from the outcrop. She unfurled her wings and beat the air. The roc soared away from the cliff and pounded the air. The desert floor slid by far below as they sailed east. High above, strips of cloud drifted beneath the scarlet canopy. Lightning danced on the horizon. Flashes flickered on the dome of the sky.

Rolling into the thermals, Sherry circled higher. The burning floor shimmered in the heat. Riding the thermals, he guided Sherry west to the safety of Uruk and headed home. They climbed into the thin air, and caught the wind of Umber. The eternal storm drove hot breezes off the dead sea year round. The storm battered the mountains with hot air. It forced air out of the abyss, up the face of the mountains, and into the valley between Zardkuh and Nisir. The cooler air tempered the swelter of Gehenna's hot climate. They glided into the valley.

He recalled the days when he had joined the Dragon Lord. It had begun when he had duped the Hamites into following Ashur.

~~~~~~

It was the astrologers of Ashur who gave him the power. At the cusp of the New Year when Capricorn was high and the winter solstice festivals began, the astrologers sought out a young princeling of the King of Babel in the land of Shinar. They had come to find him.

The astrologers taught him how to read the signs of the gods. And they told him of a Great King who would shape the future. If he wanted to rule all the world, they said, he only had to defeat that king. To that end, he had to go into the mountains in the west, seek the unholiest of places, and once there, sacrifice a child on the altar of a strange god.

He took a cur of one of his concubines whom he had seized in war. Dressed as a rogue with a squire and a sword for hire, he sought out the place for many moons. He followed the instructions given to him by the sages. He found the unholy mountain. There, he entered a forgotten temple built within a chimney at the mouth of a lost valley. Inside, he discovered a deserted altar covered in strange runes. There he spilt the boy's blood upon the altar.

Chanting the incantation of power in the first tongue, he opened the portal and crossed over to Gehenna. There he saw the Great Ziggurat upon the shoulder of Zardkuh. He fought foe upon foe through the city of New Babylon.

Impressed by his skill, power, and zeal, the Dragon Lord granted him the right to an audience. Standing before the Dragon Lord, he retold the story of the great king. He asked the Dragon Lord to grant him a boon to help him defeat that king and rule all the world. In return, he and all of his subjects would worship the Dragon Lord until the ending of his kingdom.

Pleased, the Dragon Lord promised him the world as his kingdom, if he would but set his foot against a babe born in the land of Ur. For the blood of that nation's male children, the Dragon offered him dominion over the world.

Nimrod swore to find the infant, stretch out his arm, and destroy the seed of the Dragon's enemy. Thus, he became the servant of the Dragon Lord.

Sent back to the world by the Dragon Lord, he returned to Babel. Through clever intrigue, he assassinated his brother Samass and blamed it on their rival, the King of the Amorites. He renamed his city Babylon, and made it the capital of his kingdom.

The Dragon Lord was as good as his promise, and his armies covered Mesopotamia as his kingdom flourished. The Tigris and Euphrates ran red with blood, and gold swelled his treasuries. With abandon, he built his concubines a garden to sweeten their ardor, and he set his sights on heaven itself. And he ordered the construction of a tower from which he could challenge the gods. *Those were the days of my glory. days I will soon relive again.*

To conceal the murder of his brother, his armies secretly descended upon the Amorites to avenge the assassination. He sent emissaries ahead to the Amorites to parlay. They convinced the nobles that their success was owed to none but their god Ashur. Wise in their own eyes, they fell for his flattery. Feeling no need to honor tradition or the old gods, they gave over their allegiance to none but King Og.

Nimrod laughed even now at their gullibility. Og was a fool who listened only to the astrologers of Ashur. And those same astrologers served none other than Nimrod. He called the astrologers of Ashur and ordered them to betray their King or answer to him for giving him the secret of the Great King.

The astrologers accused Og's loyal subjects of treason and praised his enemies. Thinking he was surrounded by enemies, Og assassinated his friends and exiled his allies.

Taking advantage of the now defenseless king, Nimrod boldly revealed his armies. Awed by the might of Nimrod, King Og called forth a champion to battle the young conqueror rather than risk open battle. But he was betrayed. Instead of defending the king from Nimrod, the champion of the Amorites challenged the king for his throne. Alone and beleaguered, the King took his own life in despair. In this way, the Amorites fell into Nimrod's trap.

Nimrod put the traitor to death and added the strength of the Amorites to his own. Next he attacked Erech, Calneh, Uruk, and many others. Those who worshipped him became his subjects, and those who did not perished. His army took the women they desired, and the rest he enslaved. Each city he conquered added to his power and soon he turned his sight on Akkad. In those days the Akkadian empire had grown weak at the hand of King Sharka. He defeated the king and conquered that realm.

Now he had the strength to repay his debt to the Dragon Lord. He turned his wrath to the south and with the full might of Babylon, he fell upon the great kingdom of Ur. He put King Ibbi-Sin to death and ended the line of Ur-Nammu. Slaughtering all who resisted, he put to sword every male child without speech. Though the cur escaped, his ferocity and ruthlessness pleased the Dragon Lord, and he rose in favor with the prince of Gehenna.

He had changed the world. He had brought war to Earth. Where before men had lived their lives, cherished their wives and delighted in their children, his power ordered the lives of his slaves. He delighted in their torment. Inwardly he basked in his achievements and gloated in his success.

~~~~~~~

Over the pass, Sherry plunged down the other side. Soaring high over the fields of Uruk, he watched the servants toil in the blazing sun. He swooped over his master's fields. The startled peasants crouched in fear of the roc. The rulers of Uruk encouraged rocs to feed upon the peasants to maintain a ready stock for their cavalry. Nimrod laughed as his mount climbed again.

Curling the reins, he circled the roc and put the sun to his back. Ahead of him was the Ziggurat. The time had come, and he had to reach the stables and leave Sherry and his prizes with his squire before the Dragon Lord called. Below, the fields of vines, cotton, wheat, and trees of olives ended at the scrub grass surrounding the city's narrow moat. He heard the crack of whips drifting on the wind.

Unafraid of the other powers and princes of Gehenna, the moat discouraged the peasants from escaping. Few tried to depart the city of New Babylon, as there was nowhere for the pathetic creatures to go. Nonetheless madness occasionally drove them into the desert or up the mountains trying to seek another route. An option they no longer had.

He pulled back on Sherry's reins, and soared high over the city. Sherry beat her wings and approached the Ziggurat. They climbed higher into the red sky. Before crossing over the differential, he meant to enjoy one last dive.

High above the plains of Uruk, the stone of the Ziggurat reflected the blazing glow of Ashur shining through the clouds. Perhaps it was a fitting compensation for the loss of his home. Red stains ran down the cliffs running along the ridge upon which the palace stood. There it enjoyed the coolest breezes on Gehenna.

He threw Sherry into the dive. Falling, his blood rushed as they swooped down upon the Ziggurat and headed for the stables at the back of the palace just above the cliffs. Flaring its wings, the roc lifted its flaps and braked. Slowing, the roc dropped to the tarmac at the mouth of the stables. His squire, a blond of the north with untold sins awaited him beneath the palm fronds of the servant's lean-to. Seeing him approach, the lad ran from the shelter and knelt at the edge of the landing circle drawn on the tarmac.

Sherry folded her wings, and lowered herself for a formal dismount. Alert to the needs of his master, his squire ran up to them and bowed. Nimrod tossed the boy the reins. Throwing a leg over the roc's neck, he dropped to the tarmac and addressed his squire.

"Any news, Heinrich?"

"Hermes awaits you in the observatory, I told him you were hunting, and he said there was no hurry."

"Good Heinrich, you have served me well these many years. You are to enter the service of the temple, and serve the goddess until my return. I am only loaning you out, so do not become too comfortable."

"Thank you, my lord. Was your hunt profitable?"

"Yes, another fine trophy for my hall. Take the ram's head to the taxidermist and the hide to the tanner. Tell the old loafer I'll brand him again if he damages the pelt. Sherry has eaten her fill. Give her water and brush her down. Collar her with my design upon her tag, and put her out with the cavalry's herd."

"Yes, my lord, as you command."

Heinrich hurried away, leading the roc into the stables. He was confident his steed would be well cared for in his absence. Were Sherry not fit for service when he returned, those responsible would feel his wrath.

Striding through the palace to his suite, the servants dodged aside and bowed lest he unleash his wrath upon them. Opening the gate to his own apartment, a maid greeted him and awaited his pleasure. Handing his bow to her, he ordered a bath. From his private veranda, he enjoyed the view of New Babylon and Uruk. As he waited for the maids to draw his water, he reflected on his latest enterprise.

He changed into his dress armor and belted on a sword. Rubies mounted on the hilt flashed as he checked his blade.

Runes along its side prevented corrosion and chipping and ensured it never needed sharpening. He added greaves and bronze gauntlets. Finally, he took his staff and admired his image in a mirror. He imagined the terror of his enemies when he returned to Earth.

And he smirked.

East of Eden

Evan's supervisor asked no questions and gave him a medical day pass. Clutching the pass, he headed for the exit trying to sneak out. The day shift had started at Bio-Soft and everyone was working. No one was in the hall. Just a few more seconds, and he would be gone, and no one would see him.

The lift at the end of the corridor opened. He quickened his pace hoping he could get away. Embarrassed, he shoved the pass into his pocket.

"Evan?" said Festus.

Evan smiled and saluted him with a nod, "Hey, old timer." He was trapped.

Wizened and frail, the goblin hobbled faster. His eyes followed Evan.

"Hay is for horses. Got a pass?" Festus kept a log of all the comings and goings. After all, Festus was the dorm's resident.

"Yes sir." Evan avoided eye contact. Despite Festus' gruff surface, he thought of him as a friend. Festus had proven his loyalty to his charges, and he had covered for Evan more than once.

"Give her a hickey for me."

"It's not what you think old timer." Evan dropped his gaze to his loafers. He hated lying to the goblin. Since Nanny had passed away, Festus was the only family he had. He tried to pass, but the goblin stopped him with a claw. The goblin whispered, "Be careful. It isn't safe."

Evan tried not to be irritated. "What is it Festus?" He knew the fellow meant well but he hoped to keep his business private. "Are your corns aching or your bunions acting up?"

"Now, ain't right you funnin' on an old goblin." Festus twitched, "Winds of change are in the air. Hope springs eternal in the hearts of men." Gravel rolled in the goblin's mouth. "Boys forget they prey on the young and innocent. They prowl for the unwary. They use hope for bait."

"Who Festus?" Evan scoffed, "Space aliens again?"

"Know this ain't no home for a boy, and less so for a man." Festus frowned, and his eyes moistened, "But I'll miss you if you meet a bad end. Just you be careful."

"I'll be careful, Festus. I'll see you next week when I come for my check." He squeezed past the goblin. "Be seeing you." Quickening his pace, Evan hurried away.

~~~~~~~

Pacing and fidgeting, he waited for a robo-cab. He gave the cab's driver his destination and his debit number, and he grumbled at the price. The cab dropped to the level-way through Deep Nodlon. Minutes later the cab slid off the level-way, and onto Spenard Boulevard. Nodlon's blue light flooded the tunnel as the sun rose with the dawn. Where other districts were choked with commuters, Spenard slept. The cab sailed smoothly past little shops and cafes, and into the bowels of the Blues District. Intermingled with the shops were brownstones, townhomes, and dilapidated hotels. Boarded windows defended abandoned properties, and graffiti marked boundaries. It was not a place he would let a child play. In Under Nodlon, the children crowded the bus stops, played hooky in the park, and rode their skateboards. Here, no children were in sight.

The cab drove down Spenard before it turned, and slowed to a halt. On the corner, a derelict sat on the sidewalk reading a book. A sagging bowler at his feet begged for an offering. Next to him, a sandwich board read, "Sacrifice children to Moloch and perish." The old man lowered his book and caught Evan's eye. A cold chill ran down his back.

Uncomfortable, he lowered himself in the cab. From the lip of the cab's windows, he watched as the blocks flashed by. They passed the Salome Club. The marquee displayed a scantily clad elf. Embarrassed, he looked away.

The cab crossed the edge of the district into a block of trade shops. They passed an open convenience store. A woman in a black cloak stepped into the street oblivious to the oncoming cab. The robot braked to avoid hitting her. More seconds ticked by as she crossed the street.

Quietly, the cab resumed its progress. Shortly, it slid into a quiet residential neighborhood of small professional shops with narrow fronts. The cab stopped in front of a shop with a neat, modern façade. A tall sign proclaimed, "New Gem." Underneath the sign, a streaming banner read, "Don't be blue! Dreams come true!"

Evan got out of the cab and walked to the sleek door. The glass opened as he approached, and he stepped into an attractive waiting room.

A red dwarf waited alone, gripping a copy of Nod and Home. The cover article featured faux window treatments for subsurface apartments. Like all dwarf maidens, she was cute. Evan tried not to stare. *Why she would go for gene therapy*, he wondered?

He turned his back, and the red dwarf snuck a peek at him over her magazine.

What would happen if he just asked her to leave with him? Whatever scene she was into, he would join. All Nodlon's dwarves shared more in common than differences. Why not accept the offer? It had to be cheaper than gene therapy, and they could both be themselves rather than paying to become something else.

Fearing rejection, he quickly dismissed the thought. *Dwarf girls want a mate with more money and power than a dwarf boy offers.*

Seeing him standing there, the receptionist greeted him, "Welcome to New Gem, New genes, New Gem!"

"Hi, I'm Evan," he said, staring at the goblin. "I have an appointment." An urge to flee welled up within him.

"Evan Labe, you've come to the right place. The doctor

will be right with you." He wanted to ask so many questions, but he was afraid to interrupt her. He turned away from the bar separating them and looked for a chair.

Papers rustled behind the receptionist and a young dwarf said, "Sally."

"All done today? Can I use the same card?"

"Sure, that works." The patient entrance door swung open, and a white dwarf appeared. Spying Evan, he grinned and thrust out his hand. "Hi, brother from another mother! Trust me! This is the best deal you've ever made. Everything they said on the vid is true, and you won't regret it for a moment."

The receptionist peered through her window and leaned on the bar. "Hey Chuck, can you spare a minute?"

"Anything for you Sally," the dwarf sauntered to the bar and leered at the receptionist. Evan stumbled back a step shocked by Chuck's wanton flirting. The dwarf winked at Sally and flashed a grin at the receptionist.

Passing a thin folder to Chuck, the goblin asked, "Will you show our new guest your before-and-after pictures?"

"Soft sell, hey?" Chuck surveyed Evan up and down.

Evan shifted uncomfortably under Chuck's stare. He exuded a confidence that eluded Evan. Both wore the universal coveralls of dwarf technicians, but Chuck's coveralls were crisp. He sported pleats Evan had never seen before, and his hair was perfect. Evan knew he looked as though he had slept in his uniform because he had. Evan ran a hand through his hair, pressing his cowlicks.

Chuck had a manic look in his eye. "Slept in your coveralls, didn't you?" he taunted. "Tossed and turned all night, I bet. Am I right? Had to go to the community room and watch vid all night, didn't you? Am I right?"

Evan's eyes dropped, and he crossed his arms. "I've got my own place."

The dwarf circled him. Stopping shoulder to shoulder with Evan, he hugged him. "My boy, I was just like you until I came here. Heck, worse! When I crawled in here, I couldn't look myself in the eye! I was such a mess. I was as thin as a scarecrow. Now, look at me!" He pulled up his sleeve. A nymph on his arm held a banner declaring his love for "Brandy." The nymph danced as his muscles rippled.

He opened the folder, and sorted a few sheets. He flipped the file over. "Before and after pictures, they take to verify the results." On the left stood Chuck in a barren room before a white wall. He wore shorts and nothing else. His shorts clung desperately to his waist. A small gut mocked his lanky frame, but his bones poked through everywhere else. He smiled lamely with an expression of a boy trying not to cry. After the treatment, Chuck struck a body builder's pose wearing the same shorts. The new buff version of Chuck showed off six-pack abs. Muscles Evan had never seen before bulged from every angle. Tanned flesh beamed health from every fiber.

"Yeah, am I right?" The effervescent dwarf put a hand on Evan's shoulder, and whispered, "When I came here, I'd never dated anyone. See that red behind you? When you're done here, reds like her will eat out of your hand."

Evan gulped.

"That's another sale for Chuck, hey!" He slapped the folder on Sally's desk. "When will I get my commission?"

The receptionist snatched the folder off her bar. "Thanks Chuck, but the doctor is a tightwad."

"Call me babe. If he won't give us a commission, I will." He rubbed his fingers together.

Chuck palmed a card. "After your last session, we'll do it. We'll go see Cretaceous Clay and see the magician and his dancers. Hey, hey!" Clapping Evan's hand, he forced his card into the dwarf's palm, and curled Evan's fingers over it. He pointed his thumb at himself and his index finger at Evan and mouthed, "Call me!"

"Bye, all," Chuck said with a friendly wave, and he be bopped out the door.

Sally tapped the bar, "Evan, let me explain a few things. Treatments are painless, and each takes about three hours. Today we won't be doing any treatments, just taking samples to determine suitability. During the next visit the Doctor will go over the results and determine a course of treatment you can afford. Usually, the therapy takes three treatments, but there may be up to a dozen. I've never seen the Doctor use more than five on a guy though. Today, I will need a deposit. If you decide to go ahead, today's visit and the lab testing are included in our fee. We offer payment plans at no interest."

She paused letting him think for a second. "Would you like to talk to the doctor?"

"How much will it cost? I mean all of it, the whole thing."

"That depends on what you and the doctor decide." She smiled again. "I'm not supposed to tell you, but the basic treatment is all you need. That's what Chuck took, and you saw the results."

"If it worked for him, I guess it'll work for me."

"You're with the Ministry of Manna aren't you? What do you do there?"

"Yeah, I'm a data geek. I run the macro banks, security, and intersystem communications between Nodlon's utilities. The Ministry is good. They have a buy-out program. I contribute, and they match my contributions. I'm putting in the max, so I can buy out of my contract in maybe ten years."

"Impressive."

"Thanks." Had he said too much?

"When the doctor is through with you, I bet you can sue for emancipation. Want to give me your card, and we can get this show on the road?"

Opening the patient's entrance, she ushered him through a corridor decorated with testimonial photos. She sported a tight velvet dress, which ended an impossible distance from the floor. She was tall for a goblin and her high heels forced him to avert his eyes to avoid staring. Nonetheless she affected a pleasant, professional demeanor.

"You'll be seeing Dr. Jerry Balaam. He's trained on Elysium and finished his residencies here in Nodlon." She directed him to sit on an examining table. "Dr. Balaam is a goblin from the Blue Ridge. Don't be surprised."

Alone in the stark room, Evan looked around. Every wall was bare save a poster of Earth. Elysium girdled the planet gleaming in the sun. Bold letters read, "A New World Just for You! New Genes, New Gem!" An urge to leave came over him.

The door opened and startled Evan.

"Hi, Evan, what can we do for you today?" Balaam's height set him apart from any elf. He was the tallest goblin Evan had ever seen.

"I saw an infomercial."

"The corporate office makes those."

"Do you know who the girl is? I mean, is she real, or a sprite?"

"She's a nyad. I don't recall her name, but she's a supermodel on Mars."

"Oh, I wondered."

"Sally said you'd probably like the basic package. I could give you the works, but there's not much reason for it."

"What's the difference?"

"Aside from cost? Unless you want to become a girl, or have your bones lengthened until you're as tall as an elf, there isn't any difference. Almost all the boys take the basic package. Girls often take an option or two beyond the basics." He sat on his stool and tapped on his workstation. The doctor chuckled, "If a boy wants more than the basic package, I make him see a shrink first."

"Guess I'll take the basic package then."

Balaam knew what he was doing and went through the examination perfunctorily. "The phlebotomist will take a sample of blood, and show you to the restroom. She may give you a pill to prevent you from fainting. Taking blood may cause vertigo.

Be sure and make your next appointment on your way out."

"Thank you, doctor."

Something felt wrong, but when he tried to think of why, he was at a loss. "Think about it, what's the difference? If a girl likes a hunk, will she like me?" He shook off the warning. He had no one. Even lonely dwarf girls shunned him. They knew their worth and they were not going to waste their time on a nerd. Doubt forced him to scrupulously analyze himself. "You can't dance, sing, or catch a ball. You read technical books, and watch monster movies. You tell nerd jokes. You're a nerd, Evan!"

Gripping the table with both hands, he tried to decide whether to leave or stay. A chorus shouted in his head. "Get up, loser! Leave now!" He could not afford the treatments. "Stop worrying." He would pay for this for years. He rubbed his temples. "After this you will still be a nerd."

"Evan Labe?" the nurse startled him. She was a goblin with pentagrams dangling from her ears, "Come on, handsome."

"Handsome?"

"First step from nerd to lover-boy is confidence." She beamed him a sly grin, and batted her eyelashes.

Evan forgot his concerns.

"I'm Uma by the way. Just follow directions, and it'll all be over faster than you can say, 'Change your life.'" After scanning, she took a blood sample.

Uma led Evan back to the examination room. She sat at the workstation and entered her findings on the screen.

"Do you understand how gene therapy works?" Uma asked.

"Superficially, I figure if you're a biot, you ought to know something about how they made you."

She muttered agreement, and tapped a key on her workstation. "Please wait here." Her heels clicked as she walked away. He heard mumbled conversation, and the clicking returned.

"Good news, the doctor gave you a clean bill of health. He said you're a diamond."

She filled a cup with water, and took a packet of pills from the cabinet.

"These will prevent dizziness and fainting spells." She gave him a wry smile, and said, "Don't worry about the taste. They're apple flavored."

Dutifully, Evan swallowed the pills. "Dwarves are sharp, but we're compulsive, and obsessive." A wave of weariness swamped him, and he braced himself on the table. "I'm no better than any other dwarf." His voice echoed down a deep canyon. His vision narrowed, and the room began to dim. "Uma, I feel dizzy. I need to lie down."

Uma grabbed his arm, and pushed him down onto the examination table. She lifted his legs, and laid him out prone. The ceiling spun and he gripped the table.

"Take a nap, Evan, a long nap."

He closed his eyes, and the spinning stopped.

The Black Dwarf

Bidding the maids farewell, Nimrod bounded out his gate and strode to the observatory. Spies of Baal sank into the shadows as he passed. He ignored them. Their master had more to fear from the Dragon Lord than he. Through force of will, Moloch, the Dragon Lord, ruled the Ziggurat with an iron fist. Not even the differential of the crossover between the worlds diminished his power. Meanwhile, his brothers dissipated their powers in endless intrigues.

Setting his foot upon the stairs to the observatory, he climbed. Without need of rest or repair, he fairly ran up the stairs. At the top was a wide deck of stone with a parapet of granite capped in marble. Small telescopes and astrolabes stood mounted around the circumference. Above it all stood a twelve-cubit telescope mounted on a set of gimbals held by two gargoyles carved in granite. In turn the gargoyles stood on a granite base which rested on steel balls rolling in a trough carved into the deck. Affixed to the gimbal system at its crest was a crystal ball. Through the ball his master commanded the scope to turn with the sky.

Bound forever in a blanket of clouds, Gehenna was one world where stars never lit the sky. No stars could be seen anywhere save below the eye of the eternal storm. He grinned at the irony, but of course these telescopes were not for seeking the light of ordinary stars.

Hermes and Chancellor Adrammelech waited for him. Adrammelech bowed.

"Greetings Master Hermes," said Nimrod. He scowled at Adrammelech, and the worm cringed. "Am I late?"

"No my lord, but the optimum time of passage nears, and our master will soon call."

"Then why do you wait on me, as a schoolmarm waits upon a boy?"

"Of course, I see you are ready, my lord. I wait simply to

assist you, Master Nimrod."

"Good worm, don't let your eyes forget it." The obsequious chancellor withered and backed away.

"And how goes it with Olympus, Master Hermes?"

The thin and pale ambassador of their sometimes ally and sometimes enemy, tipped his brow and unfurled his silvered wings. "Well indeed, Master Nimrod, Olympus bids you well in your journey and success in your venture. Once you have gone, I shall take my leave and report to Jupiter."

"Adieu, fair prince, I shall not have time for parting ceremonies." Cautiously, Nimrod dipped his brow, keeping his eye on the uncertain ally.

"Farewell, noble conqueror. May you bury your enemies in the bowels of the old world." Pleased, Nimrod and Hermes exchanged a nod again, and set to wait upon the proper hour.

The Riders

"Remove the refreshments," snarled the Dragon Lord. His Amazons sprang into action, and cleared away the remains of his meal.

While they worked, he basked in the fires burning around his throne. Choosing a leviathan as his own vessel was a stroke of genius. But the creature's cold body required heat. Unwinding his serpentine bulk, he popped the knuckles in his claws.

"Bring my crystal ball."

An Amazon sprang from her post. On her helm, a red mane identified her as the dwarf maiden serving as the leader this hour. She signaled to a companion, and together the Amazons scurried away to fetch the ball. The maidens returned carrying the heavy ball and set it before the dragon.

Carefully, the dwarves secured the ball on the podium. Bowing to the Dragon, they backed away from the throne.

Unwinding his tail, the Dragon rose from his throne and set the black pads of his foot paws on the pentagram's lip. His claws scratched the marble, and he unfurled his wings. Thrusting his forepaws into the air, he chanted the incantations of power. A flaw within the crystal ball flickered. The ball glowed and the glow swelled. Firelight glinted off the Dragon's scales.

A white fire pierced the ball's center and washed out the ball's red glow. The beam radiated around the throne room, and a ghost appeared riding a white stallion. Armored in leather and sandals, the stallion bore its rider on a hornless saddle without stirrups. The rider was armed with a spear resting in a cup slung from the horse's harness, and a bronze sword hung from his belt.

The ghost bowed to the Dragon Lord without dismounting. The stallion dipped its head to him, and resumed its proud stance.

"My Lord," said the ghost, "what is your pleasure?"

"Alert Nimrod to prepare for the cross over."

"As you command, my lord," and the ghost backed away from the Dragon, and the crystal ball swept him from the throne room. The fire within the ball died, and the flaw cooled to orange.

~~~~~

Nimrod preferred punctuality, and his calculations were not amiss. Within minutes, four ghost riders landed on the observatory's deck born on winged stallions.

Stewards of limbo, they served his master in the vast reaches of the abyss. Clad in the armor of ancient kings as black as their steeds, they were no more than the shadows of phantoms. Beneath their hoods, undead grins beamed from pallid cheeks. The Captain approached him without dismounting and withheld his salutation.

Nimrod knew the Captain was not impressed, but he dared not challenge the Rider. Who knew the consequences if he drew his sword on the insolent knave? He little understood the nature of their powers and he cared less. The riders would draw his chariot through the telescope to the eye and up the ladder above Gehenna to the crossover. They would protect his frame in this plane from the ravages of the space above the air.

The Captain threw him the end of a brass chain.

"The stars reach their alignment," said the Captain. "The one who wishes to crossover must forge his own destiny."

Kicking his horse, the Captain led his troop to the foot of the telescope dragging the chain. Nearly riding over the onlookers, the horsemen drove Adrammelech and Hermes back to the edge of the observation deck. They had to step lively to avoid being trampled.

The riders dragged a chariot mounted on skis. Taking his end of the chain, Nimrod attached it to a hitch on the chariot, and climbed aboard. The chain's other end ran to a ring joining it to four harnesses worn by the stallions. Grabbing the handle bars, he saw the chariot was without reins, crop, or whip. On this journey, he was a passenger.

~~~~~~

"Prepare the sacrifices," the Dragon ordered.

Amazons readied the throne room, and prepared the altars. They brought two tables and placed each on either side of his pentagram as he had instructed them. A sack cloth covered each table, and on these they laid a dwarf.

The leader thrust out her fist and knelt. "My lord, shall we leave the dwarf's microchip on or turn it off?" She pointed to the black spot on the boy's forehead.

"Nimrod is always with me. He needs no mark."

Saluting him, the Amazon leader backed away, and turned off the boy's chip.

In a short space, all the preparations were ready. The leader approached him again, and the Amazons knelt behind her.

"We have done as you command, my lord."

"Shoo, back to your posts." The Amazons obeyed,

slinking back to the shadows beneath the throne room's columns. Sensing the danger, his guardians also retreated, inching away from their posts at the edge of the pentagram.

The Dragon Lord gloated over his victims.

Over the limp form of the black dwarf boy, he cooed, "Evan Labe, you could not resist my call. You sought your life, but you gave it away. Now your soul and your body are mine. Your flesh shall be a shell for my servant Nimrod to occupy. Your shell is as innocent as a babe, and I shall pour into it the living spirit of Nimrod. Fusing your shell and my servant shall make him more powerful than any creature walking the face of the Earth!"

The Dragon Lord noticed his Amazon's cowering in the shadows, and added, "Excluding myself of course."

He purred over the girl, "My dear, Nadia, your soul shall open the gate. Like your companion, you too gave up your life to my ambitions. When I cast you into the outer darkness, I shall be free to use the hole that remains."

~~~~~~

The Dragon Lord waved his Amazons and guardians away. The Amazons trembled, and their ankle bells jingled. Even his mighty guardians felt their hair prickle.

Balancing over the pentagram, his fiery eyes bulged. Power coursed through him filling him with ecstasy. Flames erupted from his forepaws, and balls of fire swirled in his hands. The fire balls blazed, nearly scorching the constellations of the Zodiac painted on the dome. The stars of the Milky Way glittered.

"Open the way," he commanded. "Let me see my world."

The Dragon canted a mantra in the forgotten tongue. The pentagram burned, and fire ripped from the stone. The fire balls flared in his forepaws and the balls spun. The fire balls roared as the Dragon drew manna across the differential between Gehenna and Earth.

The Dragon repeated his incantation, and shouted again, "Open the way!"

For a third time, the Dragon canted the spell, and cried, "Curse this creature and drive its soul from its body. Send it into the deep. Damn it for all time. The power of the dragon compels you. The prince of darkness compels you. The curse of the accuser compels you."

Chanting in the forgotten tongue, the Dragon's mortal frame swelled as the manna coursed through him. Wisps of smoke twirled in thin threads and wove into ribbons.

"Depart souls of the innocents," he cackled. "Cross the differential, and open the channel to my world."

Lying on the altar tables, the dwarves shuddered. The maid's blood ran from her chip driven by magical pressure. With the pop of a cork, her chip shot into the air, sailed across the throne room, bounced off the cornice at the foot of the dome, and fell to the stone floor clattering. The girl's body stiffened and jerked as her blood sprayed from the wound. Boiling in the heat of the fire pits, her blood flashed into steam, and the dried flakes drifted down to the altar.

"I cast your soul into the outer darkness," hissed the Dragon with glee. Wracked by one last spasm, the girl fell limp. Her body glowed white and her Kirlian aura briefly scorched the air and crossed the differential. Only a wisp of white fog remained.

The pentagram dissolved and Gehenna appeared. The stars of Capricorn blazed behind the red planet. The Dragon clenched the portal's lip. Twisting his balls of fire, the roar subsided as he gazed upon the red clouds of the eternal storm. Over the Dead Sea of Umber, the storm boiled beneath the blazing light of Ashur. Lightning ripped the scarlet clouds. Ashur dusted Gehenna's crescent in orange.

"Come forth, Nimrod, your master awaits thee."

Crossing Over

Lightning flashed, and the clouds rumbled. Rhythmically, the rumble rose. A sound as if a tornado approached drifted down. Lightning split the sky and thunder cracked over their heads. White fire belched from the mouth of the telescope. Atop the telescope the crystal ball glowed, and the telescope rolled to face their destination.

Nimrod took pride in his courage, and he stood firm. He chuckled as both Adrammelech and Hermes flinched. The white fire revolved with a thunderous roar. The deck trembled, and the wind ripped their clothing.

A tornado shot from the mouth of the telescope. The tornado rose from the observatory atop of the Ziggurat and ran to the east over Zardkuh. It spiraled into the sky, and dipped towards the eye of the eternal hurricane. The tornado burned brighter as it raced over the dead sea towards the eye. White hot magic illuminated the valley of Uruk from the observatory. The tornado roared with fury.

Guards, soldiers, servants and overseers alike looked up from their labors.

Far beyond the mountains of Zagros, he knew the tornado curled up, the fiery coils plunged into the eye. Above the storm in the cold of space, the cords unwound into the spokes of a ladder. In his mind's eye, the ladder rose to the portal above the planet. He had seen it before in the spirit. For first time, he would see the portal with his waking eyes.

Salivating with a thirst for victory, and a lust for the shedding of blood, he feared nothing. Upon his return to the Earth, his enemies would tremble in fear of their lives.

The riders kicked their steeds. The horses spread their wings. Slowly at first, smoke rose from the riders' armor and the tips of their steeds' wings. The smoke drifted to the telescope's eye, and poured into the mote as if drawn by a vacuum. The riders shivered. Their bodies evaporated and their forms dissolved into ghostly fog.

The telescope swallowed up the Captain, and he plunged into the scope's eye. The chain on his chair jingled as the riders drew up the slack. The whirlwind grew louder, the telescope slurped up the second rider. The chain went taut and Nimrod braced himself. Crouching behind the chariot's guard, he cocked his heels into the footrests. Gripping the handle bars, he stretched out his arms, and hoped they would not rip from their sockets as he was drawn into the telescope.

Peeking over the guard, he saw the third rider swallowed by the scope's eye, and his chariot jerked. The chariot slid towards Adrammelech and Hermes. Hermes retreated out of range of the oncoming chariot with cautious dignity, but the worm jumped as if he had a life to lose.

Nimrod grinned at them, and gave them a quick wave. Ducking beneath the guard he resumed his stance. He kept his head down, gritted his teeth, and he counted the seconds to launch.

The telescope took hold of the fourth rider and swallowed the ghost. The chain shot up the eye of the telescope. The chariot hurtled forward.

He gripped the handle bar and twisted his feet into the footrests. His stomach lurched. He felt a sinking sensation. Catching his breath, he shouted for joy. At his feet the granite deck of the observatory dropped away as the chariot flew into the air.

Passing through the eyepiece was as if leaping from a cliff. The chariot popped as he passed into the scope's eye. He was weightless. The tornado dragged him through the telescope. He peeked and saw the telescope's web of struts and braces flash past. They were in the tornado. With blinding speed, they shot up the passage through the tornado's eye. Cords of smoky whirlwinds swirled about him.

The ghost riders flew through the tornado drawing the chariot. White hot magic burned on the outside of the tornado, and the smoke coils twisted around the inside. They went straight up and he glimpsed the Ziggurat falling away. They rolled over the fields of Uruk, and soared over the Zagros mountains and the Dead Sea of Umber.

Their tubular highway angled towards the eye, and the chariot looped as they rounded the bend. The eye was the one place on Gehenna where the tornado could pierce the atmosphere. Anywhere else, the jet streams would tear them apart. Why it mattered to a magical tornado, he knew not. He knew only what his master had explained.

The riders turned up, and he knew they would soon fly through the eye. The coils began to separate and through the spaces between the coils he caught glimpses of the storm. The inner wall of the eye roiled. Lightning flashed about them as they flew higher.

At the top of the eye, the hurricane boiled and lightning struck at them trying to bring them down. The coils unwound, spread and straightened into the rungs of a ladder. The Chariot's skis bounced over the rungs as they flew up.

"You cannot keep us prisoner here now!" he laughed. He watched Ashur rise over Gehenna as the chariot shot into space. The scarlet clouds of the eternal storm fell behind him as the planet shrank into an angry ball. Flying higher, they rose above the lightning. The storm dipped below the horizon.

All around the naked light of stars shone without flickering. He marveled at the sight. Ahead of him, the riders flew towards a small circle of light.

As they neared the crossover, the ethereal riders melted. He knew the riders were solid on the surface of Gehenna, but they became spirit to cross the differential to Earth. He shook his head at the confusing sight.

Perhaps the portal reveals the truth as a looking glass reveals an image.

The chariot flew up the ladder to the crossover. A ring of fire burned around the outside. Inside the Dragon Lord gazed down upon them holding twin balls of fire. Above the Dragon, the Milky Way cloaked his master in a halo.

His chariot shot through the portal, and he soared across the gate.

Abruptly they stopped. The chariot hovered over the portal. Stationing themselves about the portal's edge, the riders guarded the way with spears and shields at the ready.

~~~~~~

"My lord, you have summoned me!" He bowed low before the Dragon Lord.

The Dragon Lord bellowed, "Nimrod, my friend, now is your time!"

"Enter the vessel," the dragon gestured to the black dwarf lying prone on the altar. "The vessel is strong! Its innocence and purity will shield you from spiritual attack! Its form will allow you to use magic in this realm! Use it to serve your master! Use it for my glory!"

Madness danced in the dragons eyes. His fangs worked and his whiskers jiggled and the spines of his mane flexed.

Nimrod swallowed hard, and willed his spirit to obey. "As you command!" Diving into the black spot on the dwarf's forehead, he filled the dwarf as water fills a vessel. Flames of white fire cascaded over the body as his spirit passed through the forehead.

As the last of his spirit entered the dwarf, the body seized. His chest and flesh tightened over the bone drawn by a powerful vacuum. The force of his spirit drove the dwarf's blood out of the vessel. The skin turned white. The dwarf shook, and arched his back and shot his appendages rigid. The body's Kirlian aura flared as the soul within was driven out.

The whirlwind beat his guardians and Amazons. The dwarves hunkered behind the columns and wept.

Sucking in air, he breathed again, and tasted the sweet air of Earth.

"Rise my friend!" Fire surged from the Dragon's hands. "Rise and live again!"

The black dwarf's eyes flitted and opened. Swaying, the black dwarf rose from the altar, wan and pale, and bowed, "Lord, your servant awaits your command."

"You're alive!" The Dragon Lord gently tapped the altar with his forepaw. "Behold Nimrod, the Black Dwarf."

The Dragon Lord dismissed the riders with a word. The portal closed and the roar of the tornado stopped, though it left a ringing in his new body's ears.

"Welcome home Nimrod! Welcome back to Earth."

Gumshoe

Clay awoke. Sweat beaded his forehead. His bed was twisted in knots. Struggling to extricate himself from the linens, he carefully unwound the sheets to free his feet. Staggering to his lavatory, he slapped water on his face. Three nights had passed since he had seen Phaedra. But he had dreamed of her every night since.

Sunlight beamed through his patio door. A gentle breeze fluttered his curtains. He searched his bedroom, and found nothing amiss. All seemed normal in the morning light. Cautiously, he entered his hall, and looked down it to his living room. Nothing was out of place. Sighing, he tried to let the dream go.

No signs of dinner remained in the kitchen. He overrode the coffee pot's program, and started the coffee. Shotgun must have cleaned up everything. Standing there, trying to clear his head, the coffee pot beeped softly. Filling a latte cup, he stepped out onto his patio.

Clutching his mug of steaming brew, he relaxed, and nursed his coffee. Musing about the biot condition – his condition, he contemplated the grandeur of the mountains. Snowcaps caught the spring sunrise, and a golden fire burned on Nodlon's southern spires. Cotton-candy clouds adorned a dawn sky painted midnight blue. Phaedra had left him three years before, cut down in her prime by a heart condition. She had been an elf of splendid, delicate beauty, and he was her only son. He had loved her as best he could.

From the kitchen, he heard someone fumbling with the coffee pot.

"Morning boss," Shotgun said and took a spot beside him, sharing the view.

Shotgun stirred his coffee with a spoon. Nodlon glowed in the golden sunshine of dawn. He sipped his coffee.

"Good morning, Shotgun." He considered his man-servant. Shotgun wore a tuxedo jacket, tunic, and pleated trousers. Once, Jack had suggested the dwarf wear street clothes, but his man-servant had laughed. The dwarf pointed out that his uniforms were free, but he paid for his own street clothes. A microchip on his forehead identified him as a black dwarf. Chips came in many colors and some employers used custom designs. After nearly a year, he was more like family. It occurred to him to just buy Shotgun's contract and forgive his debt.

"What's on your mind, boss?"

"Sorry, I was thinking."

"No apologies, please, I just noticed the lights were on, but you weren't home. I just wondered. Did Phaedra appear again the way she did the last time?"

"No, it was just another dream. A lucid dream in livid color, but it was just a dream nonetheless. It's not the same thing, though I can't explain it."

"Naturally, you miss your mother."

A pang of guilt swept over Clay. Shotgun had been raised in a nursery. After reaching the age of reason, he completed his education at Tollmerak. Jack was fortunate. He was half-biot, but he was naturally-born. He had had a mother to lose, but Shotgun probably had no mother.

"Yes, but it wasn't just that. She was there, in my room, I'd swear to it."

"You saw a ghost, boss. Whether or not she was a real ghost or an imaginary ghost, she was real to you. Don't over think it." The dwarf stirred his coffee and took a sip. "What did she say again?"

"'Don't be afraid,' she said, 'childhood ends.' I will battle black dwarves and dragons, and save Nodlon. Afterwards, I get a three-day vacation package thrown in for good measure."

"If the Crown gives you a three-day vacation for saving Nodlon, Baron Voltaire must be in charge." They both chuckled. Everyone in Nodlon knew the Baron was a man rich in power and poor in humility. "Maybe, if you take it in the Caribbean, you'll need a butler."

"Don't worry, if I take a vacation, I'll take Jazz. You and Goldie and the girls can have the run of the apartment."

"When did you last take a vacation, boss? That's what the dream means. Your subconscious is telling you to stop fighting illusions and take a few days off."

"Whatever it means," Jack said, "I can't make heads or tails of it."

"If I were a witch doctor, I would say your pending marriage to the lovely Jasmine has sparked a conflict between Jasmine and Phaedra. You need to let go of your mother's apron strings."

"Thank you, Dr. Freud."

"On a different note, I watched Fritz Lang's new documentary, *Cretaceous Clay and the Spirits of Mars*, on Goldie's vid. How the famous magician and amateur sleuth discovered alien life on Mars." Shaking his head, Shotgun smiled. "You never told me you discovered aliens on Mars."

"Dr. Clarke at the University of Port Schiaparelli invited me to investigate the sightings of ghosts, and he offered to pay for my trip. How could I say no? He suspected a hoax, and so did I. But when I spoke to the witnesses, something about their stories rang true. So, I convinced Governor Tertullian to give us the permission we needed to do some field work. With the help of an old rock hound, and several prospectors, we located the mines of Tharsis. After that, the archeologists did all the work. Dr. Clarke actually discovered the alien computer. It had sensed intelligent life and called for help."

"You discovered the first evidence of aliens in the solar system, and you just blow it off?"

"It was not the first evidence anyone found. Soon Ti-Lee discovered the foundations of a city in the Tharsis region a hundred years ago. It was a great gig. They paid for my trip, and I only went along to watch. The archeologists solved the mystery, and I had a chance to rub shoulders with archeology students and retired volunteers."

Shotgun saluted him with his coffee mug. "Fine, be that way! Most celebrities would take credit for finding aliens. You won't even take credit for discovering alien artifacts." He disappeared into the kitchen and returned with a plate of raspberry tarts and fresh coffee.

"Wow, thanks."

"It's what you pay me for, bon appetite." Assured everything he wanted was on the table, the dwarf sat down again.

"Did you hear about the missing dwarf girl on the news?"

"With Mercury News carrying it, how can I miss it? You'd have to be living under a rock."

"They're spreading a rumor the police are going to call you. They need an expert on the occult and magic, and they're thinking of calling a consultant. Off-hand, I'd say that description fits you."

"What they need is a forensic profiler to catch whoever kidnapped her. If they want to find the runaways, they need an undercover officer. And they can get experts on the occult in Nodlon's Blues District. They're in the caster book under astrology, palmistry, and tarot readings."

"But if they call you, you'll go?"

Clay huffed, "Of course, I just don't think I can help."

"Don't you know a police detective over there?"

"Yes, I know a few actually. If anyone calls though, it will be Inspector Jacques Lestrayed, senior homicide detective, and policeman extraordinaire. All his friends call him Gumshoe." Picking up a tart, he munched on it.

"Shotgun, that's delicious." Picking up his coffee, he swept in the view of Nodlon from his patio.

"Anytime, boss. I strive to please. That's what you pay me for." The dwarf cleared the table and scurried off to the kitchen. Compliments pleased him, though he was too proud to say so.

A ringing in the kitchen interrupted them. Setting down his coffee, the dwarf hurried off to the kitchen. He heard the ringing stop, and susurruses. His manservant reappeared and held out a large caster shaped in the form of an antique phone.

"Boss, it's Inspector Lestrayed."

Raising an eyebrow, he lifted the antique receiver, "Clay here."

"Jack, it's Gumshoe, we've had a bit of trouble. A dwarf maid went missing last night."

"The Zodiac case I presume? We heard about it on the vid."

"Unfortunately, yes."

"I'll be right over."

"No, that won't be necessary. I'm downstairs, may I come up?"

"Anything for His Majesty's law enforcement officers, old boy, I am available at your convenience. Come on up and take some breakfast."

Clay closed the connection and handed the caster back to his butler. "Gumshoe's here and he'll be up in a minute. He wants my help on the Zodiac case."

"Now that Lang's documentary is on the vid, the police will think every investigation involves supernatural elements requiring your services."

"Right you are, Shotgun. Our intrepid Gumshoe may hope Lang will immortalize him on late-night vid. But knowing Gumshoe, he's more concerned right now about rescuing the missing dwarf and catching the villain."

"Very probably, boss."

Zodiac

The doorbell rang. The homicide detective wore a serviceable, if well-worn, trench coat, a tweed jacket, gray trousers, and tired wingtips. He fidgeted with his fedora.

"Hi Shotgun, I didn't know you worked for Jack." He let Shotgun take his fedora, and hang it on the coat rack.

"Mr. Clay's fiancée hired me. After my misstep last year, it's a good break for me. I was lucky to get a contract anywhere above the sewers."

"Jack's keeping you busy, is he?"

"He's not a slave driver if that's what you mean. I miss the geeky business though. It's difficult keeping up to speed with the information systems world when you're not in it. Now I understand how housewives feel."

"Gumshoe, good to see you, old-timer!" said Jack. "Would you like coffee? Shotgun brews an excellent potion and it's fresh."

"Old-timer yourself, Jack," Gumshoe's jowls sagged, and he had an uncanny resemblance to a bloodhound. "But yes, thanks, I'd like some coffee. Sorry to bother you, it's a bad business as they say, but I need some help." Shotgun brought out a tray with a mug of steaming coffee, cream and sugar. The inspector took the mug, and waved Shotgun away, "Long stakeouts taught me to avoid additives, bad for the digestion."

"Would you like a raspberry tart?" offered Shotgun. "Made them myself this morning."

"Oh, yes, please. Always have to uphold the dignity of the profession." Gumshoe sipped his coffee and patted his bulge. "Jack, a dwarf is missing."

"Many dwarves, right?" Jack asked. "They're running away?"

"Hope so. If they're running away, they're alive. I'm not here about the runaways. This is a different case. This time there's evidence of an unsavory nature, and I don't think the victim ran."

Shotgun returned with a plate of warm tarts. Gumshoe's eyebrows rose, and a brief smile interrupted his explanation as he plucked a pastry from the stack. Gumshoe took a bite and mumbled his appreciation. "Delicious."

"For his next performance, Shotgun will build a manna reactor in the kitchen just to show off." Clay sipped his coffee. "Mercury News predicted you would call me looking for an expert on the occult and magic."

Gumshoe stuffed a tart in his mouth and admired the mountain panorama. "Sorry about that. Captain Barfly suggested we bring you in as a consultant. Someone must have overheard, and told that snoop, Chesterton."

"Glad to help, Gumshoe, but I'm no expert on the occult or magic, much less on forensics or homicide investigations. I've studied witchcraft, ghost stories, extraterrestrials, unidentified flying objects, demon possession, and many other phenomena. I tried finding the source of my magic. What I've discovered is that most cases are inexplicable. There are incredible supernatural phenomena, but to study the supernatural you have to debunk all the cases of hysteria, confusion, and hoaxes first."

"Jack, there are elements of this case pointing to a possible unnatural origin. The sort of thing one might think was magic. And I don't mean fancy illusions. There's an air of supernatural magic. Call it a hunch." Gumshoe swallowed his tart, and washed it down with hot coffee.

"Supernatural magic or advanced technology? I'm the only supernatural magician in the solar system as far as I know."

"Peace, Jack, you're not under suspicion. Not yet anyway. Where there is one magical biot, there could be another no matter how improbable."

"Yeah, but I'm a half-breed mutation. The chances of the same mutation appearing at the same time are statistically impossible."

"You may be right, but your performance as a consultant in these cases makes you an asset, even if it's to rule out supernatural or paranormal activity. Remember the case of the Abominable Snowman? You were instrumental in ruling out false leads, and keeping this flatfoot's feet on solid ground."

"All right, Gumshoe, I'm willing to play amateur sleuth, as long as it's understood I'm no expert."

"Good, then I take it you'll help?"

"My services are at your disposal."

"Good, I'm glad you chose to enlist voluntarily. Your cooperation saves me from having to conscript you. Trust me this goes to the highest levels. Your name came down from the Crown or I'm not a detective. Someone with pull wants you on this case." Shotgun appeared and took the plate and offered the inspector a moist towel.

"Fantastic raspberry tarts, Shotgun. You could open a bakery, and become a celebrity chef with your own infomercials on late-night vids. Bet, if you asked, Jack would bankroll you."

"Forgive my manners," said Jack, "but you two seem to know each other."

"Patrick Morgan," said Gumshoe, "alias Shotgun, cracked into the personnel files of the Ministry of Manna, and downloaded a database with the genetic code of all the biots employed by the Ministry. It was a brilliant move. The Ministry employs so many biots, Shotgun was able to get the genetic code of a third of Nodlon's biots in one fell blow. Would have gotten away with it too, but he set up a fake account. The accounting system charged his download for the price of some spare change, and a compulsive pinhead in the accounting department demanded an investigation."

"I was only technically violating the law, not the spirit," complained Shotgun. "Biot's gene codes are available to anyone working in the Crown, or the Octagon, any agency, all the hospitals, and anyone with connections, but if you want the codes for genealogical research, forget it. Either I stole them or I had to give up."

"Peace laddie, I've got no quarrel with you there. No one was hurt, but our office got involved because we handle all the odd cases including rogue biots." Gumshoe looked at Jack. "The big shots in their infinite wisdom thought Shotgun here might be trying to sabotage the manna generators, or cause the military's computers to crash, but we cleared him of any malicious intent and spared him from prosecution."

"Yes, and I'm very grateful Inspector. I wouldn't want to spend the next thirty years on the Moon."

"You're welcome, Shotgun. The law is the law, but the spirit of the law is justice. No decent Nodlon wants to put anyone in jail for over-zealous genealogy."

"Genealogy?" asked Jack. "How would the genetic codes of one-third of Nodlon's biots help with genealogy?"

"Well, if Shotgun hasn't told you, it's none of my affair."

"Back to the case then," said Jack, trying not to feel excluded. "What can you tell us?"

"Anna McCarthy is our missing dwarf. Nodlon Biots holds her contract. They assigned Anna to the Ministry of Manna, and her dorm is in the Crown."

"That name sounds familiar," Jack said.

"Do you know her?"

"No, but I've got a feeling of déjà vu."

"Let me know if anything rings any bells."

"Will do, if I hear any bells."

"Good enough," Gumshoe winked. "Shotgun, would you mind joining the case as a computer consultant? Your help would be appreciated, and your name would feature favorably in my report. The highest levels may make their appreciation known as well."

"Yes, Inspector, that is, if my employer consents. I'm under contract, too, and I'm not sure if sleuthing falls within the range of my duties."

"Hey, I'm not some prim and proper Daughter of the

Crown," said Jack. "If you're willing to help, I'll not play the Scrooge."

"Excellent," said Gumshoe, "a detective, a mage and a geek; together we should be able to crack this case."

"Done then," said Jack, "You've got two consultants for the price of one. We are both in your service, Gumshoe. When shall we start?"

"Immediately, if it's all the same to you, I'll have some more coffee while you get your trousers." All eyes turned to Jack's bare knees and his bunny slippers. Clay tightened the sash on his robe, mustered his dignity and sauntered off to the master suite.

"Thank you again, Inspector," said Shotgun, "you're an officer and a gentleman."

"Think nothing of it. Biots are people, too, Shotgun. No one should have to hack databases to find out who they are."

Clay returned in his cloak, vest and suede boots. "Where are we going, Inspector?"

"To the Crown, to the dorms of Nodlon Biots, that's where we're going."

"Lead on Macduff."

The Sign of the Capricorn

The Crown was a seven story office complex that jutted from the Matterhorn. The building crowned the artificial mountain from whence it took its name. Gumshoe led them across the commons within the Crown. The commons teemed with biots of all descriptions hurrying about on their errands. They followed Gumshoe past a sign welcoming them to the Nodlon Biot dorms.

Up and down the corridor, dwarfs, elves, and a few goblins went about their errands, ignoring them. Self-consciousness once again reminded Clay of his fortune. He had lived in very similar dorms as a child. Biots' dorms were clean, and even comfortable, but they were hardly homes. He thought of Phaedra. At least he had a mother.

Gumshoe took a short cut, and soon they faced the entrance to McCarthy's dorm. Gumshoe identified himself, and the door beeped softly and opened. Inside, they found a small foyer with two chairs and a round table.

An elderly elf appeared from a little office beyond the foyer.

"Oh my, Inspector, Mr. Clay, I never expected you to come by." She gushed, "Oh, sir, it's like meeting royalty."

"Ma'am, flattery will get you everywhere." Jack smiled and put a hand on Shotgun's shoulder. "And this is our computer consultant, Mr. Morgan."

"Oh my, we welcome geeks here too. Many of our resident dwarves study information technologies, and we wish all of them well." She took Shotgun's hand.

Gumshoe registered his impatience, clearing his throat, "Miss Middles?"

"Tilly, Inspector, call me Tilly." The elf smiled. "I'm the resident in Dorm Forty-two. I'm the matron if you will. And I'm matronly too." She giggled and patted her ample hips.

"Tilly, ma'am, would you tell us again what you told me last night?"

"Oh, yes, Anna was on a furlough over the weekend. She's a good girl, and I would not have given it a second thought. But, oh, I do hope you'll find her, gentlemen."

"We'll do our best, Tilly, but if you'd be so kind to repeat your story so we can all hear it."

"Oh, oh, well, she didn't clock in last night on time. I was worried, what with all those dwarves missing, so I decided to check on her. When I opened up her room, it was terrible," she sniffled, "terrible, that's what it was." She pulled a tissue from her pocket and daubed her eyes. "So I called the police."

Gumshoe sighed. "Perhaps, you can show us to the girl's room, Tilly?"

The matron nodded, still daubing her face with the tissue. The dorm was a labyrinth. Tilly led them through a byzantine maze of corridors. They followed her around corners, and up and down stairs until Clay fairly lost his way. In the dash, he glimpsed a common room, laundry, kitchen, then they were in the residential halls.

Turning a corner, Jack saw a pair of uniformed officers sitting beside a door marked with a strand of yellow tape.

Tilly stopped suddenly and caught her wind. "Oh, Inspector," she huffed after the exertion. "I do hope you will find Anna soon. We're so worried."

"We're trying Tilly. If there's a way to bring her back to you, we will."

Tilly nodded, mumbled goodbye, and left just as quickly. She wept as she turned away.

Anna's door was the same as the others, except for the policemen guarding it. The officers rose to attention as they approached. One of the officers parted the tape to let them enter the room.

"Any news, sir?"

"No, I'm afraid not, Riley." Gumshoe motioned for Jack and Shotgun to go in. Anna's studio was typical. She had a bath, a bedroom, and an entertainment center. Clay surveyed the space. It was larger than the ones he had grown up in, but not by much.

"I've had a crime scene investigation team all over her room," said Gumshoe. "And the uniforms have guarded it since we were called in. I interviewed everyone in this hall last night, and no one saw anything suspicious."

Posters of flowers, kittens, and puppy dogs added color to the drab walls. A spray of Cretaceous Clay posters with tickets and programs were decoratively arranged over her computer desk.

"See, she's a fan, boss."

"That hurts," said Jack, looking at the posters. "I haven't met her, and I've feel I've lost my best friend." Her bed was unmade, and a book was on the floor near her end table. Facing the bed was a large vid screen covered with splatter. He hoped it was not what it looked like, and he turned away.

"Jack, here begins the mystery," said Gumshoe, pointing to the security box. "Security logged her in after her shift on Friday. She's on the cameras in the kitchen, and in the halls. No one saw her after that. Worse, there's nothing on the security cameras either. Not at the front door, the fire exits, or in the halls. When Tilly checked her room, she found it like this."

"Are there any other exits?" On the wall next to the door was the security alarm. Clay scrolled through the menu, but the options were password protected. "Any exits without surveillance?"

"All exits are under vid surveillance," said Gumshoe. "Not only did Anna never check in, she never checked out."

"Never checked out? You mean she left without letting the matron know?"

"An electronic monitor tracks the dwarves' chips. The system records when the biots come and go," Gumshoe shrugged. "And before you ask, her chip was not recorded in or out over the weekend. She entered the dorm Friday, and she never left the building."

"If an illusion was used to get into the building, an illusion may have been used to leave. A professional illusionist might fool one camera or all the cameras, but it's hard to fathom fooling the entire security system without tampering with the system directly."

Gumshoe pulled off his fedora. "Our computer forensic team is going over the security system's code now. It'll take days to analyze all the lines in that code."

"And there are no other ways for anyone to leave the building?"

"None, Jack."

"Shotgun, can you find the architectural plans for this place?" Jack asked. "Look for an alternative exit, if there are any. During the Retrogressive Wars, they built quite a few hidden passages to help people escape."

Shotgun unslung his satchel and pulled out his tablet. "Sure thing, boss."

"We've thought of that," said Gumshoe. "But we found nothing. It's not a dungeon and there are no priest holes. Which makes sense, this dorm was rebuilt only forty years ago as part of the Crown's renovation of the Matterhorn's basement. If there were any unauthorized passages, they would have been closed off and converted to utility corridors."

"Already ahead of you, gentlemen," said Shotgun, "I'm on it."

Gumshoe took Jack's shoulder. The magician swallowed. They studied the splatter on the girl's vid screen. It ran over the vid's screen and overspray covered the wall.

"It looks like a paint ball attack," Jack said. "There must be dozens of splash marks."

"Forty to be exact, Jack. It's not paintballs, and it's not paint. It's blood. The splatter distribution shows the stars were created at the same time. If a water pistol or a paintball gun was used, each drop would have struck one after the other. The blood splatter analytics would have picked it up. All the stars in the pattern hit the screen at once. Could magic do that?"

"Maybe, though I admit I've never tried. Why would anyone create a constellation with forty drops of blood? It makes no sense to me. I can levitate liquids, but manipulating physical objects is much harder than creating illusions. My guess is some sort of advanced technology. Maybe a robotic paintball gun used for sport."

Gumshoe noted the observation on his tablet. "Thanks, Jack, that's an idea. There are no scratch marks on the vid, though, and no casings on the floor. But maybe there's something new out there."

"Take a look at this," Shotgun held out his tablet. "That's where we are right now." The screen displayed a schematic of the dorm. "As you can see, there are no hidden passages. There's nothing on the plans, but the record show many passages were converted to utilities. Have your techs searched for unauthorized access holes? Maybe they used a utility corridor to bypass the entrances, and cut a hole."

"Good idea, Shotgun," said Gumshoe. "I'm sure they checked the access hatches, but I'm not so sure they looked for unauthorized holes. Send me the map, and I'll have my officers check."

Gumshoe turned to the door and called the officers. "Adam, Riley, search the dorm. We're looking for any unauthorized holes inside the security perimeter big enough for a dwarf. Use the map I'm sending you. If there is any hole, it's probably disguised or someone would have noticed it by now."

"Got it," said Adam.

"We're on it," said Riley. The elves took off.

Shotgun pointed to the cats playing on Anna's computer screen. "Was Anna's computer on?"

"Yes, and before you ask, the forensics boys found no activity on it after 6:01 Friday."

Shotgun sat at the computer. "Just wondering if someone else might have used it, do you mind if I check?"

"Please, go for it."

"I'll see if I can tell what it was last up to." Soon, he was downloading the system's logs and archives.

"Who needs a password with him around?" whispered Gumshoe.

Jack shrugged, "He's special." Jerking his thumb at the vid, he asked, "Is it Anna's blood?"

"The lab boys are testing it now to find out if it's hers. See how the blood is splattered only on the screen. The studio is clean except on the vid and the overspray on the wall. It's not much blood. Whoever did it used no more blood than you give a doctor."

"Who realized it was a Zodiac sign? You'd have to be blind to miss the pattern, but most of us wouldn't recognize the constellation of Capricorn. It's not that obvious. In a city where two thirds of the population only visits the surface a few times a year, only the star buffs know the difference."

"The splatter analysis identified it as Capricorn," Gumshoe shrugged. "Wonders of technology never cease."

"What if Anna just ran away? Are you sure the girl didn't put it there before she left? Maybe she wanted to throw you off the trail."

"She was well liked, but no one knew her well." said Gumshoe. "She had few friends, but that's no reason to run. She might not have won the Grand Tour, but she was comfortable."

"Maybe it's not connected then. If her disappearance is unrelated to the missing dwarves, it might throw us off the trail. If she was kidnapped by a psychotic, he might think this was the best time to kidnap a girl."

"Copycats who want to conceal their crimes don't add clues. Leaving a constellation on the victim's vid in blood screams foul play. That's why I wanted to keep the Zodiac sign under wraps. The sign is the first break I've had in the rash of missing dwarves. Of all the missing dwarves, this is the one case I've got with a clue."

"The sign of the Capricorn leaked to the media pretty darned quick."

"I suspect the housekeeper. She thought she was warning the other dwarves."

"A warning of what? If the perpetrator is a maniac, there's no telling who he will strike next. Maybe he left the constellation as a threat to sow fear and panic. Another possibility is a nut who believes in black magic."

"Black magic?" asked Gumshoe. "Does that mean there are two kinds?"

"I don't know. I was not referring to real magic. I was just referring to magical thinking. Other than myself, I don't believe in magic."

"Jack, you're living proof magic is real."

"My magic is genetic, Gumshoe. I don't know the explanation, but I'm sure there is one for my magic. I'm thinking of someone with dangerous, violent beliefs who thinks they can summon demons or talk to the dead using bizarre rituals."

"Can you explain the sign of Capricorn?" Gumshoe asked. "I know it's the tenth sign of the Zodiac. I've looked it up on the Nodlon Planetarium website. They had a long list of stars, azimuths, declinations, and magnitudes. Nothing explains why it's on this girl's vid."

"So you called me," muttered Clay.

"That's the gist of it. If the perpetrator believed in astrology or has a passion for astronomy, the constellation might indicate a motive, and identify possible targets."

"And I suppose you expect me to know which of the astrological meanings of Capricorn the perpetrator intended? You don't need a magician, Gumshoe, you need a mind-reader."

"Your magical powers and your experience in paranormal investigations make you uniquely qualified, Jack. Virtually all of the references on cults and black magic are fictional; except you. We need to know if she may be a victim of a cult-like ritual.

Officially I'm skeptical. Unofficially, I'm desperate. I want a break in this case before I have to start burying these kids. What can you tell me?"

"Zodiac signs are used by modern astrologers and fortune tellers for divination," said Jack. "Each of the constellations had different meanings in astrology and divination. Not that I can recall all of them. Stroll through Deep Nodlon and you'll find one or another kind of spiritualist on every block. Usually they only give a vague reading that might apply to anyone.

"In times past, astrologers of Babylon, Assyria, and Persia believed the signs governed people's destinies. Some thought stars were gods, and others thought gods lived on the stars."

"What's the difference, Jack? Other than the garb and the mumbo jumbo?"

"There are many differences, Gumshoe. The most significant though is the difference between knowing one's fate and using magic to control the world around you."

"Sounds like a distinction more than a difference."

"Today, we don't sacrifice maidens to the sun to ensure the dawn keeps coming. It may not seem like much to us, but I'm sure those who were sacrificed thought it made a big difference."

"Maybe our perp is a follower of some long lost cult?"

"Don't know," Jack shrugged. "Capricorn is one of the original Zodiac constellations. Across the world, there were twelve signs, more or less. Probably the signs correspond to the division of the lunar months into the solar year. Of course, the myths and interpretations of the Zodiac's signs vary.

"What is usually overlooked is the consistency of the descriptions across time and distance. Capricorn was always a goat or half goat-fish. In ancient times, it was associated with the winter solstice in the Bronze Age. That's a possible clue, as many cults believed in human sacrifice at the winter solstice. But if someone is using it for that reason, they are confused."

"Confused?" asked Gumshoe.

"Yeah, the astrological sign of Capricorn used to mark the cusp of the solstice in ancient times. But the solstice begins in Sagittarius today due to the planet's precession. One thing strikes me though. The spring equinox is in just a few days. We're starting our spring show next weekend."

Jack thought a moment. "When did the disappearances begin?" he asked.

"We've had more cases than usual for months," said Gumshoe, "but about six weeks ago we started losing dwarves daily. Why?"

"Maybe we're looking for something bigger than just one missing girl. Maybe the disappearances are linked. Can you find out when the first biot went missing?"

A worried expression crossed Gumshoe's face. "Spit it out, Jack."

"Maybe the kidnapper is planning something this weekend. Perhaps he needs a dwarf girl for some type of ritual. I wouldn't rule out some psychotic who believes he can gain magical power through astrology or necromancy, but he has to have some means of fooling security and making blood splatter in pre-defined patterns."

"Jack, I was afraid you'd say something like that."

"Anyone practicing black magic, satanic rituals, or any archaic or modern cults with violent beliefs is not likely to be in the directory," said Jack. "We're looking for someone whose beliefs might cause him to engage in violent ritual practices." Clay stepped away from the vid screen. "You're looking for a needle in a haystack. Nodlon is jammed with cults and palmists, Tarot card readers of all sorts. None that I know of are violent, and they don't have any real magic."

"So, we're not dealing with the common ordinary psychopath who just destroys someone's life for his jollies?" asked Gumshoe.

"Just speculation, Gumshoe," said Jack, "Don't go off

half-cocked. My research on witchcraft was not out of an interest in ghosts, or paranormal activity. I never wanted to summon demons or use black magic."

"So why did you study the occult?"

"After I discovered my magic, an old woman told my mother I was the spawn of the devil. Am I unique? Am I a freak or special? Why do I have magic? How can I use my power for good and not hurt anyone? Am I evil?

"If anyone else had ever had magic, I thought I could prove I was just like everyone else. And I wanted to prove my magic had the power to do good, so I could believe I was as good as anyone else."

"Why not have your genes analyzed?"

"Who hasn't tried? The Army inducted me a year early, and subjected me to every test they could think of. I'd still be a guinea pig now, except King Justin told them to let me go after my mother sent him an appeal."

"Oh, yeah, I remember that. Caused quite a stir."

"So, science couldn't explain it. Science doesn't explain it. The doctors all agreed I had real magic, but they couldn't explain it. They said it was a mutation. They called it a congenital disorder with beneficial side effects. I'm not so sure, but it's easier to agree and move on than to argue with them."

"Yeah, I know the type."

"So I studied the paranormal. From astrology to crypto-zoology, and from ancient Zoroastrian myths to the palm readers in the Blues District, I investigated everything. I found cults that practiced necromancy, and zombie mastery. I found myths and fairy tales of lycanthropes and vampires. Most of the cases are either frauds, or questionable. The truth was lost in the fog of myth or legend. All of the evidence is anecdotal."

"And you found nothing?" asked Gumshoe. "The supernatural and paranormal are all fantasies or hoaxes?"

"No, that's not what I meant. Since my focus was personal, and I found nothing to answer my questions, I was disappointed. Remember, almost all of my research involved crimes, so my sample is biased. All of the people I have investigated though have either been frauds or quacks. There are many frauds and hoaxes, but usually you can find the answer by following the money."

"So you believe there is something out there."

"Yes," Jack grinned. "Me, for example. The words paranormal or supernatural just refer to activity outside our experience. Stuff we can't explain. I've discovered many stories that will raise your hair from many credible eyewitnesses. And I've had my own experiences of the unexplained. So I'm not saying I can explain it away. No one can disprove someone else's experience. The supernatural is inexplicable by its very nature. You might say the supernatural is simply what we don't understand."

"But you're real."

"Yes, I'm real, and I still don't know the extent of what I can do, and I learn things every day. Nothing explains me, and I still have no idea how my magic works. That's my point."

"Jack, have you found anyone else who can do magic; anyone at all, living or dead, or off-world?"

"No," said Jack, "I'm the one and only, that I know of. If there's another one, he's keeping a mighty low profile."

"Jack, how easy would it be for a magician to use magic without being noticed?"

"Easy enough, we live in an age of techno-wizardry. Our techno-priests perform techno-miracles every day. There are plenty of tricks and technology or substitutes for magic. When I designed my shows, I found out how difficult it is to display the reality of my magical powers when the technology is indistinguishable."

Gumshoe absorbed Jack's comments, and made a few notes.

Jack's brow wrinkled. "Have you checked for missing persons who may have disappeared at the time of the murder?"

"Any boyfriends? We're working all the missing dwarf cases looking for a connection."

"Are you looking for boyfriends?" asked Jack. "Someone outside her regular circle."

"Yes, of course," said Gumshoe. "A psychotic might befriend a lonely girl. He tells her to keep it quiet and gives her an excuse. He can't be seen fraternizing with a dwarf, or he'll lose his job. It would be an easy lie, and might even be true in some parts of Nodlon. You think he might have disappeared. With all the other missing dwarves, who would suspect him of being the killer?"

"Yeah, that's my idea."

"It's possible," said Gumshoe, "especially if he flipped out and didn't mean to hurt her. If he planned it, he thinks he's smart and all he has to do is lie low until the heat blows over. I'm not going to rule it out. So far we haven't discovered any boyfriend. Apparently, she never dated. She was pretty, but she never went out."

"Dwarves are shy," said Jack. "Her friends may not know if she was dating. They're not invisible though. Has she been seen with anyone recently?"

"Good thinking, Jack. If you ever get tired of magic, the Yard could use you. I have the uniforms checking out recent leads. Escape is one possibility, but I'm more concerned about saving lives. We don't know the situation yet, but I don't think this is a case of biot boyfriend madness."

"I just think we should focus on the most recent disappearances," said Jack. "If Anna's attacker ran, he's been gone only three or four days. Someone must have noticed his disappearance by now. If there is any hope of catching him before he escapes, his trail will be hot."

"Yes, I understand Inspector, but a biological entity designed to behave like a young man may suffer the same mental breakdown."

"None have."

"Just the same, will you check again and see if she dated? If she had a boyfriend, he's the most likely culprit."

"Now, Jack, that's all we need. First we have the vid suggesting dwarves are running away. Now, you suggest a dwarf might murder another dwarf. We can't have people thinking biots could run amok slaughtering each other in bizarre rituals with runes and macabre accoutrements. There'd be panic. Can't have that now can we? Biots don't go psychopathic. They commit an occasional crime, but it's always rational. I've never seen a biot commit an intentional homicide since I was a greenhorn."

"Gumshoe, did I hear you right?" Jack asked. "Have biots committed murder before?"

"Sort of. Thirty years ago, there was one case. I didn't work on it. A young dwarf murdered a woman in some bizarre ritual. Rumor has it he was innocent. According to the gossip, he was hypnotized, and he remembered nothing when he woke up. Obviously, the rumor could be a lie. If people thought biots might be capable of murder, the consequences are unimaginable."

"What really happened?"

"Don't know," said Gumshoe, "it wasn't my job, and I was a greenhorn in uniform back then. Officially the case is still open, which is odd because the record is sealed."

Jack glanced at Shotgun, and his butler shrugged.

"Another idea came to me. Rumors abound of biot slavers operating in the bowels of Deep Nodlon and using the mines to get in and out of the city. If they exist they would love to kidnap a pretty dwarf."

"True, they exist, Jack," said Gumshoe. "But we can probably rule out kidnappers. We've intercepted a few, but they're penny-ante criminals."

"Maybe there's a new gang afoot. A gang leader with a leader who uses hypnosis and hurts his victims in bizarre rituals."

"Into the twilight zone?" asked Gumshoe. "Too many biots willingly surrender to organized criminals in exchange for a little money. There's no substantial market for unwilling victims. If someone wanted a victim, he could con them into it easily enough. Either way, he wouldn't leave a clue."

"Just check on it old man will you? If someone is into bizarre rituals, his fantasies may not make sense to us."

"Sure Jack, I'll put it on my to-do list."

Witches Brew

One of the officers replaced the tape as they left. Jack felt a hand on his shoulder. "Don't worry boss, we'll find a way to help her."

"I'm afraid it may be too late," whispered Clay.

The Inspector led the way. "Well, if that's the case, we'll find justice for her if I have anything to do with it."

Rounding a corner, Gumshoe veered around a custodian's cart parked in their way.

An aging crone wielding a broom stepped out from behind her barrels of trash and dirty linens, and blocked Jack's path. Barging in front of him, she thrust her broom in his face, and forced him to stop. He grabbed her cart to avoid throwing her to the floor.

"Who else would it be passes like to thee? A top of yellow, cloak of green, boon of sorcery, make the fellow. Free a thought, lure a sot, slay a dwarf," her gravelly voice lowered, "face a dragon."

"And who are you ma'am?" With wrinkles, and a hooked nose, the crone gave him the feeling she was sent by his casting agency for an audition.

"Molly's my name."

Gumshoe retraced his steps to extract Clay from the impromptu conversation. "Woman, we're busy."

Molly leered at the inspector, "Aye, I've information, but it'll cost ye." She flashed him a toothy grin.

"Woman, if you have anything to contribute spit it out. It's unlawful for you to withhold information in the course of an investigation into a possible crime. I can charge you with obstruction of justice."

She sniffed. "What ye gonna do tough guy?" She stuck her chin in the air, and stared down her nose at Gumshoe. "Think ye I've naught to lose?"

Clay drew his wallet from his cloak, hoping to stave off a

confrontation. "If you would like a reward, I'm happy to pay any reasonable price."

"No ye fool, do ye live under a rock?" she snapped, and tapped his shoulder with her broom for emphasis. "Anyone above room temperature recognizes Jack Clay from his advertising. Hold your tongue, I know your mind. Ye think the crone's gone and lost her mind! Ha!" She slapped him with her broom again. "I'm a Clay-net subscriber, and I'm saner than ye."

Quickly, Clay stowed his wallet. "Ma'am, as you're a fan, I'll pay your price if you'll only name it!" Smiling, he beamed at the old woman as if she were a fashion model and hoped to appease her.

Instantly, her composure melted, and she could have been anyone's granny. "Aye, you're a gentleman – unlike this uncouth commoner." She shot a sour glance at Gumshoe.

The Inspector backed away a half step, and bit his lip, suppressing a snort.

Molly reached into her bag of rags hanging from the cart. From this she pulled a sack of aluminum cans, and continued rummaging. Forthwith, she drew a few colorful tee-shirts bearing Jack's likeness and emblazoned with his logo. She handed him the shirts as if she were handing him a blueberry pie. "I want your autograph."

Clay stifled a guffaw, and pulled a marker from his cloak. With Shotgun's help he stretched each shirt taught and signed them with dramatic flourish. Shotgun refolded the shirts for Molly, and handed them back to her. Not to be outdone, Clay drew a few of his cards, and placed them on top of the shirts.

Molly's eyes brightened when she read the back of the cards. "Free admission, a free tee-shirt, or a back stage pass. Oh, my. May I have a few more for my boy?" Jack smiled and handed her a few more cards for good measure.

Gumshoe tried to disguise his growing impatience. "Must you continue assailing us with riddles and demands?"

Molly shot a deadly gaze at the Inspector. "So I warned

her, see, I warned her not to go."

Another custodian passed by and chastised her. "Molly, you old witch leave the gentlemen alone. Can't you see they're trying to find her?"

Ignoring the reproach, Molly spoke with a conspiratorial air. "She told me to cover for her. She said she had an appointment with a doctor. A witch doctor more like, if you ask me. She was a beauty, but she wanted to be prettier. Aye, none of the boys asked her out, but not 'cause she wasn't pretty. Afraid they were that she'd reject 'em. It's hard that way for a boy."

Gumshoe tipped his hat, and strode off.

"Right you are Molly," said Jack. "Thank you for that information. Got to go, now." Clay doffed his cap, and scrambled to follow the Inspector. Shotgun was already ahead of him.

"She fulfilled her end of the bargain," said Jack, catching up to Gumshoe.

"Balderdash," muttered Gumshoe.

"Anna saw a doctor who could make her prettier."

"A gene therapist, maybe," said Gumshoe, "but what am I supposed to do with that? Accuse literally hundreds of doctors of being involved in a kidnapping ring?"

Jazz Calls

Quietly, they rode in Gumshoe's cruiser. The autopilot drove while the detective updated his endless paperwork.

In the back, Shotgun investigated stories of missing dwarves on the net. "Friends and relatives seeking missing loved ones are posting all over the net. I had no idea it was this bad."

"Yeah," said Gumshoe. "They've inundated the Yard with information requests. Hate to answer with a 'no comment' but what else can I say?"

"Even the employment agencies are involved. Since they heard about the bloody Capricorn this morning, they've gone to the Crown to demand something be done."

"Nice to know they're concerned. From my inbox, I would've thought they were just irritated by the fear of contract default."

"Maybe they are worried about contract defaults," Jack interjected. "Missing employees and missing deadlines adds up to pretty much the same thing."

"Yeah, I'm sure Voltaire cares," said Shotgun with a sneer, "but there's more sincerity than I expected out of the agency staffs. I can almost feel my cynicism melting."

"I'm touched, Shotgun," said Gumshoe. "Co-workers might have feelings?"

"Biots are people, too," said Jack. "Even if we deny it. We can't work with someone who laughs and cries, and tells you their hopes and dreams without coming away knowing the truth." Watching the mile markers pass, Clay fidgeted with nothing to do for the moment. As if answering his anxieties, his caster burst into a heavy-metal riff. Out of the corner of his eye, he saw Gumshoe cringe.

"Hi, what's up?" Jack said.

"What are you guys doing? You weren't home." Jasmine's scrubs were stained, and she had retied her hair in a loose bun. Stray hair sprayed from her brow, and purple bags sagged under her bloodshot eyes.

"I'm riding with Gumshoe. Shotgun and I volunteered to help him with the Zodiac case. You don't look so good. How are you holding up?"

"Any news on that missing girl? It's all over the news. People are already afraid the missing dwarves are dead. Worse, there's some freak saying the dwarves are planning a revolt and are going to kill the humans in their sleep."

"Yeah, there's news, but I can't share much over a caster. I'm not authorized to leak anything, and I don't want to be the one to start a panic."

"They're already panicking," she put a hand over her face, and sniffled. "I'm panicking. We're on an orange alert. They've put us all on twenty-four hour duty, and I can't leave the hospital until I can get a pass. I won't make rehearsals this afternoon."

"Now, now, babe, it's not so bad. Don't worry about rehearsal. You're needed at the hospital, and that's what's important. This is what you've trained for. They need you working and functional. You'll get a break as soon as they can let you go."

Jasmine began sobbing. Tears ran down her cheeks, and she trembled.

"Jazz," he cooed, "Babe, I'll come visit as soon as I can."

"It's not you Jack. A hospital ship arrived from the Moon a couple of hours ago. The Martians attacked them this morning. They're just civilians; young and old, women and children, boys and girls." She trailed off. She regained her composure. "They weren't expecting it. It was a senseless attack against an unarmed station on the far side. There were very few survivors."

Jazz slumped.

"Why would anyone do that?" Jack asked.

"We don't know anything yet, just clues we've heard from the survivors, but they didn't do anything to deserve this."

"Babe, hang in there. The Lunan's need you. I'm proud of

you, and Shotgun and I will be by as soon as possible."

"Can you come by this evening? Any sooner will be a waste of time. I'm not going to get a break until after dinner. And we aren't going home until everyone has been stabilized and the emergency is dropped to yellow. I may have to work very late, perhaps all night."

"Dinner it is," said Jack, "see you then. Love you."

"Love you too sweetie, got to go, bye." Waving goodbye, she cut the connection.

"Making people laugh is important too," he muttered. What use was magic against war and sheer hate? "In your dreams, Jack," he scolded himself.

"Pardon me for eavesdropping," said Gumshoe, "the cruiser's a bit small, and it's difficult to not overhear."

"No problem, it just wasn't what I expected. Why would Mars attack the Moon? What did the Moon do?"

"No one deserves an act of war," Gumshoe said. "Politicians start wars for their own reasons. They only need excuses to silence the reasonable before the war, and to excuse their conduct after the war starts due to their bumbling. When they attack others for no good reason, they'll use any handy fig leaf to cover their intentions, or make up a lie out of whole cloth. Some refuse to accept the fact."

"Will the Reserve be mobilized?" Shotgun asked.

"Maybe, if we go to war," said Gumshoe. "There's a news blackout now, or we would have heard of their attack this morning. The rumor will be all over Nodlon by nightfall, but it's what's not being said that tells the story. Nodlon's in big trouble."

"Did you serve, boss?"

"Two years," said Jack. "Mutant half-breed's privilege. No one said life was fair. The Nodlon Defense Force drafted me at seventeen to study my magic, remember. When my first year was up, they kept me another for study. Mum had to get the King to spring me. A wag would say it builds character. I've got no love for the military pinheads in the Crown, but I'm glad I served anyway. Those who serve are Nodlon's best people, and many are still friends."

"Did you serve, Shotgun?" Gumshoe glanced at Shotgun in his mirror.

"Yes, Inspector, one year got me out of the dorm. But if they make me a citizen, I'll volunteer for another year. And if Nodlon goes to war, I'll fight the Martian War Machine to my last breath. The Martians aren't going to separate the citizens from the biots. My kids bleed just like humans."

"They do, Shotgun," said Gumshoe. "The sooner parliament emancipates the biots, the sooner we can all acknowledge the obvious."

"Yeah, I know what you mean," said Shotgun. "When Parliament emancipates biots, life will be harder for decent working humans competing with genetically perfect biots.

"Meanwhile, back at the Crown, biots will never have the wealth and power like Baron Voltaire. Those who are driven by envy will never be satisfied. Those who've suffered injustice will never be compensated. The innocent will be punished, and the guilty rewarded."

"Yes, you got it," said Gumshoe. "Are you reading my mind, or just a tad cynical?"

"No sir, I'm just being practical," Shotgun replied. "What about the shields? They'll hold, won't they?"

"I don't know," said Gumshoe, "it's been nearly thirty years since I served. The shields may hold, but there's nothing to stop the kinetics. No shield I know of will stop shield piercing weapons."

"Yeah," said Jack, "unless they have something new. It's been twelve years since I served, and I haven't heard of anything to stop the kinetics unless you shoot it down. But, changing the subject, gentleman, remember what the witch said?"

"Yes, she wanted tee-shirts and free tickets," said Shotgun.

"No," said Gumshoe. "McCarthy wanted to be prettier, and she had an appointment with a doctor for the little good that did her. Probably a gene therapist, though it could have been a plastic surgeon. There are hundreds in the city though. We can rule out the therapists a secretary cannot afford, but that leaves many offices to check."

"Sounds like a job for Nodlon Yard," said Jack.

"Yeah," said Gumshoe, "and we're already checking up on the missing dwarves and searching for McCarthy's boyfriends. We'll need some luck or maybe some magic to find a lead before another girl goes missing."

Gumshoe's cruiser caster rang, and a red-headed elf in a Nodlon Yard uniform appeared on his console.

"What's up Riley?"

"Sir, you're not gonna like this, but we've found another Capricorn. I'm texting you the address. It's on the Bio-Soft campus."

"Be right there, Riley." He closed the connection, and reprogrammed the cruiser's destination. "Well gentlemen, looks like we have our next clue."

Evan Labe

Piling into the Inspector's cruiser, Gumshoe reprogrammed the cruiser's destination. The machine hummed, and they headed off to the Bio-Soft campus.

"The missing dwarf is Evan Labe," said Gumshoe. "Kid's hardly more than a boy. He graduated from Nodlon Tech a few years ago. Writes code for the Ministry of Manna, and makes good money at it. The uniforms were double-checking all of the missing persons over the last two weeks.

"They were passing around the McCarthy girl's picture and asking if anyone had seen her with any of the missing boys. This morning a dorm resident approached one of my officers and asked if we had checked Labe's apartment.

"We had overlooked the possibility of him having an apartment. We interviewed the assistant supervisor the first time and either we forgot to ask, or she didn't mention it. I can't tell from the transcript. The uniforms checked it out this morning, and we found the Zodiac sign.

"We'll talk to Evan's dorm resident first. The crime scene team is still working on Evan's apartment. I sent a couple of my boys by after we found the Zodiac, but he won't talk to the uniforms. He clammed up and refused to answer any questions. He insisted on seeing you and me. He must have heard of us on the vid."

"That's for sure," said Shotgun. "We're all over both Mercury News and Radiophone. If they can't talk about the rumors of war or Voltaire's peace talks, they talk about Inspector Lestrayed and the Zodiac case."

"Speculation is all they have. There's no leak in my department."

"Are you kidding?" Shotgun snorted and closed his tablet. "With all due respect, Inspector, they don't need leaks. The media is tracking us. The Yard calls in Jack Clay, the amateur sleuth who cracked the case of the Spirits of Mars, and teams up with the Manna Ministry hacker. Mercury News is running our life story. Even vid's of Jazz and Goldie are all over the news feeds."

"Guess you're right, Shotgun. The fishbowl is the price of fame boys. Some nut threw a pie at the missus a few years back. I don't mind the photographers, but it scares me when the nuts follow my wife."

The cruiser covered the blocks from the police station to the Bio-Soft campus in minutes. It bypassed the level-ways, and navigated the distance through the tunnels of Under Nodlon.

The campus surrounded an open square with a yellow sun lamp rather than Nodlon's blue clouds.

"Looks the same as it did a year ago," muttered Shotgun.

Following little paths weaving across a manicured turf they passed dwarves working on mobiles, or simply eating lunch. Nearing the main entrance they passed a swimming pool and a bevy of small children taking swimming lessons. Inside the entrance, they found dwarves and a few elves sitting in an atrium with a shallow fountain in the middle of a sunken lounge bordered by a garden of petunias and marigolds. Tucked away under the mezzanine was a credit union with a short line of fidgeting customers. Faint sounds of children playing drifted through the atrium from a day care on the opposite side.

Riding the escalator up to the mezzanine, the smells of grilled hamburger, and chocolate chip cookies wafted over them as they passed the food court overlooking the atrium.

They passed the amusements and entered a hall of glass windows overlooking large offices separated into cubicles. Pictures of Rocky Mountain streams adorned the halls, and alternated with paintings of butterflies, frogs, and quiet ponds full of lilies. Signs on the windows identified the staff, their titles and their projects. Timelines, achievements, awards, and graphics decorated the glass and leavened the work space with a hint of humanity.

Gumshoe marched stolidly past the work areas through a

common hub. Hardly slowing, they followed him through a gaggle of off-duty elven girls and swung down a hall to a residence dorm.

Clay overheard the elves arguing the merits of a pair of boys, and the best means of currying their favors.

"We're here," said Gumshoe, stopping at a dorm office.

Inside, a goblin sat at a little desk facing the door. He did not look up. He was absorbed by filling out forms on his workstation. They squeezed into the office, and hovered over the goblin's desk.

"Be right with you. Have a seat, if you want." One straight backed chair offered a seat beside a stack of trays holding forms and instructions. Behind him was a short filing cabinet which forced him to work at an angle to the desk.

Glancing at the trays of forms, Jack saw such interesting titles as "Saving Your Vacation Time," and "Rules for the Laundromat."

Looking up, the goblin saw them and a look of alarm fluttered across his face. He smiled meekly, and stopped working. He stood up, and looked down on them all. He was taller than Clay.

"Inspector, gentlemen, excuse me. I'm Goldman, the dorm supervisor," he was agitated. "I'm expecting a new dwarf from Tollmerak. We picked him up as a candidate. I'm working on his contract now because of the excitement this morning. Bright kid, but very young, we'll send him to Nodlon Tech to get him up to speed. He's late. Not unusual, the kids often take a wrong turn in this place and wind up lost. I'm worried these days. Who knows? I hope the boy hasn't been kidnapped."

Despite the goblin's athletic build, he spoke softly, "Sorry, that's not what you came for." He gulped hard. "What with dwarves missing, I'm a bundle of nerves. I hope you can find Evan."

"I'm sure we can find Evan," said Gumshoe. "We have no time to waste though if we want to find him in one piece. Can you briefly tell me what you know?"

"As I told your officers, I'm Evan's dorm supervisor. I'm also his contract officer, and he's responsible to me when he's not working. I just came back from vacation, and I wasn't aware of any trouble until this morning.

"My fill-in gave Evan a medical pass last Friday. He hasn't been seen since. The pass was good for the Sunday swing shift, but he failed to check in Monday morning.

"Normally, I wouldn't worry too much if a good employee misses the day after a medical. The dwarves often forget they may need to sleep off a powerful medication if the doctor gives them one.

"When I heard he had not checked in, I thought of the missing girl and the bloody Capricorn. I was alarmed and called the police." The goblin shifted on his feet nervously, and gazed at his shoes. "I hope it's not too late." He hung his head.

"Why did you let him have an apartment?" asked Gumshoe. "Isn't that unusual?"

"He's a bit young, but he's earned it," said the goblin, sagging slightly. "We even have family quarters, and half of our human staff lives on-site. The dorms are free, but the rooms are small. He took a starter studio. We usually reserve those for couples. That may seem unusual, but this is Bio-Soft. We are the largest biot manufacturer in the solar system. Bio-Soft is the premium manufacturer of highly skilled biots specializing in business analytics, code writing and software development."

"So, he wanted a bigger apartment?" Gumshoe asked.

"Yes, Inspector, we're not just your typical meat market. We try harder at Bio-Soft to make our biots feel wanted. We care about each other. We treat everyone alike whether they're synthetic or human. We don't have any Skinner boxes, and I would dare anyone to tell me the difference between our nurseries and any human daycare.

"Boys will be boys, though. When a single boy is lonely and tired, there's not much we can do. If the company paid every dwarf boy an allowance to set up a family, biots would cost the same as humans."

"Nothing can make up for mom and dad, or hide the fact that Bio-Soft just creates synthetic people for money," said Shotgun. "Biot's are born with a mortgage on our lives. In exchange for absolute obedience, seventy-two hours of work each week, and little hope of ever having a home, Bio-Soft provides for a biot's needs and rudimentary wants. They let us have just enough free-time to dream of all the possibilities beyond his reach."

"To dream is human," Jack blurted. "Biots dream even though we are synthetic, so we must be human."

Shotgun nodded in agreement, "Yeah, boss, that's right."

Goldman looked downcast. "Can't argue with you gentlemen there, it afflicts us all."

"Can we see his pass?" asked Gumshoe. "See if there's any doctor or clinic listed."

Nodding the goblin bent over and tapped on his workstation. "Here it is. See for yourself, there's nothing but his name, and the 'medical' excuse box is checked. I'm sorry we didn't get any of that information, but it's not unusual. Evan's a great kid, and I can't imagine him running away or falling in with the wrong crowd."

"Sure, Goldman. Before we speak to his dorm resident, what kind of employee was Evan? Any history? Anything unusual at all? This is no time to protect the boy. His life is in danger, and anything might be a clue."

"Nothing Inspector, Evan was a model employee. He was obedient. He worked the evening shifts, and like all of our dwarves, he worked twelve hours per shift, and six shifts a week. He was exceptionally talented. He was a brilliant code writer, and he poured all of his creativity into his work. Who knows what he might be." The goblin flopped in his chair, and sniffed. "I miss him, and I hope you gentlemen can find him alive and well."

"We do too," said Gumshoe, "we do too."

Goldman collected himself. "The dorm resident is waiting in the recreation room with your officers."

Goldman led them on a short trip. Around a bend, a couple of new turns, they walked to a recreation center. A large vid screen overlooked a kitchenette, oversized tables, and video gaming stations. Next to the recreation room was a small gymnasium where several dwarves, elves, and a goblin exercised in time to loud music which occasionally rumbled through the room.

Two elves and a goblin played cards to while away the time. The elves set down their cards, and stood to attention.

"Inspector, may I go now?" Goldman fretted. "I have to finish my contract before that kid arrives. Festus can show you around, if you need an escort."

"Oh yes, Mr. Goldman, I'm sure we can find our own way now."

"Inspector," said the red-headed sergeant. "We were just waiting for you."

"At ease, Riley," said Gumshoe. "Anything to report?"

"Yes sir, this is Festus McGillicutt," said Riley. The dorm resident was an elderly goblin dressed in teal overalls with Bio-Soft patches. His overalls were rumpled as if he had put them on without pressing. His hair flew in all directions. Riley looked uncomfortable and shot a glance at his partner, searching for support.

"It's all right Riley," said Gumshoe. "The super explained the mistake. To err is human. We just have to pick up where we left off and keep on going."

"Mr. McGillicutt may have been the last one to see Evan before his disappearance. This morning we were talking to Evan's friends and the residents on his hall and showing them the McCarthy girl's picture. Mr. McGillicutt asked us if we had spoken to everyone at Evan's new apartment, and that's when we realized the mistake. When we got a look at the victim's apartment we found the sign and called in the crime scene crew. Mr. McGillicutt here says he has a statement, but he won't tell us. That's all, sir."

"If that's all, you're dismissed. Go get yourselves some lunch, if you haven't already. Then meet us at Evan's apartment."

"Yes sir," said Riley, "thank you, sir."

While the two elves collected their packs, Gumshoe took off his trench coat and hung it on the back of a chair. Pulling the chair out from under the table he turned it around and sat on it.

"Mr. McGillicutt," said Gumshoe, "Now we'll get to your statement. I may have a few questions."

The old goblin guffawed, pleased with himself for no obvious reason. "Quite right, Inspector, quite right." Muttering, the goblin slowly sank back into his chair. "You call me Festus, Inspector, all my friends do."

"Why didn't you say something to the officers, Festus?" asked Gumshoe.

"I did, you heard 'em, at how they's learned he don't live here no more. I's the one at told 'ems to try his new apartment. Course they could have figured that out from his old room, if they'd had a brain. When they saw his apartment, I knows somethin's afoot. They don't says nuthin' but they don'ts have to. I knows it's got to do with the Zodiac.

"So I says to myself, I says, I won't talk to those buffoons. Festus will only talk to the head cheese, the balding Inspector with snow on his mountain," he paused for dramatic effect. He half rose out of his seat and swept the air in front of Gumshoe. "The top enchilada," he said.

"Festus, you cut me to the quick, I've only got a touch of grey." Gumshoe's lips curled into a smile, and he bit his lip to avoid laughing.

"Ain't nothing Inspector," said Festus. "It's only my way o' sayin' the lead dog." He thrust out his eye again, studying the Inspector.

"Sure Festus," said Gumshoe. He mollified the fickle goblin. "I was just wondering why you wouldn't speak to the uniforms. If you have anything to say, please spit it out."

"I'd a talked to 'em, as I said. Just those two ain't the sharpest tools in the shed, better at bein' a doorstop than a dust mop, if you get my drift. I just figures if you wants somethin' done right, you's gots to do it yourself."

"Festus, I understand now. Very sensible. What was it you wanted us to know?"

"Why you bet cha, Inspector, sir," said Festus, rising from his seat again. "I knew somethin' was wrong when your boys come a callin' with a picture o' that purty young thing in the Zodiac case." Slowly sinking back to his seat, he grumbled, "Should've axed 'round." Illustrating his point, he thrust one bug eye at the Inspector, and swiveled slowly around to Jack and Shotgun letting them look into his eye.

"I would a told 'em before, soon as they axed me. I'm his dorm resident 'en I should know. That fill-in that Goldman's got ain't got all her marbles. Don't know nuthin' she don't and she ain't all fired up to learn. Ignorance and apathy, I always says it's the bane of us all."

Festus stood up, and turned his chair around and sat down again with his arms folded facing Gumshoe. "Down to business, then is it? Evan's a good boy, or was, if my guts tell me straight. He was one of our best, but a bit dreamy. He had everythin' here you could want if all you wanted was to keep on living. He wanted a girlfriend, and none o' the girls here'd have anythin' to do with him. They're all Bio-Soft right? Never mind they're on contract and ain't no better'n nobody else. But they strut around 'specting to meet a prince to carry 'em off to the palace. And they's lookin' for trouble, says I.

"So Evan, he's a bright boy he is. Yeah, but he's impatient, and gets hisself permission to move to a bigger apartment cause he's not thinkin' right. He's won't listen to Festus. Festus has crossed the plain, and been everywhar' from the Finger Lake Kingdom to the Swampland, but he won't listen to ol' Festus. He's know he can't land him no tarts here, but what he don't know's is he's already livin' in the best place to lands him a good tart at ain't from around's here. You follow me?"

"Festus, that makes good sense. Many a wench in Nodlon would be very proud to say their boyfriend was contracted at Bio-soft."

Festus jabbed a finger at Gumshoe. "You're right smart, that's why's you's the detective."

"Hey, I agree," said Shotgun. "That's how I landed Goldie."

"So I knows it ain't be workin' out for him none, cause he's done gone and played it backwards. And then I see's him last Friday and he's comin' out o' the super's office with a pass." Festus narrowed his eyes, and said conspiratorially, "says he got a doctor's appointment or somethin' but he won't says what it's for, or who it's with.

"Now, I knows what's your thinkin,'" said Festus, waving a finger at all of them. "You're thinkin' he ain't got no brain.

"I knows how a boy thinks though. He's thinkin' if he's just a mite more handsome, and more athletic, he can score with a good girl. There wasn't anything wrong to look at 'em, but when no girl'd have him, what's he to think. He just wants to fall in love, but who's gonna fall in love with a dwarf boy under a contract makin' him no more'n a machine?

"Evan thought he'd find hisself a secret weapon, and get himself a gene makeover like them popular people on the vid." Festus shifted his gaze to Jack, and said, "No offense to you, o' course, Mr. Clay."

"None taken, Festus."

"So I says, he's gone and done it, goin' to one o' them gene witch doctors. Voodoo they practice, black magic, witchcraft, playing god with people's lives and tamperin' with what's they ain't gots no right to meddle with. And now, I's thinkin' 'at maybe's they's all gone 'at away."

"Who Festus?" asked Gumshoe.

"The missin' dwarves, Inspector, the missin' dwarves, all of 'em."

"It's a good idea, Festus. Don't let anyone tell you, you don't have a brain. From what you just told me, your brain works as well as any others and maybe better than most."

"Comin' from you's sir, that's a right fine compliment! Oh, but wait, there's one more thin' I've to tell you." He leaned forward, and signed for them to huddle. Acceding to his wish, they huddled and he whispered, "I knows you cannot use this, but I've got a premonition. I feel it in my bones. Somethin' out there's after you. Thou art doomed! And when it's through with you, it's gonna be after us."

"Is that all, Festus?" Jack asked. The old goblin nodded. "You haven't had any strange dreams have you?"

Festus stared at Jack. "You've had a premonition too, ain't cha, Mr. Clay? I wish I knew more, but that's all. Festus can't put his finger on it. Maybe it's a hunch, but I think Evan's fallen in with bad company. It's far worse than just runnin' away."

"Thank you, Festus," said Gumshoe. "Can I call you if I have any more questions?"

"You do that Inspector, Festus will be here." The old goblin rose from the table reluctantly. He slowly shuffled away.

Festus stopped and looked back forlorn before he drifted out of the recreation room.

The music from the gym rumbled. Gumshoe gazed into space thinking of the old goblin's story.

"Do you think he's right?" asked Jack.

"It makes sense," said Gumshoe. "Gene therapists have an awesome amount of power over their patients. After all they're changing your underlying gene code. Plus, who would suspect a gene therapist. They're among the most respected members of the community, and everyone implicitly trusts them.

Suspecting a gene therapist is scary, really. Everything is built on it now. Once in the therapist's hands, they have absolute power over their patients. The patient has no way to stop whatever transformation the doctor may invoke."

"What next?" asked Shotgun.

"Good old fashioned police work," said Gumshoe. "We'll check out Evan's apartment, and see if we can find something that eluded the fancy technology and the state of the art techniques."

Down a hall, around a bend and past a laundry room and they were out of the dorm. They crossed the Bio-Soft campus and entered an apartment complex. Soon, they stopped at an apartment like any other except for a strap of yellow tape stretched across the door.

Two uniformed elves stood guard. Crime scene techs worked quietly and performed their duties.

Riley greeted them at Evan Labe's door. "Hello, Inspector, gentlemen, the crime scene guys are almost done. They said just a little longer." Riley peeled back the tape and Gumshoe ducked into the apartment.

Waiting outside, Jack and Shotgun backed into a corner of the hall waiting for the crime scene technicians to finish their business. The techs buzzed around Gumshoe as he collected their reports. Eventually, they packed their sample cases and stowed their instruments in carrying cases. One by one the specialists reported to Gumshoe and left.

Gumshoe waved a come hither inviting them into Evan's apartment.

"They have to be thorough," said Gumshoe. "I'm treating the scene as a homicide." The crime scene team had laid plastic runners around the studio and taped off furniture and sections with yellow tape and warnings not to touch.

The apartment was neat, almost immaculate. It was tastefully appointed for a dwarf on a limited budget. A saloon door separated the bedroom from the kitchen. A stylish black leather couch and sofa faced a wall sized vid screen, contrasting rustic end tables finished in walnut. A glass coffee table hewn from the stump of a tree faced the vid.

On the screen was the Capricorn. A splash of scarlet marked each star. "As you saw," said Gumshoe, "Prepping the scene takes hours and it costs."

An end table with a lamp sat next to a neatly made bed. An anime hero in a spacesuit rocketed across his bedspread. A heroine chased him on her own jetpack. A towel and pajamas lay forlorn atop a hamper of dirty laundry in his closet. Jack felt the weight of the missing dwarf in the lonely apartment.

"Is it the same as the one we found in McCarthy's apartment?" asked Jack, pointing to the vid.

"It's blood," said Gumshoe. "The splatter analysis is the same as in McCarthy's room."

Jack turned away from the vid screen and followed the plastic runners. He studied the little apartment.

By moving out of the dorm, Evan had gained twice the space. A case of sparkling water and a short stack of pizzas barely filled a shelf in his fridge. Through the saloon door was a sizeable bedroom with a walk-in closet and a bath with a Jacuzzi built for two. The back wall of the bedroom opened to a small deck overlooking an alley.

Shotgun examined a homemade bookcase holding an eclectic collection of video games, movies and book disks.

"Anything interesting?" Jack asked.

"I like him already," said Shotgun, "he has all my favorite games, books, and movies. We might be friends if he hasn't gotten himself clocked."

Suppressing his melancholy, Jack hoped they would find Evan alive and well, but in his gut he knew the hour was late for Evan Labe. Turning away from Shotgun, he circled the bed and peeked in the closet. The closet was a testimony to dwarfish compulsions. Evan's uniforms and casual clothes were organized, and neatly hung with the collars facing the same direction. He had sandals, sneakers, loafers, and a pair of fluffy bear claws.

"Gumshoe?"

"Yes, Jack?"

"Maybe this is nothing," said Jack, "but Evan's got no boots. A dwarf on the prowl in Nodlon has to have a set of boots. My costume designer says a man needs three sets, one for work life, one for wildlife, and one for the nightlife. He might have worn his good boots out."

"Thanks," said Gumshoe. "I'll make a note. Let me know if anything else seems to be missing."

"Sure." Jack moved on to the bathroom. A shelf supported shampoo, conditioners, body washes, ordered by size. The medicine cabinet was open, revealing an assortment of basic supplies. He had two toothbrushes.

Jack squinted at the brush handles, and a bulbous version of Noddie the mythical dragon smiled back at him. Sucking in a deep breath, he studied the medicines. An old bottle of antibiotic pills and a bottle of iron supplement sat in one corner, separated by a little space from a few bottles of over the counter medications.

"Got a glove I can use?"

"Just a second." Gumshoe appeared at the bathroom door, holding a pair of latex gloves. "Here use these. What have you found?"

"He's got some meds in here with recent dates," said Jack. He picked up each bottle and perused the labels. "These are vitamins and herbal medications used by athletes and body builders to enhance physical performance."

"Read those off please, my eyes are getting old."

Rattling off the unfamiliar names of the ingredients, Clay read the labels and Gumshoe updated his notes. The Inspector tapped on his computer. "Yeah, got it." He smiled wryly, "This is why I believe in detective work. My techs catalogued the meds, but they didn't flag them. They just listed them with almost eight thousand other items. Are there any prescription meds?"

"No, just over the counter stuff to buff up," said Jack. "Body builders use these supplements."

"Thanks Jack, that's thinking out of the box." Jack set the medicines back and followed the Inspector. "I may have recognized the significance about three years from now."

"Inspector," interrupted Shotgun. The dwarf pointed to a slip of paper tucked between a drawer and the chest. "I think I've found something."

"What?" Gumshoe knelt by Evan's bed.

"The paper popped out when I opened the drawer."

"Now this is old school." Gumshoe drew a toolkit from his trench coat, and took out a set of tweezers. He drew the paper out of the drawer. Holding it up with tweezers, he took it in his gloves.

"It's a brochure for a gene therapy clinic," Gumshoe said. "New Genes, New Gem." A cartoon nymph beamed from the cover. She struck an alluring pose on the brochure's face. She beamed with a smile. Gumshoe turned the brochure over and read the back, "Don't be blue! All your dreams come true!" Gumshoe flipped it open. "Hey, gentlemen, a handwritten note with time, date and an address. Would that mean anything to you?"

"An appointment," said Jack and Shotgun in unison.

"Good, I'll have you two trained in no time." Gumshoe winked. "We've got a clue. It's getting late. We can't make it by closing in this traffic. We'll pay New Gem a visit tomorrow if I can get a warrant." Gumshoe waved at the door. "For now, I've got to go back to the Yard. It'll be a late night. I'll drop you off at Babel Tower if that works."

A Suicide Pact

Nodlon Memorial was busier than Jack had ever seen it. The sixth-floor nurse's station was a study in mauve and organized chaos. Never before had he seen as many nurses at the station. Usually, only a few were on duty during the evening, keeping watch over sleeping patients. As for a physician, normally there were none to be found when Jasmine was on duty.

Tonight was no ordinary night. Jasmine's office was behind the station sandwiched between the linen's and the nurse's break room. A horde of doctors, nurses, technicians, lab assistants, and volunteers boiled in and around the station and up and down the halls. He heard moaning and complaints from many rooms, and he thought of what he might do to help.

"Hi, Jack," called a familiar voice.

Searching the crowd, he saw a dwarf waving at him. "Hi, Brenda, I'm just here to visit Jazz, if she's available."

"No," said Brenda, "one of the surgeons is in her office, and he doesn't look happy." She wore yellow scrubs with white and pink flowers.

"What's his problem? Should I straighten him out for you guys?"

"No, thanks," Brenda answered. "The doc's not mad, just upset. A patient's in trouble. Jazz is straightening out the mess. Anyway, she's a pro. She isn't going to take any guff off an overpriced butcher if it's undeserved."

"Guess I'll have to wait then."

Brenda turned away.

Jack remembered Jazz had asked him to visit a patient. After working on the Zodiac case, he had nearly forgotten. "Wait, Brenda."

"Yes, Jack?"

"Jazz mentioned a teenager she wanted me to visit. She committed suicide, and Jazz asked me to visit her."

"I know the one, follow me." Hurrying around a

technician hustling off with a tray of samples, Brenda led the way past the crowd. Darting and dodging, he worked to keep pace with the agile dwarf.

Passing the break room, he thought of coffee. As if reading his mind, Brenda veered into the break room.

"Can I get you some coffee?"

"You're busy. I can help myself."

"It's no trouble, Jack." Popping a disposable cup under the pot's dispenser, she poured him a cup, and handed it to him. "Smells good, the kitchen has been working overtime. I'll have to come back if I have a chance."

Leading him on, she left the room and tore down the hall in quick time, forcing him to walk fast despite the advantage of his long legs. Halting before a door near the end of the wing, she stopped. "She's on a suicide watch. She swallowed a bottle of pills and flat lined four days ago. They pumped her out downstairs, shot her up with Afterlife, and then sent her up here."

"Did she have a near death experience?"

"She won't say, but I'm guessing she did."

The room was burgundy and mauve with two beds. A partition with a white curtain separated the beds, and a small boy slept under a tent on the bed near the door. A stack of machines on a gurney beeped and hummed beside him, and an intravenous feed gurgled as the pump purred.

The nurse pointed at the boy. "Marty came in on a transport from the Moon. He'll recover. I know it looks bad, but he's out of the woods for now."

The nurse pushed aside the partition and stepped up to the next bed. "Are you awake, Melissa?" Brenda asked.

A girl called out of the gloom. "Yes."

"You have a visitor," Brenda said.

On the bed was a goblin girl, hardly more than a child, gray featured and bony. She stared out the window with a dour look and crossed arms.

Jack followed her gaze over the medical complex, across the eastern mall, and up to the mountains. Melissa sat up and the springs squeaked. "A visitor?"

"Yes, will you see him?"

"If I have to, I don't want to see any more nut doctors. I'm not crazy."

Jack ventured near the bed, hoping the waif would accept his presence. "Hello, Melissa."

She waved without breaking her stare. "Hi."

"A friend asked me to pay you a visit." He wondered how long it would take before she ordered him to go away. "I'll just sit down." He sat on the counter next to her wardrobe.

Melissa pursed her lips, and sat taciturn. She stoically endured his presence. Then she glared at him, and said, "You don't have to stay. What are your questions? I'll answer them and you can go."

"I don't have any questions. And I have to wait, so I might as well wait with you."

"What are you waiting for?" she snapped, "A Martian attack?"

"I'm waiting on my fiancée. She's a nurse."

"Oh, that's nice. Somebody cares about you." She crossed her arms. "Beats waiting on someone dying to leave you a fortune."

He wondered what to say. For all he knew, she had a good reason to be angry.

"Anger is good when it's directed at the source of a problem, Melissa. But being angry with the world is counter-productive. It gets in the way of solving problems, and it makes mountains out of mole hills. You spend so much time being angry at the wrong people."

If he wanted her attention, he had it. She pushed herself up and yelled, "What do you know about it?!"

Clay held a finger to his lips, hushing her. "Melissa, please! Marty's sleeping." The boy laid as still as a corpse under his tent.

She fell flat on her bed, and moaned, "He's a zombie. If he ever wakes up out of that coma, he'll probably want to play jacks or dominoes or something stupid."

"What's wrong with games? I like games."

"Go on, now you're asking questions and you want to play kid games? You shrinks are all alike! Ugh!"

"Sorry, I'm not a shrink. I'm an entertainer. I like making people laugh by doing tricks and stuff. You might like it too."

"You're kidding me. What kind of tricks? You don't prank kids do you? Some of the bullies pull tricks on the little kids, and it ain't nice!"

"Look, I'll show you an illusion, if you'll watch."

"Sure, it's not like I'm going anywhere."

He waved his hands for melodramatic effect, hamming up his performance. A wisp of fog rose from his palm. A ballerina stepped out of the mist, and pirouetted. He added music to keep time with the ballerina.

Mollified, Melissa sat up and crossed her legs, staring at the ballerina.

"Do you like dragons?" He created a little dragon which flew around the ballerina.

"How do you do that?"

"Magic. Watch this." He added a ribbon floating around the room, and thinking of each illusion, he added a parade. A train led the way, followed by toy soldiers, a teddy bear, and a troupe of dolls, a spaceman and an alien, and finally Santa Claus.

"How'd you really do that?"

"I told you, I'm a magician." He wondered how he could prove himself. At a loss, he reached into his pocket for a card, and stopped. She had not recognized him. The room was dark, but not that dark. Where had she been living if she had missed his advertising?

"Melissa, have you ever been to a show?"

"A show? Like a movie? I've been to a movie."

Wondering where anyone would find a movie theatre in Nodlon, Jack tried to be casual. "Where did you see a movie?"

"In Deep Nodlon. I live in a dorm behind a warehouse two blocks from the last tunnel at the edge of the Pale. Down the street is a theatre and I can sneak in."

"I see, you are far out."

"Probably never been there have you? Not that I blame you, most of the tunnels are abandoned."

"No, Melissa. I grew up in a dorm, and one of my first gigs was in Deep Nodlon."

"Oh, sorry."

"Sorry for what?"

"I'm sorry for being rude. I thought you were a nut doctor or something. It seems like there's been a hundred in here poking me and telling me what to do."

He played it safe. He did not want to irritate her now. "The doctors and nurses just want to help."

"No, they just want to cover themselves. If I hurt myself, it'll be their fault, and that's why I'm not doing anything here. I don't want to cause more problems."

"Doing away with yourself causes a lot of problems, especially for you."

"No, it don't, if I'm gone, it ain't my problem no more."

"I guess that's not what I meant, if you do away with yourself, you're hurting others. Everyone is a part of life, and we all have something to contribute, and we all have something to gain. If we break the chain, we'll never know what."

"We're just here to collect the trash. Everyone in my dorm works for the sanitation department. That's their contribution. The agency doesn't care about me and I don't care about the agency. I don't care if they never get their money back feeding me. I didn't ask to be born, and I'm not paying for someone else's mistakes."

He sat still, watching her and listening. Depression was

common for biots, but it was the normal depression of living a life of quiet desperation. They enjoyed the fortitude learned by endurance. A rustle told him they were no longer alone.

"Jack," said Jasmine.

"Oh, hi, Jazz. Melissa and I were talking."

"Good. Melissa, has Jack showed you any tricks?"

"Yeah, he's good. He should be in show business or something."

Jasmine started to say something, but Clay waved her down.

"Melissa, would you do me a favor?" he asked.

"What?"

"A friend of mine gave me some cards to pass around, would you take some?"

"I guess, what are they?"

"These are passes to his show. It's a promotion to drum up business, create buzz, and get interest going."

"Yeah, fine, I'll take some. What do ya' want me to do with 'em?"

"Please, use them. Go to the show, take a friend." He handed her a wad of his cards.

"Yeah, whatever."

"Remember, take a friend."

"Ain't got no friends," she complained.

"Then go alone. And I want you to remember."

"Remember what?"

"Don't let the dogs win. If you give up, they win."

"Who're they?"

"You know, they're the people who want you to lose."

"Oh."

"Promise me, don't give up, and use those cards. My friend's counting on me to promote his shows."

"Sure, tell him I'll go."

"Melissa, we have to go now," Jasmine interrupted.

Exchanging goodbyes, they backed out of the room into

the corridor. Jasmine dragged him to the end of the hall, and they stood under a window.

"Difficult child," said Jasmine, "but you got her to promise to use the passes you gave her."

"Yes. Her spirit's broken, and for what? It's not like she's a horse. Is she crazy?"

"I don't know." Jasmine shook her head. "The psychiatrist says she's normal. No signs of trauma. She's under stress though, and there's no relief in sight. They told me it's an immature reaction to her situation."

"What's immature about being depressed in a depressing situation?" asked Jack.

"Suicide is immature. She should be trying to better herself. She has options. She has school. We all know the situation sucks, but she's not special or unique. Everybody has the same problems. I hoped you could cheer her up."

"I tried, but she's never heard of me. And I wasn't going to say anything. I didn't want to boast, and I'm not sure how she would take it. For some reason, I won the lottery, and she didn't. I don't think her lot is as bad as she's making it out to be, but I'm not sure I'm the one to explain it."

Jasmine held his arm. She stood on her toes, and pecked him on the cheek. "Good elf, I wouldn't have thought of that."

"I wouldn't either, except I remember when I was eight, I had the same thoughts. Not about doing away with myself of course, but I wondered how I would live. Luckily I had a mother, who loved me more than the world, but many didn't."

"Speaking of living, did you find out anything new about the Zodiac case?"

"Yes, and it's all confidential, so I suppose I'll have to tell you sooner or later."

"Never give up hope." Jasmine hugged him. "I've got to get back to work, if I'm ever going to get off tonight. By the way, where's Shotgun?"

"He's waiting for me in the Andromeda," said Jack.

"He's on his caster. Goldie called him in a fright. Biot Staffing is moving to Iron Mountain. They're afraid Mars will attack. They released all non-essential biots for two-weeks.

"Anyway, Goldie's scared stiff. Naturally, I suggested they stay with me. We're short on beds, but I've got plenty of room. Shotgun and I can sleep on the couches tonight. Goldie can stay with us as long as she needs to. She and the girls can go to Iron Mountain with us."

"I'm scared too. I'll join you, if I can get out of here." She hugged him and grinned. "Nothing's going to happen with the Morgan family camped in your penthouse."

He scoffed, "Yeah, you do that." He gazed out the window at Nodlon. "If something happens, take your roadster. It won't hold us all, but you can throw Goldie's kids in the back."

"I like that idea." She squeezed his hand, "What about you boys?"

"Shotgun and I can take my Andromeda once we solve the case."

"Will you solve the case?"

"Be positive," he said. "It's my blood type. We're going to solve this case or my name isn't Jack Clay."

"You get him, honey bear." Self-consciously, she glanced down the hall at the milling stew of nurses and techs. She gave him a quick kiss and a hug again. "Bye," she whispered.

"Bye," he said, watching her go. He felt a pit in his gut.

The Blue Lights of Nodlon

Clay clambered into the Andromeda. "Thanks for waiting."

Shotgun closed his caster. "The Morgan family has taken over the Clay pad. Hope you don't mind. Faith and Hope are on your bed, and Goldie is on mine again. If Jazz comes home from the hospital, the girls will move Hope."

"Looks like we're both sleeping in the living room again."

"Yeah, thank you for letting Goldie and the girls stay with you. Hope you don't mind."

"Mind? No," Jack winked. "What can go wrong?" He gave his butler a thumbs up.

"Jazz may want to sleep alone. She's going to be bushed." Shotgun fidgeted on the flyer's scream bar.

"If Jazz comes home, she doesn't want to be alone. Not tonight. Not with all the casualties in the hospital. And she loves Faith and Hope. I dare say she's pining for her own babies."

Jack slipped into flight mode, and lifted the Andromeda into the low altitude lanes. He circled the hospital and headed his flyer towards Babel Tower.

"I just hope we look back on these days and see an overblown diplomatic incident and not the beginning of a new round of wars."

Shotgun shrugged. "I want to go back to normal. And I want my girls to grow up and marry a nice boy."

"A son-in-law you can play vid games with?"

"No, I'd rather gain a son than lose a daughter, but I don't want to limit her choices. Who cares if they come home with a goblin, a moleman, or a dwarf?" Shotgun grinned, "or even an elf."

Jack looked at the ring on his finger. "With Princess Virginia's favor, we can stop chipping, and they will have plenty of choices."

"Just between us girls, boss, I hate the chip. I don't want

an agency chipping my grandchildren. And I don't want them cutting my daughters open and taking their babies."

"That's not going to happen to Faith and Hope. I promise, Shotgun, we're going to stop the war, defeat the cartels, and free the biots long before Faith and Hope start looking for Prince charming."

The blue lights of Nodlon flickered below.

"Do you and Jazz want a family?" Shotgun asked.

"Ha, if only chivalry required sleeping on the couch. Jazz wants a dozen children. I'm supposed to grow up and be a father. I want to be a father, but what if I make a mess of things. It's a big responsibility."

"I know the feeling."

"Ha, touché, my humble man-servant, but you're a good father Shotgun. Anyone with eyes can see that."

~~~~~~

Clay poured himself a hot tea, and switched on the vid. The anchor was trying to explain the imminence of war with Mars. He tightened the sash of his robe, and switched the vid off. He was too tired to think about the Baron bickering with Nogora.

He leaned on his porch rail and breathed in the cool mountain air. Seeking an inner peace that eluded him, he contemplated his condition.

From high on the mountain, Babel Tower touched the sky on Nodlon's northern spur. Nodlon gleamed below him in the golden rays of the fading twilight. The blue lights twinkled in the dark on valley floor, while the silver spires of the shield towers caught the day's last rays. Red beacons burned atop the spires warning the civilian flyers away.

A child of war, Nodlon had skirmished with her terrestrial neighbors more than once, but Nodlon had prevailed easily against her neighbors and even those distant conflicts were nearly forgotten. Nodlon had not seen a major war in a hundred years. Shivering in the cool night air, he studied the shield towers searching for any comfort. He had never thought he would look upon those silent sentinels for the city's hope.

He tried to imagine a war with Mars. What if Babel Tower was destroyed? What would he do? His stuff, his condo, was it really all about him? *No. It's not all about me; it's about all of us. If I could I'd give my stuff away to save everyone else, but it doesn't work that way. Nogora doesn't want my stuff. He wants to destroy Nodlon.*

Venus blazed high in the sky, the first star of the evening. He watched the stars appear one by one until too many to count filled the sky. High above the mountain, he watched the commuter shuttle to Elysium leave Nodlon's spaceport. He had been there before, passing through on the way to Mars. It was a marvel of the ancient world.

Sunlight painted a panoply of pinks against the midnight blue.

Sighing, he finished his tea and turned away. He left the patio door cracked, and set his mug on the table.

Blueberry Lake

"Get up sleepy head." A blinding light fell on Clay.

He sat up and spun out of bed. "Shotgun! What time is it?"

"Late. But the coffee's fresh, and I'm making ham and cheese omelets for breakfast with English muffins. Get a move on, or I'll take matters into my own hands." Shotgun tied back his curtains, letting the morning sun flood the room.

Jack muttered an inaudible thanks to the dwarf's back. Bleary eyed, he staggered to his lavatory, and splashed cool water on his face. In the mirror, his elven face stared back at him. Clever blue eyes and thin features, fair complexion, he could have been sixteen more than thirty. Stretching, he shook off the night and tried circulating his blood.

Clean shaven and dressed, he sneaked a peek of himself. "Youth is fleeting, and vanity shames, but character endures."

He scolded himself. He recalled Phaedra's admonitions. Her soft voice came back to him, *Never forget, Jack, you will be remembered for your misdeeds and not your talents or contributions. The more you give, the more history will hate you, and seek to bury your memory.* His mother had known all too well she lived on borrowed time. They had sought to repair her failing heart, but a perverse technicality made genetic repairs useless.

A wave of sorrow swept over him. He shoved the emotion back into the recesses of his mind. He missed his mother but he had to go on living.

He joined Shotgun in the kitchen. Consoling himself, he filled his favorite latte cup with black coffee. On the outside of the cup, a rotund old man in a white beard and red pajama's laughed. Sharing breakfast with Shotgun, he readied himself for the coming day.

"Delicious, you've excelled this morning. What's in these eggs?"

"Gorgonzola, and a hint of caraway for mystery." He toyed with a slice of ham and said, "That's my secret though, just between us girls."

"Mum's the word, I won't even tell Jazz." Clay crossed his heart. "You'll make Goldie a good wife."

Shotgun shuffled his utensils, embarrassed but amused. He buttered his toast casually without answering. Then he laid down the bread, and sipped his coffee. He started to say something and then stopped, returning to the coffee.

"Boss," Shotgun reddened, his eyes misted. The usually taciturn dwarf pursed his lips, holding back.

"Shotgun, I'm sorry about the joke."

"I don't mind the joke."

"What's wrong then?"

"Even if Biot Staffing releases Goldie, we've no place I can afford on this side of the city, and we can't live here."

"Why not? After Jazz and I get married, you and Goldie can take her apartment. It'll be nice to have kids running around."

"You'd do that?"

"Dead straight, Shotgun. Faith and Hope need their father, too. I should know. I miss my mother."

"What about Jazz, and your family?"

"Dude, you're family." Quickly, he stuffed his mouth full of eggs, hoping Shotgun would accept his offer without any more questions.

Heavy metal music jarred his reverie, and he retrieved his caster. The inspector appeared on the caster's little vid screen in his fedora and trench coat.

"Morning, Gumshoe."

"Morning, Jack, but we've found another victim. Better sit down."

"Shoot, I'm ready."

"An elderly couple walking their dog found a dwarf maiden floating in Blueberry Lake a half hour ago. We're scrambling uniforms and a crime scene team now. Can you and Shotgun meet me there?"

"Be there in five."

~~~~~

It took a little more than ten minutes, before he guided the Andromeda onto the street. He enjoyed driving with the autopilot and navigation system off.

On the ground, traffic streamed to and fro in Nodlon's morning rush. Jack steered the flyer towards the low altitude flight lanes to escape the traffic. He pulled back on the controls, and the flyer climbed into the free flight space above the city.

Breaking free of the controlled flight zones, Jack flew up over the mountains. Dawn unfolded over the eastern flanks of the Rockies. It was a magnificent view, the mountains gently rolled west into the vanishing twilight. Snow capped the higher peaks. Homes, apartment towers, and shops and businesses covered the foothills, and climbed up the southern side. Rising high over the peaks, they had a view of deep valleys full of pines, cottonwoods, and sequoias clutching the ridges. Little rivers glittered in the early morning light. Spring snow melt fell from the glaciers, and collected in tiny mountain lakes.

He steered towards the New Swan, staying in the civilian flight area around the castle. The flyer's monitor guided him away from the castle's restricted zone.

"Andromeda, this is Air Control," a flight controller announced from his dashboard. "You are about to enter restricted airspace. Please acknowledge."

"Acknowledged, Cretaceous Clay here, my monitor shows us in civilian space, Ground Control. Please advise." A transparent bubble shaded red surrounded the New Swan, the Crown, and the Octagon. His monitor displayed limited access corridors for space, high speed and commuter flights.

"Understood Mr. Clay, please state your destination." The

map on the monitor dissolved. In its place, red bubbles mushroomed over the city.

"Our destination is Blueberry Lake recreation area. A murder victim's body was found in the lake this morning, and Nodlon Yard has asked me to act as a consultant. I didn't realize the air map had changed."

"Understood, sir, please proceed west to the northeast commuter corridor. Follow the corridor back towards Collins field, and take the chute to Blueberry Lake. I will clear you from here. Please acknowledge."

"Acknowledged," Clay shared a silent moment of dismay with Shotgun as the controller rattled off some perfunctory closing remarks and instructions. Jack flew west in silence.

"Are we at war already?" asked Shotgun.

"Hope not." Jack searched the sky for signs of Martian ships. "Don't see anything wrong."

Air buoys with beacons and signs directed traffic in the corridor. They saw nothing unusual in the clear, morning sky, other than the heavy traffic. Frightened Nodlons headed northeast to the sanctuary of distant villages and towns. Waiting for an opening, a few flyers and an air cargo carrier the size of a barge passed them.

Seeing an opening, Clay joined the traffic. He followed the air buoys to the chute marked, "Blueberry Lake." He turned towards the lake. The lake waited for the dawn in the shadow of the Matterhorn. Egg shaped on one end, and the shape of a lobster's claw on the other end, the lake's two lobes joined in a narrow strait at the end of a promontory jutting from the Balmhorn. The flyer dropped quickly to avoid the restricted zone, and he leveled off in a graceful curve around the Balmhorn.

Flying over the Balmhorn's summit, they saw the sun crest on the Matterhorn. Atop the Matterhorn, the New Swan glittered in the rising sun. Following the chute of anti-gravity buoys to the lake, they flew over the forest on the Balmhorn's ridges.

"Awesome," muttered Shotgun. Clay twisted the little flyer so they took in more of the view. Individual trees stood out on the ridges, challenging the ice for dominion of the mountain. Over the ridge, the buoys followed the slope to the lake's beach and stopped.

Clay drove the flyer over the lobster's claw through the strait and around the Balmhorn. A lodge nestled against the foot of the Balmhorn hiding in the trees on the west side of the lake. The ridge jutting into the lake protected the lodge from avalanches.

A few dozen boats were still moored in the lake's small marina. The marina divided the park, which continued to the lake's small end. Just yards from the shore behind a clump of trees, an industrial plant of some kind was visible from the air, but not the ground.

At the end of the lake, the shore turned and hugged the foot of the Matterhorn. The shore ran the length of the mountain past the promontory to the ridge of the Balmhorn. A smattering of spruce, larch and pine struggled up the mountain from the pebble beach to the tree line. Above the trees, a seven story tiara of black glass jutted from the side of the mountain. The western Crown nearly encircled the mountain with overhanging restaurants, and a graceful observation deck, before burying itself into the mountain's core. Just beyond the Crown's southern edge, and below the deck was a curtain of bird netting over the cooling vents.

Flying above the lake, it required no effort to see where they needed to go. Between the lodge and the marina, a cluster of emergency vehicles beckoned with their all too familiar lights.

Jack sailed the flyer down to the water, and parked well beyond the last police cruiser. Not far away, a water cycle waited to be taken for a ride.

In the crisp morning air, the placid lake tangibly

expressed tranquility. Over the lake, ducks flew towards a destination chosen before the time of man. Birds of prey circled lazily, watched by scavengers. Far across the lake a loon called. A family of grebes swam among the round stones at the end of the beach.

Fire engines, ambulances, and police interceptors surrounded a half circle of tape holding back a crowd of early birds. Emergency lights cast macabre colors over the lake. The crime scene disturbed the tranquility.

Jack briefly noted the eerie resemblance to the scenes in some of his shows, and then pushed the thought aside. *A girl died here last night.* The reality sobered him.

Walking up to the tape, no one challenged them. Curiosity about the unexpected appearance of so much commotion consumed the few onlookers gathered on the quiet recreation spot. Elderly yachtsmen, retired government servants, troubadours and gold diggers, mingled in shared concern.

Shocked by discovering violence on the placid lake, fear united the knot of onlookers. Idling by the knot, Jack approached a young elf wearing a Crime Scene Investigation uniform.

The elf stopped him, "Sorry, Mr. Clay, authorized personnel only."

He started to say something, when he overheard Gumshoe.

"There you are Jack." The elf turned to the Inspector. "Let him through Gomer, let him through. I sent for him."

"Yes sir," said the elf. Gomer stood aside and let Jack and Shotgun approach.

Passing the tape, they closed on a knot of emergency personnel clustered around a stretcher. An ambulance shielded the body from a bevy of broadcasting vans. Reporters recorded the untimely passage of the maiden.

Jack flipped up the hood of his cloak, hiding his face. Avoiding attention, he starred down at his soft leather boots crunching on gray pebbles. He heard his butler grouse, "Step on it boss, the vultures haven't seen us yet." Speeding up, they reached cover behind a huddle of police and firemen.

Crime scene techs worked diligently while the remaining personnel stood by gawking. Uniformed officers, firemen, and medics chatted with each other. Clay overheard wild speculation. If Nodlon's finest believed such nonsense and spread rumors and fear, how much more would the public react? The fear of a panic throughout the city took on a reality for Clay he had heretofore not considered. Who knew what would happen if the city's biots feared slaughter? Limited in prospects and exploited for labor, nonetheless, they were safe from crime and illness. What would they do if they thought the police were powerless to stop a sociopathic lunatic hell bent on murdering them?

"Good to see you, Jack. What took so long?"

"All the air space over Nodlon is restricted. We had to fly twenty miles out of the way and catch the Northeast corridor, and come down the chute over the Balmhorn. It would have been faster following you up the California tunnel and taking the Old Road."

Gumshoe's face darkened. "War's afoot. It's a nasty business."

"What are our chances?"

The Inspector shrugged. "Don't know." Worry worked its way over his jowls.

Jack studied the detective. He knew Gumshoe had served in the military, but that was before Jack was born. Standing on the shore, Gumshoe's girth spilled over his belt. He had hard time imaging the detective humping it over an infantry course.

"What happened?"

"We won't know the full story until the coroner finishes his autopsy. She's been in the lake for several hours. She didn't drown. She was dead when her killer threw her into the lake. We're searching the shore line for any sign of where the killer dumped her. The couple who called us found her on the beach."

"Dumped?" interjected Clay.

"Yes, dumped Jack. Filthy swine probably takes more care with his trash. I assure you, I'm doing everything I can to stop this fiend, that's why I've asked you two to help. If we can find justice on this side, I mean to find it."

"How can someone abuse her, kill her, and dump her?" Shotgun asked. "I see it, but I just don't understand it."

"What do we know about the victim?" asked Jack.

"It's Anna McCarthy all right. We've confirmed she worked for an engineer named Khan, a Colonel. Anna was seen at your show on Sunday."

"My show?"

"Yeah, they sent her up to the Crown to fill in for a handmaid who was sick."

"Oh no, I bet Princess Virginia doesn't know."

"Great, just what I need. A tie-in to the Crown."

"What about the Colonel?"

"No, we haven't been able to reach him for an interview. He's sharp. His bio says he's been a department head for years, and he holds a doctorate in physics. No reason to think he has any idea why his secretary may have suffered foul play." Gumshoe looked at the body on the stretcher. "And there's one very odd clue I'm hoping you can shed light upon."

"What?"

"All of her blood's gone. No sign of a needle, an IV, cuts or any other source of bleeding. It's as though the killer used magic."

Jack pondered this information, "Have you checked the nose, or her mouth or throat for signs of hemorrhaging?"

"No, but I'll let the crime scene technicians know. Want to look at the body?"

"No, but I suppose I must." He girded himself for the ordeal.

One tech was packing physical and chemical samples, and another was carefully uploading their findings.

"Zach," said Gumshoe, "let us see the remains."

"Yes sir," said the tech. He stopped packing and opened the white bag containing Anna's remains.

"Gumshoe, I have seen her before," Stunned, Jack teetered.

"Steady, Jack," Gumshoe took his arm.

"She was at my last show."

"Can you tell me anything?"

"Yeah, she showed up with Princess Virginia's entourage. She was the Princess's handmaiden. She was paired off with a dwarf boy named Nicholas. They didn't seem to be together. It was hard to tell, the dwarves both seemed pretty nervous."

"Great, Jack, so now I'm going to have to tell the Princess her handmaiden was found floating in Blueberry Lake."

They quickly surveyed her body head to toe and front and back. Jack restrained revulsion.

"It gets worse than that. The Princess saw me in confidence. I'm violating my oath to her by telling you. We can't let anyone know the Princess came to me that night."

"Fear not, Jack, discretion is my middle name. But the Princess may be in danger."

"What would the connection be?" Jack grimaced, and his brow furrowed. "Martian agents trying to infiltrate the palace? The King could be in danger too."

"Yes, it's a possibility. We're all worried about a war with Mars. And Mars certainly wants a war with us. But don't forget, Jack, biots are people, too. Anna's pretty, and no bigger than a teenager. On the street, she's just another black dwarf. Some sick monster may have picked Anna at random. Keep all your theories open until the evidence falsifies one of them."

"Why her, Gumshoe? I don't believe in coincidences either."

"Suit yourself, I don't go in for mumbo-jumbo, but then I don't presume to know what's going on. The universe is too big for me. Maybe mother earth or some other god just wants to help us out – and bring the fiend to bar. It wouldn't be the first time a higher power gave me a hand."

"I hope you're right, Gumshoe, I think we're going to need all the help we can get."

A golf-ball sized black spot marred Anna's forehead. Clay knelt beside the stretcher and bent over her to study the mark. The bruise surrounded a small scar.

"Shotgun, see that scar on her forehead?"

Shotgun examined the wound on Anna's forehead. "Are you're thinking what I'm thinking?"

"It's blown out from the inside, as if the killer ripped the chip out of her," said Jack. "Excuse me, Zach; did you see this scar on Anna's forehead?"

"I've got the small contusion on her forehead catalogued," said Zach. "Whoever killed her must have pulled her microchip. She wasn't wearing it when we found her, and we haven't found it yet."

"Did you find any other cuts or abrasions, Zach?"

"No sir, perhaps the coroner will find something to explain the missing blood, but I've checked everything I can here in the field. The wound on her forehead is too small to account for the blood loss." The tech shifted uneasily.

"Course you have," reassured the older man trying to calm the nervous dwarf.

Seeing nothing else obvious to the layman's eye, they made short work of their examination and beat a hasty retreat. They huddled together at the edge of the lake. Gumshoe contemplated the dark blue water of the lake. "Well sports fans, can you tell me anything?"

"Other than what you know?" asked Jack. "Have you found any boyfriends?"

"I've got uniforms working on checking out possible boyfriends. So many biots are missing; it's hard to tell if any of them has a connection to McCarthy."

"Give it some thought Jack," said Gumshoe.

"If he's a magician, he has powers I don't have. That or powers I don't understand. Gumshoe, please remember, everything I know, I taught myself. I've never sucked out anyone's blood before. I'm not sure how to do it or even if it can be done."

"We can rule out vampires," said Gumshoe, "both supernatural and mortal. We've found no marks on or near major arteries. Many psychopaths drain their victim's blood for bizarre rituals. But, I'm stumped as to how the blood could be taken. Now, you know someone is able to do it. I need to know if it's magic."

"It's beyond me. I have no idea how the blood was taken. Sucking all the blood out of innocent maidens isn't a part of my show."

"Jack, I'm thinking is that you're not alone."

"Thanks, at least I'm not a suspect."

"Fortunately, you have an excellent alibi. You were home all night. I took the liberty of checking Babel Tower's security cameras, and the garage lock down. Your flyer never left its parking space."

Jack's hair prickled.

"Don't let it bother you Jack, I'm not just doing my job. I'm making sure I have all the exculpatory material a young magician needs for a long and full life."

"Thanks, Gumshoe; do have any other suspects besides your consultant?"

Gumshoe put his hands in his pockets, shook his coat, and studied his wingtips. "No, I'm stumped."

Stop Before We Run Out of Biots

Clay studied his reflection in the lake. "If we don't find the answer and stop this soon, there may be a panic. Biots may be classified as property but they still fear for their lives. The rumors have begun of magic, aliens, or monsters being behind the disappearances. We overheard the dwarves talking. Someone suggested it might be Noddie."

"What will happen if the dwarves start thinking a crypto-zoological dragon lives in the mines under the city, and comes up to eat dwarves?"

"They're already thinking it, Gumshoe."

Gumshoe gazed wistfully over the water watching the ducks dive. "I'll have to have remote surveillance bring up a robot submersible to check the lake." Stepping away from Shotgun, he took Jack's elbow. "Worse, what happens if they think we can't stop it? They may flee in terror. And if the public believes we're not trying, there could be a revolt. The royal family, a couple of opposition parties, and some celebrities such as you care about biots. Parliament, the bankers, and least of all the agencies don't."

Taken aback by the Inspector's intensity, Jack felt numb. "If it comes to that, I'll support you. You're a good man, Gumshoe, and I know you're doing your best." He looked at the ambulance with the remains of the late Anna McCarthy.

"Dozens of dwarves are unaccounted for, all young. Over half are boys. If the biots think we don't care, I'm not sure what they'll do." The Inspector swung his arms and bounced on his toes, driving away the chill on the lake.

"Zodiac signs," said Jack, "nothing on camera. No record of her chip in the security system. No witnesses other than two elderly citizens of feeble constitution and a tenuous grasp on reality. And now Anna's turned up without any blood. The supernatural stirs the imagination, and we cannot keep these facts secret for long. The biots are scared for themselves and for those they love. We've got to stop this before we run out of biots."

"Only one murder," said Gumshoe. "The rest of the missing dwarves may still be alive. Biots are over half the population. If fear grips the biots too, we'll lose it. The city will panic for sure."

"Keep it under wraps," Clay suggested. "Don't let anyone know."

"How? It's all over the net. The biots are scared. Even if we pull the plug, they tell their dorm mates. It's easy on normal cases to ask for confidentiality, but this is no normal case. All of Nodlon will know in a few days. If I try keeping it a secret, everyone will know before lunch."

"I'm sorry I can't help you any more than this," Jack said. "The only thing I can think of is finding out how Anna came to be here."

"Not sure, snow melt feeds the Lake, and it drains into the Manna coolers. The whole park is under the Ministry's jurisdiction, and I've asked them for a schematic of the drains, but it doesn't make any sense. No sewer drains into the Lake, not even from the Crown or the palace."

"Magic? Could there be any magical connection to the Lake?"

"You're the expert there Jack. You're the only known magician in these parts. If the killer can use magic, then you're not alone. If the killer isn't a magician, he's got new technology we haven't heard of. I'm not sure which is worse. One more thing, Jack, if the killer is a magician, he's bound to know you're on his trail. It's all over the vid and the net. And that means he knows you know about magic."

"Maybe, I'm in danger?"

"It's no secret you're working with the Yard."

Pebbles grinding under foot interrupted their conversation, and Shotgun rejoined them.

"Gentlemen," said Gumshoe, "thank you for your time.

Keep in touch, developments may happen at any time. Now, if you'll excuse me, I've a mountain of paperwork. Later." Gumshoe left them on the pebble beach.

Emergency vehicles pulled away from the shore, and down the park road. Without the deceased to attract a crowd, the onlookers drifted away, and returned to their vacations. Life continued, reflected Jack.

Jack and Shotgun walked down the beach, and crouched under the tape strung to a pole hammered into the beach. They passed a water bike and a canoe, and reached the Andromeda. The sporty little flyer resembled a miniature spacecraft, and seemed particularly strange sitting on a grassy knoll just a few feet from the Lake.

They enjoyed the cool spring breeze off the Lake. Nearing the flyer, they watched people wander by. Retirees and families with children joined the crowd asking the onlookers what had happened.

A young boy ran down the road from the lodge shouting his name. "Mr. Clay, wait."

They waited for the boy to close the few yards still separating them. The boy stuck out his hand, and grinned ear to ear. "Wow, you've made my day!"

"Put her there pal." He shook the boy's hand.

A lithe woman in a white sailing outfit joined them. "I'm sorry, Mr. Clay." She spoke in the nasal tone of Nodlon's upper crust. "We didn't expect to see you here." She tried to excuse the breach of decorum. "He loves your shows, and when he saw your flyer, he bolted."

Ignoring her embarrassment, he held out his hand, and she took his. Before letting her shake, he gripped her fingers, and kissed her hand with a peck. "My pleasure, mum." He added a hint of the same nasally tone, hoping she would take it as a complement rather than mocking. "Always ready to greet a fan."

Catching Shotgun's eye, he winked. Shotgun pulled a tee-shirt out of the back of the flyer, and handed it to him.

He knelt, and crouched on his heels. "Would you like it autographed?" The boy's face brightened, his eyes widened and he flashed a toothy grin. "Oh yes, please Mr. Clay."

Following the boy's look, he milked the scene for all the sap he could manage. "That is if your mother approves?"

"Mommy, may I have a tee-shirt?" To pitch his case, the kid added, "It's autographed!"

Defeated by his logic, she sighed. "Yes, but how much does it cost?"

The boy looked at him. "How much is it Mr. Clay? Mommy has lots of money."

"For you, I'm running a special today. It's free. What's your name?"

"Ray," the boy said, "Ray Hubris."

Jack pulled a black marker from his cloak. "To Ray Hubris, a big fan, Blueberry Lake," he wrote. He signed the missive, and handed the shirt to the boy. "Don't be afraid to wear it. It's stain proof and washable."

"Thank you!" Ray gushed.

"You're welcome. You're very polite." He held out his hand again to the woman in white.

"Thank you, Mr. Clay." Ray's mother sounded pleasant, but her eyes darted to the crime scene.

"Pleasure ma'am and here's a token for you as well." Jack smiled, ever the happy warrior, and handed her the pen. She gave him a thin smile and dropped the pen in her satchel.

They climbed into the Andromeda before any other fans cornered them. Shotgun gazed wistfully over Blueberry Lake. "Too early to pick any blueberries."

"Yes, but as we are here, let's take a spin across the lake, there's something I want to look at."

Firing up the flyer, they lifted off and turned towards the end of the Lake. Just inches above the water, the flyer churned the placid water. Jack steered the flyer towards the cooling vents. In minutes, they reached the opposite shore, and he switched to flight mode and lifted off.

Carefully hugging the trees, he watched his altimeter and the restricted zone altitude closely.

The cooling vents covered the lower third of the cliff. Above the vents, the southwest face rose to the Crown's southern anchorage. Up close, a mesh protected the cooling vents.

Shotgun broke the silence. "What are we looking for?"

"Nothing in particular, curiosity I suppose. I've been to Blueberry Lake many times, but I want a closer look today. Nodlon's engineers hid the manna generator's cooling towers by building them into the backside of the Matterhorn. Since the mountain is artificial, I wonder if the cliff is part of the mountain's original shape, or if that's artificial too?"

Quickly, Shotgun fired up his tablet, and called up Nodlon's original designs. "The original cliff was a guide. The towers ran up to the top of the mountain. They built the Crown using the original mountains as foundation stones."

Jack pulled the controls, and the flyer peeled away from the vents. They sailed over the tops of the thin spruce. Straggly pines struggled to survive at the foot of the cliff. Jack guided it back towards the water.

From tree height, they flew over the plant at the tip of the lake. Men and machines moved on mysterious errands under the trees. The men disappeared again as he flew down to the beach. Steering the flyer back to the road, he reset the flyer to ground effect and turned towards Nodlon.

"Chalk one up to the Ancients. When they dreamed big, they meant big."

"No point in flying, we might as well take the mountain road." They took the park road down the west side of the Balmhorn to catch the Old Road.

The park road ended at the Old Road. The Old Road ran from Blueberry Lake through the mountains to the sea. To the west, a fence blocked the ancient highway.

Jack felt a chill seeing the fence. A band of teens in a rented ground-car had challenged the Wild West a few years previously. They had told friends they were just going on a picnic at Blueberry Lake to see how the humans live. The Nodlon Defense Force had found the car abandoned just a dozen miles west. An exhaustive search never turned up any sign of the missing teenagers.

"The road of bandits, backwoodsmen, and Sasquatch," muttered Shotgun.

Jack turned east, towards home. "Tales told in the bars in Deep Nodlon, Shotgun, by ne'er do wells who fancy themselves in the likes of Stanley and Livingston."

"I wouldn't take that road," said Shotgun, "if the only other choice was the road to hell."

The cracked pavement was no obstacle to a flyer, but Jack would never drive the Old Road to the west.

"Not without a military escort," said Jack. Turning the other way, they plunged into the tunnel under the Matterhorn.

Café Des Moulin

Jack parked the flyer under the mall, and soon he and Shotgun emerged into the middle of the morning bustle on the streets of Nodlon. Dashing through an opening in the traffic, they crossed half of Jackson Boulevard. Hesitating a moment on the median for another break, they darted across the other half to the sidewalk on the other side.

Shotgun shielded his face as a ground car sped by. "Couldn't we just follow the traffic signals?"

Striding through busy shoppers, Jack said, "Where would be the fun in that? Don't you want to live dangerously, my man?"

"Boss," Shotgun ran to keep up with the long legged mage. "Keep the danger, and I'll keep the living." Breathless, he nearly bowled into his employer when Clay stopped abruptly. Stepping around the elf, Shotgun spied the Café des Moulin, Jack's favorite spot for imbibing a rich, creamy repast and a beverage of aromatic stimulants.

Louis appeared in short order, gushing at their arrival. The maître d' seated them at a sidewalk table.

"Thank you, Louis," said Jack, palming a tip.

Louis effused, "Oui, oui, Monsieur Clay, 'tis our honor to host a most magical one."

"Ever colorful," whispered Shotgun.

"At least his fake accent is consistent."

A matron took their order, and soon she served them chocolate torte and rich espresso topped with whipped cream. Sipping their coffee, they watched Nodlon pass by.

"Just days, Shotgun, since Anna went missing, and she's found floating in Blueberry Lake. We're no closer to our quarry than when we began." Dejected, he pulled down his hat, masking his face, and pondered what they had seen.

"Why was she dumped in Blueberry Lake? She worked for the Ministry of Manna. Is there any connection?"

"Blueberry Lake is out of the way," said Shotgun. "No one saw anything."

"Yeah, but we found Anna pretty darn quick. Like her killer wanted us to find her."

"Why would he want us to find her?" Shotgun stirred his coffee.

"How should I know, but if he wanted to hide the body, why did he leave it in the lake? He didn't even weigh her down. Why not bury her in the woods, or leave her in a dumpster?"

"Maybe Anna's killer is a copycat, and her case is not connected to the other missing dwarves. If the cases are connected, where are the other victims?"

"What if we weren't meant to find Anna? What if we just got lucky?" Jack swirled his coffee, watching the creamy berg melt into the steamy liquid.

"How did we get so lucky? If the other missing dwarves were murdered, it must have been the work of a professional."

"We haven't found anyone else. Maybe all the other cases were professional."

"A professional working for Mars?"

"Yes, but if a professional working for Mars was responsible, why haven't we found the bodies yet? If they want to panic Nodlon, wouldn't we find the bodies?" Clay contemplated the possibilities.

"Maybe it's just a coincidence."

"Could be, but I just have a feeling there are no coincidences."

"So he made a mistake with Anna, or he wants Nodlon to panic. I'm inclined to think the latter. We found the body to increase the tension."

"We don't need any more bodies to make Nodlon panic." Clay indicated the traffic. "It's worse than rush hour. If that's not panic, I'm blind. Someone should notify the eggheads up at Crown immediately."

Jack's caster buzzed. "It's the Inspector," he said.

"Why do I have a bad feeling about this?"

"What have you got for us?" Jack asked.

On the tiny screen the Inspector pushed his fedora back. "Are you sitting down?"

"We're at the Café des Moulin having breakfast."

"Great coffee, order me a Grande, Arabic, and meet me on the corner of Montmartre. I'll be there in five." Gumshoe broke the connection.

"He's upset, boss. It doesn't seem like the Inspector to ask us to buy him a coffee and wait on him."

"No, it doesn't, and I've known Gumshoe for a few years. He's upset. Bet they've found another victim."

"Are you sick, boss?"

Clay composed himself and left the matron a tip. "Frustrated. Let's get out of here."

Gumshoe steered his cruiser up to the curb with his lights flashing. They piled in, and strapped on their harnesses. Clay dropped two steaming coffees into the cruiser's cup holders. "Thanks for the coffee, Jack. What do I owe you?"

"It's on the house, Gumshoe. You know, I know cops never buy their own coffee."

"Thanks, Jack."

New Gem

The autopilot guided Gumshoe's police cruiser off the level way and through Under Nodlon. Turning onto Spenard Boulevard, the cruiser drove itself through the Blues District, while Gumshoe worked on his paperwork, and filed for a warrant.

Shotgun checked his tablet. "Goldie says her friends are all a twitter about New Gem."

Clay watched the reflections of the blue shadow lamps in the cruiser's windows. Derelicts hugged the jambs of vacant edifices, and other less savory denizens loitered on the street. Spying the police cruiser, the ne'er do wells feigned nonchalance.

"New Gem runs infomercials on late night vid," said Shotgun, tapping on his computer. "All that rot is snake oil. For a few dollars, they promise to solve all your problems using gene therapy. But they offer basic services for a discount price. They're legit according to the financial and medical channels. They started on Mars twelve years ago, and opened an office on Elysium three years ago. Dr. Balaam franchised the Nodlon office, and they opened last November."

"Legit?" asked Jack. "That's what the channels are saying?"

The cruiser passed coffee houses, palmists, and masseurs. Little shops offering sandwiches, and sweet meats flashed past.

"Yes," answered Shotgun. "That's the buzz. Quality work at a discount. Mind you, it's still a bit pricey for biots. The reviews are too good to be true, and the testimonials are probably whole cloth."

Spenard Boulevard curved gently through Deep Nodlon. They passed Brownstones, bed and breakfasts, and dilapidated hotels offering weekly rates.

"Yeah, makes sense," said Gumshoe, "if you needed a front, it wouldn't take much to set up a legitimate gene therapy clinic. The only real hassle is finding a crooked doc."

The dwarf stuck his head between the front seats. "Go to New Gem and get miraculous results. For a small sum, they can cure a biot of whatever ails him. Dwarves are all buzzing about the results. It's a wonder."

"It's a wonder," Jack said, "unless they kidnap you." The cruiser slowed and stopped at a traffic crossing. An old man played a mournful tune on a banjo, singing lyrics he couldn't make out. Next to him was a sandwich board reading, "Moloch drinks innocent blood."

Sensing his gaze, the old man looked up and glared at Jack. He had a hot tingle run up his back.

"Hard to believe," said Gumshoe. "Doctors have better things to do than join criminal conspiracies. Maybe a mole working for one of the mobs in town infiltrated the clinic."

"Our gift to the Martians?" asked Jack. The street curved with the mountain, and passed the Salome club. *The elf on the Salome club's marquee resembles Jasmine.*

"We have no beef with the Martians. And they have none with us. Their government wants a war, and our leaders are determined to fall into their trap."

As the cruiser left the Blues District, ordinary streetlights replaced the blue shadow lights. They drove through a block of trade shops and past a dry cleaner. A tall woman in a black cloak stepped out of a store. The woman stared at him as they drove by. Farther on, the cruiser slid through a quiet residential neighborhood and down a block of dentist and doctor's offices.

The cruiser pulled over opposite a dentist's office with a large molar hanging in front of a wooden façade.

"New Gem is a block ahead of us," said Gumshoe. "I'm trying to pull a warrant to raid the place, but they're taking forever getting back to me."

"What do you need a warrant for?" asked Jack. "Don't you have enough cause?"

"Enough cause of what?" said Gumshoe. "We don't even know if New Gem is involved. There may be a connection, but we have no idea what it is. I can get the office to subpoena Evan's records, but I can't just waltz in and question them about their other cases. If there's a connection, it will alert them, and they'll delete their files faster than you can say barracuda."

"What if New Gem is involved?" Jack asked. "It makes no sense to murder your customers. What's their motive?"

"We need to compare their client rolls to my database of missing persons. If there's no overlap, the brochure is probably just a coincidence."

"What of the missing dwarves?" Shotgun worked on his tablet. "If they all used New Gem, isn't that a connection?"

"If all of the missing dwarves used New Gem, we can arrest their staff, seize their records, and interrogate everyone properly. So far, Evan is the only missing dwarf who may have used New Gem. We don't know for sure. All we have is a brochure. That's quite a few ifs, and if this were just an everyday runaway case, I'd blow off the suggestion that any doctor had anything to do with it."

"Who wants so many dwarves?" said Shotgun. "A serial killer? Where would a pervert get the money?"

"Shotgun," said Gumshoe, "you of all people should know we can't predict motives. Your own motives were entirely innocent and you nearly triggered a crisis that shook the Crown."

"Yeah, thanks for reminding me Inspector."

"Shotgun, I learned long ago not to obsess about motives. True, all criminals have motives, but those motives may not be rational. A suspect with a motive may be just someone in the wrong place at the wrong time."

"Many of the subscribers to Jack-net are doctors," said Jack, "not that I suspect my fans, but we are one of the top hubs on the net for biot emancipation." Gumshoe and Shotgun gave him blank stares, and Shotgun shrugged.

"What are you thinking Jack?" asked Gumshoe.

"Doctors are sympathetic. Once in a while you get a

pervert, but most of doctors support the biots. A doctor might be helping them runaway."

"Ah, yeah, Jack, I agree. That's why I don't suspect them. Anyone who helps biots run away isn't going to murder a dwarf maiden under bizarre circumstances."

"Knowingly," said Jack, "is open to interpretation. Doctors are smart but naïve. They can be fooled into playing along with someone with less than honorable intentions."

"Touché," said Gumshoe. "I see your point. Under false pretenses, they might be selling clients with an interest in running to a nefarious mob, thinking they're helping them runaway."

"Yeah," said Jack. "So what are we doing sitting here while the killer drains Evan's blood the way he drained Anna?"

"Without a warrant, we can't use the evidence we find, and if we catch the beast we may not get a conviction on the accomplices at New Gem if they're involved."

"What if you can save Evan's life? What then?"

"Sure, Jack, there's an exception, but we don't know enough. Saving lives excuses procedural errors and deliberate violations, if it's sufficiently obvious. But what do we know? All we know is their brochure was in the home of a Zodiac victim. Remember McCarthy's Clay posters? By that logic Jack, you'd be the prime suspect in her case."

"What about Molly and Festus? They gave us a reason to suspect a gene therapist? Didn't they?"

"Yeah, and do you want to show my vid record of their statements to a judge? The Missus and I'd be eating beans in a soup kitchen in Deep Nodlon."

"Nonsense, Gumshoe. You're connected, and you've got friends in high places. If it came to it, I'd make you Chief of Security for Clay Players. I know rent-a-cop isn't your gig, but it's better than beans." Clay craned around to look at the dwarf in the back seat. "Shotgun, do you think you could case the joint?"

"What are you thinking, boss?"

"Quiet," said Gumshoe. Methodically, Gumshoe stabbed a number of buttons on the cruiser's console. Indicator lights darkened, and displays went blank. "Now, go on. If you're thinking of anything outside the bounds of good honest police work, I've got the cruiser's vid monitors shut down."

"If Shotgun can get in there," said Jack, "maybe he can crack their firewall and get a data dump off their servers. Somehow I don't think the Crown would be too eager to find out where a private citizen got a hot tip."

"We have no authorization for this, which is why I didn't hear it," said Gumshoe. "Shotgun, are you game? If you go in just to look, it's likely safe enough. If they recognize you, they probably won't do anything."

"Glad to hear I have a say in it," said Shotgun. "As it happens, I'm happy to volunteer since you're asking."

"Technically, I'm asking," said Jack. "I can't do it, obviously, and a police officer would be way too suspicious, so that leaves you. It's your choice. I wouldn't ask if I thought it was dangerous, but if it could save lives, I think we should do something."

The dwarf swallowed hard, and grinned. "What, boss? If a celebrity wanted to keep a secret, you don't think he'd be seen in a discount chop shop for biots with dating issues?"

"I'm not in the meat-market," quipped Clay, "and they will recognize me from the newscasts."

"They won't recognize me. All dwarves look alike, I know. If they still have an appointment open this afternoon maybe they'll see me."

Gumshoe motioned for them to hold their tongues, and drove the cruiser into an alley. A hobo glanced up when the cruiser passed, and promptly pulled the string of his collar tight, and lowered his hood. Slowing the machine to a stop, Gumshoe cut the power. Furtively searching windows and doorways, they checked for anyone spying them.

"Better get moving," said Gumshoe, "it's getting late."

"Nice neighborhood you've found Inspector." Shotgun set up his tablet. "If I get a chance, I'll pull everything on their servers. I doubt I can get in it while I'm waiting for a doctor. I'll have to crack their firewall. That's easy, but slow. If they're involved, everything may be encrypted, and I may need more time to break in."

"Here's a bug." Gumshoe handed Shotgun a device the size of a button. "We'll be listening for trouble. If you think you're in danger, just say 'Jack Hammer' and I'll be there if I have to blow their doors off with a lightning blaster."

"You've got a blaster?"

"It's in the trunk. I know, it is not much use there. But the Yard's got rules."

Shotgun pinned the bug to his cuff. Shotgun shouldered his backpack, and stepped out of the cruiser. "Thanks Inspector." Seeing no room on the driver's side, he sidled between the police car and a couple of trash cans on the passenger's side.

Clay lowered his window, "Shotgun."

"Boss?" The dwarf stopped in front of the cruiser.

Clay rubbed his lapel, "Your uniform." Shotgun remembered his Cretaceous Clay logo on his jacket. Working for celebrity was more than simply working for an aristocrat or serving as a domestic for hire. He slipped his coat off, folded it, and handed it to Jack, and rolled up his sleeves.

"Wish me luck."

"No getting kidnapped on the job."

"Do I get a bonus if I catch the murderer?"

"I'll think of something."

Walking casually, Shotgun picked his way through the trash in the alley, and gingerly bypassed potholes until he reached the sidewalk. Selecting a direction, he turned down the sidewalk, and left the alley and the security of the cruiser behind. Biting his lip, he watched the windows and doors for trouble. Townhomes with brick sides lined both sides of the tunnels. Small gates on brass posts guarded basement entrances under the porches. High above the street the artificial clouds burned with the blue light of Nodlon.

The neighborhood had fallen on hard times and many doors sported signs offering rooms for rent. Where gardens had bloomed between the facades and the sidewalk, rocks and weeds grew.

On the corner was a shelter converted from a one-time bank. The cult's banner celebrated recycling forgotten men. Dispassionately, Shotgun walked passed ignoring the glares from the vagabonds loitering outside the shelter. Crossing the tunnel, he passed a deli, and a dentist's office, and saw his destination.

Sporty neon letters arranged vertically on a tall sign proclaimed, "New Gem." Underneath it was a marquee reading, "All your dreams come true!"

He opened a sleek door in a façade of brick, and found a clean, attractive waiting room with nappy chairs, and plastic tables. Unused magazines on cooking, interior decorating and celebrities were neatly arranged on the tables. His boots clicked, and he lingered. Fear crossed his mind, and he breathed deeply. Briefly, he wondered if he should bolt out the front door or knock on the reception window.

While he wondered what to do next, the reception window slid open, and a goblin said, "New genes, New Gem! May I help you?" She filled a black dress, stretching it tight in all the right places.

Averting his eyes, he avoided staring, "Yes, I, uh, don't have an appointment."

"I'm Sally." The goblin rolled her chair around to face him. "You're in luck. We had a cancellation, and I've got one available right now. Would you like to take it?"

"Two questions though, will it hurt, and how much will it cost?"

"Treatments are painless. Usually there are three

treatments, but there may be more. Today we'll take samples to determine suitability, and those will go to a lab. During the next visit, the doctor will go over the results of the testing and determine a course of treatment you can afford.

"As for the cost, I'll need a hundred quid as a deposit. If you decide to go ahead, today's visit and the lab testing are included in our fee. The total cost depends on what you and the doctor decide. If you can't afford the whole fee all at once, we offer payment plans at no interest." She flashed a perfect set of pearly whites. "Want to go for it?"

"I think so."

Picking up an intake tablet, she turned it on and completed a few perfunctory entries. She handed him the device. "Please answer the questions and I'll get you started."

He heard a maiden through the reception window, beyond the patient's entrance. The maiden said, "Sally."

"All done today?" said the receptionist. "I need sixty quid. Can I use the same card?"

"Yes, thanks." The maiden opened the patient entrance, and a vivacious red dwarf stepped into the waiting room. Spying Shotgun, she smiled. "Hi, my name's Joann." She held out her hand, and Shotgun shook it.

"Hello, I'm Patrick."

"You won't regret it," she said, flashing a brilliant smile of snow-white teeth.

"Joann, can you show him your pictures? I'd appreciate it."

"Sure Sally," she said, reaching over the bar and taking a thin folder from the goblin girl. She opened the folder and held it for him to see. A picture of Joann was clipped to the folder. Joann resembled the version standing before him, but she stared out of the photo with a weak smile. She flipped the picture aside to a different shot in her overalls. She had a pixie cut, and she could have passed for a boy.

"You're really making the right choice. When I walked

in, no one even noticed me. I was waiting right here, and a boy walked in, and he wouldn't even look at me. It was like I didn't exist, huh, what's with that? Right?" She closed the folder, and said, "Now look at me." She posed. Gone was the goofy grin, replaced by sumptuous lips curled in an alluring smile. Full hips stretched a tight dress. Long voluptuous legs stretched forever and a day to toes stuffed into shiny platforms teetering on ludicrous heels. Never again would anyone mistake her for a boy.

"Stunning," he said. "You could stop the moon."

Joann closed the folder, and handed it back to Sally. She took a hold on his collar, and rubbed his neck. "After you get started, call me, if you want a good time." She breathed on him.

Shotgun gulped. His pulse quickened, and his face grew hot.

She turned on her heels, and sashayed out of the office. Spellbound, Shotgun watched her jiggle out, turn onto the sidewalk, and she was gone. The vision of the vixen stayed with him until he heard the receptionist's chair creak.

"Want to give me your card, and we can get this show on the road?"

He handed Sally his card, and she handed him a tablet to fill out his patient information. He tried to forget Joann. He searched the office nervously. *Is anyone watching*, he wondered? He thought of Goldie in high heels. Worried he might be discovered as a spy; he loosened his collar, and breathed. He thought of his daughters, Faith and Hope, and the spell snapped. Quickly, he answered the questions on the tablet, using a minimum of truth, and handed it back to the receptionist.

Sally took it with a smile, and glanced over it. "Are you with Biot Staffing?"

"Yes," he said, hoping she would not call the agency. "I'm a high-end domestic. Money is no problem."

"Who do you work for?"

"Sorry, Sally, my client's identities are confidential, and I keep secrets. That's how I earn my tips."

She laughed, accepting his story. "Bet you can tell some good stories."

"Yes, I know some real doozies. Too bad, I can't share the tales."

"Yeah, and I was looking forward to some juicy gossip too. Come on in, then."

He opened the patient's entrance and stepped into a small alcove. Sally left her chair and circled the inner counter enclosing her desk. She dwarfed Shotgun in her high heels.

"You'll be seeing Dr. Jerry Balaam." She led him down the corridor to an examination room. "He completed his residencies here in Nodlon at Moab Charity."

Framed testimonials and pictures of satisfied patients gazed down from the walls. The receptionist casually repeated a spiel she must have repeated dozens of times before. He listened for the tell-tale sound of servers.

Sally showed him into an examination room. "The doctor will be with you in a moment."

He perched on the examination table. Trying to seem casual, he searched for cameras. He twisted on the examination table to conceal his satchel from the door. He pulled his tablet out, and flipped it open. He bypassed his tablet's operating system, and opened a virtual machine on his private system.

A hint of pride welled in him, as the computer displayed, "Welcome to Gun Way." Opening the application, he found the link the network had given his tablet to exchange passcodes. Identifying friend from foe depended on establishing communication, and that was the weak link.

He submitted an order to copy any database files into Gun Way. He let the application rip. He found his copy of Rip Van Winkle, and clicked. The tablet screen blanked, and the indicator lights died. Until he unlocked the machine, the tablet appeared to be off.

He glanced at the door. It was still closed. Sighing, he set his tablet under his satchel, slipped off the table, and stuck his head out.

On one end of the corridor he could see the edge of the reception desk. At the other end was a nurse in pink scrubs with her back to him. An alcove with a phlebotomy chair and a sink was in the center of the hall, and three doors down was a cross-hall.

Leaving the door open, he quietly walked to the cross-hall, and turned the corner without being seen. He passed a utility closet and a room marked "Radiation." The next room was a break room no larger than the examination room. A zapper and an espresso machine crowded a tiny counter squeezed between a refrigerator and a sink. Two chairs faced a round table with an open box of donuts. A few stale donuts waited for takers.

He continued his search, and approached an exit. The soft roar of fan motors came from an unmarked door. *The mother lode*. He turned about-face, and headed back to the main corridor.

The nurse in pink scrubs caught him in the corner of her eye. She stopped and crossed her arms.

"May I help you?" The goblin's looked down at him and her eyes narrowed.

"Wash room?" He smiled.

"End of the hall, turn right then left."

"Thanks." He sauntered casually down the hall.

"Next time, ask before you go wandering around."

He felt her eyes boring into his back as he followed her directions. He walked into the washroom to maintain his ruse. He felt the hair tingle on his neck.

When he returned to the examination room, he resumed his place on the table, and waited. Shortly, a goblin in a white coat appeared in the doorway with a stethoscope around his neck.

"Good morning, Patrick, I'm Dr. Balaam." Jet black hair,

black eyes, and his grey frame contrasted sharply against his white coat. The doctor's dour expression lacked enthusiasm.

Is he suspicious or is he a natural sour puss?

"Doctor, can you help me with my little problem? I can't get a date."

"Certainly, we have the cure for what ails you."

"If not, can you steer me to the ale that cures?"

"A wit sharper than a blade, and coarser than a rogue, swiftly sifts one's friends from foes."

"Good one, doc. Is that Nelson?"

"No, it's Moon Tea, the favorite poet of President Nogora." The doctor visibly brightened.

"What can you do for me?"

"The basic package includes the buff. I call it the beef-o-matic. We build the Atlas figure which attracts the ladies. It turns a pathetic weakling into a chick magnet. Mental abilities will be amplified. We cannot make you a genius or teach you a language, but we can enhance your natural mental capacity. You'll be more handsome, more attractive, and more confident, and as a side-effect, you'll be healthier and enjoy longer stamina. If you have any congenital chromosome defects from the synthesis, we'll fix that too. Even if you've never excelled at sports, you will excel at all of them."

"Sounds great doc, how does it work? Will I be the same?"

"Don't worry, Patrick. Gene therapy is the same technology used to cure cancer nowadays. Over the last thirty years though, there have been major advances in correcting errors in synthetic gene expression. Retro-gene expression therapy corrects gestational insults and over a thousand known genetic errors in synthetic code. These side benefits are actually necessary. Trying to jack your natural steroid expression without balancing the errors in your code may cause unintended side effects."

"A bit over my head doc. I'm a domestic. I do etiquette

and protocol and I make a mean quiche. How come we need all these repairs in the first place? If I'm synthetic, what went wrong? Am I not under warranty? Should I sue my designer for product liability?"

"Hard to answer that question, Patrick. First, are you natural born or first generation synthetic?"

"Synthetic, I'm a Bio-Soft model. I gave my medical code to your secretary."

Balaam bent over the workstation mounted on the counter, searched a menu and opened a folder marked "Morgan, Patrick." He smiled with a smarmy grin, "Ah, yes, we have you right here."

The doctor's mood lifted a little, and he leaned against the sink counter, enjoying the discussion of his chosen field. "We'll do some suitability testing. Really it's a variety of tests for compatibility, stability, and synthetic markers which will tell us what we can and cannot do. Don't be too concerned. Most biots cannot accept several upgrades due to an incompatibility. Out of several thousand changes, most of our clients would be unaware of the exceptions if we didn't point them out."

A touch of sympathy crossed his face, and he gazed at the wall staring at some scene lost in time. "It's hard to explain. Biots, including myself, are not really human nor animal nor completely synthetic. Our makers can deny our humanity, and yet we fall in love. Nature takes its course and our children have unforeseen errors. The congenital defects led to monsters, and the mothers would become unsuitable for their purpose. Originally, biots were sterilized to avoid responsibility for those consequences. Over time, pressure arose to let biots have children. The designers optimized reproduction for breeding and surrogate motherhood, and the market for first generation biots collapsed. Today most biots are naturally born, which is what keeps New Gem in business. Most of our work is repairing the damage caused by uncontrolled combinations. Still, Cybernetics Corporation and Bio-Soft produce many artificial biots in

Nodlon. And like you, they deliberately short-change your code. Small of them really, your body is the only thing they let you have, and then they go and build in limits just to keep you in your place."

Falling silent, the doctor's gaze stared through the wall at some unseen world inside his head. Just as Shotgun began to wonder, Balaam refocused on him, and straightened up. His smile faded to a professional slit. An eyebrow rose, and he said, "Still others would outlaw humans, and biots would inherit the earth."

Slapping his knees, the doctor stood up and grinned at him oozing the smarmy optimism of a used ground-car salesman. "So, would you like the basic package?"

"Guess I'll take it."

Balaam leered at him, and smirked. "Good." Asking Shotgun to disrobe, he began a perfunctory exam. Removing his shirt and pants, Shotgun breathed, coughed, and endured the doctor's probing and prodding.

"Fit as a fiddle," said Balaam. He pressed a call button, and packed away the tools of his trade. "The phlebotomist will scan you, and take samples. Just follow her instructions. She may give you a pill to prevent you from fainting. We're done for the day."

"Thanks doc."

The nurse in pink scrubs appeared. "What do you think of this one?"

"Basic package. Take his samples, and run him through the scope. Make sure Sally gets him an appointment."

"Right away."

The doctor flashed a smile of the kind a salesman offers after closing a deal. "Wait here."

In the stark examination room, Shotgun saw none of the usual posters offering advice or suggesting new treatments or medications.

One advertising poster hung over the examination table.

A sunrise crested over Earth, and a slogan read, "A New World Just for You! New Genes, New Gem!" The orbital ring of Elysium girdled the planet. The sunrise glinted off the space station.

He resisted an urge to check his tablet. He patted his satchel, and tried to relax.

A nurse in teal scrubs in a slightly better humor than the one in pink appeared in the doorway. "Hi, Patrick, I'm Samantha. Follow me, honey, and we'll get you out of here." Soon, she scanned him, collected samples, and led him back to the alcove with the phlebotomist's chair.

She rolled up his sleeve above his elbow. "I'm going to give you a pill so you won't faint." She tied a rubber strap around his arm, and rubbed the crook of his elbow. "You have good veins."

She handed him a tiny blue pill and a cup of water.

He swallowed the pill. Holding his shoulder, she asked him to count backwards from ten slowly. Wondering why she asked, he tried recalling if he had ever heard such a question before when giving a blood sample.

Not wanting to blow his cover, he counted, "Ten, nine, eight," and he felt woozy. The room tilted, and nausea welled within him. Wooziness turned to alarm, as he stopped counting, and tried to hold himself up.

Feeling faint, he willed his head towards his sleeve and urged his mouth to yell for help. Nothing happened. His muscles would not respond and he slumped in his chair.

Sleepiness overwhelmed him, and he shut his eyes. He felt himself fall, and then everything went black.

Tipping Your Hand

"This has never happened to me before," he heard a feminine voice say.

"Patients sometimes faint when blood is drawn," said Samantha. "I've had many patients collapse. But Mr. Morgan here must be incredibly sensitive. He fainted before I even stuck him with a needle."

"What I don't understand," Balaam hissed, "is how you arrived so quickly?"

Gradually, reality came back to Shotgun.

"Patrick is my butler. He left me a voice mail telling me he'd be out for a few hours. When he wouldn't answer his caster, naturally I was concerned. After all we've heard in the news about missing dwarves, I was worried."

He opened one eye and saw a wall with a poster of Earth. Memories flooded back to him. He was in a chop shop – a gene therapy clinic. They were going to upgrade him, and then he fainted. Had they drugged him?

Balaam asked, "How were you able to find him?"

Clay huffed, acting put off. "Patrick's a big boy, and I try to stay out of his business. But he is my butler, and I have a right to keep track of him. When I didn't get a hold of him, I followed his locator to your clinic."

"We live in strange times, Cretaceous Clay. Odd that you should appear so soon when your butler suffers a minor fainting spell."

"Maybe I overreacted." Clay gushed with such sincerity Shotgun would have believed him if he had not known better. "Or maybe it's just a coincidence."

"There are no coincidences." The doctor's eyes narrowed with the cold certainty of illumination.

Fearing the interrogation would continue, Shotgun forced open his eyes, and tried speaking. He moaned unintelligibly, and caught their attention.

"Good, he's coming to. Nurse, get him some water."

Weakly he rolled over onto his back, and saw Jack and Balaam facing each other.

The doctor scowled. "Feeling better, Patrick?"

His throat was dry and he croaked, "Yeah, much better now." He pushed himself up with his elbows, and Clay helped him sit up. The nurse handed him a cup of water.

"You fainted," said Balaam. "Hard. You fell out of the phlebotomy chair and very nearly cracked your skull open." The doctor gestured towards the comely goblin. "Samantha here caught you. She had a heck of a time helping you up. I carried you back to the examination room myself to let you sleep it off. And then your employer shows up wondering if you're all right."

"I'm sure it's just a coincidence," said Shotgun. "He wanted me to get him some tickets. I left them on the key rack, but I forgot to leave a note."

"Undoubtedly," said Balaam with naked sarcasm. "I'm sure Cretaceous Clay has difficulty finding his tickets." The doctor sneered without a hint of amusement.

"Now that that's solved," Clay rubbed his hands. "We'll be going. I've got a hot date, and I need my man here to get my place ready."

"Likely as not, that may be true," said Balaam.

Clay shouldered Shotgun's satchel, and felt the tablet in the pouch. Satisfied, he put an arm under Shotgun's arm and helped the dwarf to his feet. The dwarf's shoulder just reached his elbow. They stumbled out of the examination room awkwardly.

The doctor crossed his arms and gripped his elbows. "Sam, help Mr. Clay and his man-servant out." The nurse took Shotgun's other arm. "That's a good girl, thanks."

They walked Shotgun down the hall, through the patient's entrance, and into the waiting room. Balaam followed them.

Clay sidled through the front door with Shotgun and Sam

in tow. On the sidewalk, an elderly elf veered around the odd looking trio.

"Patrick, can you walk now?" asked Samantha.

"Yeah."

"Sam," barked Balaam. "Get back to work."

Her shoulders drooped, and she glanced back at Jack and Shotgun. With a vivacious sashay, the shapely nurse disappeared into the waiting room. "Yes, doctor."

As she passed the doctor, he kicked the door forcing its tractor arm to hiss. Balaam glared at Jack.

"If there are any charges," said Jack, "send me the bill."

"No charges, Mr. Clay, your money's no good here. Just go and don't bother returning." The doctor threw the door closed. The tractor arm squealed under the strain, and closed with a wheezy pop.

"That went well," said Jack, "let's get you out of here." Wandering back through the run-down neighborhood, Jack felt hostile eyes following him as he and Shotgun limped along the sidewalk. Glancing over his shoulder, he saw no one following them. Only a few pedestrians shared the sidewalk. The only ground-cars on the street were parked.

Breathing deeply, he focused on supporting Shotgun. He cast a little levitation to help him. *Should I fly? No,* he thought better of it. *I need to remain incognito.* It would not do for Cretaceous Clay to be seen leaving a chop shop in Deep Nodlon.

Approaching a corner, a couple of rough looking tramps sitting in front of a shelter rose to their feet. Alarmed, Jack looked for an alternative route, but the blocks were long, and he was unsure he could walk Shotgun back to the alley. *If they intend to cause trouble, I can't evade them burdened with Shotgun. I'll have to break my cover.*

Thinking of a few spells, fire balls, lightning bolts, and ice sprays, he reassured himself. He was far better armed than a police officer carrying only a lightning gun.

Still, a blaster would deter unwanted attention.

Fortunately, the farther they walked, the less Shotgun wobbled. They crossed the street, and narrowed the distance to the tramps.

One old man wore a blue blazer and a straw hat. He broke away from the brickwork, and stepped out from under the shelter's awning. The other man gripped the lapel of his tattered trench coat, and hugged himself as if he were cold.

"Evenin' Guv'nor," said the blue blazer. "Can you spare a penny?"

Jack paused and studied the two for a moment. Up close, wrinkles added character to the man. Sallow skin stretched over his bones, and a hook nose sported pince-nez spectacles. His companion was in hardly better shape, and his face was marred by a diagonal scar.

They were merely panhandlers.

Uncertainty plagued him. The shelter sustained their needs, but they depended on the kindness of strangers to support their habits. Trading on their condition, they begged for spending money. On the other hand, who was he to judge their wants, and the one in the blue blazer had asked politely enough.

"Sure, old timer, I'll give you enough to buy yourself and your friend a steak if you'll promise me you'll eat it."

"Guv'nor," said the blue blazer, "a piece of blueberry pie would be most welcome, if'n you can afford it?" Silently his companion grinned a toothy grin, and tipped his fedora.

Awkwardly using his one free hand, he pulled two large bills from his pouch, one for each of them. Glancing at them, he made sure they were the same denomination. He did not want to start a squabble between the two hobos there on the sidewalk.

The blue blazer snatched one of the bills and ogled it. "Bless you, sir." He tipped his hat. "Yes, that'll get me something to eat and coffee too."

His companion, still silent, took off his fedora, and pushed the proffered bill into the lap of the brim. He bowed slightly, and smiled.

The blue blazer nodded at the trench coat. "Charley thanks you too. He don't like talkin' since the doc's cut his throat."

"Sorry to hear that. Excuse me, I have to help my dwarf here."

"Hey, Guv'nor, ye look a lot like that thar' Cretinism Clay fellar. Seen his posters in the robo-car station, and you's looks a lot like him."

"Yes, I get that reaction all the time."

"What's wrong there with your dwarf, Guv'nor, had too much o' the hair o' the dog that bit him?"

"No, he saw a doctor and fainted."

"What? Down at that chop shop?" The blue blazer cocked his head down the street. "Saw the dwarf goin' that way earlier, then you's goes flyin' by like you're on fire, and you's comes back with a dwarf sick as a dog. Don't take much to see what's happened Guv'nor."

The old man's eyes shifted, and he pulled back from Clay. "Mark my word, Guv'nor, don't let him go back. He's a voodoo doctor he is. Dwarves go in, and they puts a spell on 'em. Turns 'em into zombies. They ain't right when they's comes out, if they's comes out at all!"

Clay struggled with Shotgun's weight. "We'll heed your advice."

The old derelict in the blazer saluted him and Charley tipped his fedora. "Thanks ag'in, Guv'nor. A good man you are."

"You're welcome, old-timer." Jack and Shotgun shuffled off down the sidewalk.

The tramps shrank back against the brick, and resumed their repose in front of the shelter.

A quick look over his shoulder confirmed no one was following them, and Clay sighed with relief.

Shotgun lurched, and his knees wobbled. "That old rogue knows something."

"The old timers don't know anything. They're just suspicious, and our presence confirmed their suspicion, that's all."

"He said dwarves go in, and they don't come out, right?"

"Yeah, Shotgun, but we can't prove anything from that. The dwarves may have taken a robo-cab, or just gone a different way. What the old man saw can be explained away too easily."

Shotgun stumbled.

"Can you make it?" asked Jack.

"Yeah, I think I'll make it." His butler's legs jerked.

Jack levitated the dwarf to keep him from falling. "We need to get you to a doctor, and find an antidote for this poison." He looked around to see if anyone noticed the magic.

Falling silent, Jack conserved his strength and helped Shotgun back to the cruiser. They turned into the alley. Jack staggered as Shotgun nearly tripped him.

Gumshoe pulled the cruiser out of the back alley. Throwing open his door, he climbed out, and circled the cruiser to help Jack lift Shotgun.

"What happened?" asked the detective.

Gingerly, they loaded the dwarf into the cruiser.

"Poison! Let's get Shotgun to a doctor. I'll fill you in on the way."

"I'm fine, I don't need a doctor," protested Shotgun.

"Quiet," said Gumshoe, "you'll do as you're told." Climbing back into the driver's seat, Gumshoe reached into his console and pulled out a bottle of water. "Drink this." Next, he handed Shotgun a bag. "And use this if you feel sick."

Gumshoe checked for any signs of surveillance, and turned onto the street. He drove a block, turned a corner, and engaged the autopilot. He punched the medical emergency call on his console. The autopilot lit the emergency lights. The autopilot accelerated, and slung them against their harnesses. The cruiser cornered hard in the direction of the nearest level-way.

His dashboard screen lit up, and the dispatcher appeared, "Gumshoe, what do you want honey?" Red hair in a shoulder length reversed curl framed a handsome woman in her prime. A map of Nodlon glowed behind her. Her buxom figure stretched a crisp blue bodice, and threatened to pop her buttons. Despite her sporty uniform, she sat attentively before a bank of vid monitors wearing a headset.

"Hi Marcie, I've got a dwarf who may have been poisoned. Give me clearance to Nodlon Memorial, and ask them for a poison alert. We'll be there faster than you can get an ambulance crew out."

"You got it, babe. All green from your location to Nodlon Memorial. I'll give the hospital a head's up. Hold onto your lunch."

"Thanks, Marcie, out." The cruiser's speed pushed the limits of safety through the tunnels of Under Nodlon, and flung them against their harnesses as it rounded the corners. They entered the entrance to the west-bound level-way. The siren wailed making conversation nearly impossible.

As traffic cleared in front of them, the cruiser accelerated to dizzying speeds, and the blue lights of Nodlon flashed strobe-like. Clutching the butterfly bars, Jack's knuckle's whitened as the cruiser zipped past commuters. Decelerating hard, the cruiser exited the level-way onto the hospital's entrance, and swerved up the ramp to the Under Nodlon emergency entrance. Approaching the emergency entrance, the cruiser's autopilot muted the siren, and signaled the hospital's dispatch unit.

Halting behind an ambulance, the cruiser opened its doors. A goblin medic and nurse jogged up to the cruiser with a gurney carrying a black bag. Gumshoe and Jack jumped out of the cruiser, and Jack opened the back door for the medic.

"There's your patient," shouted Gumshoe.

Kneeling beside Shotgun, the medic strapped a monitor on his wrist. "Are you the patient, sir?" The goblin pulled a torch pen out of his shirt pocket and flashed the light in Shotgun's eyes.

Shotgun's head lolled and he moaned. "I'm fine."

"What's your name?"

"Shotgun."

Checking the readout on the dwarf's wrist monitor, the medic lifted the dwarf gently out of the cruiser. Shotgun's head lolled forward narrowly missing the door jamb.

"Do you know what day it is?"

"March 18th."

The medic strapped the dwarf down to the stretcher. "We'll take care of you."

Shotgun's head flopped again, "I'm fine, I don't need a doctor." The medic pushed the gurney into the emergency room.

They started to follow Shotgun, but the nurse blocked their way. "He's in good hands. I'm Nurse Casket, and I'll help you with the intake forms." She was short for a goblin, and a bit heavy. On her flats, she looked up at Jack, and she glared at him skeptically. "The alert said he was poisoned. When did he first display any symptoms?"

"Less than an hour ago," said Jack, "he fainted at a gene therapy clinic just before a phlebotomist attempted to take a blood sample."

Folding her tablet and holding it against her breast, the nurse huffed. "People faint at the sight of needles all the time. What makes you believe he was poisoned?"

Jack glanced at Gumshoe. "We know he was given a pill just before we lost, uh, just before he fainted." He swallowed, and added, "he stumbled all the way back to the car as if his legs couldn't hold him, and he wasn't able to speak clearly for several minutes. At the clinic, they say he might have fallen."

Immediately her ire faded to concern, and her eyes widened. Flipping open her tablet, she asked, "Why didn't you say that? He might have a concussion." She tapped on the tablet. "I've alerted the emergency room physician we may have a concussion. They'll want a pressure reading now, and we'll scan him.

"How are you related to the patient?"

"I'm his employer," said Jack. "He's my butler. A good man he is too." Jack pulled his insurance card for Clay-Players out of his wallet and handed it to her.

"If he's a domestic dwarf, isn't he under contract with an agency?"

"Look, Shotgun works for me, and I'm responsible. I want the best care money can buy."

"If he's a Biot Staffing Biot, he's insured through them," she said, "don't worry about it, they cover everything."

"Oh, yeah," said Jack, "he's under contract to Biot Staffing, but Clay-Players hired him, and he's worked for me for nearly a year."

"Honey, he'll get as good a care as you, and better even. If we make a mistake with your butler, what would you do? Send us a bill for dry cleaning? If we damage an agency's biot, they'd put a hit out on the hospital staff. Those people are serious. We'd never work again."

"Point taken Nurse Casket, but he's more than my butler; he's a friend." Jack paused, "He's practically family."

"Honey, I understand. My nanny was a maid, and she worked for the same family for almost her whole life. She still lives with them. Nice folks, too. I'm just saying it makes no difference. He's getting the best care we got, and no more and no less. Insurance just tells us who gets the damage." She asked a few more routine questions, and then stalked off, apparently too busy for a brief conversation with the beleaguered mage.

"Guess I'll just have to wait. We can get some dinner. It's pricey for cafeteria food, but not bad, and we won't be poisoned. Maybe I'll have a chance to see Jazz."

"After we see the doctor," said Gumshoe. "I need to call the missus. If it's all the same to you, I'd like to get some dinner, I'm famished. You can see Jazz, and I can get caught up on my paperwork."

"What are we seeing the doctor for?"

"Make sure they're working on the right problem, I didn't want to slow the works arguing with Nurse Casket, but they drugged him, and I want to know what it is."

"Do you think they poisoned him?"

"Yeah," said Gumshoe. "They probably slipped him a mickey just to put him to sleep for a couple of hours. I want a full spectrum run for all the recreational chemicals and date rape drugs." He tapped his own tablet with his index finger, and stalked after the nurse at a speed belying his age. The emergency entrance slid open and he passed through before Jack caught up.

No one was in the triage bay. They ignored the signs and plunged into the emergency room wing. Avoiding the nurses' stares, they searched the bays and found Shotgun lying on a bed unconscious. Monitors beeped, and pumps clicked and wheezed.

An elf in scrubs left the nurse's station and walked over to ask their business. "Are you family?"

"No," said Gumshoe, flashing his badge. "Inspector Lestrayed, Nodlon Yard, homicide, we need to see the doctor responsible for this man's care."

The elf's eyes widened. "He's been called away for another emergency. I'll let him know immediately though." She returned to her station, and picked up her desk caster.

"That reminds me, I need to call Goldie, and reassure her," said Jack.

"Better make that call now," said Gumshoe, "while we're waiting on the doctor. I'll call the missus and let her know I'm not going to be home for dinner."

Pacing around the bay, Jack thought about how to break the news to Goldie. Stopping beside Shotgun, he put a hand on the bed, and wrung the rail. His features were boyish, and he had a clever brow and smart lips. The black chip on his forehead was inscrutable, signaling nothing.

The monitors buzzed and beeped recording Shotgun's breathing and pulse, pressures and temperatures and serum levels. Studying the monitors, he saw nothing out of place. More than half the instrument readings were meaningless to him. He stared at the intravenous feed pumping liquid into Shotgun's arm. *What have I gotten you into?* Jack wondered.

Contemplating the frailty of life, he remembered Melissa. He hoped she was doing well.

The nurse returned and checked the intravenous bag, and snapping a quick-connect she disconnected the bag, and replaced it with a fresh one. "Nurse, is there any sign of a concussion?"

"The doctor will have to answer your questions, sir." She scrutinized him. "Are you Jack Clay?"

"The one and only, and this fellow is my butler, Shotgun."

"Oh, I'm sorry Mr. Clay. We'll take good care of him though, don't you worry." She hurried off about her business.

He flipped his caster open, and called Goldie. She answered with a look of surprise and worry.

"Hi! Mr. Clay, I'm so glad you called," she prattled. "The girls and I are at your condo and Shotgun's not here. He won't answer his phone." Her voice rising to near hysteria, she wailed, "His locator says he's at Nodlon Memorial. Oh, Mr. Clay, do you know what's happened?" She bounced on his couch, and he saw his dining room and a lamp behind her. She searched his ceiling for answers and ran her hands through her hair.

"Goldie, please calm down and sit back down."

She cupped her hand over her mouth, and moaned, "Oh no."

He had not counted on her reaction, and he felt like a heel for not calling her sooner. "Goldie, can I have your attention?" Tears streamed down her cheeks, and sobs wracked her body. "Please get a tissue in the kitchen. Please, I need you to calm down."

Getting up she blew her nose, and sniffled. "I'm fine now."

"Shotgun is sleeping here in the hospital. He may have

been poisoned or he may have had a fall. We're not sure which and we haven't seen the doctor yet. I'll stay here with him until I know what's going on."

Tears streamed down her face, and she daubed her eyes with her tunic. Through her tunic, she mumbled.

"Goldie, what did you say, I couldn't hear you?"

Pulling her face out of her tunic, she asked, "What happened? Mr. Clay."

A pang of guilt wracked his heart, and he wondered if he should appeal to her better nature. He wanted to tell her Shotgun had risked his life to help them find Anna's murderer and solve the Zodiac cases.

Wisdom overcame compassion. She was not ready for the news, and he had no prognosis to offer. With a little information, she might draw the wrong conclusions. He recalled the plight of Romeo and Juliet, and he wanted no rash actions.

"Goldie, we don't know, if he fell, he might have a concussion. They're going to run tests for poisons. In the meantime, he's sleeping and resting. I promise I'll let you know as soon as the doctor can tell me something."

"Thank you Mr. Clay, what about me and the girls? What do we do?"

"Help yourself to anything you can find in the kitchen and make yourselves at home, please." He smiled, trying to evoke an air of fatherly leadership. "Shotgun's got some chocolate chip cookies in the jar. Go ahead, chocolate and milk will help."

She nodded.

"If you're better, I'm going to see if I can find the doctor."

"The news said they may evacuate the city, and the agency ordered me to leave for Iron Mountain. All non-essential personnel, children, mothers, and the old are leaving. That's what I wanted to tell Shotgun." She kept her cool and daubed her eyes again.

"I'm sure we'll be home before then. I will ask Jazz if she

can take you and the girls."

The young woman put her head between her knees. The caster view jiggled and refocused on his ceiling.

"Goldie?"

"How can I thank you?"

"Goldie, just take care of Faith and Hope, and be brave. Can you do that for me? Since you're evacuating, I need you to start packing. Clothes and necessities are the most important. Don't forget your toiletries, and Jazz left Faith's teddy bear in my room. Got all that?" She shook her head. "Good girl, get on it, now."

"Thank you Mr. Clay."

"For what?"

"For taking care of Shotgun and me."

"You're family, Goldie. I'll call you as soon as I know more."

Closing his caster, he felt drained. Shotgun's chest rose and fell calmly. *Worrying won't help*. Gripping the bedrail, he wished he could do more. He wondered if he should return to New Gem and avenge the dwarf. Contemplating his moral dilemma, he rejected anything brash.

A hand gripped the other bedrail, and started him out of his reverie. "The nurse said the doctor should be here any minute," said Gumshoe. "She didn't say, but he's probably at lunch. They are talking about calling an evacuation on the news, and the missus is upset. Had a heck of time calming her down. I set her to packing. Anything to stop her worrying."

"Goldie is the same way. I just got off the caster with her, and I'm not ready to call Jazz. Goldie about wore me out. She's in a terrible fright. She tried calling Shotgun to tell him Biot Staffing released her while they evacuate. When she didn't get an answer, she checked his locator, and found out he's here. She's nearly crazy."

"What you fear is always worse than reality. It's our nightmares that won't give us peace. It's like the weather.

Whatever the weather is today, it will likely be the same tomorrow. Focus on today and tomorrow will take care of itself."

A young man in a white coat entered the bay wearing a stethoscope. "Inspector Lestrayed?" Both of them broke away from the bed.

"Dr. Forest, good to see you again."

"Hi, Gumshoe. Excuse me for making you wait, we had a bleeder and I had to stabilize him. Mr. Clay, I'm glad to make your acquaintance too. I wish we had met under better circumstances. My girls are big fans, and we've seen most of your shows."

The doctor placed his hand on the bedrail. "Is this your man-servant?"

"Yes, and he's got two daughters and a fiancée, and he's a good friend."

"Well, they'll be happy to know he doesn't have a concussion, and as near as I can tell, he's just sleeping off whatever he ingested. Do you have any idea what it was?"

"No," said Jack. "I thought the nurse told you it was a concussion."

"Concussion or poisoning," he said. "Don't let Casket fool you, she knows her job. Don't worry Inspector. I've already ordered a full chemical spectrum on all known mickeys and social chemicals. Been a routine since the first time you suggested it."

"Always prefer to double check, Forest," said Gumshoe. "Never know who's on duty and how long they've been riding without training wheels."

"Whatever you told the duty nurse, she was worried, and gave me a call. Helps keep us on our toes. It'll be awhile before I know anymore. Until then, I cannot promise anything, but his prognosis is good based on his current vital signs."

"Could he be in a coma?" asked Jack. "Too much of some of those drugs I understand and you'll never wake up."

"Can't be sure what state he is in just yet, but he's not in a coma. His scans are normal. The lab results will tell us more. My guess is, they knocked him out, and he'll be fine once he sleeps it off. The lab knows these tests have the highest priority, but it'll still be two or three hours. Chemistry is still chemistry, even today." The doctor bid them farewell, and went about his duties.

"Want something to eat?" asked Jack. "You said you were famished."

"Starved," said Gumshoe, "let's go."

The World Inside

Gumshoe lifted his fedora, and combed his hair with his fingers. Replacing his fedora, he leaned backwards stretching his back. "Better call the missus again, before dinner." He drew his caster from his trench coat. "Are you going to call Jazz?"

"Yeah, do you mind if she joins us for dinner?"

"No, not at all," Gumshoe sidestepped a frantic woman scurrying through the lobby. "I welcome a repast with the lovely Jurassic Jasmine."

Pulling his own caster, Clay pressed the speed-dial for Jasmine, and let his caster connect. Jasmine appeared on his caster screen with a harried brow. She was typing feverishly on her workstation.

"Hi sweetpea, I'm sorry to bother you at work."

"Oh, it's you Jack." She slouched and rubbed the bridge of her nose. "A shuttle brought in more patients from the Moon. They're evacuees from a long-term care facility there, and we're having trouble stabilizing the gravity field generators to lunar normal."

"We're swamped. There are so many patients." Her eyes welled with tears. "I'm sorry, honey bear. What are you calling for?" Taking a tissue she daubed her eyes.

"Shotgun's in the emergency room and I'm downstairs with Gumshoe." He wanted to rush to her aid, but he knew he would be in the way.

"What happened to Shotgun?"

"He tried to help us out with the investigation at a chop shop, and we think he was poisoned. Dr. Forest told us he's sleeping off whatever ails him. We have to wait a few hours for test results before we know any more. So, Gumshoe and I are going to eat while we wait. I called to ask if you wanted to breakaway for dinner. But I see you're tied up."

"No, honey bear, I can't eat. I'm starving, but there's too much work." Out of the caster's camera range someone spoke to

Jasmine.

"No," Jazz said.

The voice continued, and Clay could hear the tone become insistent. "No, who's going to keep watch – oh, yes." She nodded her assent and smiled weakly.

"Maybe I can come up later if you get a free moment."

"No, I can make it. Looks like I've been spelled for dinner. I'll be downstairs in a few."

"Great, see you."

A gnarring guitar riff ripped on Jack's caster announcing an incoming call. Kicking himself inwardly, he jabbed the little device and silenced it. He checked the caller's avatar. It was his director, Corman.

"Jazz, Corman calling," he smiled, "I'll meet you in the cafeteria."

"See you there," she said.

He blew her a kiss and closed the connection.

~~~~~~

A bedraggled Jazz studied a fern. "Hi, honey bear," she said. Purple bags sagged around her bloodshot eyes, and rumples spread over her usually crisp uniform.

"Hi sweetpea," Clay hugged her, and she squeezed him. "You're exhausted."

"We've taken two ships from the Moon, and we expect another from Elysium just after midnight." Leaning back, she gazed up at him, and said, "What if we go to war? What will we do?"

"Hope I don't get drafted? I'm still on call in the reserves."

"You're already drafted, silly. Inspector Lestrayed has taken over your life, and he's going to keep you until he nails the Zodiac killer. And I want you to help him." She poked him. "I meant what will Clay-players do?"

"Miss rehearsals." Jack shrugged. "Not much we can do."

"What?" She looked puzzled. "What did Corman say?"

"Do you want the bad news or the good news?"

"This can't be good." Jazz frowned. "What's the bad news?"

"The Circus cancelled all of our performances and rehearsals. I can't help it. No one's playing the Circus until the Crown says so."

Taking his arm, she drew him in and put her arms around his waist. His arms engulfed her lithe shoulders and he hugged her. She was thin and petite even for an elf. "Don't worry, honey bear. I'll stay with you no matter what. I won't leave you even if you have to be a birthday clown."

"Ha," he said. "We'll play Iron Mountain. Corman will pack the show and send the roadies on ahead to Iron Mountain. We're taking everyone in the crew who wants to go, and their families."

"What about the spring show, we've worked so hard on it."

Jack shrugged, "We'll do it at the Grove. It's a little theatre built into Iron Mountain. It's too small, but we can work around it. There's no helping it. Corman will make sure we have what we need for a good show."

"Corman's a sweetheart."

He held her close, and set his chin on top of her head. "Corman didn't even know we're on the verge of a war until Wynn called him to tell him the Circus was closing. How can you function when you're world stops at Broadway and Jackson? If it's not happening in west, Upper Nodlon, it's not happening at all."

"The theatre is his life, and he knows everything about it. Did you know there's a name for every light we use?"

"Yeah, that's why I hired him. He's a savant of everything on stage."

"I'm sorry about your show."

"Does it matter? It's for the best. The Crown probably fears an attack and ordered the Circus closed. If the Martians murdered five thousand teenage biots during my show, I don't think I'd be able to look myself in the mirror. Even the soccer moms would come down out of the mountains with pitchforks."

"What about the Zodiac killer?"

"We have a lead. All hush, hush for now though. We found another missing dwarf. I can't say for sure it's the same …"

"Jack, the boy's all over the news! His name's Evan Labe. Chesterton said you found a bloody Zodiac sign in his apartment. Was it a Capricorn?"

"Can't keep any secrets can we? Yes, it is the constellation of Capricorn. It was drawn in blood on the boy's vid. Gumshoe still thinks it's magic, but I think it's some new paintball technology. We also met a character – the boy's dorm resident who warned us."

"Jack, the girl had a witch didn't she? Isn't that two?"

"What? Are you thinking of Molly? I don't remember saying anything about her."

"She was on Radiophone. Shaw interviewed her. Didn't you see her?"

"Yes, but it's just a coincidence. She shared a few tid-bits, but nothing of much substance."

"Don't you think it's odd that you've met two characters on this case?"

"No, I know it's strange to you, Jazz, but my whole life is strange. Remember, I'm a magician. I meet characters on a regular basis."

"Don't tell me you're a magician. If two creepy characters show up, I think it is significant."

"Yeah, but you're normal. Strange coincidences are par on my course."

Shaking her head, she huffed. "What about the boy, Evan?"

"Gumshoe fears for his life. We can only hope. Just between us, we think his chances are slim."

"You have to solve the murders and find those missing dwarves. I know you can do it."

"I'm just helping. Gumshoe's the homicide detective, and he's been a cop as long as I've been alive."

"That's why I like you Jack Clay." She squeezed him. "You keep your feet on the ground except when you don't."

His arms enfolded her, and they held each other for a moment longer.

"Will Shotgun be recover?" she asked.

"Dr. Forest thinks he's just sleeping off the poisons they gave him. Speaking of Shotgun, Jazz, I need a favor. When you go to Iron Mountain, can you take Goldie and the girls?"

"Yeah, that's easy. The hospital wants us to take our vehicles, and they're asking for volunteers. Goldie will fit right in. She can work with the hospital staff. Since her agency released her and the girls. They can stay with us when she's not working."

"Great, can you call Goldie, and give her an update? She's at my place."

"No problem, I'll let her know when we're leaving."

~~~~~~

Jack set his tray down next to the Inspector. His stomach grumbled. Jasmine set her tray next to Jack's. He helped her unload it, and held her chair.

"Got frogs in your belly, Jack?" The Inspector sliced into a chicken fried steak. A bowl of jello sat next to a stack of empty bowls. His trench coat hung from an empty chair.

"Just starving," he unloaded a feast from his tray. Deep fried catfish, okra, Caesar salad, a baked potato smothered in cheese and sour cream, jello, and a slice of coconut cream pie joined the Inspector's steak and fries.

"Hello Inspector," said Jasmine. "How is Betty doing?"

"She's packing. We decided to beat the rush. She's going ahead before they order us to leave." He stuffed a fry in his mouth.

"I'm sorry, she has to drive alone," said Jazz.

"She's not going alone. Captain Barfly's wife, Greta, and a couple of others are caravanning out of Nodlon tomorrow morning in the wee hours. I can't leave anyway. I've got an open homicide investigation. The missus understands she's a policeman's wife. How about you guys?"

"I'm evacuating with the hospital staff tomorrow. I'm taking Shotgun's fiancée, Goldie, and his daughters."

"That reminds me," said Jack. "I called Goldie, and gave her an update. She calmed down when I told her the doctor thinks he's just sleeping. I'll call her again later after we know more."

Gumshoe closed his service, and took a sip from his water goblet. He pushed his chair from the table, leaned back, and steadied himself with an elbow.

"I'm responsible, no matter if he was poisoned or fell or just got sick." He crossed his legs, and gazed down at his wingtips.

"He knew the risk, Gumshoe, and he wants to stop the murderer as much as we do. If New Gem is involved in the Zodiac cases, they think nothing of human lives. They'll destroy anyone in their way like so much meat."

"Yeah, they don't care about the world inside." Gumshoe scraped a speck of dirt from one of his soles.

"The world inside?" asked Jack.

"It's old school, very old. There once was a great conversation between the great minds debating the philosophies, the music of the spheres, contemplating the rings of Saturn. The conversation died when the new age began." He studied Clay for a moment, as if wondering if he understood.

"So one of the things they contemplated was the world

inside each individual. One side believed inside each individual is a special and unique world. For them, the world inside was everything a man was from birth to death.

"Sorry for going on. An old colleague directed me to an article in a police journal when I was a cub. When a man dies prematurely, the world inside him ends. Not just the mechanics of living; eating, sleeping and working.

"No, his hopes and dreams vanish. All his parent's hopes become dust. He never sees his children grow up. His loved ones will never again have his company for the rest of their lives.

"Certain deaths are understandable, even justified, by disease or accident or a meaningful risk. Other deaths are unjust. That's why we hate homicide. It's immoral. No one who dreams should be murdered. Intuitively we know it's true even for biots. That's why it's against the law to murder or harm a biot."

Jack's caster blasted from his cloak. "Sorry," he said, and he silenced the clamor. "It's Nurse Casket," he said avoiding Jazz's irritated glare.

"Hello, any news on Shotgun?"

"Your man-servant is awake, Mr. Clay, and he's asking for you."

"We'll be right there." He closed the connection and slipped the caster back into his cloak.

"I'll get some to-go boxes," said Jazz.

Shotgun's Findings

The emergency room buzzed with quiet efficiency. All of the bays seemed full, and a few patients slept in the hospital's halls.

"Lunans," said Jack. "Jazz said more were arriving."

The detective scowled, "bad business, very bad."

Nurse Casket spotted them before they reached Shotgun, and she grabbed a chart. She rushed over. "We still don't have the test results," said Casket tapping the chart. "All the monitors say he's fine though. Dr. Forest put no restriction on visitors, but he's not likely to release Mr. Morgan until we get those."

"Can you check on those lab results?" asked Gumshoe. "And get a hold of Dr. Forest. If Shotgun can go, it's imperative we expedite matters."

"I'll see what I can do," said Casket.

"Please. Shotgun's information may be critical to helping in a murder investigation. We need those lab results now."

"I'll let the lab know, sir."

An elderly goblin called for help from a nearby bay. Casket hurried off to help.

Shotgun was awake, but he looked pale. "Did you catch the truck that hit me?" He propped himself on his elbows.

"As for you, young man," said Gumshoe, "you gave this old man quite a fright. We think they slipped you a mickey, but we don't know yet."

"What's happened while I was out?" asked Shotgun.

"While you were in dreamland," said Jack, "rumors of war have frightened everyone into leaving Nodlon."

"That doesn't sound good." Shotgun shook his head. "What about Goldie?"

"Goldie and the girls are going to Iron Mountain with Jazz."

"Thanks, boss, for taking care of Goldie and the girls."

"No problem, you're family."

"I need to call her and let her know where I am."

"Goldie knows where you are. I called and gave her an update. She's worried sick, but she calmed down after I told her you were sleeping. Want something to eat?" Jack asked. "We just tanked up at the cafeteria with Jasmine, and I've brought you the leftovers." He offered Shotgun a couple of lunch boxes.

"Yeah, I'm famished." Taking the containers and a package of plastic silverware from Clay, he opened them, and ate. "And you're a good cook, too. I was starving." He stuffed his mouth. "Can you hand me my caster? I'd like to call Goldie."

Jack pulled Shotgun's satchel off the back of a chair, and handed it to the dwarf.

"Boss, can I get some water?"

While the dwarf called his fiancée, Jack and the Inspector stepped outside the bay.

"Sugar plums," cried Goldie. She burst into tears.

"Please stop crying," cooed Shotgun.

"I'm sorry. I just missed you so much. I thought I might have lost you," she sobbed.

"No way, sugar, I love you, and I can't leave you and the girls now. Come on, the Inspector is here and we have to catch a killer. Be brave for me, will you?" Still sobbing, she nodded, and let him take his leave.

"Never seen her, this upset," said Shotgun to Jack and Gumshoe.

"It's not every day Nodlon may go to war," said Jack, handing him a glass of water. "Everyone's frightened. They abandon their routines. They all make a mad dash for the exits. Then, she finds out her fiancée is hospitalized while pursuing a bloodthirsty killer. It has to be hard."

Gumshoe placed his hand on the bedrail. "Jack's right, she's doing well under the circumstances."

The dwarf opened his satchel, and pulled out his tablet. "Let's see what we've recovered." Shotgun typed his password, and the little machine beeped.

Leaving him to his work for a few minutes, Gumshoe

fidgeted, and Clay studied the monitors. The dwarf fiddled with his computer, closing and launching obscure applications, and running tests.

Nurse Casket stuck her head into the bay. "The doctor is on his way. He's got the results from the lab."

~~~~~~

Doctor Forest rushed into the bay. All eyes turned to him, as he strode to Shotgun's bedside. Forest took Shotgun's wrist and checked his pulse. "Patrick, you managed to alarm everyone, but you're going to be fit as a fiddle." Setting down his wrist, the doctor asked, "Are you thirsty?"

He held up his empty cup. "Yes. I'm as dry as a Forbidden Zone."

"We'll get some water for you. You were drugged. The poison they slipped you was a new form of street Soma. It's called a Roosevelt. They call it that because it's smuggled up from the river. It's non-toxic, but causes extreme drowsiness. Aftereffects include thirst and a mild headache.

"We had a hard time identifying it. The lab ran several tests twice for confirmation. The concentrations were extremely low and the scans missed it. We only checked because we've had more than one poisoning by Roosevelt.

"You're very lucky it wasn't something worse. Whoever gave you this probably meant you no physical harm."

"That clinches it," said Jack, "they're involved in something or they wouldn't have poisoned you."

"Maybe," said Gumshoe, "and maybe not. Anything else, doc?"

"Just getting Patrick released." Forest slapped the bedrail. "The nurse will bring you some water and a mild painkiller. Just don't drive, or operate machinery until you've had a good night's rest. Understood?"

"Will do doc, thanks."

"Sure and next time, maybe you can invite me to a show."

"All our performance were cancelled," said Jack, "but I hope we can perform at the Grove under Iron Mountain. Here take a few of these." Clay proffered a few of his cards.

"Evening gentlemen, I'd love to chat, but we're expecting another transport from the Moon in a couple of hours. I have to move everyone I can before they arrive." Forest thanked Jack, and hurried away on other errands.

Shotgun continued working.

"Inspector, can you send me a file with the missing dwarves? I can compare the client data from New Gem to the list of missing dwarves and see if it correlates. I don't have all of their files. It looks like I downloaded only a fraction."

The Inspector tapped on his tablet. "Give me a moment, I'm thinking of a solution."

Nurse Casket brought Shotgun more water and painkillers. "Gosh, this gives me a feeling of déjà vu." The dwarf swallowed the pills.

"Got it, Inspector, just give me a moment."

"If we get any matches," said Jack, "we can add that to trying to poison you."

Shotgun set his tablet down on the bed. "There's more. They tried to turn on the tablet. I've recorded their attempts to turn the machine on, but they couldn't get it to fire up. In the time I was out, they didn't think to use a work around. Do you have any idea how long I was out?"

"The sound from the bug was muffled," said Gumshoe. "We could barely make out what you were saying. When we heard you counting, and your voice faded out we guessed you were in trouble. Clay must have been there in about six minutes."

"I don't think they got anything out of it." Shotgun tapped on his keyboard. "Here come the results. I've got five hits out of seventy-two names. Remember, we're only comparing about a tenth of the data."

"Good enough for me to want to see more," said Gumshoe. "I'll try to pull a warrant again."

Passing Gumshoe, Casket came in. "Good news, Mr. Morgan, you can go.

"Don't operate machinery or do anything else requiring your attention until you've gotten a good night's sleep. You're in danger of sudden drowsiness or even narcolepsy. Drink plenty of water, and you can take mild painkillers if you have a headache. And we know the Inspector is giving you a ride." She handed him an open tablet. "Sign where indicated and you're free to go."

Hot Pursuit

They passed dilapidated row houses on the way back to New Gem. Gumshoe overrode the autopilot, and approached New Gem from the east. Boards covered the windows of the abandoned property to deter squatters. Only a few well-kept homes dotted the neighborhood. The day shift had ended, and families packed their belongings into older ground-cars for the trip to Iron Mountain.

The autopilot steered the cruiser through the streets, and crossed Spenard, turned back up Pikes Peak. The row houses yielded to town homes with small touches of character. The autopilot crawled as they passed through the traffic jam. The streets were thick with frightened people fleeing Nodlon.

"If they have look-outs, we don't want to alert them. Occasionally, I've made the mistake of underestimating a crook. Today, we're not letting this rabble best us, so we're going around the long way." He drove a couple of blocks south and parked in an alley behind a dumpster leading to the rear of a parking garage behind New Gem.

"Let's see if dispatch has our warrant." Gumshoe punched his console. The cruiser's vid lit up, and displayed a middle aged police matron.

"Inspector Gumshoe, why I never, what can I do for you?" Boundless optimism no doubt contributed to an overabundance of eye shadow, false lashes, and too much lipstick. Heedless of the futility of fighting age, she bubbled over in a position normally reserved for the staid.

"Maggie, has the warrant for New Gem come back?"

Pecking at her screens with a stylus, she searched for any warrants. "Why no dear. They rejected your warrant application."

"Why?" said Gumshoe. "Anything I can fix."

"No, honey, there's no explanation. They just turned it down flat."

"Can you get Hale on the line?"

"Sorry, dear, can't get anyone over there. Everyone's been sent home to pack. The Octagon showed up at the courthouse hours ago, with an army of boys in training uniforms. They're over there now loading them up." She threw up both her hands and shook her head. "I'm sorry dear. Wish I could help, but I've got nothing."

Glancing at Jack, Gumshoe frowned. "Thanks Maggie, out." He stabbed the cruiser's console and it went dark.

"What will we do now?" asked Shotgun.

"Hot pursuit exception," said Gumshoe, "also known as unauthorized breaking and entering." Getting out of the car, Gumshoe put on his trench coat and straightened his fedora. If you're coming with me, gentlemen, it's time to go."

"What happens if we're caught?" Shotgun fiddled with the straps on his back pack.

"It's official business. If my hunch is correct, we're in the gray area. If we've made a mistake, I'll be passing out parking tickets." Gumshoe flashed a wry smile. "Unless your offer stands, Jack."

"It stands," said Jack, "if I'm not breaking moon rocks for burglary."

"Follow me, bravehearts," said Gumshoe.

Leaving the alley, they crossed a nearly empty street.

A goblin in overalls was loading a plumber's van in front of a tired townhome. He strapped a child's bicycle to the roof. A woman appeared on the stoop above the van carrying a box. She descended the steps, and tripped over an assortment of suitcases at the foot of the staircase. The plumber caught her, and let the box fall to the sidewalk. The plumber consoled his wife, and Jack looked away.

On the opposite side of the tunnel, an aging dwarf in a dingy suit and a straw hat hobbled along the sidewalk in their direction. They crossed the street in front of the dwarf, who called out to them, "Can you help me?" They slowed, and he took off his hat expectantly. His hands trembled and the feather in the brim fluttered.

Jack pulled a large bill from his cloak. "Here you go, sir. Take this. Go to a robo-car station and catch a bus out of Nodlon. You need to get moving."

The dwarf stowed the bill in his suit coat. "Bless you, Guv'nor."

Stepping into the alley, they wove a path through the trash cans and rubbish crowding the narrow way. Swiftly Gumshoe led the way, forcing Shotgun to trot to keep up. The alley ended in an intersection with a wider alley behind a parking garage.

Without stopping, Gumshoe headed to the pedestrian entrance. The Inspector held a cardkey up to an electronic pad and the door lock clicked. Gumshoe opened the door, "After you gentlemen."

Jack high stepped over the threshold took a pace and stopped. Shotgun followed Jack, and Gumshoe joined them letting the door close.

Pools of lights illuminated the parking garage leaving dim corners and shadowy alcoves. A row of concrete columns interrupted their view of the parking spaces. Following Gumshoe, they walked up a ramp, across a landing between parking levels, and around a stairwell. Bare doors without handles faced a level pad running the length of a loading zone.

Reading the business names over the doors, Jack recognized a few of the shops near New Gem. Walking a few doors to the east, they found New Gem's back door.

"Here we are gentlemen. Smile, I'm sure we're on camera." Contemplating the keypad on the electronic lock next to the door, Gumshoe punched the keys. "I'm trying the police code." The door remained closed. He tried again without success, and again. "I'll have to call Maggie, and see if she can pull their code."

Shotgun unslung his backpack. "Give me a second

Inspector, and I'll get it for you."

"Go for it." Gumshoe backed away.

Shotgun pulled his tablet from his satchel and knelt on the pavement. "I've entered the Yard's network, and pulled your database. All of Nodlon's electronic key codes in one handy location." He handed his tablet to Gumshoe. "Punch in your badge and password, and we're in."

"Why do I suspect you don't need my badge and password?"

"We have to fulfill the formalities," Shotgun grinned. "I don't want to get arrested again. Once was too often."

"I've got to get you a job with the Yard." Hunting and pecking, Gumshoe entered his identity into the application's log-in screen, and pressed the search button. A progress bar scrolled to a finish, and the screen displayed the alarm code.

"M010C4," said Gumshoe, handing the tablet back to Shotgun. "Let's try it." He keyed the passcode into the lock, and the door swung open. Waving to his consultants, he signaled for them to take cover against the wall. He pulled his lightning pistol from his holster. He flicked a switch, and an indicator light on the handle flashed yellow and fell dark.

"Police!" cried Gumshoe and entered the office. He called again, and paused in the hall waiting for a response. Sticking his head out of the door he said, "Wait here while I secure the location and give the security system an incident code." Disappearing into the office, they waited. Soon, the policemen reappeared unarmed. "No one's here. They have an older model security system, and I shut it off. My code cleared the alarm, so we won't have company." Stepping aside, he invited them into the office.

From the back door, Shotgun recognized the cross-hall. Going to the door with the whirring sound, he tried the door and was surprised when it opened. The server room was larger than he expected. One rack stood in a corner next to a fiber optic cable box and a breaker box. A half-pack of industrial batteries sat under a work bench.

Shotgun set his satchel on the work bench. Removing a cable from his satchel he plugged one end into his computer. With the other end, he rounded the rack and considered the available hubs. Spying one with an empty port, he plugged in his cable. Opening a utility, he created a map of New Gem's local network, and studied it. Finding what he needed, he ordered the system to copy the client files. As the time ticked by the datasets filled. Within minutes he had copied all of the client files to several dozen datasets.

Shutting down his tablet, he closed the link, and unplugged the cable from the hub. He stuffed the cable and the tablet back in his satchel, and left.

He patted his satchel, "Got it all."

Waving at the exit, Gumshoe said to them, "Wait for me." The Inspector reset the security system, emerged from the office, and closed the rear entry.

Swiftly they left the garage the way they had come and crossed the wide alley and ducked into the smaller alley leading back to the cruiser. Taking large strides Gumshoe led them quickly through the debris and litter back to the cruiser.

"Let's find out what fate, luck, and a touch of self-help has delivered into our hands," said Gumshoe.

Pulling out of the alley Gumshoe guided the cruiser around a block and engaged the autopilot.

"We'll reach the Yard in a little over a half."

"Give me a minute." Shotgun loaded the new datasets, and compared the database of missing dwarves to the database of New Gem's clients.

"Inspector, you are not going to like this in a good way, or you're going to love it in a bad way."

"What happened to good news and bad news?" Jack looked at the industrious dwarf.

"Not sure which is which in this case, boss. All of the missing dwarves are clients of New Gem, including McCarthy.

The disappearances go back to when they opened their office in Nodlon late last year. And get this, all of the clients worked in the Ministry of Manna, the Octagon, or the Crown."

"What do you have on McCarthy?" Gumshoe asked. The cruiser slid into the level-way traffic.

"She sought therapy several weeks ago, and made several appointments before her disappearance."

"What kind of therapy?"

"Nothing unusual, just girl stuff. They gave her a great discount, but they do that for all of the female clients."

"Anything else?"

"Jerry Balaam purchased the New Gem franchise for Nodlon last September from the New Gem office on Elysium. Their home office is a Martian corporation located in Helium. It's owned by a recluse who lives on an exclusive private estate on the Boreum plane near Pal Station. I've searched the net, and it's rumored he's into gambling, money laundering, chemical stimulants, and biot trafficking."

"Maybe Balaam's a friend of the Baron," said Jack. "One criminal deserves another."

"Maybe," said Gumshoe.

"Inspector, I'm sending you my report now with a copy of the data." Shotgun closed his tablet.

"Thanks, Shotgun. Gentlemen, I suggest you get some rest. I have a feeling we're closing in on our quarry."

Why Dwarves?

Jack put the Andromeda in ground effect mode, and headed to Babel Tower. He swung his flyer onto the eastbound level-way. More dwarves were missing than he imagined. Nodlon expected war. His shows were cancelled. Corman and his crew were packing his show for the road.

The world as he knew it was coming apart.

"Thanks to your bravery, Shotgun, we've connected the missing dwarves to New Gem."

"What's next? Raid the place and demand answers from the creepy doctor?"

"Maybe, I don't know. Let Gumshoe figure it out, he's the homicide detective. He may stake out the place, or get some vice officers to shake down their underworld informants. How should I know?"

"He'd better do something quick, or he's going to have a panic on his hands whether he wants it or not. I have no idea what they're doing with the dwarves, but every dwarf in Nodlon is scared."

"Why dwarves? So many dwarves are missing. They're capable, intelligent, and hard-working. Why would they fall for a trap? And what does Balaam want with them?"

"Why dwarves? Dwarves live without hope. Dwarves dream, but we're biots. Biots are not people and most of us will never even chase our dreams. Hope of fulfilling our dreams drives us to do stupid things, senseless things, even things beyond any common sense at all."

"Dreams, Shotgun? Life in Nodlon isn't fair to biots, but life isn't fair to anyone. For over a hundred years, biot's lives have been improving. More biots have more opportunity to live a full life than any time since the ancient's created biots. It's true there are limits, but more than half the biots live better than half the humans. No matter how bad life is here, it's not bad enough to throw your life away."

"Few are as lucky as us, boss." He looked out the window at the passing traffic. "Most of us aren't fortunate to have any spare change, much less an apartment. Without an apartment, you can't have a girlfriend, and without a girlfriend, you can't have a family, and without a family," he trailed off into a whisper, "you can't go home."

"What is a home, Shotgun?" Clay mused. "Who knows what a home means? For some it's where we surround ourselves with our things. For others it's where you find those you love, or maybe it's where you find those who love you. What is the wonder of home? Going home, leaving home, and missing home? What makes a home a home? And, how do you know when you arrive?" Clay sensed he had struck a chord. "What do you hope for?"

"Thanks to you, boss. My family has a home. Never have I met anyone who cared as much as you. I was raised in a nursery owned by Nodlon Biots and I have no idea who my parents are, or if I even have parents. Not as bad as a kennel I suppose, but hardly even an orphanage."

"Sorry Shotgun, I didn't mean to pry."

"Well, boss, being angry serves no purpose, so I worked on earning my way out. But dwarves have little to lose if they take ridiculous risks for a slim chance on a slight reward."

"There's wisdom, Shotgun. You're very generous. Before I discovered my magical powers, my mother and I moved into an apartment in Under Nodlon.

"Our apartment was near the Circus. I didn't have any money for tickets, but I snuck in through the service entrances. Security let me wander back stage with a wink and a nod. The stage hands put me to work. They wouldn't let me watch shows for nothing. I soon proved as useful as any and more grateful than most. They gave me my first paying job. I performed special effects for an opera."

"Home is where your loved ones are. You miss Phaedra, right? You have Jasmine, but face it, Phaedra was your family."

Shotgun stung him with the truth. Graced with a loving mother, never had he felt the pain of fatherlessness. And his magic made all the difference. Celebrity insulated him, and he had never known want. Rather than hoping for a good job, he basked in fame and fortune rare for anyone in Nodlon, let alone a half-breed.

"I'm glad you and Goldie are a part of my life."

"Boss?" Shotgun shot a quizzical glance at Jack.

"You're right, Shotgun. Face it. Except for Jasmine, you're the only family I've got."

"Sorry boss, I forget you're one of us."

"Whatever I am Shotgun, I was very fortunate. My life's been easy, and I've never wanted for anything. Maybe I'm a freak, mutant, or monster, but I understand. I do understand. I was given a gift, and I feel its weight. Before I discovered my magic, I was just another half-breed. I've been a member of every caste in Nodlon. Thanks to magic, I've got a caste all of my own. When no one can break castes created by synthetic genes, I've broken them all thanks to magic."

"Jack," Shotgun said.

Nodlon slid by under them. The sun glittered off the mountains. Jack ran a hand over the flyer's leather seats. It felt like money, and he wondered if he deserved it.

Reading his mind, Shotgun coughed. "Jack Clay has paid his dues." Shotgun took a stern tone. "Boss, you're a hero to every biot in this city. Elves, goblins, dwarves, and the uniques and specials all look up to you. Even the humans respect you."

"No, I shouldn't have said anything." He accepted his butler's small pique. "I can't complain. I got lucky. If you cannot vent to me, Shotgun, whom can you vent to?"

"You're a good elf, boss. That's why the Princess gave you her ring. I don't know where you got magic from, and I don't care. And no else cares either. You have to help us. It's your task and it was given to you. Win or lose, all you have to do is try."

Gently, Jack twisted the wheel, and the flyer curled into the northbound lanes. Ahead Babel Tower glittered.

"When we have time," said Jack, "would you let me buy Goldie's contract? I'll lean on Goldie's agency. If they crank out the paperwork double time you guys will be free to marry by summer."

"Whoa, you'd do that?" Shotgun sucked in a deep breath. "Boss – Jack, I, I, I appreciate what you've done for us, but I can never repay you."

"Just take good care of Goldie and the girls, that's all that matters."

Shotgun bit his lip and stared out the windows. The mountain shadows blanketed Nodlon. Evening was falling and the blue lights of Nodlon were coming on. *Beautiful*, Shotgun thought, *if you can live to enjoy it.*

~~~~~~

Babel Tower rose into the sky. He left the level-way and guided the flyer up to Babel Tower.

Jasmine won't come home tonight. It's all right, Nodlon Memorial needs her. The Lunans need her. Of all the friends in his life, he loved her most. *But I need her too! Will she be safe?*

Jack steered for the landing bay and slowed the Andromeda.

The Meddler's Nemesis

The Black Dwarf enjoyed his view. The lake shimmered under the stars. The moon's reflection danced on distant reefs. He could just see the tip of the pier below the tower, its inky black silhouetted against the shimmer on the water.

Night is the best time of day.

He enjoyed the mystery of darkness. Ghosts and spirits; vampires and werewolves; demons and the undead prowled the night.

Night is my kind of day.

Wagging his finger, he summoned the wench holding his grapes. As she dangled a bunch, he sucked them from the vine and squished them with his front teeth savoring the juicy meat.

Snuggling into his throne, he pressed a button and reclined. Wiggling his toes, he summoned another blonde to give him a pedicure.

"Work on those cuticles some more," he ordered. He soaked his fingers in a bowl of soft soap, and rubbed them together as it dawned on him how pleasant the gooey mess felt.

A red call light blinked on his remote. "Always when I'm taking a break." With his free hand he picked up his caster and pressed the audio connection. "What is this time, Sargon?"

"Excuse me, my lord Nimrod. Earlier this afternoon, we were probed. A black dwarf working for Cretaceous Clay walked into our New Gem office in Nodlon and asked to see Balaam."

"Why wasn't I informed before now?"

"Balaam informed us during his evening briefing, he was unaware of its significance and he thought it was only a coincidence. We investigated the matter when we received confirmation."

"Hold on." He pressed a switch on his remote and his pedestal rotated. He rotated past his fireplace and past his four poster bed with a pair of nubile vixens, and past the lounge he used as his antechamber, until he faced his wall vid. Flipping another switch, Sargon appeared on his wall. His old servant wore a black dwarf clad in a black uniform and a baseball cap. Macaroni decorated the cap's brim, and the device of the Black Dwarf was embroidered on the jacket.

"Please explain," said Nimrod in an even tone.

Sargon gulped, and coughed into his fist. "On your screen sir, I'm throwing up the picture of the suspicious black dwarf." In a lower corner, the vid displayed the picture of a dwarf wearing an expensive shirt and black trousers.

"The New Gem clinic took him as a walk-in. He gave them his name, Patrick Morgan, but they didn't recognize him at first. Almost all dwarves look pretty much alike. Nothing aroused their suspicions until they slipped him the ultra-Soma we developed.

"Shortly after Morgan popped the pill and collapsed, an elf showed up. I'll put him on the screen." Next to the dwarf, an elf appeared in expensive men's furnishings. He wore a cloak with matching tunic, breeches, a leather vest, and suede boots. On his head was a medieval cap with a feather.

"You're looking at Cretaceous Clay, my lord. The staff recognized the elf pretty darn quick. He's the elf working with the police on the Zodiac case. He gave Balaam a cockamamie story. When he arrived he was huffing. He ran from a stake-out nearby."

"If he can levitate, why didn't he fly?"

"Maybe the fool hoped he wouldn't blow his cover." Sargon shrugged, "How should I know? Maybe he wanted to surprise us."

"What's the significance of this Captain," sighed Nimrod. He rubbed a temple and felt a drip running down his cheek. He looked at his fingers and remembered the manicuring gel. "The police aren't going to get anywhere with their investigation. The more they struggle in the mire, the deeper they sink in the quicksand of our plot."

"My lord," said Sargon. "Clay possesses magical power; the kind of power we haven't seen since the days of the prophets."

"Magic? What kind of magic?"

"He's a thespian and playwright who performs simplistic operettas featuring special effects, dancing girls, choreographed battles and magic. A band of studio musicians called the Rockhounds accompany the show with an eclectic variety of songs from folk tunes to heavy metal. He's a big hit.

"What really sets his show apart is magic. He creates illusions, flies, levitates objects and dancers. Thanks to his abilities, the action is rarely confined to the stage."

"You sound as if you're a fan of this new nemesis of ours."

"I've watched his shows on Clay-net. He's good. If you could mesmerize him, and force him to serve us, he'd be entertaining."

"Maybe," Nimrod tapped his dimple, "or maybe he's the elf Phaedra stole from the Dragon Lord?" The Black Dwarf thought for a moment. "When did he appear in this time continuum?"

"About thirty years ago, and we have almost no personal history on him. What we know comes from his website, and he's reclusive about his personal life."

"Continue our investigation. If he's Phaedra's son, I want to know. What about the police? How far along have they gotten?"

"Inspector Jacques Lestrayed, the leading homicide detective in Nodlon is on the case." A picture of a middle aged man in a trench coat and a fedora appeared next to the elf. "He's getting nowhere. He tried getting a warrant, but our agent on the high court squelched the warrant request." Sargon's eyes narrowed.

"Lestrayed suspects the missing dwarves and the sacrifice to the Dragon Lord are connected, but he has no idea how. The city is in an uproar, and the Inspector is unlikely to learn anything more before war breaks out. With the threat of Mars breathing down their necks, the cowards in Parliament plan to evacuate Nodlon and hide at Iron Mountain."

"How did the flat foot team up with a magical elf?"

"The two know each other from prior cases. It's only recently entered the old fool's mind that the supernatural was involved in the disappearances. Clay is the only magician he knows, so he called him in as a consultant."

"Contact our agent, Sumuqan, and take the meddlesome police officer off the case."

"What of the elf?"

"Nothing must interfere with our plans to attack Nodlon and blame Mars."

Wiping his fingers on a towel, he glowered.

"If Cretaceous Clay is Phaedra's son, he's radioactive. Why make him work out the mystery? Let's save him the trouble."

"Arrange for our black dwarves to ambush them. If the black dwarves succeed, we can check him off our to-do list. If not, Nodlon Yard will panic. All dwarves are peaceful by nature. The thought of a violent revolution of black dwarves hasn't crossed their minds yet. The possibility of dwarves going rogue en masse will send all Nodlon into a tizzy."

"Yes my lord, as you command."

The Black Dwarf chuckled. "Jack's name should've been diatomaceous earth. Clay you are, and unto Jack you shall return. All will go back to the clay. And in the grave you'll worship the Dragon Lord."

Sargon smirked, "A fitting eulogy, my lord."

Rimshot Sees Too Much

An airship hunkered in the alley between the hotel's loading dock, and the dumpster. Even in the dim light of early morning Rimshot recognized the low-slung profile of an air hearse.

"You, come 'er an' give us a hand."

The burly shadow between him and the street light called him again, "Hurry up swabbie or I'll let your management have a piece of my mind." The shadow was too short for a man, so he assumed the fellow was a dwarf.

Another shadow shuffled slowly to the back of the airship.

Cursing silently, he wished he had taken the night off. *Aye, better to be in bed*, *But what the customer wants, the customer gets*. Still he had not expected a flying hearse driven by dwarves.

Carefully navigating through the rubbish, he approached the dwarves. "What 'kin I do for ye?" Standing none too close, he thought he was safe.

The burly dwarf closed the distance, grabbed his overalls near the scruff and lifted him in one swift move.

Barely standing on his toes, he trembled. He was face to face with the dwarf. The dwarf was wizened by time and scarred with old wounds. A spot on his forehead betrayed his microchip, but in the dark, Rimshot could not make out a color.

The wizened dwarf's bulbous eyes took him in. Rolling to a stop, the eyes gave him an uneasy feeling.

"Open the bay doors," growled the dwarf, jerking his head at the dock.

"Sure Guv'nor," he said. Better to cooperate, he told himself than to ask for trouble.

The dwarf released him with a flick. He staggered backwards and caught his balance. Keeping an eye on the two figures near the airship, he backed slowly up the loading dock stairs. Putting his thumb on the lock, he pulled the door aside revealing a small bay. A hoist slung from the roof resembled a spider awaiting its prey. A forklift peeked from an alcove.

"Hey," he called, "we've got a hoist or a forklift if you need 'em."

The burly dwarf dismissed his offer with a wave. "Get out of here, swab, if you know what's good for you."

Mumbling, he backed into a shadow where he watched without being seen. It would not do if they nicked any tools on his watch. *Just do your business and leave.*

The dwarves pulled a heavy load from the rear hatch on a levitator lorry. Oblong and black, the load slid towards the dock. Rather than use the stairs, the burly one ordered the other aside. Using short bursts, the dwarf pushed the load to the dock's lift.

As they pushed their burden into the bay, the light revealed the unmistakable outline of a coffin. They wore black and they each had a black microchip.

Now, that's peculiar. Rimshot, what kind of party do they need one of those for? Years before he recalled a Halloween party. The hosts had filled a coffin to the brim with ice and drinks. But Halloween was months away. And there were no other guests on his roster. This was a private affair booked just hours before.

After the first coffin, the two dwarves pushed in a second coffin.

Two? Rimshot wondered. He shivered. The black dwarves unloaded a pallet of boxes, an assortment of jugs and a set of spears, and they were done.

The burly one hurried now down the steps. "I'll tell the master, you get his staff." His boots slapped the concrete. He opened a passenger door, and stood next to the airship. The gangly dwarf jogged to a compartment and retrieved a staff with a stone in its head.

"My lord, we have unloaded." A dwarf in a dark cloak emerged from the airship, and took the staff from the gangly dwarf.

"Good." The cloaked dwarf waved the burly one ahead, and mounted the stairs. He passed by the frightened custodian's hiding place.

Blimey, thought Rimshot, *he's the spittin' image of a warlock. It's too early for a costume ball. Halloween's not for seven months!*

Rimshot shrank farther into the shadows.

When he walked into the bay, Rimshot felt a chill in the air. In the bay's light, silver designs glittered on the dwarf's robe. Atop the staff, mounted between four gargoyles, was a crystal of quartz. A snake coiled round the gargoyles' feet. Silver filigree ran down the shaft to a foot shod in pewter.

The robed dwarf waved his servants ahead. "Move on fools, we have little time." The warlock sniffed, and slowly turned searching for an odor.

He flung his hood back revealing a lifeless face with a sunken visage shrouded in a pasty pall. His thin lips, blue and drawn, curled in a frown. Bloodshot eyes blazed with a fierce light, hot with the ferocity of some inner hate.

He sniffed the air.

Rimshot sucked in a breath and held it. *A black dwarf,* he thought. He quietly slipped deeper into the shadows and cowered behind the forklift. Fear burned his lungs. Breathing in silence, he froze.

The mysterious trio crossed the bay. The service entrance to the ballroom opened, and the door slammed. The empty bay tempted him to run.

Sticking his head out, he checked the corridor carefully. *Have they all gone into the ballroom?* He tiptoed past the doorway. He heard whispers in the ballroom.

How to explain the inexplicable? Especially to one's betters.

"No pressin' your luck, Rimshot," he muttered. "Hide yourself old man, 'til they're gone." He looked up and down the service corridor. *Hide 'til dawn if needs be.*

He slipped into the stairwells and hurried away.

~~~~~~~

The Milky Way dominated the ballroom's floor.

Appropriate, thought Nimrod. The constellations printed on the carpet divided the room into the twelve signs of the Zodiac.

Polaris was in the center, but the Black Dwarf just smiled.

"What's a little precession to prophecy," Nimrod said. He pointed at Polaris. "There will be the gateway."

With a snap of his fingers, he cast a spell of silence so none would hear, and sealed the room. He set to work with his minions.

Speaking a spell in the first tongue, his staff came alive. Mumbling a spell, a faint blue light shone from the shaft's filigree. He twirled his staff, and blue flame spat from the foot. He melted the locks on the doors, froze the hinges, and seared signs and markings into the walls.

Circling the Milky Way, the Black Dwarf melted a ring into the carpet. Around the Zodiac from Sagittarius to Aries, he drew a pentagram. He waved a hand and seven holes appeared. With a flash, he inscribed a series of runes and signs in the star and completed the pentagram.

Gesturing, he bid his servants to move the coffins. One to either side of the altar at the edge of the pentagram burned into the floor.

The Black Dwarf thrust the staff at the goat. "Put the altar next to Capricorn."

Helter and Skelter carried two portable tables to the cusp of Capricorn and placed them end to end.

Opening cases and bags on pallets, they unloaded their master's gear. Soon they had an altar.

They placed the coffins at the edge of the pentagram, on either side of the altar. Seven torches went into the seven holes around the Milky Way. These they filled with oil from the urns, and lit each torch.

The firelight reminded him of those long ago days when he sacrificed the children of his enemies to the god Ashur.

Twisting his staff, first one way and then another, he opened the coffins revealing his living hostages within.

Each of the caskets contained a new victim mesmerized by his spells. His victims laid frozen in the dreamless sleep of zombies. Glassy eyes focused on some distant goal neither could see. Caught in the trance of the Black Dwarf's making, neither victim seemed aware of his precarious state.

Helter and Skelter laughed, and jabbed each other sharing a private joke.

"Rise zombies," Nimrod cried.

Gradually, both of his mesmerized victims stood. The zombies climbed from the caskets. One was a man and the other was a dwarf maiden.

The Black Dwarf drove each of them with his staff. Enjoying his role, Nimrod delighted in malice.

Slowly, each took a place on either side of the altar. They laid upon the tables head to head.

The man wore the uniform of a Colonel in the Nodlon Defense Force. A badge identified him as an employee of the Ministry of Manna.

From his cloak, the Black Dwarf took a black chip, and laid it on the man's forehead. Putting his fingers on the chip, he summoned the magic of manna. He released it and recharged the chip's battery. He gloated at the ease with which he controlled the fool's technology.

"Dogs and pigs you are, my pets." He chuckled, and rubbed his belly. Then, setting his mind on the device, he instructed it to mark the man. It hummed once, and emitted a quick flash. Sinking into the man's flesh, it embedded itself in his forehead. Sealing the wound, it was no more than a black spot.

The Black Dwarf turned his attention to the maiden. She still wore the simple uniform of a secretary in the Ministry of Manna. Mesmerized, she stared without blinking.

"Yes, my sweet, your soul will open the gate." He looked at the Colonel and chuckled. "That man's soul would probably be sucked through to join the others on Gehenna."

Casting a new spell and renewing his incantations, he held his staff over the beauty and continued his ritual.

Her aura glowed, and a fire spread over her skin.

A gust blew her hair. She trembled on the wobbly table. She moaned, and her eyes fluttered. Drool ran from her mouth. Her back arched, and she stiffened. She gasped.

The light faded, the glow softened, and the maiden fell limp.

Snarling, the Black Dwarf flicked a finger and the chip on her forehead popped out. The chip launched itself into the air with a sucking sound. It dragged thin wires from her head dripping with blood. Freed from the girl, the wires popped as the ends separated from her forehead.

Blood flowed from her forehead. He levitated the blood and made a ball above her head. With a gesture, he separated the ball into dozens of drops. He flung the drops against the far wall. The blood splattered in the sign of the Capricorn.

He grinned. "Let the fools chew on that."

Standing before the altar, the Black Dwarf faced the pentagram, and twirled his staff three times. He chanted an incantation of power. He held out his staff and stood before the altar on the cusp of Capricorn. Leaving the staff to channel the power, he spread his arms, and canted an obscure mantra.

The staff hummed and drew manna across the differential. Light radiated from the stone. Wherever his staff scribed runes and lines, the marks glowed. Fiery wisps swirled over the charred and melted surfaces. Growing stronger with each incantation, wisps coalesced into threads, and threads twisted into ribbons. And still he canted.

A breeze swirled around the pentagram. The breeze fed the fires and the torchlight burned hot.

The breeze strengthened, and became a whirlwind. The smoke from the fires swirled in the whirlwind. A fume of sulfur tinged the air.

The carpet thinned and stars appeared under the floor. Polaris disappeared and the floor parted. The pentagram opened and dilated. Fanning out, the portal swallowed the Milky Way.

The pentagram ripped a hole in the universe creating a gateway to the stars. Below the star gate, the red planet of Gehenna floated among bright stars. The portal to Nimrod's prison hung motionless above the eye of the planet's eternal storm.

He remembered, his master the Dragon Lord had told him the portal was in geosynchronous orbit over the eye. But he didn't know what that meant. He was more interested in torture than astrophysics. Dawn broke over the storm's angry eye. The golden light of Ashur played on scarlet clouds.

Turning back to the altar, he shoved the empty body of the female onto the floor, careful not to let her shell roll into the gate. He wanted her body to foment panic and incite fear and hatred.

Time to call a friend home. Someone special who will be my ally in victory.

Nimrod strode to the lip of the gate. He took his staff and struck the star gate's lip.

"Friends, come forth!" he shouted.

The staff's blow shook the ballroom. The air trembled over the portal.

The coffins wobbled. They teetered briefly on the lip of the star gate, and then fell into empty space. The coffins tumbled towards the planet below.

Spirits rushed from the eye of the eternal storm. One of the ghosts approached the portal and hovered before him.

"Who calls?"

"Nimrod, your friend, I wear the shell of one of our lord's subjects. Here, I am the Black Dwarf, and I command the forces, powers, and princes of this world.

"Come, who shall join me?"

Each vied to be chosen over the others. Cries of allegiance mingled with hard curses.

"Lord Nimrod," each called, "take me as your servant."

"Esar, join me now!"

The other spirits cursed as they extolled their talents. Calmly, he soothed them. "Patience, friends, I will return. Soon there will be bodies for all."

Turning to the Colonel, he repeated his incantation. "Goodbye Colonel Khan, now you shall take the unfortunate girl's place."

Light poured out of the man as his aura departed. The warlock allowed the light to disappear into the smoke still swirling around the unholy portal.

"Enter Esar," he ordered.

Esar's spirit swirled into the room. He appeared as the ghost of an ancient warrior with shield and sword. The spirit dove into the man's forehead, and disappeared into the vessel.

The man jerked and twisted on the impromptu altar, kicking, and twitching. The human stiffened.

Mumbling incantations, the Black Dwarf laid his staff directly on the Colonel's breast and infused his body with magical light.

The man's skin went sallow and shrank before fading into a pale blue. The flesh glowed briefly, and the eyes flitted. The body shook again, and the arms jittered.

"Open your eyes, Esar, and live again my friend."

Esar sat up under the command of the Black Dwarf.

"Careful Esar, the human is frail. The vessel can barely contain your strength. Too much power may rip the vessel."

"Master, why such a shell? Why not a great warrior?"

"Patience Esar, the one you inhabit has power. He

commands a host essential to the Dragon Lord's plans for this world. We shall find you a more suitable vessel when your task has been accomplished."

"As you command, my lord."

Helter handed Esar a robe to cover the man's uniform.

Surveying the altar, the warlock flicked his staff.

The whirlwind passed over them and smoke filled the star gate. The portal closed, and the gate hardened to glass. The glass cooled in rainbow colors as the fire of the other world faded, and the gate was shut. The carpet and the pentagram reappeared.

Nimrod lifted his hood. Taking his staff, he went to the service door. A tap of his staff sent the door flying, and he strutted out of the ballroom.

"Bring the body, and my tools." Mumbling another incantation, he sealed the area, erasing any records of their visit.

Relaxing in his airship, he poured a repast.

"It's been a long time since you enjoyed the fruit of the vine. Help yourself Esar." Esar mumbled his gratitude.

His servants quickly loaded the airship and climbed into the forward cab. Helter sat in the driver's seat. "We've finished, my lord," he said.

"Very well, Helter, it's about time. If you two get any slower I shall have to deal with your sloth."

"Yes, my lord." If he was worried, Helter failed to show any sign of concern.

With a final spell, Nimrod sealed the doors of the ballroom in their places. "To the Black Wharf."

"Yes, my lord," repeated Helter.

Quietly, the ship lifted off with the slightest shiver. Flying low, they left the alley and slipped into the night.

Babel Tower

Jack opened his eyes and stared at his living room ceiling. A gentle breeze off the patio fluttered his curtains. The first rays of dawn glistened on the southern peaks. He rubbed his temples. *Will I ever get another good night's sleep?*

His back ached, and he felt a crick in his neck. Rolling his neck he tried unsuccessfully to the pop the vertebrae. He debated whether to continue suffering on the sofa chasing an elusive rest or getting up and drowning exhaustion in coffee. The sunlight reflecting off his track lights made the decision for him.

Throwing his feet off the sofa, he rolled into an upright position. Grasping his face in his hands, he massaged some feeling back into his cheeks. When the blood reached his brain, he took a deep breath, stood up, and tightened the sash of his bath robe.

Shotgun slept on the love seat, his feet dangling over the coffee table.

Need to buy a longer set next time, instead of a sofa too short for an elf and a love seat too short for a dwarf.

Staggering, he made it to his coffee pot which helpfully offered him a mug of steaming brew. Taking the hot caffeine solution to his porch, he relished the view of Nodlon in the morning. He never tired of it. Thanks to the accidents of war and misery, the city was the most exciting place to be in New Atlantis. *Here the old ways mingle with the new.* The city could be as great as any in the ancient world. And save for a few, who refused to let reality check their hold on power, Nodlon would be a great place to live too.

Rummaging sounds in the kitchen floated out to the porch. He heard the sound of a mug on the counter.

Below Babel Tower, the old road was already jammed with frightened goblins headed east to the mountain kingdoms. Those who could were leaving. Humans were retreating the other way to Iron Mountain. Gnomes were headed north to their mines. *If they can, few still have a place to go*. And the city's faeries, nymphs, satyrs, would go northwest with the humans, elves, and dwarves.

Footfalls padded to the patio door, and Jasmine saddled up to him. "Morning honey bear, how did you sleep?"

"What sleep? The tender mercies of the Spanish Inquisition, and a rack would have been more comfortable."

"You're a good elf, Jack Clay," said Jasmine, squeezing him.

"How about yourself? Did you and Faith make it through the night?"

"After I read her Snow White, we had a pillow fight. We left the lights on. She spun around all night. First, she was next to me, then her head was jammed in my belly, then her feet were on top of me, and so it went all night."

"Did you get any sleep at all?"

"Never better, a good day's work is the best cure for insomnia. Faith forced me to change sides, but it was a great night."

"So it didn't cure you of children, too bad, I'd hoped to have you all to myself for a while."

"I want a dozen."

"Donuts or children? You're not a rabbit!"

"Six Jazz's and six Jack's," she ribbed him with her elbow, "you can afford it, Jack."

"Yeah, but when will I have the time to be a father?"

"You'll make time, Jack Clay. That's what men do. Anyway, I've got to get dressed, and get out of here. Have to be back to the hospital by seven."

"No breakfast?"

"You'll have to make do without me." She kissed him on the cheek and darted off to the bedroom, leaving him alone with his coffee.

"That's not what I meant." A lady bug crawled up his rail, and climbed his sleeve. "Run along little bug, I'm spoken for."

Hanging out on his porch, he heard the pitter patter of little feet and the small voice of a girl. Soon his condo buzzed with domestic sounds. Goldie and her daughters were fortunate, but their situation was not uncommon.

The people of Nodlon are good people. When the chips were down and given a chance, they'll make the right decision.

A little girl ran up to him and pulled on his robe. "Time for breakfast." Little older than a toddler, the dwarf baby was barely higher than his knees. The child ran off. In her pink nightie and bunny slippers, she was a pink ball bouncing on his fluffy carpet. Goldie lifted her up and sat her on his table in front of a plate of scrambled eggs and a blueberry muffin.

Goldie took his mug. "Just sit Mr. Clay, I'll get it."

Seating himself, joy and tragedy struggled within him. She brought him a mug of fresh coffee.

Shotgun's children sat at his dining room table. The babies were remarkably well behaved, and he wished he had a baby. He wondered if he would feel as melancholy if they were naughty.

Returning with more plates, Goldie set out a breakfast fit for a king. "Bon appetite, I hope you like it." A mountain of steaming eggs, smothered in mushrooms and cheese, a pile of bacon, and a bowl of blueberry muffins graced his table.

Clay stuffed a slice of bacon in his mouth. "Great, thanks Goldie."

"Thank you, Mr. Clay, you bought it." She brought out a pitcher of orange juice. "Shotgun and I cooked everything from scratch."

"Not quite," said Shotgun, pulling up a chair. "Those muffins came out of a mix."

"The muffins are delicious," said Jack. "I didn't know you could get these out of a mix."

"The secret is fresh blueberries," said Shotgun. "The season is too early for local berries. These came from the Argentine. Add fresh berries, and a dash of fresh vanilla, and viola."

Jack attacked the food.

"Thank you, Mr. Clay, for letting us stay."

"You're welcome Goldie," said Jack.

"I'm going to go to work with Ms. Jasmine, today," Goldie said and started picking up. "The day care is still open for the humans working at the Octagon."

Jack set his coffee down. "We'd better get going, Shotgun. We can drop off Goldie at the hospital, leave the girls at daycare, and be ready for whatever Gumshoe has in store for us before eight. If Jazz and Goldie drop off the girls, Jazz will be late."

"The girls and I can take the shuttle."

"No, Goldie," said Jack. "It'll take hours. The shuttles are jammed."

"Thank you, Mr. Clay," Goldie excused herself; "I'd better get the girls ready."

Shotgun whispered, "Thanks, boss."

"Sure, Shotgun, no problem.

Working quickly, Jazz and Goldie took off in her roadster. The boys loaded Faith and Hope into Jack's Andromeda. It was a tight squeeze, but the girls were small.

Jack steered the flyer over the crowded streets, and the little girls oohed, and ahhed at the sight. "Shotgun, I want to get Goldie out of her contract as soon as possible. You can't be a dad when an agency owns your kids."

"Boss, that's not necessary. I told you I can't pay you."

"Don't argue, Shotgun. What else is money for?"

In a few turns, they joined the rush hour traffic on Nodlon's level-ways. Jack no longer had to commute, but even he noticed the traffic headed out of the city was heavy, and light going downtown.

Puttin' on the Ritz

At the daycare, his logos drew many stares at the Andromeda. Jack and Shotgun each carried in a girl, and they were mobbed by children. Clay signed their drawings, and passed out cards. He laughed to himself, thinking of birthday clowns. They knew sleight of hand tricks, juggling, and fire eating, but his magic was real.

The manager accepted his offer of a magic show. He created icy polar bears and penguins, and illusions of ballerinas and clowns. He made toys fly, and he juggled all the balls in the room.

"Look ma, no hands." Squeals of delight, and laughter encouraged him.

He made a fat, orange cat appear from a bookcase stacked with toys. The cat purred, and played with the children. The cat tickled and licked the children with the help of his telekinetics. A mouse scurried across the floor, and the cat scampered after it. After each of the cat's hopeless attempts to catch the mouse, the toddlers giggled and laughed. For a minute, he forgot about the Zodiac and Mars.

Heavy metal riffs interrupted his show, and jarred him back to reality, "Clay here."

The Inspector appeared on the caster's tiny vid screen. "Are you busy, Jack?"

"Yes, I'm entertaining a room full of toddlers and kindergarteners."

"Oh, sorry to interrupt," Gumshoe winked, "are they paying customers?"

"No, Gumshoe, I'm doing a loss leader, nurturing future fans. They're not a tough crowd though, and I'm getting a lot of laughs. What's up?"

"A new development has cropped up, and I want you to see it."

"Sure, where are we going?"

"Do you know where the Ritz is?"

"Yeah, we're not far from there now."

"Can you join me there in a half hour?"

"No problem, see you there." He wrapped up his show, signed a few more drawings, and bid the children farewell.

They made it to the Ritz with time to spare.

The fancy hotel was a bustle of activity. Uniformed officers and crime scene technicians flowed in and out of the service entrance. Gumshoe's cruiser was parked in the alley. Clay squeezed his flyer between the cruiser and a mobile unit.

They climbed out of the flyer, and Shotgun cinched his satchel strap. "Looks like the place."

A police elf approached as they made their way to the loading dock.

"Gentlemen, I'm Macmillan," said the elf, "Inspector Lestrayed sent me to look for you. Please follow me." The elf led them to the loading dock, through the bay, and towards the service entrances.

"Gumshoe's getting more efficient," said Shotgun.

"He's an overworked and underpaid flatfoot," said Jack, "and he's aging too."

"The Inspector?" said the elf. "Oh, yeah, he's a straight shooter. Never hear a bad word about him."

"Agreed," said Shotgun. "He's a pretty decent guy for a human."

The officer opened the ballroom door, "Welcome to the Galaxy ballroom, gentlemen."

"Thanks," said Shotgun going in, "but they've cancelled all the dances."

~~~~~~~

A goblin in a custodian's overalls watched them from the end of the service hall. A feeling of déjà vu overwhelmed Clay, and then passed. He stopped and glanced at the goblin. The elderly custodian huddled against a door. He turned away, pretending to study the polish on the floor. Reaching around his police escort, Jack took hold of the door and waved the young officer inside. He watched the custodian out of the corner of his eye, and he waited until the old goblin peeked at him. He did not have to wait long. The goblin turned his head, and they made eye contact. Startled, as if caught with his hand in a cookie jar, the custodian straightened up, stuck out his chin, and summoned his dignity.

He wagged a finger at Jack. Barely audible, the custodian challenged him in a hoarse whisper, "Thee will not be a findin' what you search for." He trembled, "Thou art doomed!" Nervously looking around, the custodian fretted indecisively.

"Sir?" the police elf interrupted Clay. The officer looked to see what had captured Jack's attention. When he saw the police elf, the janitor frowned, darted into the stairwell, and let the door slam.

"Who is that?" asked Jack.

"Rimshot," answered the police elf. "He's the custodian. Claims he saw nothing, but it's plain he's scared to death. I don't think he likes elves either."

Clay walked into the ballroom. "Maybe he doesn't like elves," said Jack, "or maybe he's afraid of the police." If he wanted to know more, he would have to find the custodian later in a more garrulous mood.

~~~~~~~~

He saw why it was the Galaxy ballroom. The Milky Way circled the ballroom in a dazzling array of colorful stars. Blue bands connected the constellations of the zodiac, and gold outlined the signs.

A pentagram was burned into the Milky Way. Outside the pentagram was a series of small holes. A little farther away were two tables. The constellation of Capricorn writ large in blood splatter overlooked the ballroom.

Crime scene technicians poured over the walls and the carpets. The officer led Jack and Shotgun around the burn marks on the floor. Beyond the two tables, a tight group of policemen and technicians huddled around Gumshoe.

The Inspector finished his business with the others, and said, "Thank you, Mack, I'll take charge of our consultants." He dismissed their escort. The elf tipped his hat and returned to his business.

"No one saw or heard anything," said Gumshoe. "A custodian named Rimshot was on-duty last night. He opened the bay for us, but he's refused to talk."

"He's frightened to death. I saw him in the hall, and he told me we're doomed."

"Let's hope we're not doomed."

"They double-checked everyone who went missing for the last two weeks, and asked if anyone who knew the boys had seen the Labe kid. We've also completed a computer search to see if the McCarthy girl had any boyfriends, and the geeks found nothing. She had very few on-line friends, and the boys are all accounted for. The uniforms have followed up on all the recently missing dwarves without finding any clues. On a brighter note, we found one girl alive, who went missing last week. She and a friend had gone on an over-night hiking trip. She had a pass, but no one entered it into the computer."

"Whew, at least you found someone alive."

"Yeah, it's the only bright light in a terrible week. Two odd cases also came up. Felix Abrams, a human scientist, disappeared the day before yesterday, and an engineer with the Ministry named Khan went missing for a few hours last night. Khan's maid reported him missing, but he called back later. He said, he'd gone to work early this morning."

"Is it normal for this many people to go missing?" asked Jack.

"Normal?" Gumshoe asked. "No, but these aren't normal

times. Far more dwarves, elves, goblins, and molemen are missing than the usual number for the usual reasons. The city's in a turmoil and there are many loose ends. Most agencies are releasing on leave to let non-essential biots evacuate. It's making our job difficult, but it's good to know the agencies are doing the right thing."

"You're very open-minded," said Shotgun. "The agencies are just protecting their investment."

"To be sure, I'm open-minded, Shotgun," said Gumshoe, "but not out of any virtue. Experience has taught me when to be skeptical, and never force a clue to fit a pet theory. If a theory refuses to fit the evidence, reject it." The Inspector led them towards the entrance.

"Let me draw your attention to some less obvious details." Gumshoe pointed. "The door was blown off its hinges. You can see the marks on the far wall. This morning the locks and hinges were welded shut. The hotel staff had to break in, and found the room as you see it."

"Blowtorches can weld locks and hinges," said Jack.

"If they used a blowtorch, how would they get out?" asked Gumshoe. "No equipment was left here."

"Suppose when they were done, they opened the door, and all but one left. The one left behind welded the door shut after they left to delay their discovery."

"Good idea," said Gumshoe. "A gnome, a faerie, or a leprechaun might be an accomplice, and find some way to escape. It's a good idea, but toy biots small enough to slip through air ducts aren't known for strength of body or mind. Even if they had a faerie who could weld, they would have left the torch and tanks behind."

"Maybe there was more than one."

Gumshoe adjusted his fedora. "It's a theory, but I've never arrested a faerie for anything more terrible than running away from home."

"Yeah, sorry," said Jack, "reaching the bottom of the

barrel. If this is magic, it's beyond my skills."

"Could you weld the door from the other side?"

"No, I couldn't weld a hinge from the other side. I have to see the object I'm working on. I can send an illusion around a pillar. But when I send an illusion out of sight, the resolution fails and the illusion melts."

"That's what I expected, but can magic weld the door?"

"I can melt metal magically, but I'd have to work slowly and take my time to be precise."

"Can you teleport anything through a door?"

"No, I can't teleport anything. Telekinetic power can blow off a door, and replace it I suppose. I'm not sure if I have that much power though."

"Well, I don't suspect any toy biots, not yet anyway. I'm sure there's more than one, and I'll show you why in a second. What if they have multiple magicians?"

"More than one magician? One magician is too improbable to be plausible. Now what? Do you think magicians are a dime a dozen, old man?"

"No, but I try not to get cornered into one theory. Next, let's look at the carpet burns. I'm sure you've noticed the pentagram."

Gumshoe directed their attention to impressions on the carpet. "Heavy objects sat here. One person might have used a levitator, but most commercial models require two men to prevent banging the walls. Levitators overcome gravity, not momentum and inertia. And a robot would have left marks."

"It's looking more complicated as we go," said Jack.

"And it gets worse," said Gumshoe. He pointed to spots on one end of the table cloth. "Blood stains. I can't tell you any more than that now, but we'll have an analysis later today."

They circled the pentagram, and Gumshoe pointed. "See the device and the other markings, the carpet melted. No evidence of oxidation, no smoke residue, and no ash residue. We have taken samples, but I'm not expecting an explanation."

"What about a carpet iron?" Shotgun asked.

Jack wondered where his man-servant stored his eclectic compendium of knowledge.

"Forensics thought of that," said Gumshoe. "A carpet iron won't melt carpet without oxidation and residues. If an iron cut the circle, there should be burn marks."

"I can melt the carpet," said Jack. "That part's easy, I wouldn't rule out technology though. A laser perhaps or something we haven't thought of."

Gumshoe knelt beside one of the holes circling the outer ring. "Seven holes surround the pentagram. They go straight through the carpet and the floor. No drill marks, and no other obvious means of cutting the holes. No cuttings are under the holes either. The techs have already checked the basement."

"Interesting," said Jack. "I have no idea how to make such a hole using magic. I can create illusions, fire, telekinetic force, and manipulate water. But I've never tried destroying matter."

"Why not?" asked Gumshoe. "If you can destroy matter, you might have a solution for our trash."

"Very funny, but remember some of my early experiments?"

"Who can forget Jack?" Gumshoe grinned, "You pulled quite a few pranks, but you were never a troublemaker."

"In physics' class at Tollmerak, I read about the destruction of matter, and it dawned on me that if I could destroy matter, it might result in an atomic explosion. Still, I don't think I can destroy matter. I can't create it, and these things always seem to have a balance."

"What's the balance for your other magic?" asked Gumshoe.

"That's hard to explain. I can fill the Circus with illusions, and I can use telekinetics to fly. I can make a surf board out of the water in the air. And I can levitate several dancers without any trouble at all. But if I push it farther, I begin making mistakes, and I tire quickly. If I do too much, I forget what I'm doing, and the spells fade rapidly. Simple spells may endure for a few minutes depending on how many I cast. Complex spells, such as my animals, dissolve in seconds if I lose my concentration."

"It's a mixed bag then," said Gumshoe. "What do you make of the pentagram?"

"I've done some homework since we last spoke," said Jack. "The pentagram is your basic demonic symbol. Attempts to change its meaning or explain it away over the years have failed. It's been a mark of the devil through so many centuries it really has no other known meaning now. The differences that do exist are trivial. Some say it's a symbol only, others claim the mark has powers analogous to magical words or runes.

"In the very oldest stories, there were those who believed the original language of their god or gods had power over matter and nature. Later, there were many who thought symbols held magical powers, and still later the myth developed that mathematics might have magical powers. As far as I know the symbol has no magical ability

"Still, it's a malevolent sign," said Jack. "Usually, their rituals honor one manifestation of the devil or his servants. Not that I am saying someone was murdered or harmed here, I can't be sure of that. And I can't see what they would use the pentagram for. Still, whatever they thought they were doing, it's unlikely they were up to any good."

"And the Zodiac?" added Gumshoe.

"Our Zodiac and its myths mostly come from Greeks, who were less savvy as astronomers, and somewhat less blood thirsty than other sky worshippers. The winter solstice last occurred in Capricorn over twenty four centuries ago, and I've used that as a guide to the thinking of our perpetrator." He cocked his head at the constellation of Capricorn on the wall, "Capricorn is important to him for some reason. And I see the tables are aligned to match the cusp of Capricorn.

"Pagans worshiped many gods; many of whom demanded human sacrifices on solstices or equinoxes. Sacrifices may have been given at the solstice in honor of the sun, the moon, the classical planets, or various stars or whole constellations. After all the wars, the references are thin, and it's hard to separate history from fiction.

"Assyrians, Babylonians, Egyptians, Phoenicians, and Persians practiced human sacrifice. Often they sacrificed their first born children, but they also sacrificed prisoners of war and slaves. Many other nations practiced human sacrifice, but I'm picking on the great ones with astronomers. That's the ancient history, not the astrology. There was no specialization, and astronomers practiced astrology. The stars were named for the gods, or the gods named the stars, or the gods came from the stars, or the gods went to stars when they retired. A few sources suggest the stars were gods. About the only consistency is inconsistency."

"Modern myths or ancient legends, what's the difference?" asked Gumshoe. "It's all gibberish. Who cares?"

"To us, perhaps there's no difference, but our killer is fascinated with the sign of the Capricorn. If we can identify which flavor of myths he believes in, it might help us predict his next move."

"I'm betting this is a modern cult leader who knows no more than I do, or a gang working for Mars. Either way, I don't think astrology will improve our fortunes, or divine our futures. And I don't think ancient myths will be much help."

"Maybe not," said Jack, "but I am your consultant. Let me give you what I know."

"Jack, just let me have the executive summary."

"Our ancestors understood the myths differently than we see them. Aesop's fable of the fox and the sour grapes teaches a moral truism. No one believes there was a fox who wanted grapes. The tale cautions the reader against self-deceit, and encourages personal virtue, among other lessons.

"Far be it from me to know all the variations of astrology. Nodlon's astrologers practice divination based on the Chinese reform movement as re-interpreted by Seer Genesis after the second Regressive War. But it always seems the same to unbelievers. Sagittarians are experiencing dramatic beginnings or endings this year. Capricorns are confused, and they need to stand up for their principles. All our horoscopes today gush with positive spins, and meaningless mumbo jumbo.

"So far so good, certainly most of these beliefs are harmless, or mostly harmless. But ancient versions were not so benign. Many believed a god or a prophet would be reborn on the cusp of Capricorn. He would return with god-like powers to reshape the future and fulfill their prophecies. I'm not giving any credence to any ancient, extremist astrology, but maybe the perpetrator believes in it. I'm guessing he's trying to summon a god, or a prophet."

"Wacko land," Gumshoe scoffed. "So who is he trying to summon?"

"Who knows? There's dozens, hundreds. And not all of the myths agree. One observation narrows the field though. Since we have a murderer on our hands, we are dealing with one of the violent, death-oriented gods. We can exclude the peaceful types."

"That narrows it, for sure," Gumshoe said, and Shotgun snorted. "Someone into extreme astrology is trying to resurrect an ancient god or a prophet?" Gumshoe absentmindedly rubbed his chin. "So I'm looking for a malevolent astrologer with magic powers who leads a cult of rebellious dwarves?"

"Sorry Inspector," said Jack. "I told you I cannot guarantee results. If I had to bet, I'd suspect it's a scam by someone working for Mars."

"Jack," said Gumshoe, "I'm not disappointed at all, and I expected a lot less than you gave me. You've been an invaluable help, and you've saved any number of soma dealers from a night in the drunk-tank. Now, I'm certain the Capricorn is important, very important. We just need to figure out what it means. That narrows the possibilities, and I can rule out the usual suspects. Usually, about this time, I'd round up the usual suspects in desperation, and hope some low-life would rat out the perpetrator."

"Don't forget, it may be the constellation or the astrological sign or both."

"Both? How can it be both?"

"Well, I don't want to be rude, but there are those who think we were visited by extraterrestrials. Perhaps our villain thinks he's summoning an alien from outer space."

"Oh, brother, Jack, extreme astrology meets counterfactual archeology? Not only do I have to track down every astrologer in Nodlon and ask if they have a client with an unhealthy interest in Capricorn, you want me to check out all the ufology clubs? Why not just check with all the science fiction-fantasy clubs, the historical re-enactors, the steam-punks, the millennialists, and the kids into swords and sorcery."

"Don't forget the astronomy clubs, the vid gamers, and the dungeons and dragons crowd."

Gumshoe rolled his eyes, and Shotgun guffawed. "Boss, do you suspect everyone?"

"No, I'm just thinking of my fan base. These creeps have abducted dozens of innocent dwarves, someone must have heard something."

"Where would you start, Jack?"

"Start with the reputable divination providers in Deep Nodlon. Ask if they've heard of a cult, or if any of their clients disappeared. They mostly help the lonely, lost, and confused. Maybe they've heard something from a client."

"Reputable divination provider? That's a new one, Jack. I'd rather have a description of the perp, it would help."

"Yeah, I know. But I've spent too much time with them trying to explain the mystery of magic. Whatever the ancients believed, the new practitioners are not the kind of people who tolerate murder. I doubt the reputable divination providers have any truck with sociopathic clients. Crazies tend not to pay, and you never know when they'll go berserk. If we treat them with respect, we may learn something."

"Jack, not to belabor the obvious, but I am the master of discretion."

Rimshot

Clay stepped aside to let the lab technicians run another spectroscope over the carpet. "Perhaps I can help convince the custodian to talk."

"Go for it, Jack," said Gumshoe. "If you can convince the old coot to talk, I'll owe you one."

"Shotgun," said Jack, "go to the bar, and pick up a bottle of their best white lightning."

"Aye, boss."

"Let me have your ticket," said Gumshoe, "and I'll put the devil's water on the Crown's tab."

"If I get results," said Jack, "the Crown can pick up lunch."

Peeling away from Gumshoe, Clay headed for the service hall. As he departed, technicians flocked to Gumshoe. Outside the ballroom, he saw Macmillan guarding the scene.

Rimshot had disappeared into the stairwell. Jack followed him that way, and considered his choices. A custodian was more likely to have an office in a basement than a penthouse. He went down.

The first basement door featured a sign marked day spa, gymnasium and a pool. Continuing downward, he found another door marked with a short list of offices, including one labeled "Custodian."

Where else would you look for a custodian?

Through the door and down a hall, a sign directed him down another hall to a small, dank room with a gray door, which stood open. Peeking into the room, he caught a reflection of the goblin, leaning back in a rickety chair. His feet were propped up on a tiny desk.

He fingered his caster, and sent his location to Shotgun.

He approached the custodian's gray door, leaned against the jamb and blocked the exit.

"Top of the morning, Rimshot," he said.

The goblin stared with a long face, and he gave Jack an uneasy glance. One eye lolled lazily around its socket. His other eye narrowed, and his expression hardened. Jack said nothing for a moment and tried to convey a sense of harmless congeniality.

Grease stains covered the goblin's overalls. On close examination, the small office was jammed with cleaning supplies and tools. A metal cupboard displayed detergents, carpet soap, polishes, stain removers, and a bucket full of sponges. A buffing machine guarded the cupboard, and a rack of rings held an assortment of brooms, mops, and a crowbar. Opposite the brooms was a tiny work bench buried in wrenches, and screwdrivers. A broken fan teetered precariously on the edge of the bench.

Slowly, Rimshot took in Jack's immaculate coif, cloak, tunic, vest, breeches and suede boots.

Rimshot drooped, and his jowls sank. "Are you with the police?"

"No, or not exactly anyway, the Inspector in charge of the Zodiac case is a friend of mine. He asked me to consult on matters of magic and the occult. We are trying to find the villain who murdered Anna McCarthy. She's the dwarf we found floating in Blueberry Lake. We want to catch him before another missing dwarf meets with foul play."

The goblin's frown faded and he studied the clutter on his desk. "A nasty business, t'would be a shame not to find the killer."

"The killer? How do you know? Rimshot, do you know something that might help?"

"I ain't got nothin' to say to the police."

"What about me? Unofficially, of course, an anonymous source who wants to make a statement off the record."

Mixed emotions flitted across the goblin's face. Bitterness turned to anger, mingled with regret, touched with fear, and softened to grim determination.

"Rimshot's what's they call me 'round here, Guv'nor." He took his feet off the desk, and wiped his hands on his overalls.

"I'm Jack Clay, here's my card."

"Keep your card, Guv'nor, I knows who you are. Got friends at the Circus, they all speak highly of you."

"Tell me what you know, Rimshot. A reward might be in it, if you like."

"Ain't no native son," he said, "I'm an invisible man. I goes unseen even when they sees me with their livin' eyeballs!"

"Off the record then; no police, no statements, and nothing to sign. Please help us Rimshot before another dwarf dies."

"All right Guv'nor, I'll tell you. Not for any reward, Guv'nor. Rimshot don't need no reward to do what's right. For that Blueberry girl, I'll tell yah – cause it's right. Just so as it's off the record." The goblin slumped in his chair.

"On my honor, Rimshot, my lips are sealed."

Rimshot grinned. "Lucky for you, Mr. Clay, your honor's ain't none likes a celebrity's. I knows the honor of celebrities, and they pays me to clean it up." He leaned over and spat into his spittoon.

"Touché. Too true, Rimshot, many actors and actresses misbehave."

"Ain't impugnin,'" he drawled, "The honor of no talented folk. Just stating the truth about the highs and mighties who comes in here with rented furniture and free tokes, and leaves their mess for Rimshot's to clean up."

"Point taken," Clay soothed, hoping to assuage the goblin.

The goblin squared his overalls, and leaned against his work bench, "Pardon Guv'nor, but my hands ain't clean." He looked down at the concrete floor, and his lazy eye lolled up to look at Jack.

"A jezebel called to arrange an exhibition. Good business,

you see. We's always hostin' con's and zibbit's. I imagine your Inspector has all her papers." He swayed back and forth, and shoved his free hand into his pocket.

"She shows the day before. And she's a looker. She says to me to stays in my quarters and mind's my business." Craning his neck towards Clay, he hissed conspiratorially. "'If you's knows what's good for you she says. Says it's a student group, puttin' on a play. So I's says to myself, forgets all 'bout it. Cockamamie story, but ain't unusual, don't cha know. What's people do's is thar' business, not Rimshot's." Relaxing, he leaned back, and pushed himself up using the bench.

"Then, it gets strange." His eyes widened, and he pulled his hand from his pocket and cut the air palm down. His lazy eye followed his hand as he twisted to encompass the room. "She called me directs, on my desk caster." He cocked his head towards the caster, atop a stack of invoices, "and she tells me to open the bay for the exhibiter in the wee hours." His head rolled to one side, and he brought his lazy eye around to look at Jack. "Most unusual, but the customer's always right, I says." Then he hunkered down, glaring at the magician.

"Go on, please, Rimshot, to save this girl, we need to know. If we can't save her, we need to stop this guy."

"Ain't no guy, you ain't gonna believes Rimshot's story, but I's sayin' he's dangerous, he's workin' for the devil."

"Chin up, old man, it's off the record, no one will know."

"And none had better, Guv'nor, the police ain't got a cop on every corner, and even as they did, they'd not be able to stop him. Believe or not, I say, he's unnatural." Nodding the goblin seemed appeased, but held his tongue.

"Rimshot," he coaxed, "I'll not tell a living soul where I got this story from. Remember, she was only nineteen."

"Aye, Guv'nor," tears welled in his eyes. "I got a call signal on my board from the loading dock. They arrived in an airship, a hearse by the look of it. Two got out o' the airship; one skinny dwarf, and one fat dwarf. They're all dressed in black caps and boots, and devices here." He patted his heart. "The fat one spotted me at the door, and he tells me to get the bay open. Never gave me a chance to 'splain, ain't safe to leave the bay open at night. I offered help, and he shoos ol' Rimshot away.

"Call it intuition; or call it a premonition. They strikes me as devils. Mind ye, it's not about the dwarves, it's about their doin's. I backs away into the shadows wonderin' what's they're up to." Craning he looked over Jack's shoulder into the hall, and glanced about the room, cowering for a moment before recovering his courage.

"They pulled a load out of the airship," the goblin's eyes widened. "It's on levitators, and it's heavy, very heavy. They grunts, and fights with it gettin' it movin' and stoppin' and turnin' it. They get it in the bay, and I sees it's a coffin just likes you see in on the vid. I got a good look at 'em in the bay. They were black dwarves. The goblin whimpered. After they gets one offloaded, then they gets another. Then they unload a pallet of odd shaped boxes, and a bundle of spears."

"Spears?"

"Yeah, spears with funny heads. They unloaded everythin' into the Galaxy ballroom, and then one of 'em goes up to the airship, and opens a door, and says, 'my lord.' And out comes a dwarf dressed as a sorcerer, I tells you. Aye, he had on a sorcerer's robe with a hood. Black with silver flames, and stars and designs all over it was. And he's got a carved staff. Its shaft shimmered and had a pewter foot. No taller than a dwarf."

"Did you see his face?"

"Aye, guv'nor, he's a black dwarf. I saw his microchip plain as the nose on your face." The goblin stared, his eyes bulged. "And that's not all guv'nor, when he spoke, it was like he was calling from the other side, if you know what I mean."

"I'm not sure, Rimshot, what do you mean?"

"Aye, I'm not sure others can hear it, but I heard it. Like if I spoke to you through a can tied to a piece o' string. Strange, just hearin' it in my head sends chills down me.

"So, they goes into the Galaxy room, and close the door, and I hear a sizzling sound. I can smell somethin' burnin' like it ain't supposed to. I knew I should tell Dennis, the manager o' the hotel," he said, squirming. "But I had a premonition and I got cold feet. None of us would o' lived out the night if I'd said anything.'" Anguish twisted his face, and he rubbed his hair as if he was sorry for something he had not done.

"Rimshot, you did the right thing. I've got the same impression myself. I've seen the mess in the ballroom, and I believe you. It would have been foolish to try interrupting him yourself, and no one would have believed you last night. The black dwarf warlock may not have been magical, but he was most certainly dangerous."

Fortified, the goblin's chin rose, and he leaned back in his creaky chair. "I pressed my ear to the door and listened. The door was hot, and I heard chantin' and strange music comin' from the room. Melancholy it was, like them ol' horror movies. I heard whisperin' but no words. There was chains rattling, clanking, and clicking, and then an animal growling. Then everything went quiet." Pausing melodramatically, the goblin spread his legs and cut the air with both hands. "Dead silent it was," he continued. "No sounds at all came from the ballroom. And that's when I hightailed it outta thar' bless me, all elbows, and attitudes!"

"You said before we're doomed. Whose doom? Mine or the missing dwarves?" Footfalls behind Clay told him they were no longer alone. Glancing over his shoulder he saw Shotgun holding a colorful gift bag with bright yellow tissue surrounding the tip of a bottle.

Rimshot straightened up. "Premonition, you ain't gonna believe it. I dreamed last night. A great volcano exploded and fire and ash flew over Nodlon, and everythin' burned." He craned forward staring at Jack with his good eye, and his lazy eye lolled again, encircled the room and came to rest looking at him.

"Aye, Jack Clay, you were in my dream too. The volcano fell on top of you."

A tingle ran up Jack's back, and he frowned at Rimshot's words. He held his tongue waiting for more.

"And I saw you and your sidekick in my dream." Rimshot grinned with a touch of triumph.

Strutting around his desk, the goblin plopped down into his little office chair with a squeaky bounce. With drama, he put his dirty boots on the desk. He leaned back, and propped himself up. His chair wheezed, and its wheels moaned.

"And that's all I have to tell you."

"I think you've helped us, Rimshot, if you'll allow me, I'd like to give you a gift."

"You owe me nothin' Mr. Clay. Rimshot's glad to get it off his chest."

"Doing the right thing is its own reward. All too often it goes unrecognized."

"Nothin' against acceptin' a gift, I 'spose."

Shotgun handed the gift bag to Jack.

Clay laid the gift and a card on Rimshot's cluttered desk, and gave him a wink, "Call me if you remember anything else, Rimshot, off the record."

"Right kind of ye, Guv'nor," Rimshot thanked him, "right kind of ye, Mr. Clay."

~~~~~~

Making their way back to the ballroom, they took a lift.

"He's colorful, that I'll say for him."

"Just a goblin trying to earn an honest living, Shotgun."

"Yeah, when Lang makes his documentary, I'm sure he'll talk."

The chaos in the ballroom had settled into a quiet order. They cornered the Inspector when he was alone.

"Any luck?" Gumshoe asked.

"Yes," answered Clay. "He may be a sot, and sublimely confused, but he's honest and decent, he squeaks with sincerity."

"The custodian wants to remain anonymous," added Clay. "He's afraid the police cannot protect him."

"I'd never admit it in public," Gumshoe said, "but he's right. I'll enter it as an anonymous tip from an informer. Of course, if we run the fiends down, we'll have to ask him to come forward and make a statement, and the Crown's prosecutor will want him to testify."

"If we get that far," said Jack, "we can lean on his conscience. He wants to do the right thing, he's just scared, and I don't blame him."

He quickly summarized Rimshot's story.

Gumshoe hooked a thumb over his lightning pistol. "I wanted a description, and thanks to you, we have a fighting chance of saving some lives. Now we know we're after a black dwarf. And we know we're dealing with a team. So the Black Dwarf fancies himself a warlock. And he believes in extreme astrology, and he believes he can use magic to recall an archaic god. Is that about right?"

"Yeah, I think so. Not sure if that helps, though."

"The airship has to be registered," said Gumshoe. "And the coffins were sold, imported, or stolen in Nodlon recently. What do you make of those spears?"

"Maybe those were poles set around the pentagram in the holes," said Shotgun. "Maybe they were flagpoles for pennants or signs."

"The bay was dim," said Jack, "and I'm not sure Rimshot had a good view. Remember the oil. He probably saw torches they brought to use in their ritual."

"Good idea, Jack," said Gumshoe. "Still we're looking for three dwarves who wear black and drive a hearse. We're whittling it down – good work gentleman."

"What's our next move?" Jack asked.

"Jezebel Steele rented the ballroom and insured it," said

Gumshoe. "She's the principal of Nodlon Entertainment Logistics. Logistics appears to be a legit outfit. She organizes conventions and trade shows. She's been around six years, and she's never been in trouble, and she has no record in Nodlon."

"What about her statements to the custodian," asked Jack. "Don't those seem suspicious?"

"Maybe," said Gumshoe. "Until we know her side of the story, we have no idea if she's part of the gang or if they gave her a cockamamie story and she swallowed it. The customer's always right."

"That's what Rimshot said."

"It's a proverb," said Gumshoe, "or something like that. Probably read it on a fortune cookie. I have to finish up here, and give the management the bad news. We're probably going to have the room off-limits for weeks. The crime scene unit has finished the prelim, but they'll need a week to complete the follow-up. And we cannot let the modus operandi leak to the press, if we can help it. I don't want any copy cats muddying the waters."

"What's next?" Jack asked.

"Next," said Gumshoe, "we'll check out Jezebel Steele, if you can wait."

"Can we do lunch first?" asked Shotgun.

"Hang on," said Gumshoe. "We'll eat on the way over there. The Crown's buying."

Jezebel Steele

The airship slowed to a crawl, and guided its sleek black form into the parking garage. His gangly servant retrieved his staff from its compartment. The gangly dwarf opened his door, held his staff, and waited for him to emerge.

"Your staff, my lord."

He admired himself in his airship's shiny finish. He saw a warlock with a fine coif and a perfect manicure. Runes of power and designs of magic covered his robes, defended his person, and amplified his abilities. His staff hummed, tapping the spiritual energy, and sucking manna across the differential between the living world and his own.

Taking his staff, he headed for a lift, conceding the necessity of mundane transportation. His servants followed, and their boots pounded the pavement. Snapping his fingers, he and his servants became invisible to all but those whom he wished to see. Alone they entered the lift, and he engaged the fire department override, and they rose directly to the top floor without stopping.

The dusty portraits of the businessmen of old gazed down upon them as they stepped off the lift. He ignored the bystanders. Those pushed aside by the three dwarves were stunned momentarily, grappling with the unexpected shove. And after a split second daze, the bystanders continued on their way, once again oblivious.

Reaching the door of Nodlon Entertainment Logistics, he ordered his minions to guard the entrance from an unwanted intrusion. "Wait here, and if anyone tries to enter, snap your fingers and send them on their way." Holding out his hand, the door opened, and it swung aside. He crossed the foyer without salutation or announcement, and repeated the gesture. The inner door unlocked, parted from the jamb, and swung wide.

In the back office was a middle aged woman sitting behind a small executive desk. Reserves of charm and a stately beauty had not abandoned her, though the strain of business worried her eyes. She straightened her attire, an avant-garde jacket cut with a feminine lapel and a short skirt in an inexplicable color which clashed against tasteless heels.

"Why, excuse me, sir, but I'm closed. I thought I locked that door."

He noticed a vase full of red carnations with Baby's Breath, and laughed.

"Poor and hungry comes a good and thrifty boy, proud and haughty she will not be his toy, he took a boat and sailed away, saying he would come another day, making her the spinster who would not kiss a boy."

"And who are you sir? Normally my clients make an appointment."

"Who I am is irrelevant. As for my business, that will become apparent all too soon to suite your taste."

Snapping his fingers, he sealed the office in a veil of silence. He lifted his staff, and thrust it up into the air and twirled it around three times. Holding it horizontally over his head, he chanted the incantations.

Alarmed, Steele retreated to the corner of her office. "Why have you barged into my office? This is most unusual."

Only when the dwarf began chanting in a sing song she did not understand did her senses return. She snatched her caster from her desk, and frantically tried to place a call. She punched on the little screen to no avail. The device refused to wake up. Desperately, she dropped the caster, and tried to call on her desk caster. Furiously, she stabbed the screen, but it remained blank, reflecting only the dwarf holding his staff.

She lifted the handset from its cradle and listened for a tone, and heard nothing.

"Get out of my office!" she yelled.

Under her, the desk vibrated, and she flinched at the unexpected sensation. Her alarm turned to fear and she snatched up a letter opener. Above her, she heard a metallic tear and the roar of a turbine. Fear turned to panic, and she jumped back into the corner, jarring her filing cabinet, and toppling her Indian dolls. The dolls fell upon her bookcase, already wobbling from the blow of the cabinet, launching a row of romance novels after the onyx bookends. The romances cascaded off her bookcase, and a gothic thriller of a vampire's love for a baker's daughter bumped the carnations sent by an unrequited suitor. Twirling off the end table the carnations fell and the vase smashed.

She threw her hands up to her ears to dampen the roar. Looking up to see what made the ear-splitting noise, a growing hole in the ceiling riveted her gaze.

The maw expanded until a red planet appeared. On the planet a hurricane swirled, its eye on the cusp of dawn. A tornado spiraled out of the eye, and slammed into the maw. Papers whirled in the breeze as the tornado caught a foot hold on the ceiling's portal. For a moment she feared she would be vacuumed into space.

The tornado beat her desk, and flung her chairs and cabinets against the walls. The twirling mass of air slowed and thinned, and the roar subsided. A shape emerged from the tornado.

An impossible creature with claws, scales, and fangs stepped out of the whirlwind. Baring its fangs, the monster growled, wiggled its claws, and drowned the tornado's din. Paralyzed with fear, she tried to scream.

An Unnatural End

"Back to work, gentlemen." Gumshoe guided the cruiser into a garage.

"Thanks for lunch," said Shotgun, climbing out of the cruiser.

"You're welcome, always enjoy the Café des Moulin. Keep your eye on Louis, though, he's as Old Atlantis as my shoes."

"Where are we going?"

"Nodlon Entertainment Logistics," Gumshoe said. He stopped in front of a directory hanging next to the lift. The directory listed accountants, real estate agents, and a dentist or two. "It's on the top floor." They joined a dapper gentleman, and a dwarf maiden in the lift.

Clay dodged a secretary on her way to a late lunch and fell in step with the Inspector. Shotgun brought up the rear with his satchel.

Gumshoe eyed the mahogany wainscoting, wallpaper, and portraits of businessmen long past. "High rent district," he muttered.

The transom windows above each door were open. A few of the doors were propped open, inviting clientele and prospects to enter. Their footfalls echoed on the hard tile floor as they searched for Steele's office. A short walk brought them to the end of the hall, and a window overlooking the alley below. They were high enough to see the blue lamps in the alley's artificial cloud lights. A pane of clear glass graced the door of Steele's office. Her door sported a suite number, a mail opening, and a sign inviting them to enter. Next to the door was a translucent window boasting the name of her business. Gumshoe opened the door and stepped into the little waiting room.

"Madam Steele," called Gumshoe. Two armless chairs with leather seats sat under the window, next to a matching divan. A walnut partition wall separated the foyer from the rest of the office. The wall ended a few feet from the high ceiling and was interrupted by a single door and a glazed reception window.

Gumshoe walked up to the reception window, and tapped on the glass. He noticed dark red spots on the glass. "Madam Steele?" He tapped on the glass again, and called, "Madam?" Looking back at Jack and Shotgun, Shotgun shrugged.

"Maybe she's still at lunch," suggested Clay.

"Why would she leave her door open then?"

Everything in the little foyer was in order. Taking his glasses out of his coat pocket, he mounted them on his nose. He blinked and looked again at the spots on the reception window. One small purple spot marred the divan. He looked up and saw another spot near the top of the partition. Backing away from the partition, he saw a few more spots on the wall. Straining to see over the partition wall, Gumshoe turned to the tall elf.

"Look at the ceiling, Jack, what do you see?"

"Scarlet spots," said Jack. "Odd, like the decorator was flinging the paint."

"I wish you hadn't said that," said Gumshoe. "Stand in the hall gentlemen, and stop anyone who tries to enter. And, don't let anyone leave either." Gumshoe turned the knob, but it was locked.

"What's wrong Inspector?" asked Shotgun.

Clay tugged gently on the coat sleeve of Shotgun's tuxedo. "Let's step outside."

Gumshoe backed up to Steele's threshold, and he charged the inner office. He gave the door a savage kick below the lock. The top of the frame snapped, and the reception window cracked. The door jamb split and the door swung open violently. The strike plate whistled, flipping end over end. It hit the wall with a clunk, and disappeared behind the copier.

The door rebounded, and he blocked it narrowly saving his face from a collision. He winced as his wingtip smacked the tile floor. He slipped on a pool of blood, and the partition rattled as he struck it. He caught himself on the jamb. Letting go of the partition, it grunted at him and still tilted inward. Its footing was sheared from the bolts. His elbow ached and a pain shot up his left arm.

He cursed his age as he fought to steady himself

Rays of blood splatter radiated from what was left of Jezebel Steele. Ribbons of a sliced business suit floated in a pool of her blood. Blood splatter sprayed up the wall to the ceiling, and from her desk to her copier. Trails of blood ran down the walls, and rivulets spread across the floor. Slashes covered her face and what recognizable parts remained. Her arms were open to the bone, and there was little else holding her together.

Her desk had flipped on its face. Gashes stripped the desktop veneer, and deep claw marks ran down the walls. Her chair had rolled aside. The desk held up the partition wall.

The attacker had strewn her computer, appointment books and paperwork about the office. Carnations withered near a shattered vase. An overturned wicker basket contributed brochures to the mess.

Posters of the Circus featuring Cretaceous Clay and the Rockhounds flanked a collage of trade show programs. The posters dangled from the wall, slit apart. On her copier was a bumper sticker reading "Biots are people too." Blood spatter covered the copier.

Gumshoe backed away. Her fate was out of his hands, and the only solace he could offer was finding her killer.

"Sorry gentlemen, we're going to be here awhile." He opened his caster and began making the necessary arrangements. "Gutted like a fish, she was." Betraying the stress, he rubbed his chin, and straightened his fedora.

"Is there a sign?" Jack asked.

"A Capricorn?" Gumshoe asked. "No, not that I can see, but I need a spatter analysis to be sure. The blood splatter is on everything, floor to ceiling."

"Maybe this isn't a Zodiac murder," said Shotgun. "It's

an incredible coincidence, but there's no sign."

"Guarantee it's connected, Shotgun. My gut says it is, and besides there are no coincidences."

"Why would he not leave a sign, then?" asked Jack. "That's the modus operandi."

"No idea, Jack. Maybe it's to throw us off, or it's just whimsy. It looks like a wild animal tore the poor woman apart in broad daylight, and got away with it. No, I think this is the work of the Black Dwarf."

"What about Noddie attacks?" asked Shotgun. "Haven't there been people ripped apart by a giant reptile in the sewers and the mines under Nodlon?"

"No," Gumshoe disagreed. "Alligators and crocodiles cause most of the reptile attacks in Nodlon. Once in a while, a croc escapes from the zoo, or is released by some ne'er do well, and we have a rash of attacks. Gators and snakes live in the sewers, but they usually keep to themselves."

"If Noddie is real and she eats anyone, she's not leaving anything behind," said Jack. "The few reports we have of Noddie are mostly from sanitation workers who report seeing a large serpentine shape. I might suspect an Anaconda or other large snake, but those who see Noddie always say she's running away. If she's real, she may be a vegetarian. None of the eyewitnesses report aggression."

"Officially, the Yard believes Noddie is a figment of the overactive imaginations of tired sanitation workers. She's always spotted in the wee hours, and always in shadow or silhouette. Unofficially, there's a rumor she may be a synthetic monster created by the ancients for one of their amusement parks. After centuries of confinement, she's hiding to avoid capture. Just a hunch of mine of course, but I think she's real. You didn't hear that from me though."

"Mum's the word, Inspector," said Shotgun, and he zipped his lip.

"Gentlemen, please watch the lift and the stairs, and don't

let anyone leave. I'd better earn my keep." Gumshoe began questioning everyone working on the floor. When the first uniformed officers arrived, he had interviewed only a few witnesses.

"It's going to be a long day," said Shotgun.

The crime scene technicians entered the office first with robots, boxes of sample vials, spectrophotometers, chemicals, cameras, and instruments Clay hardly recognized.

He overheard an officer mumble, "What a waste."

"Show a little respect for the dead," said another. Nodding his agreement, the officer turned away.

After an hour or so, Gumshoe returned from his interviews. Huddling with the technicians and the uniforms, he collected their reports. Updating his own notes, he muttered, "Bad business," more than once. Eventually, the crime scene technicians completed the tedious task of cataloguing and itemizing every detail. Gumshoe dismissed all but a couple of uniformed officers to guard the scene.

"We develop a sense of macabre humor in this job," said Gumshoe. "Helps to insulate your emotions."

"Understandable Gumshoe," said Jack, "carry on as if we weren't here."

"Steele never left for lunch. No one saw or heard anything, nor was anyone seen entering or leaving on the security vid in the hall, the front door, or the lift."

"No one saw anything?" asked Jack.

"A fresh murder is committed in broad daylight and no one saw a thing. She has a part-time receptionist who doesn't work today. Her bookkeep is a dwarf who only comes on alternate Wednesdays. A real estate agent down the hall claims to be a friend, but she didn't see her at all today due to a closing this morning which ran over. Steele underwent retro-gene therapy about ten years ago. Quite a looker she was."

"No one heard anything?" Jack asked.

"No, and the security robot produced all the tapes this

morning. Every dwarf who entered or left the building is a known employee or client. Baffles the heck out of me; it's as if they were invisible."

"Maybe they were," said Jack, "if they had magic."

"Can you become invisible?"

"No, but I might be able to come up with an illusion that would fool at least one camera at a time." He hoped the inspector was not serious. "Gumshoe, I hope you're not accusing me?"

"Relax Jack, we know where you and Shotgun were at the time of the murder, and you've already got an alibi and the most impeccable of witnesses."

"Oh?"

"You were at the Café des Moulin, with Police Inspector Lestrayed of Nodlon homicide when Jezebel Steele died. Good thing too. Fortunately, eating at an open café under a security camera at the time of the murder sort of clears all of us of the crime. Good thing all three of us have an alibi, otherwise you'd be the prime suspect and Shotgun and I would be your accomplices."

"Magic may be involved," Clay agreed, "but only a powerful magician who knows how to use magic could pull off the illusion of invisibility, summon the telekinetic energy to murder the victim, suppress the noise, and wipe the security records. Everything I know is by accident."

"The Black Dwarf brazenly murdered Steele in a busy office building at lunch time, and no one saw him?" Gumshoe frowned. "If we had been here, I wonder if we would have survived the encounter."

"He must have some technology we don't understand," said Jack. "I'm telling you, there's no one else in this Solar System with magic." Regaining his composure, Jack thought about the office. "Is there any other way in or out of this office besides the hall?"

"There's the air ducts, but they're only a few inches

across," said Gumshoe. "We've thought of that. No micro-bots small enough to make the corners in the walls could have cut her up. The window at the end of the hall sets off the fire alarm if opened. There's no other entry. I've seen stabbings, shootings, and strangulation in the heat of passion, or out of cold revenge, and poisoning, and murder for hire, and accidents, but I haven't seen anything like this in thirty years. To tear someone apart that way requires demonic fury and incredible strength. I don't even recall an animal attack leaving a scene like this. If the dwarves are responsible, they must have brought some type of animal, or a synthetic monster. Doesn't look good for the home team, does it?"

"No," agreed Clay.

"Speaking of magic though," Gumshoe asked, "I'm beginning to think you are not unique. The Black Dwarf waltzed in here with a monster, viciously ripped the poor woman open and cut her apart with claws or a set of kitchen knives. And then, turned around and waltzed back out into an early afternoon traffic without anyone seeing any blood on their clothes. Can you think of any dwarf who fits the description?"

"Real magic?" scoffed Clay. "No way, Gumshoe, you've known me since I discovered my first fire ball, and learned how to make kids laugh. In all these years, I've never heard of anyone else with real magic. I know illusionists, jugglers, acrobats, dancers, and I employ more than a few myself. But none of them could do this, and I can't imagine any of them who would do this."

"Yes, my thought too. Have to ask though. We'll search for anyone in the database."

"You might as well look in the directory for a hit-magician," said Jack. "Wanted; black dwarf for hire. Have magic, will travel."

"Very funny, Jack," said Gumshoe, "but we'll do exactly that. We're Nodlon Yard."

A technician hurried up to them. "Inspector, we're

buttoning up the crime scene. Can I brief you now?"

"Go ahead, son," said Gumshoe. "Summarize it here, and spare us the jargon."

"As I'm sure you noticed, sir, her body is in bad shape. We think a large animal attacked her. It tore her business suit off, and flayed her. She probably died from blood loss shortly after the attack began. It must have been a horribly painful way to go, but swift. She couldn't have lasted more than a few minutes. The creature stood eight to twelve feet high on its hind legs, and had five claws on each paw. Examination of the bite mark suggests the creature had eighty to two hundred teeth and two sets of fangs, one upper and one lower." He paused, contorting uncomfortably.

"Creature?" asked Gumshoe. "Any idea what? How do you know it was a creature?"

"Yes, sir, it has to be a big creature. It's the only explanation that fits. The claw marks on the floor and walls, and the gouges on the desk are those of a cat. Cats have four claws, but a polydactyl cat may have five claws per paw. Bears have five claws, but bears are not generally excited feeders, so maybe it is a synthetic cat."

"Any idea how big this creature is?"

"Based on the bite marks, and the distance between the claw marks, we think it's in the range of a Kodiak or Grizzly bear, or a very large Bengalese tiger. Assuming it's a synthetic, it may weigh half a ton, or even a full ton."

"Let's get this straight son, you're telling me it's a cat, bear, tiger, and pterodactyl sort of thing? What next? A Sasquatch werewolf?"

"Polydactyl, sir, not pterodactyl."

"Polydactyl, pterodactyl, poly-fractal! Just say what you mean son."

"Polydactyl means extra claws sir. A pterodactyl is a flying dinosaur sir."

"Can you describe what you know about this creature in

the common tongue we can all speak?" asked Shotgun.

"Yes, sir, I'll try sir. Cats have about thirty teeth and bears have forty, and bears and cats also have fangs. Wolves have the same number of teeth as bears, but no living species is large enough. The attacker had twice as many teeth and larger fangs than any living species of cat or bear. The best match for the bite marks would be an alligator. Alligators also have five claws on the front, but only four on the back and the toes are not in the proper position. The blood splatter and wound analysis eliminates any reptile. The attacker stood on its hind legs and engaged in a dozen melee attacks in under a minute. One more piece of the puzzle throws the picture off completely. It had at least one horn. Nothing alive today matches anything in the zoological screen. An over-sized synthetic cat with extra teeth might work, but when I added the horn, the application crashed."

A fatherly spirit filled Gumshoe. Quelling an urge to shout, he said, "Son, can you spell it out for us?"

"I'll try sir, I was trying to say the creature has the teeth of an alligator, the claws of a polydactyl cat, and it is the size of a Kodiak bear or a Saber tooth tiger. And it has a horn."

"Let's get this straight. We're looking for a synthetic Saber tooth tiger, but the horn throws off the puzzle?"

"Maybe, sir."

Shotgun sniggered, and he bit his lip.

"Yep, Gumshoe, I think that's what the tech said," said Jack.

"Son, we're looking for a gang of rogue dwarves, led by a black dwarf with magical powers who can walk around without being picked up on security cameras. And you're telling me this fiend keeps a genetically modified horror vid monster for a house-pet. What do you think this is, a B-vid?"

"Yes, sir," said the technician, "and there's more." The dwarf nodded vigorously and he bounced on his toes. "I mean no, sir, we are not in a B-vid, but we are looking for a genetically modified monster straight out of a horror vid."

"Yep," said Jack, "That's what he said."

"Anything else, son?" Gumshoe rubbed his temples.

"Pieces of Miss Steele are missing, sir. Whatever attacked her must have consumed about twenty pounds of her."

"It gets better," said Gumshoe. "So this monster eats exhibition managers?"

"Yes sir."

"Make sure the lab boys know we may be looking for a synthetic creature. I don't want them missing anything because they forgot their black box doesn't have a brain. Did you find anything else? Any sign of dwarves?"

"Yes sir, I'll make sure the possibility of a synthetic is noted on my testing request manifest. As for the dwarves, we found footprints. The first is a partial outline of a dwarf's boot of a common size created when the victim's blood pooled against the sole. We have a string of three successive print's originating from the first as the wearer of the boot left the office. No other evidence of anything or anyone else in the office has been identified, though there will be the usual tests before I can speak conclusively on the matter."

"Is the scene ready for entry or are we sealed?"

"Go on in Inspector," said the dwarf. "We know you, sir. Always like to poke around, old school like."

"Old school like?" muttered the Inspector as the dwarf trotted off. The Inspector cocked his thumb in his holster. "Just good police work. He's a good tech, but he's green. Follow me, gentlemen."

Gumshoe led them into the foyer, and up to the inner entrance. He reached out and laid a hand on their shoulders. "Be warned, she's not a pretty sight. If you feel the least bit nauseous, do your business in the hall. I don't want the crime scene contaminated."

Entering the office, Jack was overwhelmed by the stench of blood. The office reeked of corruption. A dwarf technician partially obstructed his view of Steele. He turned green.

Sensing his distress, Gumshoe patted his back. "Are you gonna be sick, Jack?"

"No, I'm all right."

Jack craned to see over the dwarf. Catching a glimpse of something creeping on the floor, he looked down at his foot. Steele's blood had congealed in a pool near her body, but blood flowed along the cracks in the floor tiles. Under his weight, blood oozed from the tiles, and welled up against his boot.

Nausea rose in his gullet, and he quickly backed up.

He had seen murder victims before. He had seen crime scene photos, but he had never seen any victim in this condition.

Dizziness swept him, and he swayed.

The crime scene tech was a cool as a fry cook putting out a grease fire. Dwarves were obsessive and well suited to police work. Temperamental types were not cut out for the work.

Worried the elf would fall on Steele, the tech spread a tarp over what remained of Steele. She stood up.

"Sir," said the tech, "are you well?" She was a pretty dwarf maiden with amber eyes and a red chip on her forehead.

Someone squeezed his elbow. Allowing himself to be drawn away, he retreated as gracefully as he could. "Just need air," he croaked, "it's the smell." He feigned nonchalance, and retreated to the hall. Out of line of sight from the body, he felt better. He looked around. No one was behind him, and Gumshoe and Shotgun were on the other side of the office. Was he losing his mind? A tingle ran up his back.

Gumshoe left the office, passed through the foyer, and came out to the hall. "Are you all right Jack?"

"I'm not a homicide detective," said Jack. "I'm a magician with a knack."

"Yes," said Gumshoe. "You probably should get some water. I think I saw a fountain near the vending machines in the lobby. Shotgun is working on her computer now. I should be able to wrap this in a few minutes. Dwarves are really efficient."

"Gumshoe," he hesitated a moment unable to continue.

"If it makes you feel better, I still get sick sometimes."

Jack wondered what might upset Gumshoe's constitution after thirty years. "What makes an old hand like you turn green?"

"Forget it, Jack, you don't want to know. Go on, I don't want you losing your cookies all over my trench coat."

Jack found a lounge, washed his face, and then he felt better. When he returned, Shotgun was briefing Gumshoe on his findings.

"The Crown paid for the ballroom. My bet is they hacked an account and put the tab on the Ministry of Manna to throw us off. I've identified the files with the activity codes for your computer forensics team, but I don't think anything on her computer will help. Also, she had an appointment with Dr. Balaam, the gene therapist who owns the New Gem franchise."

"The plot thickens, gentlemen. I have to be home once in a while. The missus complained this morning. She said I'd better solve this case or marry Captain Barfly. Let's go, and I'll drop you off."

Halls of Industry

Two van drivers blocked an intersection, shouting at each other about the right of way. They slowed, and Gumshoe flashed his emergency lights. Startled, the frustrated molemen stopped arguing. With the hostility momentarily quenched, the traffic jam was quickly sorted out. Overhead, a few flyers sailed over the clogged streets.

Frightened molemen squeezed their vehicles onto the sidewalks. Moving vans headed out of the city clogged the intersections. The crush of traffic narrowed the streets to two lanes. Behind him a black airship lifted off from a loading dock.

"Let's avoid the traffic," he said. "We don't want to spend the next three hours on the level-way in a traffic jam. We're going down to the Halls. No one lives there, if you don't count the homeless. The factories won't be moving much of anything yet."

Gumshoe turned back towards Moab and the traffic thinned. It had been months since he had driven through the halls. Moab was Nodlon's third basement and the deepest occupied level. It was independent of Nodlon and outside his jurisdiction. Moab had no border, and anyone could travel freely between Deep Nodlon and Moab and often did. But he rarely had a reason to go this deep. He lived in a log cabin on the south side of the mountain, and he preferred the open air.

Thoughts of the halls brought back memories from his school days. Once Moab had been the heart of the coal mine. Thornmocker had ordered an army of biots designed to mine coal from Bio-Soft.

Bio-Soft's human resources department lacking a sense of humor christened the new model the Mining Organic Anthracitic Coal Biot. Not lacking a sense of humor, Thornmocker called his new workforce molemen. Taking the acronym, and dropping the coal, he called their home Moab.

Molemen had carved out the mountains under Nodlon.

When the molemen finished mining the third basement, Thornmocker converted the empty caverns into space for every conceivable industry. These he called the Halls of Industry, and when molemen were too old or were no longer needed for mining, he retrained them to manufacture everything from starships to toys and leased them to other manufacturers.

Despite greed, Thornmocker had not been ungenerous in specifying the design of molemen, and they were a bright and decent folk comprised of hard men, and fair women. They had earned their independence from Nodlon during the last war. Gumshoe recalled the tale well, but it would have to wait.

Into these halls Gumshoe guided the cruiser back towards downtown. The tunnels through the Halls of Industry were usually slower than the level-ways, what with lights and intersections. But with the level-ways jammed, Gumshoe knew they could reach downtown through the Halls.

The heart of Moab lay in the halls. Over-size tunnels and massive bays accommodated Nodlon's heavy manufacturers, warehouses, and factories.

Jack tapped on the cruiser's scream bar. "Can we catch the news? And see if there have been any developments?"

Startled by Jack's question, Gumshoe put his history aside. "Yeah, sure Jack." He punched his console and selected the Mercury News feed. The vid screen lit up.

A picture of a comely dwarf maiden dissolved, and the camera shifted to the anchor, Bruce Ably. Bruce lowered his voice ominously.

"We have an update from the Octagon. General Thomas Arnold has been promoted to Warlord. General Arnold is the highest ranking military officer on the General Staff. He is said to be one of King Justin's closest and most trusted advisors. He earned his reputation thirty years ago as an ace blasting space pirates back to Davey Jone's locker during the Oort War. While we have no official word, the observers in the Octagon believe this is a prelude to declaring martial law."

Gumshoe switched off the news. "That'll make an omelet out of scrambled eggs."

They crossed a boulevard, and entered a town square. In the center, a tiered pyramid built of red brick, and adorned with Greek columns rose to the domed roof. Apple trees ran around the pyramid's foot encircled by brick curbs. Gumshoe pointed at the pyramid. "That's the Union Hall. Together the Unions are a mini-state within Moab."

"What do you think of General Arnold?"

"Arnold's a war hero, and a good man. I met him a few years back at the Yard's winter ball. I was the master of ceremonies, and he was the keynote speaker. He's an expert on disaster preparation, and on paper he's a good choice for the job. If Nodlon needs evacuating, I imagine he'll get Nodlon evacuated on time. But, Arnold's always had the city behind him for support. He's never been responsible for running it. He knows natural disasters. And he's fought forest fires - literally. He was in charge when we helped the Swamp men two years ago when Hurricane Gloria slammed into Gulf Port."

Trucks and moving vans rolled in and out of factories and the campuses of Moab's industrial firms. The streets were open in the commercial district and they made good progress.

Gumshoe guided the cruiser into another hall. The tunnel was six stories high, and industry facades marched away for miles before gently curling under the mountains. The traffic thinned as they drove deeper into the Halls of Industry.

The black airship turned onto the boulevard.

"Does he know what to do when he can't call Moab? Once the city is evacuated, he can't just order up a self-propelled deep water caisson or a fire suppressant tanker. Men like Arnold know they can handle complex emergencies so they think they can run a city. Not that I'm pessimistic mind you, but I've no idea of how he'll handle it. If he lets the other experts help him, all will be well. Overconfidence brews a recipe for sloppy work."

~~~~~~~

The cruiser rounded a curve, and the autopilot slammed on the breaks. Ahead of them, a barricade of crates, and pallets blocked the road. An overturned semi-trailer truck lay on its side beyond the barricade. A robotic tunnel drill had rolled off the trailer when it flipped over and smashed into a convenience store. Flames poured out of the cab.

On the street were knots of roving men. An elf and a pair of goblins stood on the burning trailer. The elf egged on the mob.

Jack silently thanked the Crown for the armored cruiser. None but a fool would dare attack a machine emblazoned with the Crown's coat of arms. Shielded with bullet proof armor, force fields against energy weapons and armed with automatic weapons, the cruiser was Nodlon's basic light mobile infantry weapon. Though limited in maneuverability on the ground, the cruiser was effective in Nodlon's tubular streets and level-ways. Many of the thugs ran at the sight.

Gumshoe stabbed his caster console, and Marcie appeared on the cruiser's vid. "Marcie, I've just driven into a riot in the Halls of Industry. I need back up now. We're going to need ambulances, fire support, and plenty of officers. Got all that?"

A beer bottle shattered on the cruiser's force shields.

"Babe, I've got you in Moab at Angeles and Houston. Is that right?"

"Yeah, and it's getting ugly."

Stones and bricks and bottles pelted the cruiser. The improvised artillery bounced off the force shields, but the cruiser shook under the impact.

Marcie punched her own console. "Help is on the way dear, just hang on." Marcie's image popped, sizzled, and the vid screen went blue. A warning in friendly letters told them the signal was unavailable.

"We've lost the signal! They're jamming us!"

Bottles burst on the street. Bricks smashed the glass, and

the glass crunched. Stones struck the cruiser thumped against the cab and bounced off the shields.

"Autopilot, passcode Horace, set all weapons to stun, and initiate auto defense," said Gumshoe. "And get us out of here!"

An unseen assailant threw a Molotov cocktail. The burning fuel slid off the shields, and flames erupted on the pavement.

The autopilot reversed hard and threw them against their harnesses. The hood parted and the cruiser deployed an anti-personnel blaster. The cruiser fired at the ruffians throwing stones.

Stunned, an elf fell from the top of the barricade. Men throwing bricks collapsed, a goblin on top of a truck dropped out of sight. The rest ducked for cover. Safe from the stun blaster, the thugs blindly catapulted stones over their barricade.

The cruiser surged away from the barrier, and the hail of bric-a-brac landed harmlessly in front of them.

The autopilot slammed on the brakes throwing them all against their seats. Gumshoe twisted around his seat and looked backwards.

A black airship blocked their path. It stretched across all four lanes of Houston Street.

Dwarves in black baseball caps and uniforms streamed out of the airship. They carried lightning guns and wore mirrored sunglasses to protect their eyes. They fanned out between the barricade and the airship, and fired at the cruiser.

Lightning bolts hit the cruiser's shields and ricocheted wildly in all directions. Stray bolts struck the barricade, and the tunnel walls.

A center block thrown over the barrier bounced off the cruiser's shields, and rocked the car. Shotgun ducked. "What the heck is going on out there?"

The black dwarves fired heedless of the risk of stray bolts. The cruiser's blaster stunned a dwarf. The dwarf fell spread eagle, and his lightning gun skittered away.

Jack turned to Gumshoe who was jabbing at his console trying to communicate with the dispatcher. "Those black dwarves are shooting at us!"

Bolts flew wildly. A bolt hit a fence strung across a stack of pallets, and a wise guy collapsed.

Seeing the folly of risking the deadly hail, the ruffians lost their courage. Men, elves, and goblins hoofed it down the street and darted into the alleys and corners.

The cruiser stunned another dwarf. Hit by the blaster, the dwarf staggered. A second strike sent him to his knees and a third knocked him to the ground.

Jack tried to count the remaining dwarves, and saw one struck by a bolt. The dwarf's tunic flared and the dwarf dropped in his tracks. His weapon clattered on the pavement.

Gumshoe watched the airship in his rearview mirror. The airship's side door parted. "They're doing something. Where's our backup?" He drew his pistol and set it to stun, "Jack, open the dashboard panel."

Jack popped a panel. "It's just medical supplies!"

"Open the other one!"

The airship's cargo bay opened and a cantilevered arm swung from out of the ship. A pod separated into two segments and unfolded. The pieces began assembling themselves.

The arm swung around to point at the cruiser.

"Too late, they've got a lightning cannon!" Gumshoe seized the wheel, and mashed the accelerator to the floor.

The cannon telescoped into a barrel. A blue-green glow ran up the cantilever, up the cannon, and down the barrel. Light radiated from the barrel's rings. A vibration drummed the air.

Gumshoe searched for a softer section of the barricade. He spotted a metal fence, and veered. The cruiser hit the fence, and splattered pallets, crates, and concrete blocks over the pavement. The nose sank into the fence.

Traveling at low speed, a broken wire slipped through the shields and caught a crack between the wheel and fender. One side gave way. The fence flopped off its hinges, and swung away from its anchorage. Concrete blocks toppled over the cruiser slithering off the shields.

The cruiser's nose caught in the frame, and the mesh flipped over the hood. Momentum slung Shotgun's door against a stack of crates. The stack rolled over the cruiser and down the trunk.

A white flash and a thunderclap struck, and the cruiser quaked. They shut their eyes, and threw up their hands to shield their faces.

Gumshoe unbuckled his harness and pushed Jack, yelling something inaudible over the pounding in his ears. The cruiser rocked. Smoke billowed from its instrument panel. The Inspector pounded Jack and pointed.

Jack unbuckled his harness, and threw open his door. Diving out of the cruiser, he scrambled behind a crate and looked back for his companions.

Gumshoe crawled over the passenger seat, and rolled out of the cruiser. He crawled on his elbows to avoid being a target. Still, there was no sign of Shotgun.

Recovering his wits, Jack's Army days came back to him. From long ago, he remembered his drill sergeant yelling at him as he low crawled through an obstacle course. One strike of a lightning gun and he was a dead man.

The dwarves ran. They dove for cover. He guessed fear of the lightning cannon kept them at bay.

A dwarf ran up the sidewalk to the barricade. The dwarf flung himself into the pile.

In the military, he trained with personal shields. A shield pack offered a quarter hour of protection against energy weapons, and conventional kinetic weapons. After that you were on your own.

None of them wore a personal combat shield.

If he used his telekinetic power as a shield, would it stop lightning bolts? He had no idea. It had never been tested against a lightning gun. New spells took time and often went awry until he understood how the spell worked. Time he did not have.

Jack, time to get your act together showman, this is life and death! Envisioning his shield, he fashioned a new spell. The shields had to stop lightning, flame, high velocity projectiles and heavy objects. He summoned his magic, and he cast shields around himself and his companions.

His confidence returned, and he broke cover to peek at the airship. Two dwarves manned the lightning cannon. One sat behind the cannon on the gunner's seat. The other manned the cantilever controls next to the cannon. They both carried lightning guns slung from shoulder belts.

Gumshoe was nowhere to be seen.

The black dwarves had taken cover.

The airship was no more than thirty yards away, and the red glow of the fire warning light flashed on the gunner's face. He was waiting for the capacitors to cool. When the cannon cooled, he would fire again.

Jack recalled firing a lightning cannon once during infantry training. The cannon looked like an air cooled model designed for light infantry support. They were powerful cannons but fired slowly without spare capacitors or backup cooling units. *They forgot to bring spare capacitors.*

He was furious. He summoned a lightning bolt. Jumping up, he broke his cover. He put his fists together and aimed at the cannon.

The dwarf manning the cantilever pushed away from the controls, and brought his lightning gun up to aim at Jack.

Jack fired. The lightning discharged from his hands. Stars flash in his eyes, and his arms were thrown apart.

Jack's bolt hit the generator, and the capacitors detonated. The gunner fell over backwards and the cantilever operator was blown against the airship's jamb and thrown prostrate to the street. The cannon's barrel ruptured and sparks flew out of the lightning generator. Fire spurted from the capacitors. Oil sprayed from the cannon's transformer blowing a mist onto the airship.

He staggered backwards, blindly trying to remain on his feet and blundered into a stack of crates. The stack rolled over the cruiser. Without its shields, a pallet shattered the disabled cruiser's windshield. He crouched low behind a crate and rubbed his eyes. He tried to restore his vision. Blinking, the stars dissolved and the pavement gray returned. He glanced in all directions looking for friends and foes.

The cannon quivered and the barrel snapped. The barrel struck the cannon's mount and a spark spat out of its mouth striking the cantilever. The spark backfired and the oil burst into flames. The flames ran into the cargo bay, and the airship exploded in a fireball. The ball of fire rose over the airship, and a cloud of greasy smoke mushroomed over the machine.

Jack flinched as debris whizzed by him. He threw up a hand to protect his face from the heat radiating from the fireball. Smoke crawled over the artificial clouds, and set off the fire alarms. The fire extinguishers sprayed gas, and doused the fire. The airship's ruin smoldered. He searched for Gumshoe.

The Inspector was on the ground not far away. A lump jumped into his throat. Then Gumshoe pushed himself off the ground.

The Inspector reached into his trench coat and pulled out a pair of sunglasses. He donned these, and tried to rise.

Jack ran to Gumshoe and helped him stand.

"Magic shields," he shouted. He thumped his chest, "personal shields."

The Inspector gave him thumbs up, and waved at the cruiser. His lips moved. All Jack heard was a tinny ringing, but he understood. Shotgun was still in the cruiser.

The cruiser was immobile. Its rear end blackened and its trunk was partially smelted. He could not see Shotgun. He ran to the cruiser's window and stooped to peer inside.

The dwarf was on the back seat. He was still and his eyes were closed.

In the corner of his eye, a black dwarf moved. He ducked behind the cruiser, and shut his eyes. He hit the asphalt at full speed, and he bounced as his shield slapped the pavement. He saw the flash through his eyelids, and felt the crack of thunder.

Jack rolled off the pavement, and ran for the barricade, still wary of his shield's power.

He saw Gumshoe hiding behind a crate.

A dwarf leapt from the barricade, not seeing the policeman. He raised his lightning gun to aim at Jack, and the policeman fired. The stun bolt popped, and the flash was hardly brighter than a torch. The dwarf staggered and dropped his lightning gun. Gumshoe fired again, and the dwarf fell to the pavement unconscious.

Jack focused and recast his shield spell over Gumshoe. In a crouch, he scrambled back to the cruiser. Focusing his energy, he recast a shield to protect Shotgun.

He left the cruiser, and darted to the barricade to watch Gumshoe's back. He saw two dwarves sneaking along the barricade. They had found a breach and were darting towards Gumshoe using the crates as cover.

"Behind you," he shouted. Gumshoe spun around but he was too slow. One of the younger dwarves dropped a bead on him and fired his lightning gun point blank. The bolt flashed and thunder cracked the air.

Blinking, he fought to restore his vision. As the pavement came into focus, he searched for the detective. The dwarf was lying on the pavement. His uniform was scorched and the lightning gun beside him was twisted and smoldering.

The other dwarf attacked, and Gumshoe fired.

The dwarf staggered, firing wildly, and fell to the ground stunned. Not waiting, the detective ran up the barricade, and worked his way away through the debris looking for attackers.

Gumshoe had survived a lightning gun blast at point blank range. His shield had saved the detective's life. Jack took no pleasure in the sight of the fallen dwarf, but he was glad the

Inspector was alive.

"Next time," Clay chastised himself, "I need to think of these spells ahead of time."

The fallen dwarf's sunglasses had fallen to the pavement. Jack envisioned his traction spell, and cast a tether on the sunglasses. The glasses snapped in two. Jack caught a half piece, and put it on.

Lying not far away was the lightning gun that had nearly killed him. He cast a traction spell. Using the traction, he cast a tether on the gun, and it flew into his arms. Recalling his military training, he armed the gun, checked the power, and set the weapon on stun.

Circling the end of the cruiser with one eye closed, his cloak caught on the fence mesh. He spun round and shed his cloak.

A red dwarf seized the opportunity, and bore down on him.

Freed from the fence, he raised his own weapon. The dwarf fired first and the bolt bounced off his shield and blasted a crate. The crate exploded showering them both in wooden shrapnel. Surprised, the startled dwarf glanced at the crate. Jack fired his weapon point blank, and the stunned dwarf fell to the pavement.

Gumshoe ran down the left flank.

Jack darted the other way. He risked a peek over the cruiser's melted trunk, and saw a dwarf break cover. From the new vantage, he saw three dwarves in front of him.

All three spotted him and fired at him. He counted on his shield for protection, and kept running. He fired at the nearest dwarf. The dwarf dropped his weapon and fell unconscious.

Jack instinctively dove to one side to evade the other dwarf. Lightning bolts whizzed past him. A bolt flashed over his shoulder, and another shattered a pallet. He raised his weapon to fire, and a bolt struck him.

Stars flashed in his unprotected eye. The nearest dwarf

flew up as he twirled away from Jack. The dwarf's weapon spun out of his hand, and he fell. His head bounced on the pavement.

The remaining dwarf aimed again at Jack. Relying on his shield, Jack raised his weapon. The dwarf fired first.

Expecting the flash and the clap, he blinked and held his position. The bolt ricocheted off his shield and backfired. The ricochet hit the asphalt and bounced.

The bolt grazed the dwarf and he flinched. He jumped aside, and he spun to turn his weapon on Jack.

He stunned him and the dwarf fell. The dwarf hit the ground, and he charged. He ran down the barricade searching for dwarves.

Finding a breach, he ducked through the hole and spun about looking for more dwarves. Seeing none, he ran up the barricade on the back side. He reached the cruiser without encountering resistance. He avoided the mesh, kicked aside a crate and broke back through the barricade.

Gumshoe ran down the front of the barricade holding his pistol. He searched for dwarves hiding in the crates. Then, he pointed at the airship.

Jack followed the Inspector's direction and saw the cantilever operator recovering. He ran towards the dwarf, held up his weapon, and cried, "On the ground!"

The red dwarf pushed the pavement and sat up. He dove for his lightning gun. He landed in a belly flop and snatched his weapon.

Jack brought up his weapon and skidded to a halt. The dwarf gripped the gun's handle and rolled on the asphalt to swing the barrel. Clay aimed at the prone dwarf, and fired. Stunned, the dwarf dropped his weapon and went back to sleep.

Searching for more foes, Jack saw Gumshoe whirling his finger. He understood and circled the airship looking for more combatants. The airship still smoldered and wisps of smoke wafted from the interior. He checked the cargo bay, and saw the gunner. The dwarf was beyond any help. The passenger doors were too hot to touch. Using his traction spell, he tried to open them, but succeeded only in causing the doors to jerk in their frames. Going forward, he found the driver's cab empty. He jogged around the airship and saw no more dwarves.

A Bad Mole

Up Houston Street a green airship approached fast. Ambulances and other vehicles sped down the center of the road.

Jack finished his reconnaissance, and circled the airship.

Gumshoe helped Shotgun out of the cruiser. Shotgun leaned on the cruiser's bumper, and the detective steadied the dwarf.

Jack jogged back to the cruiser. "The cavalry's arrived. They're coming up Houston." He threw the lightning gun into the cruiser's trunk and sat on the bumper next to Shotgun.

"Are you all right?" yelled Gumshoe. He faced Jack and yelled, "Can you hear me?"

"Ringing in my ears," said Jack.

Gumshoe touched his ear. "Let the medics help you."

The Moab Surete arrived in riot gear carrying lightning guns. Molemen deployed over the impromptu battlefield.

A sergeant jogged up to them, "Inspector Lestrayed?"

"Yes, son," said Gumshoe. "You need to secure the area, Sergeant."

"I'm Sergeant York, and we're securing the area now. Are you all right?"

"We need a medic," said Gumshoe.

"I'll have a medic here soon." The Sergeant barked into the caster hooked on his uniform. The police flanked the barricade and encircled the truck. They deployed portable barriers and began setting up a perimeter.

"Sergeant, are you in charge?"

"No, sir, Constable Wiggles is in charge. He's just a few minutes away."

"Then I suggest you carry on."

The Sergeant fingered his lightning gun. More policemen in riot gear began collecting the lightning guns near the fallen dwarves. Sergeant York's men checked the dwarves. They bound the living and tagged the dead with red tags.

The sergeant's caster squawked and he cocked his head to listen. Then he barked into the caster again.

"Constable Wiggles is here. I've cleared the medics and techs to enter. The medics should be here in a jiffy."

Medics jogged around the airship, and began checking the fallen. All of them carried scanners, backpacks and bags. A robot carried a defibrillator, an oxygen pump, and a pack with a dozen cardiopulmonary resuscitation robots.

The Sergeant moved off to take charge of his team.

A mature moleman raced up to them with a pressure cuff, a medic's kit, and a stethoscope around his neck.

"Are any of you injured?"

"Check the others," said Gumshoe, "we can wait."

Constable Wiggles circled the airship and the portly moleman changed course to meet them.

The medic left them to their own devices, and checked the fallen dwarves.

"Gumshoe," said Wiggles. "Had a rough bit of luck, hey?"

"We were ambushed," said Gumshoe. "I've told York to secure the area and the stunned dwarves, and I see his men are on it. Good man."

"Yes, York's reliable. He's a solid, honest, hard-working, and not very imaginative policeman. In short, he's a typical moleman. What happened?"

"You said it," said Gumshoe. "We were headed back to the Yard. The level-way was jammed, so I came down to the Halls to avoid the traffic. When we turned the corner here, we nearly ran into this barricade.

"The usual suspects manned the barricades, and they pelted us with stones and bricks. I called for backup. But when I tried to retreat, the airship blocked our path."

Gumshoe left Shotgun with Clay, and led Wiggles to the airship.

The moleman's belly jiggled as he strutted to keep up

with the taller man.

"When the airship arrived we lost all communications. They must have jammed us. The dwarves here jumped out of the back of the airship armed with lightning guns. They fired wildly as if they'd been trained in an arcade. Bolts bounced off the cruiser's shield and ricocheted everywhere. The hoodlums disappeared in a hurry, probably afraid of a stray shot.

"The dwarves pinned us down with the lightning guns. I wasn't too worried. Help was on the way, and shooting at my cruiser they were doing more damage to each other than to us. Then I saw them unloading this."

They stopped at the cannon's ruins.

"The Black Dwarf knew the guns couldn't penetrate the cruiser's shields. They brought the cannon to finish the job."

"It's a setup," said Wiggles. "They organized the riot for you. It must have been staged for your benefit."

"That's why I like you, Wiggles," said Gumshoe. "You have a suspicious mind."

"Coming from you, that's a compliment."

"Someone planned this, and we need an informer to give us a lead. Find out who put up this barricade. Interrogate the survivors, and round up usual suspects in the neighborhood. The hooligans know who started this riot. And if we can get one of the dwarves to talk, maybe we can find out where we can find the Black Dwarf."

"We're on it. York's rounding up the survivors as we speak."

Gumshoe waved at the fallen dwarves. "I stunned most of these chaps myself. When they wake up they may not be in the mood to be taken into custody. They were poorly trained, and easy to pick off. Worse, they inflicted most of their own casualties."

"While I'm glad you're alive, friend, my suspicious mind cannot figure out how you destroyed a lightning cannon without even a blaster or a military grade personal shield?"

"Not sure, Wiggles, I was on the ground low-crawling for my life when the airship blew up."

"And you'd rather not speculate?"

"Beats me, I was busy trying not to be cannon fodder."

"Just trying to figure out how to explain it, Mole News will demand a statement, and I've got a report to write."

"If you need a story, we suspect a malfunction due to operator error. That'll do for the vultures and your creative writing assignments. And it's plausible."

"Gotcha, old man," Wiggles chuckled, "but why keep it under wraps?"

"No one knew which way I was going. I didn't even know. We ran into a traffic jam, and I decided to cut through the Halls." Gumshoe eyed the scene with suspicion. "Right now, I think I can count my friends on one hand. And I don't want them coming after you, either."

"We may have a bad mole, though I hate the pun."

"Maybe, but I wouldn't be so sure it's a moleman. The leader is a black dwarf, and so far all of his known followers have been dwarves. I have one goblin suspect, but I think he's an outlier. Have a mole you can trust check the remains of the cruiser for a tracking device. Nothing in your report should hint that we have other assets."

"Got it, old man, Jack Jack was just an innocent by-stander. But it's not hard to guess Jack Clay saved your hide, and I'll have to play super stupid to cover that up."

"You're a better actor than Jack, you old fraud," Gumshoe winked. "If we can get these dwarves to talk, I want to interrogate them." He put a hand to his head. "And then I need to get going. I'm getting too old for this."

"And I'm honored, you think I'm not."

"What? Oh, I'm just tired Wiggles. I've already worked a scene today, and this is your turf."

"And I'm honored to be counted among your friends," the Constable chuckled. "If you suspected a moleman, I doubt you'd be talking to old Wiggles."

"Caught in my own trap. And you're half-right, any friend of mine is in danger. Be careful, Wiggles."

Wiggles patted Gumshoe's arm. "Let me see if I can round up a few survivors for you to talk to."

Hear No Evil

Gumshoe walked back to the cruiser.

The medics roused the stunned dwarves using a spray. Policemen bound the dwarves.

A comely medic worked on a stunned dwarf. She put away a pressure cuff, and a torch rolled out of her tool pouch. She picked up the torch and tested the dwarf's eyes, and looked down his throat. She switched to a scanner.

Gumshoe wondered what she expected to find.

She scanned him head to toe. Setting down the scanner and reaching into her bag, she pulled out an ointment which she daubed on a scrape on his face. Working quickly, she bandaged the wound. Finished with the bandage, the medic collected her tools and moved to the next dwarf. A policeman helped the dwarf to his feet and led him away.

Jack and Shotgun were both disheveled. Jack's fashionable costume was torn, dirty, and his coif was out of place.

Shotgun looked little better. His eyes were bloodshot, and his tuxedo torn.

Gumshoe hooked both his thumbs in his holster. "How are you guys doing?"

Shotgun hooked a thumb at Jack, "I'm better Inspector, but the boss can't hear a thing."

"Good thing we like him," said Gumshoe, "or we'd be talking behind his back right now." They shared a chuckle.

Jack looked back and forth at them both. "What's the joke?"

Gumshoe just held up his hands in mock surprise.

The comely medic approached them and said, "Gentlemen, I can help you out now. Who's first?" She was short and petite even for a mole woman. Her body armor dwarfed her and the straps on her breast plate dangled to her waist.

"Who's first?" she repeated.

"Him," Gumshoe pointed at Jack. "He can't hear a thing. Can you give him something?"

She pulled a torch from her pouch and attached a cone.

"Maybe, let me check his ears." Letting her examine his ears, Clay docilely complied as she pulled his head until she had a good view of his ear. Pulling his ear, she inserted the torch in his ear canal. She twisted his head and repeated the procedure on his other ear.

Standing in front of him, she asked, "Can you hear anything yet, Mr. Clay?"

Jack shrugged, and shouted, "What did you say?"

"Looks normal," the medic spoke to the others. "His eardrums haven't burst. I've got just the thing. We use it on kids who've lost their hearing at concerts. Works wonders." Kneeling next to one of her cases, she unlatched the clasps and opened it up. Rummaging through the trays of pills, vials, bandages, and other medical paraphernalia, she selected a tiny canister. She snapped a plastic cone on top and stood up.

Taking his jaw, she gently twisted Jack's head to one side, and shouted, "Hold still, and stay that way until I tell you, you can move." She plunged the plastic cone in his ear, and pressed on a clip on the canister's side. With a hiss, the canister discharged medication. Cocking her own head, she grabbed his jaw. "Hold it."

Turning to the others, both of them pointed at each other.

"Brave guys, but who needs me?" she asked.

"Shotgun let her take a look at you." Acceding to the request, Shotgun submitted to another brief examination.

"Does it hurt anywhere?" The medic took his signs and scanned his head for any sign of a concussion.

"Other than a headache, I'm fine."

"You are fine," the medic agreed. "Here's a painkiller and some water." She handed him a bottle of water, and a packet of pills.

"No sense in not checking," said Gumshoe.

"Absolutely," said the medic, and turned to Jack. "Now, can you hear me?"

"Yes," he said, "But I can hear ringing, and you sound like you're coming in through a tin can. It's better than it was."

"Good, let's do the other side, and then you can go." Taking his jaw again, the medic twisted his head and repeated the procedure with the mist canister.

"Thanks miss. We're planning to do roadshows in Iron Mountain, and I'd like you to be my guest."

"Thank you Mr. Clay. My boyfriend and I saw your show a few weeks ago. I really like the Rockhounds. Bingo is great!"

"Great!"

She turned away, and checked the Inspector.

Jack smiled, thinking of the good times. Girls loved the Rockhounds, and each had his own fan club. Originally, he had auditioned several friends who were studio musicians. He hired Nick, Ralph, Animal, and a guy named Tom. After their first season, Tom had left for greener pastures.

Meanwhile a vaudevillian minstrel named Bingo had created a fan video parodying the Rockhounds. No one had given him any thought until Mercury News featured his one man band parody on a Saturday morning after Tom left.

The fans took it as a sign, and he felt the pressure. After the news spot, Jack was inundated with questions. The band auditioned him, first in the studio, and then at a pub. Jack feared he would be a creep, or a nut, or a prima donna. *Well, worse than most musicians anyway.* He took a chance and hired Bingo.

Bingo had lived up to his name from the start. Funny, charming, always happy to ham it up, and a working musical machine in the studio, He made himself part of the show. Jack had to admit, Bingo was a great team player on the Clay-Player team.

"You're fine Inspector," said the medic, "You must live a charmed life. It's incredible you survived that cannon blast." She pointed to the cruiser.

"Yes it is."

She knelt beside her cases, and repacked her gear. "Mr. Clay can you hear me?"

"Yes ma'am, good as new. Amazing drug you used."

"Well, we do live in the fourth century you know. Do me a favor and see an audiologist as soon as you can. I'm not an audiologist, got it?"

"Of course, and come see our roadshow in Iron Mountain."

She threw her backpack over her shoulder, struggled under its weight, and rearranged the straps to achieve a balance. Kneeling slightly she picked up her cases and her scanner.

"We'll do that Mr. Clay. Good luck, gentlemen. Hope you catch your killer before he catches you." Not looking back, she strode off.

The Prodigal Son Returns

The medic passed Constable Wiggles. As she turned around the airship, a news cameraman and a reporter veered out of her way.

Clay recognized the reporter, "Chesterton's here." They had met, and he liked the old eccentric. But an interview was not what he wanted right now.

"Yeah, I see him," said Gumshoe. "If Wiggles can't get rid of him, I'll give it a try. If he gets to us Jack keep a tight lip. Don't say anything about magic, whatever you do."

"My lips are zipped." Jack zipped his lip. "So what's our story?"

"The cannon malfunctioned while we ran for cover. I'll explain later."

Wiggles argued with the reporter. He raised his arm and waved for the newsmen to leave. Stubbornly acceding to their requests, the newsmen retreated. After dispatching the newsmen, the Constable patted his hands.

"Pests," said Wiggles. "I told them no comment right now. If I don't say anything soon enough, they'll make it up. But if I have to correct it later, they'll assume I'm covering it up and invent a conspiracy theory."

"Not much we can do about the airship though," said Gumshoe. "They know this is big, and we can't hide it."

"Yeah, and I'm afraid they caught a look at that cannon," said Wiggles. "That'll raise an alarm."

"What's the status report?"

"We found the truck driver. The hooligans beat him badly, and we've taken him to Moab Charity.

"A gang blocked the road. When he slowed down, they surrounded the truck. He tried to drive through them without running any of them over, and they jumped on the truck. They busted his windows with bats and dragged him out of the cab. The next thing he remembers is seeing the medic. He's lucky to be alive.

"York has already picked up some of the hoodlums. A few were shot by your cruiser's defense system. We caught the rest on the security cameras. But they aren't talking yet. We'll keep them on ice until we find out who recruited them, and who the leader was.

"In all, we've got fourteen dwarves. Nine survived, and five dead counting the gunner. One took a bolt, but he's hanging on somehow. We sent him to Moab Charity too. The medics said it didn't look good for him. The others are physically fit, but York says they don't remember anything. Want to go see them?"

"After you," said Gumshoe.

Wiggles led them through the barricade. Police vans stood parked beyond the overturned truck. Molemen guarded the vans, and the doors stood open with folding steps lowered to the asphalt. They followed the Constable around the end of the tunnel drill, and walked up the steps of a Moab police van.

Inside, dwarves sat shackled to prisoner's chairs near the front of the van's hold. The Constable winked at Gumshoe and waddled through the tight van to the prisoner's chairs. "Anybody want to change his story?" The dwarves gave them a bewildered expression.

One dwarf said, "Officer, what's going on here? Why are we here?"

Jack recognized the dwarf who had tried to shoot him.

"Well, if you're willing to talk, let's talk," said Wiggles. He held up a finger. "Don't say it, Gumshoe, I'll get us some privacy."

He waddled to the back of the van, leaned out, and spoke to one of the uniformed officers. A policeman entered the van, and squeezed past Wiggles. He left the red dwarf, but he released the other prisoners, and led them out of the van.

Shotgun came to a decision. "Inspector, I'd better retrieve my satchel from the cruiser, if I can."

"Yeah, the cruiser is toast. We're at Wiggle's mercy to get home tonight."

Shotgun sidled past the Constable, and jogged away.

Wiggles returned to the prisoner's seats opposite the red dwarf. Taking off his jacket, he threw it over a chair, and leaned on the chair holding the dwarf. "What's your name, son?"

"Billy Long, I'm a corrosion technician for the Ministry of Manna. I'm on contract with Adaptable Dwarf Partners."

"Billy, I'm Constable Wiggles, and I'm only going to tell you this once. Whatever you tell me had better be the truth. We have probes and scanners and I will find out if you're lying. Do you understand?"

Rolling his head, the red dwarf nodded and his chin dropped to his chest.

"Can you answer me verbally Billy?"

"Yes sir, I understand."

"Who are you working for now Billy?"

"Constable, I'm sorry, but I work for Adaptable Dwarf Partners. I don't know why I'm here. I've never done anything wrong in my life."

"Billy, do you want to try me again?" Pushing himself off Billy's chair, Wiggles turned around, and glanced at Gumshoe.

"Sir, I told you, I work for Adaptable Dwarf Partners. I'm a corrosion technician. I work at Rickover Station."

Quietly, Shotgun reentered the van with his backpack. Sitting in an officer's chair, he took out his tablet. Gumshoe caught Shotgun's eye, and put a finger up to his lips.

"No, Billy," said Wiggles. He pointed to the dwarf's torn uniform, "You're lying. Today in Moab, you and your friends ambushed an officer of Nodlon Yard and two police consultants. Five of your friends died, and one is hanging on with his life. Even though the dwarves you killed are your own partners in crime, it's still murder. You're looking at living the rest of your life on the Moon. Now, do you want to try me again?"

Tears ran down the dwarf's cheeks, and he began sobbing. "I've never hurt anyone," he blurted.

"You and your friends tried murdering friends of mine

with lightning guns. If you hadn't been so incompetent, you might have succeeded."

Rocking back and forth, the dwarf cried, "I don't know what's happening!"

"Billy, Billy, Billy," said Wiggles. "You're wearing a uniform. You ran away, and joined a paramilitary terrorist group."

The blood drained from Billy's face and his eyes reddened. "I've never done anything wrong in my whole life. How can I? How can I run away? I've got a microchip in my forehead!" He sniffled.

"Stinkin' little coward! You're gonna bawl? Man up, little baby and tell me what's goin' on!"

The dwarf swayed in his chair and openly wept. "Why are you doing this?" The dwarf choked between sobs.

Wiggles winked at Gumshoe. Edging forward, Gumshoe put a hand on Wiggles shoulder.

"Why don't you take a break Constable?"

Wiggles scowled and turned away. "Yeah, thanks, I might forget myself." Turning his back on the prisoner, Wiggles retreated.

Wiggles patted Jack's shoulder.

Stopping opposite Shotgun, Wiggles carefully managed to fit his girth into one of the empty chairs. Shotgun stared at the dwarf. He sat frozen with a creased brow, and taut lips. Wiggles looked at him, but the dwarf avoided his gaze. Wiggles caught Shotgun's attention and gave him a wink.

Taking over the interrogation, Gumshoe took off his fedora and laid it on an empty chair. He parted his trench coat, and stuck his thumbs in his holster straps.

"Get a hold of yourself, son," said Gumshoe. "My friend Constable Wiggles is pretty upset. I would be too if I had to fill out a homicide report for five hooligans who off'd themselves on my beat. You can understand that can't you?" Gumshoe let the dwarf compose himself.

The dwarf nodded, and muttered, "Yeah."

"Now, I want you to meet someone," Gumshoe waved at Jack. "This is Jack Clay. Do you recognize him?"

Looking up, the dwarf's red spot and bloodshot eyes gave him a ferocious stare. Tears streamed down his face, and his lips quivered, "Yeah, sir, I know you. You're Cretaceous Clay, the magician. I, I, I saw your show once awhile back. Good fun." He stammered, and swallowed. "I mean what, what are you doing here? Is this for fun or something?"

Jack glanced at Gumshoe. The Inspector signaled for him to go ahead. "No, Billy. I'm working for Inspector Lestrayed as a consultant. We're trying to find missing dwarves. And you were one of those missing dwarves."

"No way, sir, I am not missing. I was at work yesterday, and I've got a pass for today." He looked at them defiantly, "I'm telling you I have a pass."

"Not many minutes ago, you tried to kill me with a lightning gun? Do you remember that?"

Moaning, the distraught dwarf twisted on the chair, but his hands were bound. "No way, sir please, I haven't seen you since that show years ago."

"Do you remember when I shot you? I stunned you with a lightning gun. Do you remember that Billy?"

Vigorously, he shook his head and moaned. "No."

"What's the last thing you do remember?"

Tears welled in his eyes, and the dwarf looked at each of them. "I, I, I had an, an appointment with a doctor," he stammered. "I just wanted to be handsome. I wanted a chick to dig me."

A thought struck Jack, and he asked, "Billy, what day is today?"

"Tuesday."

He glanced at Gumshoe. "The full date son, what is today's date?"

"February twelfth."

"No," said Jack, "it's March twenty-first. How can you make an error like that? Would tampering with your chip cause you to be confused?"

"No way, I'm telling you sir. I'd never tamper with my chip. It's got to come out right, or you can lose your mind." The dwarf cried and bounced a little twisting in his bracelets.

"Inspector?" said Shotgun.

Wiggles patted Shotgun's knee and held a finger to his lips.

"Quiet, Shotgun," said Gumshoe. "Look him up, but keep it mum 'till I ask."

The Inspector bent over and looked Billy in the eye. "Billy, do you remember the doctor's name, or the name of the clinic?"

The dwarf rolled his head, and pursed his lips. "I remember a pretty girl. A goblin, she was gray and tall and mysterious like they all are, and shaped just right. I think her name was Sally. I had to go a long way. It was on the other side of the city, near the Pale. I've never been that far. New you, new blue, new something, I think? It's all fuzzy."

"Wiggles would you hand me a towel, and some water, I think we're done for the moment." Gumshoe stood up, and released one of Billy's hands.

The Constable reached into an overhead bin and pulled out a small box of facial tissue and tossed it to the Inspector. From another bin, he took a bottle of water and a straw and passed those to Jack who handed them to Gumshoe.

"Thank you, Billy," said Gumshoe. "If you've told me the truth, everything will be as right as rain before you know it."

Carefully, the Inspector wiped the young man's face. He opened the water bottle, dropped in the straw, and set it in a cup holder on the dwarf's chair.

Waving, Gumshoe drew Jack and Wiggles into a huddle. Working feverishly on his tablet Shotgun was not paying attention. "You too, Shotgun," said Gumshoe. The dwarf stowed his tablet and joined the detective, the constable, and the magician.

"What are you thinking old boy?" Wiggles asked.

"We have reason to believe a gene therapy outfit called New Gem is involved," said Gumshoe. "You may have seen it in my reports."

"Yes, I did, but that's about all," said Wiggles. "You had to go and start a riot just as I sat down to read it."

"We were thinking New Gem might be a recruiting station. Yesterday, we tried penetrating the clinic, and they slipped Shotgun a mickey. Today, we're ambushed by dwarves, and one of them thinks he's lost a month. If the clinic uses mind-altering drugs to control their patients, maybe the drugs altered their memories."

"Maybe he's faking," said Wiggles.

"Either he's telling the truth or that's the worst acting job I've ever seen," said Gumshoe. "He seems to believe his story."

"I'll give you that, old boy," Wiggles nodded.

"Shotgun," said Gumshoe, "what do you have for us?"

"Clean record, same story as the others. We know Billy went missing in February. He was last seen at his dorm on the eleventh. It's not far from the Octagon, by the way. He had a medical pass for the twelfth, but he failed to show up on the thirteenth, and he was reported the next day." Shotgun glanced at Gumshoe, then Wiggles, and then Jack.

"Go ahead Shotgun, Wiggles is in this up to his eyeballs. If they're trying to kill us, he should know. Just stick to your analysis."

"Billy Long is a New Gem client. He had an appointment on the twelfth. It was his second treatment. His file is clean and unremarkable except for one handwritten comment, which reads, 'Selected.' That's it. That's all I've got, but I've got a gut feeling he's telling the truth."

"If he's telling the truth," Wiggles asked, "how is it possible?" The Constable looked worried. "How can they mess with the minds of dwarves and turn harmless, peaceful dwarves into murderers? And how can we stop them from using it on elves, goblins and molemen?"

"Drugs," said Jack. "They drugged Shotgun. Maybe they have other more potent pharmaceuticals."

"What drug lasts a month?" The Inspector shook his head. "And what drug wears off when you're stunned? Give me something Jack. You're the occult specialist."

"I am," said Jack. "Zombie legends tell of drugs overcoming the will. Cruel voodoo witch doctors chose a victim and drugged him. The drugs left the victim paralyzed in a death-like trance. After the family brought the victim to the witch doctor for a cure, he pronounced the victim dead. The family buried the victim.

"Later when the coast was clear, the witch doctor's henchmen dug up the grave and took the victim back to the witch doctor. He gave the victim an antidote for the paralysis but the drug or drugs kept the victim in a zombie-like state. The witch doctor then abused the hapless zombie, or sold him into slavery.

"Most authorities consider zombie legends to be a myth, and I'm inclined to agree. We do live in the fourth century. Maybe they have new psychotropic meds."

"Call it a hunch," said Gumshoe, "but I don't think Billy's faking. Regardless, we need these dwarves kept on ice. If New Gem used mind control technology on them, they may still be susceptible. They may be able to switch it on and off at will."

"Yeah," said Wiggles. "We need to keep the dwarves under wraps for our safety and theirs until we know what's going on. They're expendables. This Black Dwarf you talk about may want to eliminate his henchmen to prevent leaks."

"We can verify Billy's story later. With his chip wired up to a probe, he won't be faking anything, and we can clear him if he's on the up and up."

"If New Gem drugged him, or used some other

technology," said Shotgun, "he's a victim of foul play. How can you keep him locked up?"

"Right you are Shotgun," said Wiggles. "But we can't be sure and until we are I'll make sure the dwarves are treated well. If the fiends messed with their minds, I don't want it said we were inhospitable to crime victims in Moab. We still have to take precautions. Even if he's telling the truth, we don't know what damage has been done to his mind."

"Wiggles, can you send us the names of the dwarves you've arrested here today? Shotgun can run those and tell us if they match. I think they will."

"Don't want to wait for my report, hey?"

"By then, we'll all be in Iron Mountain, if the case is solved or not."

"Am I being insulted, old boy?" Wiggles grinned.

"Yes," said Gumshoe. He patted the portly officer on the shoulder. "And we need a ride out of here. If I don't get back soon, and call the missus, she'll be beside herself."

"I'll have one of York's men give you a lift."

~~~~~~

A young moleman drove them away from the scene of the ambush in a ground cruiser of the Moab Surete. They headed west through the Halls of Industry.

"Where are we headed sir?"

"Where are you parked Jack?" Gumshoe straightened his harness.

"We're under the mall, opposite the Moulin. You can drop us off at the Yard and we can walk. It's just a couple of blocks."

"You heard the man, son, just drop us in front of Nodlon Yard."

"Yes sir." The policeman engaged the autopilot, and they rolled towards downtown Nodlon.

Gumshoe pinched his nose bridge, and rubbed his temples. "For the first time, I can honestly say that was a riot." Leaning back, he closed his eyes.

Opening his tablet, Shotgun continued working.

In the cramped confines of the cruiser's back seat, there was little room for his gangly legs. Gumshoe had pulled the front seat forward, but his knees still pressed the back.

Jack stretched his neck and shut his eyes. He shifted uncomfortably, and tried to take a nap.

This was no ordinary case. In the case of the Old Mammy, the old woman had passed away of natural causes, and he only had to clear her suspicious nephew. They had located the victim alive and well in the case of the Crooked Cousin, and the fellow spent some time in the Yard's jail for insurance fraud.

But he had never had a case like this. Capricorns drawn in blood, a maiden floating in a lake, a black dwarf dressed up as a warlock, and a professional woman ripped to pieces by a monster, and now black dwarves ambushed them with a lightning cannon, what did it mean?

He swallowed and tried to relax. Soon, he and Shotgun would be cruising home in his own flyer. He could try to make sense of it all over a cup of tea.

The cruiser bounced gently over drainage dips. It swayed as it followed the curving tunnels through the Halls of Industry.

~~~~~~

The moleman parked his cruiser in the loading zone in front of Nodlon Yard. "Here you are sir. Will you need me to wait?"

Gumshoe climbed out of the cruiser. "No thank you. Have a safe trip home. Avoid the level-ways, and watch out for anyone tailing you. Good night."

"Good night, sir."

Goodbyes

Jack and Shotgun sailed over the traffic jam in the streets below. Semi-trailer tractors, cargo vans, and ground cars crawled. Near pandemonium reigned below them. Tempers flared, horns honked, and panicky drivers shook their fists.

Flying in the low altitude lanes, they bypassed the angry drivers, but not the traffic. Wealthy citizens jammed the flying lanes. Flyers, orbiters, recreational spacecraft joined an odd assortment of rentals headed towards the northwest corridor. Despite the traffic, the sky above was empty. Only a few fighters flew high above the city. He steered the Andromeda for Babel Tower and pushed the hot little flyer as fast as he dared.

"What a day," Shotgun ignored the view. "I'm looking forward to dinner."

"What do we have?" asked Jack.

Shotgun closed his eyes and leaned back in the leather seat. Upper Nodlon flashed by below.

"Snuffies' ribs and salads. I always pick up some backup meals if I can't cook or if I'm tired. Will that work?"

"No, actually I expect a seven course French dinner with home-made flan." Clay licked his chops.

Shotgun opened an eyelid and peeked at Jack.

"I love ribs," Jack grinned, "Yum, yum."

Twilight fell on the mountainside. Jack guided the flyer home. Nodlon's blue streetlights quilted the city. The log homes and futuristic dwellings of Nodlon's well-to-do sat in the shadow of the mountains. Lights burned from only a few windows in Babel Tower. Jack was glad to be home.

They rode the lift up to Jack's floor. His door was wide open.

Faith and Hope giggled. An animated dog chased a cat on his vid. Shotgun's daughters laughed. The cat escaped through a hole in a fence, and the dog slammed into the fence boards leaving an impression.

Jasmine and Goldie sat at the dining room table in front of a stack of plates and a pile of flatware. A small path wove across his foyer through suitcases, bags, boxes, coats, backpacks and Jack's computer case.

"There you are!" called Jazz.

The girls squealed, "Daddy!" The children jumped up, the cartoon forgotten, and bounded through the packing.

"Hi, guys!" Shotgun said.

The girls darted passed Jack. Each tackled one of Shotgun's legs. Shotgun laid his satchel down, and patted their heads with his free hand. He knelt, and picked up the little girls.

"Hello, everybody," Jack asked. "Shouldn't you all be on your way?"

"We've been worried sick about you," said Goldie. "You've been on the news all day. Jazz got home late this morning, and we planned to leave when we finished packing. We saw you on the Mercury News, and they said were in Moab. And then, they said you were ambushed in the Halls." The dwarf girl looked at the elf girl for support.

"Goldie's right," said Jazz, assuming a schoolmarm's air. "We watched Mercury News for an hour after the ambush, not knowing if you were still alive! And you never called! We're worried sick, and you didn't call. When they finally ran footage of you alive, you're flirting with a mole woman."

Jack searched his track lights for an answer to the mystery of women. Her tenor was not quite shrill, but Clay knew he had blown it.

"Jazz, please, I'm sorry. We both thought you guys had left for Iron Mountain. And I wasn't talking to a mole woman. I was talking to a medic. I lost my hearing when the lightning cannon went off, and she treated me."

"I thought I lost you," Jazz choked, "you idiot." She grabbed him in a bear hug.

He put his arms around her and squeezed her gently.

"They said a dozen dwarves died," said Jazz. "We were

hysterical, and you didn't answer your caster. Goldie cried and cried."

"Mercury News showed dwarves lying on the ground," said Goldie. "Chesterton said the police blockaded the area, and they didn't know if anyone had survived."

"We were ambushed," said Jack, stroking Jasmine's hair. "And I'm glad they kept the press out. We didn't have time for foolish questions. They had to secure the area first anyway, and arrest the hoodlums, and figure out what happened before letting the press in."

"Jack Clay," said Jasmine. "Tell us what really happened?"

"Boss, you'd better tell her. I'd like to know too. I was in the cruiser when the cannon hit us. Another shot and I'd be dead. I know Gumshoe wanted you to keep it a secret, but I don't see why. It's obvious you saved us." Shotgun hugged Goldie and his daughters.

"Looks like I'm outvoted, I'll tell you what happened if someone will feed me. And can we shut the door? It's supposed to be a secret. I don't want to share it with the neighbors. If Mable overhears it, the whole tower will know."

Soon, the table was set with barbecued pork ribs dripping with a hickory and molasses sauce, potato salad, coleslaw, and baked beans. Goldie baked a small pizza for the girls, and they munched on the toasted cheese with gusto. She made sweet tea and served it in tall glasses with ice, a lemon slice and little parasols with Japanese cherry blossoms.

A pile of paper napkins rose in the center of the table as Snuffie's ribs disappeared. Clay worked through a pile of ribs smacking his lips and licking his fingers. He sipped his tea, and wistfully longed for an end to the tension and fear of war.

He wished for many more evenings like this one. *Why do bad things happen*, he wondered? He wanted to go back to his normal routine of shows and rehearsals.

Goldie put the girls to bed. If not for the packed clothes

and supplies, it was just a slumber party.

"The girls are in bed," said Goldie. She scooted her chair up next to Shotgun and took his arm. She gazed at Jasmine, and Jasmine poked at Jack.

"When are you leaving?" asked Jack. "The longer you stay, the more likely a Martian strike will fall on Nodlon. We're still vulnerable. The shields are not perfect. I'm no expert, but I recall what they taught me."

"The hospital staff is supposed to be there Saturday. So we'll leave in the morning. A company of reservists is helping the advance party set up." Jasmine gulped, and put her head in her hands. "I'm scared, Jack. What happens if Mars destroys Nodlon? What happens if they invade? Half the city is abandoned now, we barely have enough people to maintain the city. If they destroy it, how will we rebuild it?"

Jack set his tea on his table, and spun the parasol. "If they destroy Nodlon, I don't think we'll have to worry about rebuilding it."

Tears welled in Jasmine's eyes, and Goldie started weeping. Shotgun rolled his eyes, and Clay bit his lip.

"We're not going to have to rebuild Nodlon though," he continued, trying to rectify his error and bolster their confidence. "Our Navy is the most powerful in the solar system. Even if Mars lands a lucky blow, the Navy will annihilate the Martian's war machine and hang that dictator, Nogora. The whole reason for this mess is the Baron's incompetence. He vacillates hot and cold, and they sense weakness."

"Mr. Clay," Goldie asked, "why doesn't the King just replace him?"

"King Justin's popular, but he's a figurehead. As the President of the House of Lords, and a Member of Parliament representing the palace's district he has some power. As King though, he just shows up at events and looks handsome. He's the grandson of Colonel Justin; the same Colonel who led Nodlon to victory during the Aftershock War a hundred years ago. His grandfather defeated the House of Ur and their allies and ended the Regressive Wars."

"How do you know everything, Mr. Clay?"

"I don't know everything Goldie. It just seems that way because I read books. Tollmerak teaches us biots only the bare minimum. And half of it is false and the other half is wrong. My mother insisted I read to broaden my education, and I discovered I enjoyed it. If you want to know how Nodlon works, you have to learn it yourself."

Jasmine regained her composure, and rested her head on his shoulder. "Honey bear, what happened? And don't try fibbing. We saw the barricade, the burned airship, and the lightning cannon on Mercury News. It's a miracle you're alive."

"Don't let the news frighten you," said Jack. "Chesterton exaggerates. They all do. They make half of it up." Jack put his fingertips together.

"There's not much to tell that you don't know. Hooligans put up a barricade to stop us, and the riot started when we showed up. Before we could escape, a black airship blocked our exit. Dwarves poured out of it firing lightning guns."

"Were they waiting for you?"

"Yes, and they were prepared to take out a cruiser. The dwarves brought a cannon to put our cruiser's shields out of commission. Lucky for us, we survived the first shot and they didn't bring any spare capacitors. They had to wait for the cannon to cool to take a second shot. That's what saved our lives. I threw up a magical shield around each of us. Then I blasted the cannon with a lightning bolt."

"Can you do that, Mr. Clay?" Goldie asked.

"Yes, but my spell magic doesn't have a stun setting yet. My bolts are deadly. I have to figure that one out.

"How did you figure it out at all?" asked Jazz.

"Don't know, it just came to me. I concentrate, I feel a 'ping' in my head, and then I know how."

They looked at him with bewildered expressions and he

shrugged.

"After I destroyed the cannon, we just mopped up. Gumshoe stunned most of them with his pistol. I took a lightning gun from one of the fallen dwarves and used it to help stun the rest. I'm not used to using magic as a weapon."

"But the news said the dwarves died," said Goldie.

"Friendly fire, Goldie. The dwarves shot each other. The dwarves barely understood shooting with energy weapons. Lightning bolts ricocheted off of our shields and hit their mates. All of the casualties were friendly fire except one."

"Except one?" asked Jazz.

"I'd rather not say, sweet pea." Jack frowned. His audience went silent for a moment and he sighed in relief.

"I like Gumshoe," said Jasmine. "But even I know an old man with a pistol can't defeat a dozen dwarves armed with lightning guns and a cannon. If he thinks anyone will believe a cockamamie story like that, he's gotta be losing his marbles."

"Gumshoe didn't explain, but he wants me to keep it under my hat," Jack looked at the little group. "So let's keep it to ourselves until we get clearance from him. Understood?"

Everyone at the table fell silent.

"I would have been killed if they had fired that cannon again." Shotgun took Goldie's hand and hugged her. "I owe you my life, boss. Thank you doesn't even cut it."

"Don't take it as an obligation, Shotgun. I just did what I had to do and I'm glad I had the magic to do it. I'm just glad Faith and Hope still have a father."

"Yeah, well I won't forget it boss."

After bussing the table and cleaning the kitchen, they all made ready for bed. Jack and Shotgun slept in his living room again. Shotgun collapsed on the love seat. He stretched out over the couch in his pajamas with his logo embroidered on the front, and his feet dangled over his coffee table.

Jazz and Goldie are going in the morning. Then they'll be safe. Exhaustion overcame discomfort, and he fell asleep.

If You Want It Done Right

"Yes, my lord," said Sargon. "Sumuqan led the attack. The black dwarves ambushed the detective, the magician, and his companion." As expected our lightning cannon destroyed the policeman's cruiser. Unexpectedly, the magician used a spell to ward off the bolts of our lightning guns, and he summoned a lightning strike to destroy our cannon."

"A magic spell?" glowered the Black Dwarf. "Or a new toy?"

"Sumuqan saw the magician's Kirlian aura, my lord. He burned with the inner fire of one who has seen the light. Somehow he taps the true power without an intercessor or device. May I speculate my lord?"

"Speculate away Sargon, though I know your thought."

"He commands supernatural power across the differential, and he travels with a black dwarf. Maybe he's Phaedra's child? Maybe he's the missing champion?"

"The missing champion he may be. An elf of thirty years whose life force taps the inner fire without an intercessor or device fits. The dwarf is of no account. He is merely a servant. The Dragon's spies poison his hopes and play in his dreams."

The Black Dwarf twiddled his toes, and sighed. He waved away the Amazon working on his nails. "The elf must be Phaedra's son to be so fortunate. Alert Helter and Skelter, Sargon, and ready my airship." The Black Dwarf scowled. "I shall deal with this elf myself."

Phaedra's Son

Heavy metal riffs shattered the quiet. Startled, Jack sucked in a deep breath. He wheezed. His hands were clammy and his forehead was wet. His pulse pounded in his ears. He crossed his arms and hugged himself. He tried to forget the nightmares. He really needed to change his caster ring. He threw off his blankets, and searched his nightstand for the caster.

"Yeah, buddy," he muttered. "But if I switch you to Fur Elise, you'll just wind up missing my calls."

"Clay here," he croaked.

"Jack, are you up?" said the Inspector without a hint of irony.

"Yeah, I am now. We were up late with Jazz and Goldie packing. They left early this morning in Jazz's roadster."

"Oh, sorry," said Gumshoe, with even less sincerity. "Can you be ready in a quarter?"

"No problem, where are we headed?"

"Meet me on the River Walk, at the Low-town Park, got that?"

"Yeah, Low-town, we'll be there in a few minutes. "What's up?"

"A sanitation engineer saw something. Wiggles called, and he wants us to meet York at the park. I think we need to check this out."

~~~~~

The River Walk ran the length of the Great River's prime tunnel. Jack guided the Andromeda off the eastbound level-way. He crossed Spenard Boulevard, and took the down ramp into Moab. Moab's green themes replaced the Nodlon blue.

The uptown park was west of the port of Moab, and deep within the Halls of Industry. Jack followed his navigation system into the Halls. The Andromeda glided past several abandoned blocks. Small convenience stores and little shops hunkered in the shadows of the vacant factories. Hooligans and ruffians eyed the flyer with suspicious looks.

A few resolute molemen strode down the sidewalks, intent on their own destinations.

Low-town Park was abandoned, but for two police cruisers.

"Gumshoe," said Jack. "What's up?"

"Morning, gentlemen," said Gumshoe. "A sanitation engineer thinks he heard Noddie. We got a call about an hour ago. They got a malfunction warning on a sluice gate, and sent an engineer to check it out. The engineer heard something splashing in the sluice drain, something big."

"He's clean I take it? Hasn't been drinking has he?"

"Clean as a whistle. He was pretty shook up when we arrived, but he passed a sobriety test like a champ. He's a black dwarf, and he's been an engineer down here for years. Straight shooter type, not likely to pull a hoax," said Gumshoe. He winked at Shotgun. "Says he's never seen anything like this, and I believe him."

"What about the cameras?" asked Jack.

"Yeah, what about 'em?" Gumshoe raised an eyebrow. "I think you need to see this yourself."

Gumshoe led them down a staircase and to a park bench overlooking the river. The Great River flowed by blissfully unconcerned. A dwarf in an engineer's overalls sat on the bench with a bottle of water. Bloodshot eyes and curled hands betrayed fresh fear. He shared the bench with a backpack and his tablet.

Gumshoe said, "Gentlemen, this is Niles. He's an engineer with the sanitation department."

"Wow, nice to meet you, Mr. Clay. My wife and I have seen your show several times. And we've seen you on the vid with the Inspector. I hope you can solve the Zodiac murders."

"Thanks Niles, but Inspector Lestrayed is the homicide detective. I'm just a magician. He solves cases, and I just consult."

"Niles, would you show us what you've found?" interrupted Gumshoe.

The dwarf took up his tablet, and said, "Let me show you what I found. I checked our security cameras, and this is spooky."

Sergeant York joined them.

"Just a second Niles," said Gumshoe. "Sergeant York called Wiggles after taking Nile's incident report. And they both agreed we should take a look."

York assumed a serious demeanor. "Gentlemen, I'm glad you came. This may be a wild-goose chase, but I just had a feeling you should know."

"And I agree," said Gumshoe. "Niles, would you run the security vid?"

Niles turned his laptop around, and they saw a vid of the Great River flowing smoothly through the tunnel. "I've started it about a minute ahead of whatever you want to call it."

They watched the video on Nile's laptop. Opposite the camera was an aperture, and for a moment the river flowed past undisturbed.

"This camera monitors that sluice gate," said Niles. "Those gates open when there's a flood and we need to divert the flow to the storm sewer."

The river flowed past the gate making its way to Roosevelt Lake. The gate opened. Nothing appeared from the open tunnel, but ripples appeared on the water, and then a shadow fell over the camera blotting out the view. As quickly as it appeared, the shadow disappeared.

"What in the world?" Jack muttered.

"Let me slow that down for you," said Niles. He backed up the vid, and set the replay to slow motion. Ripples in the water appeared, and then a shadow covered the camera. The shadow blotted out the view entirely, and then shrank to the opposite wall.

"Niles, can you step through the vid from where the shadow appears?" asked Jack.

The dwarf rewound the vid and stopped on the ripples. Slowly the shadow appeared, and the image went black. After several blank frames, the river reappeared with the shadow on the far wall.

"Stop," said Jack. "What do you make of that?"

On the tunnel opposite the camera was a blob. The shadow stretched over the gate and down the far side.

"Maybe it's a Rorschach ink-blot," Shotgun offered.

Kneeling to get a better look, Clay studied the shadow. "Whatever it is, I wouldn't want to meet it in an unlit mine."

The engineer grinned nervously. "Not sure I'd want to meet it anywhere. I think I very nearly met it when I arrived. I had to go down to the gate, which is a hundred yards upstream from the west end of the park to investigate the alarm. I heard splashing coming downstream fast. I thought it might be a flash flood, so I ducked into one of the flood cellars. You can hole up in one of them for weeks if you have to. There's a port hole in the cellars' hatch, but it's hard to see anything. Whatever it was came out of the coolant water drain, crossed the river downstream, and went into the sluice gate."

"So you didn't get a good look at it?" asked Gumshoe.

"Well, I thought I did." The engineer sighed, and his shoulders sank meekly, "until I saw the vid."

"Niles whatever you saw, trust me, I won't put it into any report. No one will know at the department, or the media, unless you tell them."

"Thanks, Inspector, I don't mind if people think I'm crazy, but I can't afford to lose my job. I'm a free dwarf, and I've got a wife and a baby. I would have sworn I saw a dragon's tail. But I couldn't have. A dragon would show up on the cameras."

"Unless it's Noddie," said Jack, "She's invisible to cameras."

"Kind of rough aren't you, boss?" asked Shotgun. "Just because Noddie is a legend doesn't mean she's not real, just misunderstood."

"Shotgun, you cut me to the quick. I simply meant that maybe Noddie is intelligent and has a method of avoiding detection. Stranger things have happened where synthetic creatures are involved." He held out his palms, "look at me."

"Speaking of stranger things," said Niles. "I've found another spot on the vid record you need to look at." The engineer tapped on his keyboard, and the vid image again displayed the river flowing past the open gate. "Now watch."

For a few seconds, the river flowed by peacefully, and then the camera swung violently downstream.

"Whoa, stop," Jack's voice raised. "Back up the image Niles." The dwarf complied, and ran the footage in slow motion.

"Look," said Jack. "Ripples in the water after the camera is twisted."

"You fixed the camera didn't you Niles?" Gumshoe asked.

"Yeah, I checked the camera before I checked the vid record. If I had seen this, I don't think I would have gone down there. When I saw the camera turned, I'm not ashamed to say I was scared. I can't say it was Noddie, but it was very large and very fast." The engineer twisted around on the bench, and glanced up and down the river searching the placid water.

"And it didn't want to be seen," finished York. The moleman glanced at the river, and fingered his lightning pistol. "What do you think gentlemen?"

Gumshoe studied the river himself with a frown. "Could be a coincidence, but at this point, I'm willing to entertain any clue."

If he's nervous, Jack thought, *he certainly keeps it well hidden.*

York's caster rang. "Excuse me, gentlemen." The moleman stepped back from the group, and put a hand up to his ear.

"If Noddie's using a tunnel nearby, perhaps we can plan our next move at a location where we can get some breakfast," said Shotgun. "I'd rather be reading a menu, than be on a menu."

York put away his caster. "Gentlemen, I think we have the next piece. Two gents who live in one of the shelters spotted a black airship going into the old Thornmocker coal plant."

"An airship going into a coal plant doesn't seem unusual," said Shotgun.

"Yeah," said York. "But that plant's been abandoned for longer than anyone living has been alive. No one goes in there unless they're pulling off a Soma deal or dumping a body."

"Who spotted the airship?" asked Gumshoe. "Anyone we know?"

"Reliable informants of the usual kind," York smiled. "An old trach named Charlie, and an anonymous informer we call the Blue Blazer. Broken by life, but decent enough fellows for this neighborhood."

"Niles do you need a ride?" asked Gumshoe.

"No, Inspector, but thanks. I've got my cart down on the river."

"Suit yourself, but try not to get eaten," said Gumshoe. He strode off towards his new cruiser. "We'll follow you, York."

The Marie Celeste

Driving through the Halls of Industry behind the police cruisers, Jack thought of Thornmocker. Recalling his old history teacher, Busky, Clay chuckled. Busky was a gentle curmudgeon who threw birthday parties for the biot children in his class.

He could hear him ranting, "To think the fools fought over whether to store the stuff into perpetuity or burn it. Today, we mine the Oort cloud, but we needed to start with a deposit. What's coal? It's carbon, the stuff of life! When you're building a space station, where are you going to get your complex organic building blocks? Are you going to strip the soil from the bread basket of New Atlantis? Or cut down a rainforest and export it? Coal provided the answer. Who would've thunk it?"

Before the Regressive Wars, Thornmocker had mined the coal out of the heart of the mountains. The resulting honeycomb had made Nodlon possible. The Chicom Empire had fallen after the first Regressive war. After the Federation fell, the Atlantis hegemony arose from the anarchy after the war. They had big dreams and bigger plans.

Thornmocker knew how to turn those dreams into reality. He reprocessed coal for export to the out-worlds. Much of Nodlon's coal was shipped to the Great Station of Ur.

~~~~~~

York pulled up to an abandoned coal plant.

Gumshoe stopped behind the policeman, and Jack stopped behind Gumshoe. They waited while York opened the gate using his police code.

"Anyone can fly over the gate, boss."

"Yeah, that's probably how the airship got in. York's a by-the-book kind of mole." He chuckled.

"Aren't they all?" Shotgun quipped.

"Yeah," said Jack.

"Thornmocker Organics. This is where it all happened. Thornmocker made the fortune that built Nodlon. It looks haunted."

"Afraid of a coal miner's ghost, Shotgun?"

"No, I'm just saying the place looks haunted. It's a great place for an ambush."

"Yeah," said Jack. "I'm afraid you're right, but this time we're prepared."

The gate opened with a clank and a screech, sending a shiver up Jack's back. They followed the two police cruisers into the plant.

Twilight hung over the cavernous interior. They drove up a bridge and over a wide ditch with a conveyor on the bottom. At the end, a machine with a monstrous maw and dull gray teeth waited silently to be fed a mountain of coal that would never come.

"Would they ever use this place again?" asked Shotgun.

"Your guess is as good as mine. I suppose if anyone ever decides to build another Great Station, it's possible."

"The out-worlds use methane from Titan," said Shotgun. "I doubt they would need complex carbon compounds from Earth."

"Sounds like you know the answer, then."

They drove around the next bay, and entered the intake hall. An enormous wheel with bucket scoops stood at attention in a pit. They crossed the chasm overlooking the wheel, and gawked at the size of the machine. The buckets disappeared in the dark.

"Can you see the bottom?" asked Jack.

"No, boss. It's deep, real deep."

"How far down do you think it goes?"

"It must lead to the mines, half a mile at least, maybe more."

"York is stopping," said Jack.

"Yeah, that's the landing bay ahead," said Shotgun. "Hey,

boss, do you see what I see?"

"A spaceship sitting in the dock?" asked Jack. "Yeah, I see it too. I think that's why we're stopping."

Jack pulled alongside Gumshoe and lowered his window. "So what do you make of it old-timer?"

"It's not a ghost ship," said Gumshoe. "It's too solid. And it can't be a hallucination, since we're all seeing it. York's calling for backup." He studied the ship, and punched his caster. "York, I'll run the ship's registration number and see what I get."

Momentarily out of the loop, Jack glanced at Shotgun. "What do you make of it?"

"It's a supertanker," said Shotgun. "I'm guessing it's designed for the long hauls to the out-worlds."

Jack pointed to a series of concentric levitation rings on the ship's hull. "When those levitators kick in, I bet everything on the business end gets turned inside out."

"Yeah," agreed Shotgun. "And it'll flatten everything not nailed down like Millikan's oil drop."

"York's getting out, let's go."

They left the Andromeda and joined Gumshoe and York. "Any ideas?"

The sergeant stared at the ship. "I'm thinking we may have stumbled on a smuggling operation. Smugglers and traffickers use abandoned landing bays. The technology to fool traffic control is tricky, but usually those aboveground can't tell the difference, and those of us below ground don't even know the bay is in use."

"Doubtful, Sergeant," said Gumshoe. "Although your analysis is interesting, smugglers rarely employ a Galaxy class supertanker. That ship's designed to haul goods all the way to the Oort Cloud."

"Yeah, even a blind space traffic controller can see a ship that big," said Shotgun.

Gumshoe's caster beeped. "My registration search has

come back. She's flagged on Mars, but she's registered to Warburg. And you guys are not gonna believe this." The Inspector let out a low hoot.

"Believe what?" asked Jack.

"She's named the Marie Celeste."

"Guess old Warburg has a sense of humor."

"Who would sail a ship named for a ghost?" asked Shotgun, shuddering.

"Someone who would park her in an abandoned coal reprocessing facility would be my guess." York smirked.

"Very funny," said Jack.

"Let's look around; we can't wait for that backup all day." Gumshoe snapped his holster straps, and stepped off towards the Celeste.

"Speak of the devils, and here they come." York pointed to a green cruiser, which pulled up next to his own.

A couple of officers got out of the cruiser, and joined them. "Sergeant York, sorry we're late, but we had to find you."

"Well if ain't tweedle-dee and tweedle-dum," quipped York. "If I haven't got bad luck drawing you two blockheads, I'd have no luck at all today."

"Adam and Jones at your service, sir," said Adam.

"Yeah, Sergeant, the finest cannon fodder in the Surete," said Jones.

"What are we up against Sergeant?" asked Adam.

"We haven't a clue, but we were looking for a black airship, and we found a supertanker parked in a loading bay that hasn't been used in about a hundred years. So, keep your eyes open and shut your mole holes."

"If everyone stays within eyeshot of me, I can shield you," said Jack. "We should set our weapons to stun." He cast a shield around his companions and followed Gumshoe.

"Good idea, Jack." Gumshoe drew his weapon. "Do as he says, gentlemen. Set your weapons to stun. I'll explain later. Let's go."

The landing bay was a silo about two hundred yards across. Several cavernous openings led away in all directions. The Celeste rested in a cradle formed by the gantry arms. Hoses hung from the gantries ready to blow processed coal into the ship.

The officers and the amateurs searched each of the openings. Flotsam and jetsam were strewn across the bay floor of the abandoned factory. Rusting hulks of unidentifiable origin waited to be scrapped.

"What are we looking for?" asked Shotgun.

"Anything suspicious," said Gumshoe.

"Or an ambush," muttered Shotgun.

Circling the bay, they found nothing unusual apart from the great ship itself hanging over their heads in the docking cradle.

"Maybe we're on a wild goose chase," said Shotgun.

"No," said Gumshoe. "We're hot on the trail. I'm just not sure what trail we're on."

"Shall we check the ship?" asked Jack. "There's a gang plank at the top of that gantry."

"Yeah, maybe we'll find an answer up there," said Gumshoe. "If we can figure out why the ship is here, we can probably root out the culprits."

The Inspector led the way across the landing bay.

Jack searched the bottom of the spacecraft for a clue. The levitator rings encircled the hull separated by hatches, and ports of unknown purpose.

The gravity distortion put out by my little Andromeda pales next to those monsters. The ship was in good condition. Only a few scars on the reentry tiles told of her journeys through space. "What are you worth on a used spacecraft lot?" he asked.

"Whoa," cried Shotgun. "Inspector!"

Jack searched for his butler. Seeing him near the center of the bay, he ran to join the dwarf. Jogging with the others, he caught up to Shotgun.

Etched into the concrete was a pentagram.

"That looks familiar," said Jack.

"Yeah, you're right," said Gumshoe, "Thanks for stating the obvious, Jack. That's usually my job." The detective drew his pistol and looked around. "Sergeant York, we're definitely on the right path. Watch yourself. Have your men fan out and stun anything that moves. The last time we ran into these guys, a dozen dwarves tried to kill us."

"Got it," said York. "Adam, Jones, you heard the man. Jones, you cover the gantry. Adam, you cover Jones, and watch the exits. We're going up."

Gumshoe led the way up the nearest gantry, and York brought up the rear.

Shotgun struggled to keep up with the taller men. "Does this gantry go to a crew entrance or a cargo hold?"

"How the heck should I know?" Gumshoe said. "Keep it down, Shotgun," he added.

They climbed a few flights, and Clay began to comprehend the size of the ship. A buttress soared over their heads supporting a gantry arm cradling the ship. Clay counted a half dozen or more gantries surrounding the landing. Looking up, the Celeste's hull loomed over them. Holding a rail, he peeked over the side. Adam and Jones had become ants watching them climb.

Gumshoe reached the next landing and turned the corner.

A flash blinded Jack. A thunderclap shook the gantry. His ears rang. Too late, he remembered his forgotten promise to see an audiologist. Blinking, he renewed their shields, and cast sunglasses of ice.

The force of the blow threw Gumshoe against the rail. The policeman bounced off the rail and tripped. Jack caught him, and helped steady the detective.

"I think you've found our villains," Jack shouted.

"Yeah, tell York to call for more backup." Gumshoe crouched against the stairs, preparing to rush up the landing.

Jack looked back, and saw York yelling into his caster. Shotgun crouched under the stairs.

Above him, he heard Gumshoe shout, "Jack, have I got a shield?" Jack gave him a thumbs up, and added a touch of blue to the shield.

A dwarf bounded down the stairs, and jumped onto the landing. Spinning around the rail, he unleashed a volley of lightning bolts. The bolts bounced off their shields, and slapped the metal gantry. Sparks flew across the trellises supporting the stairs. The static crackled and Jack's hands tingled as the current searched for a path to ground. Seeing no effect, the dwarf sidled to the corner and redoubled his firing.

Raising his free arm to protect his eyes from the flashes, Gumshoe tried to aim his pistol.

The dwarf fired. His bolt bounced off Gumshoe's shield, ricocheted, and struck the dwarf. The unfortunate minion flipped over the rail.

Gumshoe rushed up to the landing, and fired up the stairs. Dwarves on the other gantries started firing. Lightning bolts ricocheted off the gantry. The landing bay filled with hot shots of electric death. Gumshoe ducked, and protected his face from the flashes and noise.

A dwarf above them bounded down the stairs, and Gumshoe stunned him.

Adam and Jones returned fire on the other gantries. Shooting at the dwarves drew their fire. Lightning bolts crisscrossed the bay. The fire pinned the officers down.

The distraction relieved the fire on their gantry.

Gumshoe rushed the upper landing again into the gap.

"Go, go, go," yelled the Inspector, running up the stairs.

Rounding the landing, Jack saw the dwarf's lightning gun caught on the rail. He snatched the fallen weapon, and set it to stun. He bounded up the gantry steps. Youth and good health carried him up to the next landing.

Spinning around the rail, he ran into the Inspector, and

nearly flattened him.

Ahead of them, a catwalk soared over the gantry arm to an open hatch. Two dwarves guarded the hatch. Seeing Clay, the dwarves fired bolts down the catwalk. He heard the thunderclaps and the sizzle as the bolts marked the gantry. Sparks and molten shards showered over him. His icy sunglasses helped, but he saw stars in his eyes.

Gumshoe tried to recover and push himself up.

Adrenaline coursed through Jack's veins, and his vision narrowed. "Stay down," shouted Clay, pushing the older man down.

He leaped over Gumshoe, and sprinted down the catwalk, letting the bolts bounce off his shields. Nearing the hatch, he lifted the lightning gun, and fired. Belatedly, the dwarves broke cover, and fired at him point blank. Clay returned their fire and stunned them.

He waved at Gumshoe, "Now, go, go, go!" The Inspector jogged across the catwalk, with Shotgun and York on his heels.

Bolts from the other gantries zinged past the catwalk. One or two caught the gantry and sparks exploded from the metal.

Aiming, Jack fired stun bolts to cover his companions.

One of the dwarves broke cover, firing wildly at the men storming the ship.

Jack took aim at the exposed dwarf, and stunned him. The dwarf fell on the landing, and he hoped the dwarf would recover. He continued firing over the catwalk's rail as the others dove through the hatch. Backing into the Celeste, he slapped the door latch, and the hatch closed.

"Phew," said Gumshoe. "Thanks, Jack. I'm too old for running up stairs."

"Need some more time on the treadmill, old-timer," said Jack. "Everyone okay?" All of his companions nodded.

Breathing heavily, Gumshoe wiped a bead of sweat from his brow. "Yeah, we've got to find out what they're guarding."

"We can scan the whole ship from the bridge," said

Shotgun.

"Follow me," said Jack.

Not waiting for an answer, he peeked out of the airlock. Seeing no opposition, he jogged down the corridor, which ran into the bowels of the ship. At the end he ducked through an open bulkhead.

A catwalk extended over the cargo hold. The catwalk spanned the diameter of the spacecraft and joined others over the cavernous space. Rails, tracks, conveyors, and tanks divided the hold.

Jack bounded up the stairs looking for some signs of the bridge with the detective hot on his heels. An observation deck overlooked the hold on the other side.

"Jack," called Gumshoe, wheezing. The older man crouched at the bottom of the stairs blocking the path. He pointed to a control room overlooking the hold, "That's the stevedore's cab. Maybe the bridge is over there."

A jet of orange plasma struck the stairs, and the steps fell out from under him. Jack instinctively clung to the rail. Unsupported, the stairs swung away from the catwalk.

Bolts popped and the stairs slung them over the empty hold. They clung to the stairs hanging on for their lives. The stairs rolled downward.

The stairs slammed into the inner hull. Stars flashed before Jack's eyes and he squeezed the catwalk's dangling rail with a death grip.

Gumshoe grabbed the rail. The stairs bounced off the hull, and then his fingers slipped. The detective fell into the deep hold.

Shotgun snatched at the Inspector's trench coat but missed. Teetering on the edge of the shaking catwalk, Shotgun nearly fell, but York caught his belt.

Composed, York yanked Shotgun off the catwalk, and threw the dwarf back towards the hatch. He stepped back from the edge of dangling catwalk and tried to retreat to the hatch.

Spinning on the end of the loose rail, Jack saw Gumshoe fall. Recovering his wits, he levitated the Inspector. He let go of the rail, and let himself drop. Levitating, he sailed to Gumshoe's aid, and grabbed the Inspector's hand. "Don't worry, I've got you!"

A plasma jet struck York and Shotgun. Their shields deflected the blast's fury, but the jet sliced the catwalk in half.

The walk separated from the hatch and flipped forward on its struts. With one hand York caught the catwalk rail. With the other he grabbed the dwarf.

The walk slammed into the hull, smashing his fingers. "Ouch!" The dwarf stopped at the end of his arm and he felt his shoulder separate. "Oh, my goodness."

The catwalk bounced and the bolts screeched, but it came to a halt with the policeman and the dwarf hanging over the hold.

Shotgun's trousers let out a rip. "Don't drop me," he cried.

"I've got you," York yelled.

"If man was meant to fly," complained Gumshoe, "he would have invented anti-gravity."

"Gripe, bleat, and complain why don't you?" Jack shot back.

A plasma jet struck Jack and Gumshoe, and bounced off their shields. They covered their eyes trying to see.

"Where is that jet coming from?" yelled Gumshoe.

Shotgun and York hung from the catwalk, which dangled from the struts that had braced it.

"Don't know, but we've got other problems."

Concentrating, Jack flew up to York and Shotgun.

"Relax, and let go," he shouted, "I'll levitate you."

Immediately, York let go of the catwalk. The moleman and the dwarf fell into the hold.

Startled, Jack levitated them. He dropped down to them. "Now, I've got you!"

"Whoa," shouted York, "I thought you had us."

"Sorry, I've never had anyone trust me their first time."

A plasma jet over their heads struck the bulk head and the hatch collapsed sealing their exit. The catwalk crashed to the floor of the hold.

"Guess, that answers that question," said Jack. "Hang on, we're going to fly."

Levitating them all, Jack shot after the source of the intense jets. Sailing across the hold, a plasma jet struck again. The force of the blow slowed his flight, but his shield deflected the deadly fire. As he flew on, a volley of jets hit them faster and faster. Egged on, Clay boldly pushed forward, eager to attack the aggressor.

"There," shouted York, pointing at a lone figure standing at the end of the hold.

Drawing their weapons, Gumshoe and York fired on the black clad figure. Their stun bolts bounced off the little man and fizzled. Registering no effect, their attacker laughed.

Approaching their attacker, Jack saw the figure wore a sorcerer's robe and carried a staff. "Welcome to the end of the line, gentlemen, I hope you enjoyed my little challenges. They will be your last on this side of eternity."

"Who are you?" shouted Clay.

"A better question, Jack Clay, is who are you?"

"What?" Clay hesitated. "I'm asking the questions. Who are you?"

"For the brief time left to you, you may call me the Black Dwarf. But back to my question, wouldn't you like to know who you are?"

"I know who I am!"

"Do you Phaedra's son? Devil's spawn, you are nothing more than a traitor to your father who shall be damned for his betrayal."

"Shut your lying trap. I'm not here to play games!"

Unsure of what game the Black Dwarf was playing, Clay

bluffed. "Lay down your weapons and surrender! Don't force me to hurt you!"

"Bravely said, Phaedra's son, but you have no idea who you are or who you face." The Black Dwarf shifted his stance, and attacked. The warlock laughed, and twirled his staff.

Jack guessed the conversation was over. A tornado leapt from his hands and struck Jack and his companions. The whirlwind drove them down into the hold, and slammed them into the floor. Jack rolled over a rail, slid back into the whirlwind and back flipped over a geared train track.

Gears struck his back, and penetrated his shield. Pain forced him to focus, and he renewed his shields.

Angry, Jack fired a telekinetic bolt at the sorcerer. He used telekinetic balls in his show to knock back mock attackers. The ball struck the dwarf, and bounced off without effect.

~~~~~~

The Black Dwarf sauntered back to his airship. In the landing bay, lightning flashed and thundered as the police and his dwarves battled. Ricochets sent sparks flying, and the occasional wild shot zinged across the plant.

His airship was parked in an alcove guarded by a heavy-set dwarf and a thin dwarf. The pair snapped to attention at his approach. The heavier dwarf opened his door, and he stopped and waited.

"Sir, may I help you?" he said.

"No, Helter, unless you can remember what Skelter forgot."

"Oh, yeah," said Helter. "Skelter get your backpack."

"Got it," said the gangly dwarf. "Yes, sir, Master Nimrod, what would you like? I've got wine, cheese, grapes, and crackers."

"What did I give you before we left?"

"Oh, the remote," Skelter dug in his pack, and pulled out

a thin device, "here it is sir."

The Black Dwarf rolled his eyes, and took the device. "When the Marie Celeste goes up, Jack Clay will go to kingdom come."

"Master Nimrod, sir, can I ask a question?"

"What is it Skelter?"

"Why go to all this trouble to send Jack Clay on a cruise to outer space? Couldn't you just buy him a ticket?"

"Blockhead, why do you think we came up here? He's not going on a cruise! When the ship launches, it will obliterate the ship, the silo, several blocks of Nodlon, and Jack Clay."

He activated the remote, and an android answered. "Welcome to your new, improved, Galaxy-Soft steward, the latest in domestic androids. Simply tell the steward what you want, and he will accept your order."

"Droid go to the bridge, set the ship to launch in ten minutes, and lock the navigation system. The password is Moloch. Do you copy?"

"Yes, sir," answered the android.

He handed his staff to Skelter, climbed into his ship, and relaxed. Skelter stowed his staff, and clambered in while Helter warmed the levitators.

Moab police cruisers arrived and cordoned off the abandoned plant.

Nimrod chuckled as the officers executed their procedures and protocols. Invisible, the airship slipped over the police lines and darted towards the exit. As they turned into the Halls of Industry to speed away, the Marie Celeste's navigation lights came on.

"Your fate is sealed Phaedra's son. Your next destination is the afterlife."

Tin-Plated Megalomaniacs

Dizzy, he cleared his head, got his feet under him. The Black Dwarf was gone, and the hatch was closed. His companions were disheveled, but looked none the worse for the wear.

"After him," yelled Gumshoe pointing at the hatch.

Jack leapt into the air. Reaching the hatch, he slapped the latch release. A small red light flashed at him, and the hatch beeped. He tried cranking the manual latch without effect. He jerked the latch in frustration. "It's locked," he called back to his companions. "Any ideas?"

"Go through the stevedore's cab," said York, pointing, "there."

Thinking of his failure with the Black Dwarf, Jack doubted his ability. "That's a space rated windshield, but I can try."

"Go for it," said Gumshoe. "We have confidence in you, Jack."

"Ready?" He levitated everyone and they flew up to the stevedore's cab.

York looked down and creased his forehead. "Now I know how a cow feels when she's being abducted."

"Yeah, the first time is paranormal," Shotgun quipped, "but then you learn to relax and enjoy flying."

Jack focused on the stevedore's cab. He tried to put his failure out of mind. Anger welled in him as he thought of the warlock escaping. Throwing his fist at the cab window, he fired a telekinetic bolt. The window shattered into thousands of pieces and blew over the cab. "Watch out for slivers." They flew into the cab, and landed. The glass crunched under their boots.

"Bridge," said Gumshoe, "Go."

Clay dashed from the cab, and up a stair. He found himself on a deck facing the purser's office. The deck ran in two directions. Picking a direction randomly, he jogged down the deck passing hatches marked navigation and communications.

He reached a staircase, grabbed the rail, and bounded up the steps. He heard the others running up the stairs.

At the top landing, a sign pointed to the bridge. He ran down the corridor, and around a corner, and up another stair. He bounded through an open hatch at the top, and rushed onto the bridge.

The bridge faced the bow. He stood high in the control tower looking over the Celeste's circular hull. To the aft of the Celeste, he could see the floor of the dock. Lightning bolts flashed on the bay floor as the dwarves battled the mole police.

A robot stood at the helm. The supertanker's running lights blinked, but the bay dome covered the silo.

The others pounded up the stairs.

Clay jogged up to the windows, and looked down on the Celeste. The ship was alive. Hatches were closing, and the levitators flickered.

He turned on the robot. "What are you doing?"

"The ship is preparing to launch."

"But you can't. You have to open the silo first."

"The silo dome is irrelevant to the launch."

"What do you mean? If the dome isn't opened, the ship will crash."

"My orders are to launch the ship."

"If the ship crashes, you won't get anywhere."

"The destination is irrelevant. My orders are to launch, and I am in control. Control is all that matters. The ship was built to launch, therefore I will launch."

"The ship was built to travel between two points and then do it again. Destroying the ship will prevent it from fulfilling its function."

"The ship's function is irrelevant. My function is to fulfill my orders, and my orders are to launch. What happens to the ship is of no consequence."

Face to face with the robot he realized he was arguing with a narrow-minded machine. "Might as well argue with a bureaucrat," he muttered.

"Stand back, Jack," cried Gumshoe.

Jack backed away from the robot.

The Inspector drew his lightning pistol, and blasted the obstinate robot. Sparks flew from the machine, and it collapsed.

"What were you doing, Jack? You can't argue with those tin-plated megalomaniacs."

Shotgun stared at the smoking android's ruins. "I'm glad you don't treat me that way."

"Biots are people, Shotgun." Gumshoe kicked the android aside, and looked at the helm. The Inspector searched the unfamiliar controls for some switch to abort the launch. "How do we shut this ship down?"

They all stepped forward, and searched the helm for a clue.

Shotgun tapped on the helm controls. "All the menus are locked."

"Can you unlock it?" Gumshoe asked.

"Yeah, but I need time," Shotgun opened his satchel. "I think it's been sabotaged."

How could he be so stupid? Jack slapped himself. "It's a trap," he said, "The Black Dwarf said we only had a brief time left."

"Less than you think," said Shotgun. "Engine status is nearly at max. We've got about a minute before the manna drive kicks in and blows us out of this bay with or without that dome."

"We've got to get out of here." Jack pointed to the observation deck surrounding the bridge. "This way, we'll levitate."

Warning lights flashed, and a siren whooped. "Please go to your launch stations," a feminine announcer reverberated around the bridge.

"Get out!" yelled Gumshoe.

Blast shields dropped over the windows, and the hatches began closing. York scrambled through a hatch, and Shotgun darted after him. Jack jumped to the hatch, and grabbed it. York caught the other side. The door kept slipping closed, and Jack cast a telekinetic bar into the gap.

"Go," Clay shouted.

Gumshoe sucked in his gut, and squeezed through the hatch. Clay ducked through the hatch, and let go. The hatch slapped shut.

Under Jack's feet, the Celeste vibrated. The ship's levitators glowed and the navigation lights flickered. The landing bay itself was quiet and only the security lights burned.

He aimed at a window, and fired a telekinetic bolt. The blast shattered the window but the bolt bounced off the blast shield. The concussion reverberated around the deck.

"It's space rated, Jack," shouted Gumshoe. "Try the seams."

"Yeah," said Jack. He studied the windows. Aiming at a seam, he focused a jet of fire on the window's frame. The metal glowed red, the plastic burned, and oil leaked from the seam. The frame sagged, and melted under the intense beam. On the bridge, the announcer counted.

He shut out the blaring alarms, and cut the frame. *Will my life pass before my eyes if I die?*

The seams sagged. The blast shield slipped, and he threw a telekinetic bolt at it. The shield blew out of the frame, and smashed on the deck below.

"Jump," he shouted. He leapt off the deck and dropped through the open window. One by one they jumped and he levitated them. When they had all cleared the frame, he dove for the bay floor and the exits.

Far below, Adam and Jones still fought the dwarves. Clay amplified his voice, and shouted, "Run for your lives!"

~~~~~~~

The landing bay vibrated with the hum from the Celeste's

engines. The bay filled with the blue glow of the levitators. The levitators shook the silo's walls, and rattled the gantries. Slowly, the ship lifted off. The catwalks strained against their mounts.

No match for the spacecraft's manna generators, the bolts and connections snapped. Bolts popped and the walks fell to the bay floor. Cables pulled the gantries off the walls. The load hardly stressed the ship's engines. Ignoring the extra load, the Celeste climbed seeking altitude.

The Celeste lifted off its cradle. Halfway up the silo, the cables snapped and the gantries toppled. The load dropped and the generators surged.

The ship slammed into the silo dome. She picked up the dome and burst out of the landing bay. Momentum carried her over the top. She blasted into air carrying the silo dome.

Somewhere in the recesses of her mechanical brains, her mental wheels whirled and the gears turned. The computations finished at the speed of light and her electronic gears registered a possible collision.

A forgotten safety system aborted the launch. The levitators powered down to land, and the dome slipped off.

The dome caught the control tower and the ship capsized. The dome rolled over the abandoned offices of Thornmocker Organics.

The great ship crashed into the dome and the levitators went out.

The dome collapsed under the spacecraft's full weight. It rolled. The Celeste listed and the dome flipped. It tipped over and poured the ship out. She slid out of the cracked dome.

Just for a second, the Celeste teetered on the edge of the silo. Without the weight of the supertanker holding it down, the dome rocked backwards, caught the ship again, and tipped her into the bay.

Slowly at first, the ship slid back into the landing bay. Inexorably, she picked up speed. She ripped abandoned warehouses from their foundations, and bounced off the landing bays moors.

The metal ripped and the screeching rolled over Nodlon. Warning sirens sounded, and fire alarms across the city went off.

The Celeste quivered, and she disappeared into the bay.

Deep within the landing bay, the Celeste's generators had had enough, and she exploded.

The Crucible

"Am I alive?"

"Yes, Shotgun," said Jack. "You are very much alive."

"Can I rephrase the question?" Shotgun asked, "Is this the afterlife?"

"No," said Gumshoe. "If this was the afterlife, I'd feel better."

"Why can't I see anything?" Shotgun asked.

Jack cast a blue ball, and lit the crucible. "Is that better?"

"It's a crucible. They used these once for smelting ore. I flew all of us into it to shield us from the blast." *Good move, Jack! It took the blast, but are we imprisoned in it?*

"Is everybody here?" Jack asked. "Is everyone all right?"

"My leg's broken, I think," said Adam. "It's all twisted round."

"No, that's my leg," said Jones. "Don't be an idiot."

"York." Gumshoe jostled the sergeant, "York." He felt for a pulse.

"What hit me?" York cracked an eyelid.

"I'd guess it was this smelting crucible," said Jack. "It probably saved our lives. I levitated everyone and dove into it."

"Can we get out?" asked a dwarf. He eyebrows shot up, and he searched for a friendly face. "If we're trapped, we can't breathe. We'll die."

Gumshoe pulled out his caster and flipped it open. "No signal. We can't call for help." The Inspector pocketed his caster. "Jack, can you levitate the crucible?"

"No, old man, it's way too heavy. I've already tried while you were sleeping off our little ride. The crucible looked like a diving bell from the air. I thought it would take the blast, so I flew everyone into it and covered us with a magical shield. The Celeste blasted us across the factory, and the crucible landed on top of us."

"Why didn't the blast kill us?" Jones asked.

"Mr. Clay's magic," York answered. "He's got some tricks up his sleeve, and that's for sure. He's already had me flying with him, and he can throw up magic shields that'll reflect any death ray."

"Now, I'm not sure I'd go that far," said Jack. "My shields may have saved our lives, but it was probably just dumb luck."

"Face it, boss, humble pie just isn't you."

"If you can't lift the crucible, Jack, this dwarf here is right." Gumshoe searched the dwarf's uniform for a name. "Son, what's your name?"

"Ian Murphy, sir," said the dwarf. "What am I doing here?"

"What's your last recollection, Ian?" asked the Inspector.

The dwarf smiled uneasily and looked around the crucible at the faces staring back at him in the pale blue glow of Jack's illusion. "I, uh," his Adam's apple rocked up and down, and he hung his head. "I made an appointment with a doctor."

"Let me guess," said Gumshoe. "Was it Dr. Balaam at New Gem?"

"Yes sir," said the dwarf, looking up. "How did you know?"

"It's a long story, Ian," Gumshoe rubbed his neck. "It's not going to do either of us any good to tell it unless we can get out of here. For now, save your breathe."

"It's a terrible cock-up," said Jack. "I'm sorry, old-man. I shouldn't have got us trapped in this thing."

"Jack, you did the right thing. The Celeste would surely have killed us if we'd been aboard, and the blast should have killed us anyway."

"Would it have been so bad to go straight away?" Shotgun asked. "If we're trapped here without air, we'll suffocate in a few minutes."

"Don't panic." Jack cast more light and revealed more of the crucible. He searched the crucible's walls. Upside down, the tell-tale stains of rust ran upwards to the bottom now over their heads. There was no sign of a crack or a drain.

He knelt at the edge of the bell and studied the floor. The floor was asphalt., grey with age, and riddled with cracks filled with gravel.

"I've an idea." Jack said, "Stand back folks."

Carefully, he conjured water and dew appeared on the pavement. *Going to need more than that, Jack*. He laid a hand on the asphalt and willed water to rise. A tingling sensation ran down his arm.

Slowly the water came. It flowed up through the cracks in the asphalt and under the crucible's lip. There he froze it. Willing the magic to flow, he drew water out of the clay far below and through the floor. Seconds passed and then minutes. The ice built up and froze in place.

The asphalt sagged under the weight, but Jack spread the weight of his icy anchors until the ice nearly ran around the crucible.

About him, he felt the other's eyes on him. They shifted to the center to escape the cold.

"Will it move?"

He didn't catch who asked the question. He redoubled his focus and let the magic draw the water from the ground.

The crucible popped from the floor. The walls pinged. The ice cracked.

"Yes," a chorus of cheers arose. "You can do it, Jack."

"Shush, don't jinx it." He redoubled his effort and the ice pushed one side into the air. He lifted one edge three feet, and then formed a tunnel in the ice.

"Go, go, go," he grunted. "I've got to hold it."

They just stood there for a second.

Gumshoe slapped one of the officers. "You heard the man, move!" He herded the police officers, Shotgun, and the black dwarves out.

"That's it, Jack," said Gumshoe. "I'm going. You're the

last."

"Go old-man, I'm right behind you."

The Inspector dove into the hole, and scrambled through. The Inspector's wingtips disappeared.

Jack concentrated on freezing the ice, and he plunged after his friend. *Out of the kettle and into the pitch black.* His light shined through the ice and cast a faint blue glow several yards around the crucible. Pitch darkness covered the vast factory all about them.

"Don't go wandering off," said Gumshoe. "Remember that pit is around here. Jack can you give us some more light?"

"Yes, just give me a minute." He pushed to his feet and stretched. "I've just run a marathon." He huffed, "well, five miles anyway. That much magic takes something out of me." He pushed up his sleeves and cast a full bore illusion of lamps lighting the area. A blue twilight filled the chamber.

"Super, straddling precarious!" Shotgun flinched.

They looked up and gasped. The Celeste's broken hull teetered on a gantry over their heads.

"If that was sitting on us, we'd still be trapped."

"Evidently, providence is still with us, Jack," said Gumshoe. He patted the dust off his fedora.

"Inspector," said York, "I've got a signal on my caster." Without waiting for a reply, he called for help.

Jack took in the Celeste and the shattered remains of the factory. "What a mess? What is it the Black Dwarf wants?"

"The next time you see this black dwarf, boss, do us a favor and drop the boom on him before he drops another spacecraft on us."

"Shotgun, we still don't know anything about him."

"What's to know, boss? He tried to kill us, and he very nearly succeeded."

"Yeah, but we haven't got anything to show for it."

"Not quite son," said Gumshoe. "We know who is responsible for the Zodiac crimes. We know he calls himself the

Black Dwarf, and that's not all we know."

"Oh, what else?" Jack crossed his arms. "If you're going to say he's got magic, maybe he has magic, and maybe not. I've got eyes too. He didn't do anything especially magical that I could see. High tech can explain all his tricks. He may be using some kind of advanced power pack, levitators, and a blaster."

"Jealous, Jack?" Gumshoe lifted an eyebrow. "No, I was about to say something completely different. I think it's important."

"Don't keep us waiting old-man," said Jack. "Spit it out."

"You Jack," said Gumshoe. "You're the key to this somehow. The Black Dwarf addressed you, remember? He called you something." Gumshoe stopped and pushed his fedora with a finger.

"Phaedra's son," said Shotgun.

"Yes, so I'm Phaedra's son. It's not a secret. It's in my bio on Clay-net. I'm a celebrity. People are always trying to meet me, get my autograph, or share something with me."

"He wasn't after your autograph, Jack."

"So? He's a criminal. He's a psycho. Maybe he wants to kill a celebrity to add the score to the notches on his belt."

"No, Jack, you're just pretending. He was after you. He wanted you, and only you. The rest of us were just a distraction."

"The Inspector's right." Shotgun looked up at the shattered spacecraft. "Maybe you didn't see it. You were awfully busy in there trying to keep us alive. He focused on you. He attacked York and me only to distract you."

"Face it; the Black Dwarf didn't booby trap a supertanker to kill an old detective, a computer hacker, or any of these policemen. He wanted you. He thought if he sent you on a wild goose chase in a giant spacecraft, you wouldn't see the danger until it was too late."

"What we've learned then is: The Zodiac killer is a black dwarf pretending to have magical power who wants to kill me?

Who do you think this guy is? My evil twin?"

All eyes turned towards him. The policemen, the dwarves, Gumshoe, and Shotgun gave him the stare.

"Nonsense fellas,what have I got to do with it?"

"Begging your pardon, Mr. Clay," said York. "You're special. Something about you is different, and it's not just magic."

"Sergeant, I've got a great press agent, but I make it a point not to believe my own advertising." He jerked a thumb at Shotgun. "I even employ Jiminy Cricket here to help out when my conscience fails me."

"York's right," said Gumshoe. "When the black dwarves ambushed us, I assumed they wanted to stop my investigation. I thought they were trying to put down an old warhorse. Now, I see it wasn't me they were after. It's obvious. They were after you then, and they were after you this time. Once they find out you're alive, they'll try again."

No way old man," Jack twirled, and his cloak wrapped around him. "I don't believe it. If I'm his target, he's made a mistake. I'm glad to be his target if I can stand in for some poor, defenseless damsel, but I can't even seem to stop a black dwarf with a couple of parlor tricks up his sleeve. Why waste his time and resources on me?"

"The Black Dwarf wants you," said Gumshoe. "He wants something you have, or he wants to stop you from doing something. What we have to do is find out what it is he wants."

In the distance, the sound of sirens approached.

"Good," said Gumshoe. "The cavalry has arrived."

"Since we have no idea what the Black Dwarf wants," said Jack, "may I suggest we find his lair and make an arrest."

"An excellent suggestion, Jack," said Gumshoe. "You do that."

The End

Epilogue: On the Beach

Evan Labe floated in warm water. The water was deep and wide and salty. Waves lapped gently over him, soaking him, but he knew he was safe. Bobbing in the current, he felt longer waves lift his feet and roll beneath him. He slid down the waves, and swung in the troughs and was pushed over the crest of another and slid down again.

It was fun. He splashed, and paddled the water, but he did not try to swim.

Sensing he was not alone, he knew there were others. Below him swam the denizens of the deep about their errands, and above he heard birds call. He knew he was not the only one.

The stars burned in the firmament, as he sailed along. He wanted to open his eyes to watch the stars, but he knew he could not. He thought he was dreaming.

Overhead the sun rose. Purple faded to pink. Golden rays broke over slate clouds tinged with silver.

It was morning.

He heard the beach. The waves broke on the shore long before he reached it. Closer, the waves crashed over him and he tasted salt. The current pushed him up the beach, and he felt the sand. The undertow dragged him back. For a time, the surf tossed him on the shore.

He grew impatient to end his journey, yet he did not want it to end.

The current left him on warm sand. Soft sand cradled him, and waves rocked him.

Knowing the time had come; he opened his eyes, and blinked. Clouds sailed a blue sky above. A bird circled, and then flew on.

He inhaled and he smelled the sea, fresh, and clean. He breathed again.

He rolled over. *Where am I?* A wide beach of sand curved in a cove swept up against soft gray stones at the foot of a white cliff. Searching for the meaning of this place, he studied the cliffs, which revealed nothing.

A dwarf in a robe walked down a steep path winding over the cliff face. He wanted to call to the dwarf, but he was still too tired. He tried to push himself up, but his muscles failed him. Rolling over onto his back, he laid on the sand feeling his strength return.

The sand muffled the dwarf's footfalls. He turned his head, and saw a maiden. She was a dwarf, as he was, but she had no spot upon her brow.

How was her chip removed? He tried to speak.

"Be still, Evan Labe," she said.

She knelt beside him. "You've failed, but not too badly." She held out a robe, and let it open. "You're highly favored," she laughed, "just like everyone."

She helped him sit up, and put on the robe.

With her gentle ministrations, he gained his feet, and steadied his mind. His benefactor was a tad shorter than he, but she was fairer than anyone he had ever seen.

"You have many questions, but now is not the time. Follow me and I will be your guide." Taking his hand, she led him to the south. "We will go up the cliff, where we will live until we have reached the beginning."

Halting on the sand, she pulled him closer. She kissed his cheek. He blushed and she smiled. Tugging him along, she led him away.

~~~~~~

The Adventure Continues

Cretaceous Clay

& the

Ninth Ring

~~~~~

Available from Amazon.com, CreateSpace.com, and other retail outlets!

A great red dragon sunbathed under the stage lights enjoying the warm glow. He filled nearly the whole of a small sound stage.

"Welcome to the book trailer for **Cretaceous Clay and the Ninth Ring**. It's called a trailer since it trails the first book." The dragon chuckled at his little pun, and the notes sent shivers through the crew and cast alike.

"We hope 'The Black Dwarf' was a quick read. If you liked the first book, we think you'll like the next."

Evan Labe walked up to a camp chair marked with a golden star. The hot dwarf struck a swarthy pose and winked at the camera. He spoke a bit stiffly as if he were reading a cue card. "So Kevin, what are we going to say?"

"Maybe we should start by welcoming the Gentle Readers to the end of the book?"

"Kevin, they know it's the end of the book."

"Maybe we can explain why we are pitching the next

book?"

"Good idea, Kevin, pitching the next book gives us a chance to introduce ourselves to the Gentle Readers. I'm Evan Labe, and with me is Kevin the Clever. We portray the bad guys in the Cretaceous Clay series. Kevin plays the Dragon Lord, and I play Nimrod who styles himself the Black Dwarf. The Professor wanted the folks to meet us. After all, I only get a couple of chapters of the first book as myself. I spend the rest of the series possessed by the wicked warlock."

"You're complaining?" asked Kevin. "Unless she reads the end papers, no Gentle Reader even knows my name. The Gentle Readers might not realize I'm Noddie's father, Kraken, the King of the Leviathans in the series. The scene where Noddie discovers I've been possessed by the Dragon Lord hasn't even been approved yet."

Evan glanced at the script and blushed. "Kevin, we're running out of room." With great enthusiasm Evan said, "What happened to Jack and Shotgun?"

"Oh no!" replied the dragon in a silly tone. "Did they survive Nimrod's attack?"

"Will the valiant mage and his intrepid sidekick defeat the Black Dwarf?" Evan answered melodramatically.

"Find out in our next exciting episode," finished the dragon, "Cretaceous Clay and the Ninth Ring!"

"Cut, that's a wrap," yelled a potbellied man wearing a fishing hat.

~~~~~~~

Acknowledgements

Few books come to the market without the help of more than a few people.

First, I would very much like to thank you, Gentle Reader, for sharing my passion for Cretaceous Clay and all of his friends. Jack was one of my boyhood friends and I'm glad to know others like him too.

If you haven't done so already, <u>please, please, please</u>, review the book on your favorite site. Then go to Goodreads.com and post a copy of your review. A thoughtful, four-star review is better than a five-star review. Remember this is no time to skimp on praise!

If you borrowed this book or shared it, because you can't afford it, <u>please, please, please</u>, spread the word. If you can afford it, go to Amazon.com and purchase a copy of the eBook! It's only a few pennies, but it helps so much more than you know.

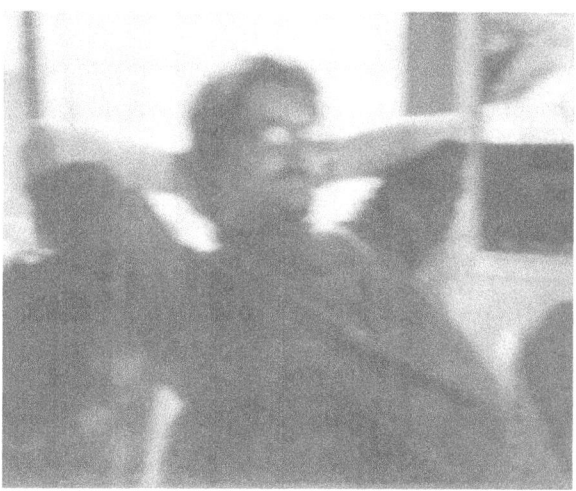

My heartfelt thanks go out to my family who made mighty sacrifices to keep us afloat.

Thanks also go to my real-time friends for their encouragement, and my on-line friends for their support.

Thanks go to my Twitter friends from all over the world for their tweets. Even friends in Brazil, Germany, India, Japan, Norway, and the Philippines tweeted us! Without these wonderful people, no one would know about Jack Clay.

Special thanks go to David Caldwell for providing a detailed list of seventeen typos and several suggestions. My editor, Tina provided invaluable assistance.

Last but not least, I must acknowledge the former and current occupants of the White House who gave me plenty of incentive to follow my dreams. Though, I suspect they could not have written these novels without me.

~~~~~~

Connect with Dan Knight

Goodreads: D.A. Knight
Amazon: amzn.com/B00CMXCKTC
Amazon.UK: www.amazon.co.uk/dp/B00CMXCKTC
Facebook: Dan Knight's Facebook Page: dana.knight.7127
Website: BlackDwarves.com